T0095477

Looking
for Lucius

VALERIE S. ARMSTRONG

Order this book online at www.trafford.com
or email orders@trafford.com

Most Trafford titles are also available at major online book retailers.

Printed in the United States of America.

ISBN: 978-1-4669-5867-8 (sc)
ISBN: 978-1-4669-5869-2 (hc)
ISBN: 978-1-4669-5868-5 (e)

Library of Congress Control Number: 2012917559

Trafford rev. 09/18/2012

 www.trafford.com

North America & international
toll-free: 1 888 232 4444 (USA & Canada)
phone: 250 383 6864 ♦ fax: 812 355 4082

Author of

Livvy

No Roses for Abby

Follow the Butterfly

This book is dedicated to my father. He was a complicated man, but the qualities I admired in him inspired me to create the character of Casey in this story.

Acknowledgements

I would especially like to thank Eileen Usher, who, under very difficult circumstances, took on the job of editing the first draft of my manuscript.

I would also like to thank Michael Fedecky, who kindly offered to help with the final design of the cover and then took great pains to get it just right.

Finally, I would like to show my gratitude to the staff at Trafford Publishing, who can always be counted on for their support.

Chapter One

Have you ever been so close to someone that you couldn't imagine your life without them? That's how I felt about my brother, Luke, when we were children. We were so close in age that people thought we were twins, even though we didn't look one bit alike. We grew up in the town of Abingdon, just five miles south of Oxford, on the west bank of the Thames. The town had been in existence for over six thousand years and had some historic landmarks, like the arched Abingdon Bridge over the river, near St. Helen's Church, which dates back to 1416.

My parents, Casey and Jane Regan, were ordinary folk and ran a small bed-and-breakfast, the Trout River Inn. My mother had taken over the running of the inn after my grandfather Henry Parsons died and my grandmother was unable to manage without him. The inn had five guest rooms and separate living quarters for the family. Like many of the properties in the area, the house was built in the seventeenth century from natural stone, and it had high ceilings with exposed beams and leaded windows. It stood on two acres of ground bordering on the river, and we had a dock where Dad moored his old rowboat. Mum was always telling him that he should sink it and build a new one with a cabin, but Dad would just roll his eyes and chuckle.

He always said that my mother had delusions of grandeur. She had dreamed of becoming an actress, but that was nipped in the bud when she met my father while on vacation in Ireland—it was love at first sight. Within three months, they were married and settled in my mother's hometown of Abingdon.

Dad was the image of, what I believed was, the typical Irishman. He was rugged with coal black hair and blue eyes, while Mum was the typical English rose with a peaches-and-cream complexion and hair the colour of corn silk. Mum's love of the theatre never diminished, and so when I was born, she named me Ariel after a character from Shakespeare's play *The Tempest*. Dad, with his easygoing manner, raised no objection; but when my brother was born barely a year later, he wasn't quite as obliging. Mum wanted to call him Lucius, a character in two of Shakespeare's plays. Dad thought it made him sound like a sissy, but Mum said the name meant "light," and she was adamant. In the end, it didn't really matter because although the name on his birth certificate was Lucius, nearly everybody—except Mum—called him Luke; and you couldn't get more macho than that.

My father's only family back in Ireland was his aunt Molly, who raised him from the time he was still in diapers. He had no idea who his father was, and his mother ran off with a juggler from a travelling circus right after he was born. Oddly enough, being abandoned at such an early age appeared to have little effect on him. He grew up to be a well-adjusted, outgoing man who never ceased to charm everyone, especially our paying guests. Many a time, he would have them captivated, spinning outrageous yarns in his wonderful lilting Irish accent. Along with his charm, handsome features, and muscular body, he caused many a female guest to blush and lower their gaze. I'm not sure Dad even noticed because he was too much in love with my mother and the life they had built together despite the fact that they had so little time for themselves.

Dad did a lot of the heavy work around the inn and was the resident handyman, taking care of all the necessary repairs that seemed to come up on a daily basis, but his real love was making custom furniture. It had been his trade back in his hometown of Ballyclare, and he had developed quite a reputation in Abingdon for his unique chairs and tables lovingly fashioned in oak, cherry, and maple.

Mum did most of the cooking and making up of the rooms; and when Luke and I were very small, she had help in the form of a local girl, Rosie Barlow, who used to come by every morning. I was about ten when Rosie moved to Oxford to get married, and that's when I started helping Mum with the chores. I didn't really mind because I liked spending time with her. Mother was the complete opposite of my father. Barely more than five feet tall and very slight, she had a gentle, sweet nature and was always the perfect hostess. I often wished that I looked like her, but I had inherited my father's thick black hair and light complexion, while Luke looked more like our grandmother Ruth Parsons, whom we always called Nana.

Nana's hair was a lovely shade of chestnut except for the streaks of grey; and her eyes, which were starting to fail her, were hazel. She had her own room on the main floor at the back of the house; that way, she didn't have to climb any stairs, which was just as well because she constantly complained about the arthritis in her knees. When not complaining, she was a really interesting character, and Luke and I spent many hours sitting at her feet while she told us stories about her childhood. When she died peacefully in her sleep at the age of eighty-six, we really missed her. Her beloved cat, Buffy, obviously missed her too. Less than six months later, we found Buffy lying beside Nana's old rocking chair. She had passed away during the night for no apparent reason other than a broken heart.

From an early age, we had always had a dog, but my favourite was our border terrier, Sammy. He loved to play Frisbee in the park, go for long walks by the river, and sleep on my bed every night. He was just like my mother—sweet and gentle—and wouldn't dream of barking at a human or another dog, unless it looked like they might be some kind of threat.

Because running the inn was a full-time job, my parents were never able to take a break, so vacations were not an option. All of my young life, I spent close to home; and my world evolved around my parents, my school, and a few friends, but mostly around Luke. I remember sitting on the riverbank with my fishing pole when I was about nine years old, hoping to catch a trout or a carp, when I began to wonder if we would ever get to see the world outside of Abingdon. I turned to Luke, who was lying on the grass beside me, gazing at the sky, and asked, "Do you ever imagine leaving here and going to live somewhere else?"

Luke glanced over at me and slowly shook his head. "No, I haven't really thought about it. Why, would you like to live somewhere else?"

I stared out across the river. "This is my home, and I'll always come back here, but I'd like to go to some of the places we've learned about at school. Imagine going to Africa and seeing all those lions and elephants and all of those strange-looking monkeys."

"Yeah, I suppose that would be fun, but they have snakes and lots of bugs. I don't think I'd like that too much."

"That's true," I replied, "maybe we could just go to London instead. Mum says it's a fabulous place to visit. They have all these old buildings like the Tower, where they used to chop off peoples' heads."

Luke snorted and rolled over onto his stomach. "I don't believe it," he said. "Anyway, I don't want to see old buildings. They have enough of those here. Jimmy Rogers was there, and he said they have tons of picture houses and a huge Ferris wheel that's almost five hundred feet tall. I'd like to go on that. I bet you can see for miles."

I felt a tug on my line, but then suddenly, it went slack. "Mmmm," I mused, "that sounds like a lot of fun. Maybe we can go together one day."

Luke sat up and put his hand on my shoulder. "I'd rather go with you than anyone else, sis," he said.

It was always like that between Luke and me; we enjoyed each other's company and could sit on the riverbank for hours with Sammy and not even have to talk. Not only was my brother my closest friend, but also if it weren't for him, I wouldn't even be here.

Chapter Two

One of my best friends was Becky Roberts. Becky and I met on the first day of school and hit it off right away. Like me, Becky had dark hair and blue eyes; and if it wasn't for the fact that she was a little on the chubby side, we could have been sisters. Being an only child, she liked to spend time with Luke and me, and I think she developed a crush on Luke very early on. I couldn't really blame her because even as a small boy, he had developed a lot of my dad's good qualities. He was both charming and kind and nearly always in an upbeat mood. I don't know how anyone could resist him. Not only that, he had inherited fine features from my mother's side of the family and Nana's wonderful chestnut hair.

Just after celebrating my twelfth birthday, something happened in my life that I will never forget. It was a Sunday morning in mid-January, and the temperature was lower than normal, so there wasn't too much to keep me occupied. There were only two guests staying at the inn that week, so Dad was taking care of the chores while Mum went off to attend the service at St. Helen's. She wasn't really religious, but I think she just wanted to get away for an hour or two. Dad didn't need my help, and Luke was out riding his bicycle with his friend,

Jimmy, so that left me at loose ends, and I decided to walk over to Becky's with Sammy.

Her house was only about five minutes away, and when I got there, I knew her mother was glad to see me because Becky had been moping around all morning. Her father suggested we take a stroll along the river but warned us to be extra careful, as the ground was wet and rather slippery. I wasn't too enthused about walking around even though I was dressed for the cold in a thick down coat, a woolly hat, and my wellies; but it was better than staying at home.

After we had been out for about half an hour, we arrived at the Abingdon Bridge. I often fished off the bridge in the warmer months and loved to watch the boats travelling down the river; but on this day, I just wanted to keep walking. Becky wasn't very good company that morning, and I think Sammy was looking forward to getting home and lazing in front of the fire. I should have turned around right then and gone back to the inn, but I suddenly felt a little devilish and thought it was a good time to liven things up. I decided to challenge Becky. "Bet you couldn't swim across the river," I said.

She looked at me as though I was mad. "What now? Are you crazy? It's freezing out, and anyway, I wouldn't even try even if it was the middle of summer."

I thought about it for a moment and then decided to try something else. "Well, if you're too scared to do that, I bet you couldn't climb up on the side of the bridge and walk across."

Becky put her hands on her hips and glared at me. "Now I know you're crazy. If you're so smart, why don't you do it?"

I hesitated for a while, trying to look smug even though I wasn't feeling too brave; and then before I knew it, the words came tumbling out. "Okay, I'll do it. You just watch me."

Becky grabbed my arm as I turned away. "No, Ariel, you mustn't. It's too dangerous. I didn't mean it. You'll fall. Please don't do it."

I shrugged her off and started to climb up onto the side of the bridge, but it was hard going in my heavy clothing. Finally, I was kneeling on top, hanging on with my hands, and trying not to let Becky see me shaking. Sammy started to bark, and Becky started to scream, "Please, Ariel, get down!" But I could hardly hear them over the wind, which had suddenly come up out of nowhere. Slowly I managed to stand up, but I was still shaking and too scared to take a single step. Sammy was barking like crazy now, and Becky was looking up at me with her arms outstretched. "I'm begging you, please come down!" she yelled. "I didn't mean it."

I remember smiling at her and taking a step forward, and then I started to slip. After that, everything was a complete blank. I didn't remember crying out or falling into the icy water; I only know what actually happened because of what Becky told me. One thing is for sure. My brother saved my life that day.

I regained consciousness in a ward of Community Hospital after the ambulance had taken me there, two hours earlier. According to Becky, Luke had been riding along the bank towards the bridge with Jimmy when he saw me balancing precariously and knew I was going to fall. He cycled as fast as his legs would carry him and had just reached the entrance to the bridge when he saw me slip off the ledge. Becky screamed as she saw me sink under the water, but Luke didn't even hesitate. He ran full tilt down the bank, sliding most of the way, and threw himself into the water. Meanwhile, Becky was trying to restrain Sammy; but seconds later, he was in the water right behind Luke. They both started swimming frantically to where I had gone over, but Luke couldn't see me, so he looked up at Becky, who was pointing to a spot a few yards away. Luke dove beneath the surface again and again, trying to find me in the murky river; and finally, he made contact. He managed to get my head above water but was struggling to reach the riverbank. He yelled at Jimmy to cycle to the nearest house and ring 999 while he was fighting the current, which was dragging both of us and Sammy under the bridge. We had floated quite a way by the time we were rescued, and although both Luke and Sammy suffered no ill effects, I had a mild case of hypothermia. I was scared to hear what Mum and Dad would say about my stupid prank, but they were so happy to see me alive that they forgot to be cross. As for Luke, well, he was my hero.

I was released later that day and thought all the drama was over, but I was wrong. Just moments after I arrived home, reporters from the *Oxford Mail* and the *Oxford Times* arrived at the inn. Luke was sitting on the side of my bed, making sure I was all right even though I kept insisting that there was nothing wrong with me. When Dad opened the door and announced that the local papers had heard about the rescue and wanted to interview Luke, he shook his head and said, "It was nothing, Dad. I don't know what all the fuss is about."

Dad advanced into the room. "Come on, lad, you did a brave thing out there. I shudder to think what would have happened if you hadn't been there. If it wasn't for you, your sister could have drowned."

I reached over and grasped Luke's hand. "Dad's right. You should go and talk to the people from the papers, and they might even take your picture."

Luke reluctantly followed my father out of the room and met with the reporters in the reception area. I heard that they wanted to speak to me too, but Mum wouldn't allow it. She said I needed to recover from the shock of it all. It was too bad because I would have loved to have seen my photo in the newspaper along with Luke's. His photo appeared the next day on the front pages. He was not smiling and looked like he had just bitten down on a slice of lemon. Sammy, however, who was also in the photo, was sitting up poker straight and staring into the camera as if to say, "Look at me!"

Two weeks later, it was announced that the mayor was presenting Luke with an award, and it was with great pride that my family and many members of the community watched him accept a certificate at the Guildhall. Luke wasn't quite as happy about having so much attention thrust on him, and after the ceremony was over, he sank down beside me and sighed, "Thank goodness that's over. Can we go back to being normal again now?"

Chapter Three

Life didn't exactly return to normal because the Regan family continued to be the main topic of conversation in our community. I'm not sure how many times I was asked to repeat the details of my lucky escape from drowning, but I didn't really mind. It made me feel important, almost like a celebrity. Meanwhile, Luke hated being treated as a hero, especially by his school chums. He had always been well liked and was particularly popular with the girls in his class, but now they competed for his attention. At the tender age of eleven, he was already being perceived as a prize catch, and I must admit that I felt a little protective of him.

By the time summer approached, any interest in our unfortunate escapade had died down, and we were looking forward to the holidays. Becky's parents were going to Spain for a month, but Becky refused go with them and caused quite a fuss. Leaving her behind was out of the question, and then Mum solved the problem by suggesting that she could stay with us and bunk with me in my room. Had it not been the height of the tourist season, we would probably have had a vacant guest room, but we were all booked up until the beginning of October. Becky was thrilled about living at the inn, especially as she would be closer to Luke. She didn't openly express her feelings for him, but it wasn't hard to see what was going on by the way she looked at him and how she became more animated when he was close by. Luke had no idea that Becky, or any other girl, had any interest in him. If he did, he pretended not to notice and politely kept his distance.

On the first night of Becky's stay, we had our first real talk since the day we met. We'd been best friends forever, but we had never really shared any intimate moments. Thanks to Mum, all that changed. When I accidentally caught Becky in her underwear getting ready for bed, I couldn't help feeling a little inadequate and definitely somewhat jealous. Her breasts were far larger than I had ever imagined. I had only ever seen her in loose-fitting tops or our school uniform. "Wow, Becky," I said as I felt myself blushing, "I didn't realise you were that big."

Becky looked a little taken aback and then snapped, "What do you mean? I know I'm overweight. Mum's always bugging me about it. I don't need you telling me too."

I stepped forward and shook my head. "I'm sorry, I didn't mean that you were fat or anything like that. It's your boobs. They're so much bigger than mine. Mine look like a pair of pimples, and I'm not even wearing a bra yet."

Becky smiled and pulled her nightgown over her head. "I just developed earlier than you. You'll get bigger, you'll see. Anyway, it's not all good. That Benny Wallis keeps teasing me about them. He said that if I'd fallen in the river instead of you, I would have just floated."

I sat down on the edge of the bed and motioned to Becky to sit beside me. "He's just a creepy little kid. You shouldn't take notice of him. If he bugs you again, I'll tell Luke and he'll sort him out."

Becky looked panicky. "Oh no, you mustn't do that," she begged. "I wouldn't want Luke to know what Benny said. Please don't tell him, Ariel."

I hesitated and then agreed. "Okay I won't, I promise, but only if you let me know if he teases you again, and I'll give him a piece of my mind."

Just then there was a knock on the door, and Mum poked her head in. "Just checking to see if everything's all right and if you need anything. If you want to come down for some hot chocolate or prefer something cold, you're welcome to join me in the kitchen. Dad's out in the garage, finishing off that table for Mrs. Hastings, and Luke's holed up in his room reading."

I looked at Becky. "Shall we? I'm not really tired, and I am a bit thirsty."

Becky nodded and we followed Mum downstairs to the kitchen, where she had a whole selection of drinks for us to choose from. I loved to get together in the kitchen with my family because it was such a warm place. We had all the latest appliances to simplify preparing breakfast for ten or more guests, and Dad had built most of the cabinets. They were made of oak, stained a lovely honey pecan colour, and the enormous table with its ladder back chairs was built to match.

Once we were all seated at the kitchen table, having decided we all preferred hot chocolate along with a piece of Mum's delicious pecan pie, Mum asked us what we had planned for the summer. It was lovely relaxing with my mother; she was so sweet and so concerned about Becky missing her family but, at the same time, relieved that I had my best friend to chum around with during the holidays.

We must have been chatting about all sorts of things for almost an hour when suddenly, Mum took me by complete surprise when she said to Becky, "I hope you won't be offended if I ask you a question, dear. I know it's a little delicate, and you don't have to answer. I was wondering if you had started menstruating."

"Mum!" I exclaimed. "What are you saying?"

Mum put her hand gently on my arm to silence me as Becky replied, "It's okay. I don't mind answering. Yes, it started the day after Ariel fell into the river. I think it might have been the shock that set it off."

I looked at her aghast while Mum grinned. "I hardly think that had anything to do with it, but it must have been a surprise."

"Well, we had sex education at school, and my mother told me what to expect, but it's not quite like I thought it would be."

Mum looked from Becky back to me again. "So I gather you two haven't discussed this amongst yourselves?"

Becky shook her head. "No, we haven't. I wanted to tell you, Ariel, but I wasn't sure how. I felt kind of ashamed."

My mother reached across for Becky's hand. "There's absolutely nothing to be ashamed of. It's a perfectly natural part of growing up, and even though I've talked to Ariel about it, she needs to hear from someone her own age. She needs to know exactly what to expect."

Becky nodded and looked at me. "I'm sorry. Do you want to talk to me about it?"

"Sure," I said a little sheepishly, "although the way things are going, I may be out of my teens before it happens to me."

Mum threw back her head and laughed. "Oh, Ariel," she said, "my precious daughter, I'm sure you won't have to wait that long."

Later, I was slightly embarrassed but grateful that we had that conversation with Mum because it brought Becky and me even closer. We talked about all kinds of intimate things after that and did a lot of research at the local library. We soon discovered that *The Joy of Sex* and *Human Sexuality* were much more interesting to read than the books we were forced to read in school.

The day before school was back in session, I finally got my period, and I can't say I was thrilled. Even though I was mentally prepared, I felt like everybody knew what had happened. When I discovered that Mum had told Dad, I was mortified, but he didn't seem to treat me any differently. I just made Mum promise, on oath, that she wouldn't tell Luke.

I was really sad that summer had ended because it had been a wonderful holiday. We had fished, swam, rode our bikes and taken long walks with Sammy, and the weather was perfect. Most of the time, Becky and I were alone, but sometimes we met up with other school chums or spent time with Luke and Jimmy. I think Becky was hoping that I would pair up with Jimmy, and then she could pair up with Luke, but Jimmy didn't interest me that way. He was nice enough, but he was skinny as a toothpick, had acne and, like Luke, was a year younger. Anyway, I was too young to have a boyfriend.

Chapter Four

At the age of sixteen, I had acquired a lot more confidence. I had never considered myself pretty; but after going through an awkward stage when I had shot up about four inches and developed some curves, I was quite pleased with my reflection in the mirror. I was really into fashion and started designing my own clothes. Mum was always picking up odd fabric remnants and helping me with the cutting and sewing on her old treadle machine. I had a vision of being famous one day like Givenchy or Valentino, and Luke constantly encouraged me to follow my dream.

For the past year, I had been getting a lot of attention from the boys at school, but Becky and I had vowed not to date until we were seventeen. I had seen too many girls get into trouble, and the thought of getting pregnant without being married really scared me. Becky and I talked about it a lot and considered dating casually but never to get seriously involved. Then we decided that would be far too risky; after all, we were only human and subject to temptation like everyone else.

One summer evening, Luke and I were having takeaway fish-and-chips on a bench in Abbey Gardens when he told me that one of the boys in his class wanted to go out with me.

"Who?" I asked, full of curiosity.

"Gary Bowles," he replied. "He thinks you're really pretty."

"You mean the tall muscular boy with the fair hair that plays on the soccer team?"

"Yes, that's him. He's a really nice chap, and I think you might like him."

I shook my head. "First of all, he's too young for me, and second, I don't want to date anyone yet."

"Why not?" Luke asked, looking puzzled. "Most of the girls your age have a boyfriend, sis."

"But I'm not most girls. Boys seem to be after one thing, and I'm not ready for that."

"That's not really fair. Not all boys are the same. Do you think I'm like that?"

"No, of course not, you're my brother."

Luke laughed. "Does that mean I don't have feelings like the other boys you're talking about?"

"Well, are you like that?"

Luke paused for a moment. "I'm fifteen, sis, fifteen-year-old boys think about sex all the time, and I'm no exception. That doesn't mean we're going to jump a girl's bones."

"Seriously? So I could go out with someone and they wouldn't expect anything from me?"

"Yes, of course, and if they do come on to you, just tell them to back off."

"Becky and I made a pact that we wouldn't date until we were seventeen. She'll be mad at me if I break a promise, and I still think Gary is too young for me."

"I'm sure Becky will understand, and as for Gary, he's almost sixteen. Lots of women marry men younger than themselves. I don't see anything wrong with it."

"Whoa, who's talking about marriage? No, I think I'll find my own boyfriend, but I'm glad we had this talk."

Neither Luke nor I wanted to pursue a formal education, and my parents didn't try to push us in that direction. Luke took after Mum. He loved the theatre and had enrolled in the creative drama class at school. When he was seventeen, he was cast as Demetrius in *A Midsummer Night's Dream*, and the play was performed in the school auditorium. I could swear that when it was over and he took his bow, the audience applauded louder for him than for anyone else. Mum was beaming, while Dad sat there with a big smile but later admitted he'd rather have watched a good film on the telly. Mum just rolled her eyes, patted him on the shoulder and remarked, "Casey, you are absolutely hopeless."

By this time, I had started dating but had made it very clear that I didn't want to go steady. I decided to play the field believing, that way, I could avoid any serious relationship. Becky, on the other hand, had fallen madly in love with a boy she met at a barbecue the previous summer; and although they had enjoyed some heavy petting sessions, they still hadn't gone all the way. I have to admit, I thought Jordan was a really nice guy; but sometimes, I resented the fact that he monopolised so much of Becky's time and we spent less and less time together. If it weren't for Luke, I would have felt a little lost, but he almost always made sure that I wasn't left at loose ends.

Luke had no steady girlfriend and didn't appear interested in dating at all. I was beginning to wonder if he was gay, but I was sure he would have told me if that was the case. He chummed around a lot with a group of his school friends; but when he wasn't busy, we would get together to go to the pictures, play video games or spend time outdoors with Sammy, weather permitting, hiking or fishing. Often, on a Saturday night, when it seemed like everyone else was out having fun and I had no plans, he would ask me to join him and his chums, and they always made me welcome. Luke made sure of that because that's the way he was.

In January, a location scout for Elstree Studios telephoned my father and asked if he could meet with him at the inn the following day. The studio was in preproduction for a remake of *Moll Flanders*, which I learned later, had originally been filmed in 1965 and had starred Kim Novak. The scout was looking for accommodations, in the Thames Valley area for some of the cast and crew, and filming would take up to three weeks, around the end of July. Fortunately, we hadn't yet booked reservations for the summer season, and Dad was more than happy to oblige. Needless to say, when he told Luke and me, we were over the moon with excitement. Luke was down at the library the very next day, searching for Defoe's novel so that he would know what the film was all about. When he finally finished reading it and passed it over to me, I could see why he had become so fascinated with the character of Moll herself. He kept anticipating who they would get to play the part and if they would be staying at the inn. By the end of that week, word had quickly spread throughout our small community because Elstree had to get permission from the town council to film in Abingdon, and there was a sense of anticipation in the air. That's when Dad suggested we should get more help, at least for the next few months; and after interviewing a number of young women, he hired a rather mousy-looking girl of seventeen.

Marcy Pearson was forced to quit school in order to help out at home. Her father had lost his job due to declining health, and her mother had enough on her hands looking after Marcy's three younger siblings. I felt sorry for Marcy and tried to make friends with her, but she was very shy, especially when Luke was around. I think she was totally smitten with him.

In March, we learned that an actress named Pandora James had been cast for the lead. It was a bit of a letdown because we had never heard of her. She had only appeared in a couple of films but had a lot of stage experience mostly in plays by Shakespeare or Christopher Marlowe. Anxious to see what she looked like, Luke and I surfed the Internet and discovered that she was twenty-six and extremely attractive, with flaming red hair that fell below her shoulders and eyes the colour of emeralds. "Wow," Luke remarked, "I wonder if we'll get to see her."

"I'm sure she'll be around even if she doesn't stay here," I said, studying the photos. "She looks really beautiful."

Luke looked like he was in a trance. "Mmm, I hope they're going to need some extras. I sure would really love to be in this picture."

I was wondering if he was really thinking about the picture or the attractive woman who would be starring in it.

Chapter Five

We could hardly wait until the end of July; and when the trucks started to arrive with filming equipment, it was hard to keep people from gathering around to see what was going on. It was when more trucks showed up, some with dressing rooms for the cast, that the excitement really began to mount. Abingdon was bustling with activity, and it seemed like dozens of strangers had taken over our quiet little town.

Two days before the rooms that had been reserved were to be occupied, my parents received a number of special requests from a rather formidable-looking woman named Eleanor Teasdale. She appeared to be in her late fifties, stout, with short grey hair and round glasses with silver frames. She wanted to ensure that our largest room, the Willow Tree Suite, was well stocked with pillows, had ample closet space and a mini bar with a constant supply of mineral water, vodka and Shweppes bitter lemon. It had to be Shweppes—nothing else would do. It was then we discovered that we would be playing host to the star herself, Pandora James, and there were other demands. Breakfast was to consist of one boiled egg, two slices of dry white toast, half a grapefruit and black coffee. Dad remarked to me later in a whisper, "Thank goodness we don't provide lunch or supper." I figured Ms. James was a bit of a diva, but Luke seemed more intrigued than ever.

On the day that Pandora James was due to arrive in Abingdon, my father was up at the crack of dawn, helping my mother make sure everything was shipshape. By the time I got up and dragged myself downstairs to the kitchen for breakfast, everywhere I looked seemed to be sparkling. The floors had been scrubbed, the windows had been washed and not a speck of dust was anywhere. Mum had always been a stickler for cleanliness, and she even had Sammy groomed regularly to cut down on his shedding and never allowed any member of the family to wear an article of clothing more than twice without it being laundered.

I thought Luke would have been up earlier than his normal hour of ten o'clock. During the holidays, he loved to sleep in, but I expected this would be the one day that he would be too excited to laze around in bed. It was only when Dad told me that Luke had been up until the wee small hours, reading Defoe's most famous novel, *Robinson Crusoe*, that I understood why he hadn't yet shown his face. What I didn't understand was, why was he suddenly so interested in eighteenth century literature? Surely, this wasn't all for the benefit of the lovely Ms. James?

It was lunchtime when Luke eventually appeared, still in his pyjamas all tousle-haired and bleary-eyed. "My goodness," I said, "you're looking pretty rough. You'd better go and get washed up and put some clothes on before Mum sees you."

"Thanks a lot, sis," he mumbled while he reached for the coffee pot, "but I need something to eat first. I'm starving."

"Well, this is your lucky day," I answered teasingly. "I was just going to make myself something. How about a fried egg sandwich? I can even put some ham in it if you'd like."

"That would be great. Could I have two sandwiches?"

"Yes, I think I can manage that," I replied, taking the pot out of his hand, pouring coffee into a mug and then digging him in the ribs, "but you'd better watch out or you'll get paunchy like old Mr. Cringle, and then Pandora won't look at you twice."

"Who's Mr. Cringle?" Luke asked, taking his mug over to the table.

"You know very well who he is. He owns the butcher's shop on Caldecott and don't try and change the subject."

"I don't know what you're talking about," Luke replied, burying his head in the newspaper.

I had just cracked open the first egg into a bowl and was about to speak when Dad came rushing through the door. "She's on her way!" he yelled, staring at Luke still in his PJs. "Luke, get on upstairs and get changed. I don't want her running into you like that, and Ariel, whatever you're doing just stop and find Sammy. I don't want him getting in the way."

Luke frowned and slowly got up from the table. "But I haven't had any breakfast yet."

"Too bad, my lad," Dad said, waving his hand towards the door. "If you were up at a decent hour, you'd already have some food in your stomach. Just get dressed, and then you can come down and get something to eat."

Luke slunk out of the door with his coffee mug in hand while I put the eggs away. "Why are you so worried about Sammy, Dad?" I asked.

"Well, we don't know if Ms. James likes dogs. She may be scared of them."

"I think Ms. Teasdale would have told us if that was the case."

"Maybe she didn't see Sammy when she was here, but I'm not taking any chances. Just lock her up in Nana's old room for now."

Reluctantly, I left the kitchen to go and find Sammy, but I was out of luck. Wherever he was, he didn't want to be found.

Less than fifteen minutes later, a silver Rolls Royce drove up to the front entrance of the inn. Mum and Dad, both looking as though they were going to some special occasion dressed in their Sunday best, were waiting anxiously while I watched from behind a curtain at one of the large bay windows. First, the driver stepped out, attired in a grey uniform, and opened one of the back doors. I held my breath in anticipation, but the foot, encased in a heavy black Oxford, followed by a rather plump leg clad in thick lisle hose, obviously belonged to the formidable Ms. Teasdale. Once out of the car, she stepped back a few paces, and the driver extended his hand to the person remaining inside. Again, I held my breath and watched as Pandora James swung her legs out and onto the pavement and then stood up to reveal the face and figure of a woman I could only describe as stunning. She was taller than I expected, although I did notice that the knee-high black boots she was wearing had at least four-inch heels. She had on a gauzy green peasant blouse with a flowing floral skirt, but it wasn't hard to tell that she had curves in all the right places. I think what I found most startling was the colour of her hair, flame red and falling well beneath her shoulders, and the paleness of her skin, which looked flawless from where I stood behind the curtain. She smiled when she saw Mum and Dad, and I watched while they shook hands and then disappeared through the front door followed by Ms. Teasdale. That's when I decided to make my presence known; and stepping out from my hiding place, I stood in the centre of the hallway. Dad looked surprised for a moment and then took my hand. "I want you to meet my daughter, Ariel," he said. "Ariel, this is Ms. James."

I don't know what possessed me, but I bobbed down into a sort of curtsy as though I was greeting some member of the royal family and then blushed to the roots of my hair. Pandora just grinned and placed her hand on my arm. "I'm very pleased to meet you, Ariel," she said charmingly. "What a delightful name you have."

I looked over at Mum, who was grinning. "Yes, well, my mother named me after some person in a Shakespeare play."

"Yes, Ariel is a character in *The Tempest*," she responded and then turned to my mother. "Are you a fan of Shakespeare, Mrs. Regan?"

Dad didn't give Mum a chance to answer. "She certainly is," he said, "She even named our son Lucius against my better judgement. Thankfully, except for my dear wife here, we all call him Luke."

Pandora looked over at my mother and said, "Well, I think Lucius is a wonderful name, and that's what I will call him when I meet him. Is he here now?"

Nobody had any time to answer because that's when Sammy suddenly came running full tilt along the hallway and landed right at Pandora's feet. Dad started to bend over to grab him, but Pandora was already hunched down, cradling Sammy's head in her hands. "Oh, he's so adorable. Does he have a special name too?"

Dad shook his head. "Just plain old Sammy."

"Mmm," murmured Pandora, still holding Sammy's head while he looked up at her adoringly, "I can't think of a Sammy character right now, but his name certainly suits him."

"He seems to have really taken to you," Mum said. "I've never seen him do that before."

I heard a noise behind me as Pandora gave Sammy a pat on the head and then stood up. I saw her glance over my shoulder and turned to find Luke standing just a few feet away. Dad turned at the same time and called out, "Luke come and meet Ms. James."

I watched Luke's face as he slowly walked forward, but it was hard to tell what he was thinking. When he got within a few steps of us, Pandora held out her hand and smiled. "Ah, this must be the elusive Lucius," she said.

I thought Luke had been struck dumb for a moment, and then he finally found his voice, "How do you do, Ms. James," he whispered.

Pandora looked amused, and I couldn't help thinking that she must be used to adoring fans. "I'm very well—thank you, Lucius—and I'm happy to be here. I hope to see you and your sister often while I'm in Abingdon."

Dad chuckled. "Oh, I expect you'll be seeing quite a lot of them. In fact, they'll probably be hanging around the film set, trying to get a part in the picture."

I was mortified. "Oh, Dad, that's not true," I moaned.

Pandora laughed. "It's okay, Ariel," she said. "I think you would probably look wonderful on the big screen."

I should have been flattered, but she wasn't looking at me when she made that remark; she was looking directly at Luke.

Dad left the little gathering to collect Pandora's luggage from her car while Mum reacquainted herself with Ms. Teasdale and then accompanied both of our guests up to their rooms. Luke and I watched as they mounted the stairs, and it was only when they were out of sight that I finally spoke. "Well, I know what you were thinking, Luke. You were practically drooling."

Luke rolled his eyes. "Trust you to say that, sis, although I have to admit she looks every bit the film star."

Sammy was sitting by my side, gazing up at the staircase. "Sammy sure liked her," I said, rubbing the top of his head.

"Dogs have a sense about people," Luke responded. "They know who to trust and who to stay away from."

"But do you know who to stay away from?" I teased.

Luke frowned. "What do you mean by that?"

"I think you've taken to Pandora just like Sammy. Just remember she's years older than you and you could get hurt."

"What are you implying?"

"Nothing, I just don't want to see you mooning about like Marcy."

"Marcy? I don't know what you're talking about."

"She's got a crush on you. Don't tell me you haven't noticed. Every time she sees you, she lowers her eyes and goes red in the face."

"You've got a vivid imagination. She's just shy that's all. Even around Mum and Dad, she hardly ever talks, but Mum says she's a good worker and she always stays late to finish off her chores. Mum says she doesn't know how she ever managed without her."

I felt a little guilty realising that I hadn't been pulling my weight. Both of my parents worked very hard to keep the inn going, and it wasn't easy. Thankfully, Dad was doing well selling his custom-made furniture, but he had less time to help Mum out, and Luke often had to pitch in for him. Sometimes I would hear my mother sighing when she got a little stressed; and one day, I asked her if she ever regretted not following her dream of becoming an actress. She shook her head and glanced out of the window, looking for Dad, who was pruning the hedges that ran around our property. "No, honey, I never regretted it because then I would never have met your father and I wouldn't have you and Lucius. I think I'm a very lucky woman."

I got very emotional hearing this and gave Mum a hug. "I love you so much," I whispered.

"I love you more," she whispered back.

Chapter Six

Pandora didn't leave her room until evening. By one o'clock, Mum was a bit concerned that our star guest hadn't had any lunch, although we usually only provided breakfast. She was just about to ring up to the room when Ms. Teasdale appeared. My mother was at the reception desk preparing for the other members of the cast and crew to arrive when she stepped up to the counter and asked, "Is there somewhere close by that provides vegetarian meals?"

Mum shook her head. "If you need something for lunch, then I'm afraid the only places I can think of are both Indian. They serve a variety of foods, but I think you're probably looking for something lighter. If you need to find a place for supper, then I would recommend the Garden in Oxford. It's less than a half-hour drive away."

Ms. Teasdale frowned. "Thank you for the suggestion. I will pass it on for this evening, but for now I just need to purchase some sandwiches. After today, it won't be a problem because the commissary truck will be arriving tomorrow, and they will have the food that Ms. James requires."

Mum smiled. "In that case, why don't I make you both something for lunch. I have some wonderful mozzarella cheese, sun-dried tomatoes and some fresh Italian bread. How would that do with a dab of mayo? It would only take me a few minutes to make, and I could have them brought up to Ms. James's room."

Ms. Teasdale smiled back. "That is so kind of you, Mrs. Regan. It sounds wonderful. I don't know how to thank you."

"It's no bother at all. I'm happy to help out. I'll bring you a pot of tea as well, unless you prefer coffee."

"Tea would be perfect. I'll go upstairs and tell Ms. James how thoughtful you have been. I'm sure she'll want to thank you herself when she sees you."

"That won't be necessary. I'm sure she has enough to do, and if there's anything else either of you need, please don't hesitate to ring the desk."

Ms. Teasdale turned to walk away and then turned back. "Thank you again."

Mum asked me to watch the desk; and fifteen minutes later, she was back with a tray laden down with sandwiches, a pot of tea and a plate of her home-baked raspberry tarts. "How would you like to take this tray up to Ms. James's room?" she asked.

"I'd love to," I replied, just dying to see what Pandora was up to and maybe get a chance to talk to her some more.

I climbed the stairs, balancing the tray rather precariously, and when I got to the Willow Tree Suite, I tapped lightly on the door. Ms. Teasdale appeared and looked rather surprised to see me rather than my mother. "Oh, Ariel, isn't it?" she asked. "Do come in. You may put the tray on the table near the window."

I caught a movement out of the corner of my eye as I made my way over to the table and gently put the tray down. I had my back to the door; and when I turned around, Ms. Teasdale was standing with the door ajar, obviously expecting me to leave. I didn't dare look anywhere else except directly at her; but then suddenly, Pandora called out, "Ariel, why don't you join us for lunch? It looks like your mother has made enough for an army."

I looked over to see her sitting in one of the large green velvet chairs near the fireplace. She was wearing an apricot silk caftan with her hair tumbling about her shoulders, and she was holding what looked like a manuscript. "I'm tired of learning lines," she remarked. "I need a little company."

I glanced at Ms. Teasdale, who was slowly closing the door. "Are you sure it would be all right," I asked nervously.

"Oh, don't worry about Claire," Pandora replied. "She'll be happy to take something to eat and go back to her own room. I'm not the nicest person to be with when I'm studying my lines. Claire, just take whatever you want, and I'll see you at around six. I'm going to have a nap before I go out to dinner with Martin this evening."

"Very well," Ms. Teasdale said, taking a sandwich and pouring herself some tea.

I stood there not quite sure what to do until she left the room, and then Pandora pointed at the chair opposite her. "Come, Ariel, bring the tray over here to this table and have a seat. I want you to tell me all about yourself."

I carried the tray over to the other table and sat down; and as I did so, I noticed Pandora's bare feet poking out from beneath her caftan. Her toenails were painted in the same scarlet colour as her lipstick, but her fingernails were unpolished. I couldn't help staring at her face as she reached over and poured some tea into the only cup left on the tray. She had a perfectly shaped nose, a wide mouth with sparkling white teeth and flawless skin with not a sign of the freckles usually associated with redheads. I was wondering if her hair was really that colour when she looked up and handed me the cup and saucer. "Here, Ariel," she said, "you have the tea. I already have something to drink."

I thanked her as she picked up a glass containing what I could only assume was the vodka and bitter lemon she had specifically ordered to be in her room. She took a sip and then picked up one of the sandwiches. "Do have something to eat," she said. "I certainly can't eat all this myself."

I picked up a sandwich rather reluctantly, as I had already had lunch, but I didn't want to be rude and it gave me something to do while I tried to think of something to say. Thankfully, I had only taken my first bite when Pandora leaned forward and said, "You know, you're a very attractive girl. You have the same colouring as your father."

I swallowed as fast as I could before responding, "Thank you, but I always wanted to look like Mum. She's so pretty and very feminine-looking."

Pandora chuckled. "Yes, she is, but you have a lot of character in your face. It makes you stand out from the crowd, and your hair is marvellous."

Coming from someone who was so beautiful was very flattering, although my parents and even Luke had always complimented me on my looks. I felt very self-conscious, sitting there being stared at, and started to blush.

Pandora put the glass down and leaned back in her chair. "Don't be embarrassed, Ariel. By the way, I'm curious, how old are you?"

"I just turned nineteen, and I finished high school in the spring."

"And what do you plan to do now?"

"Well, I want to go to London, but Mum and Dad want me to stay home for at least a year before I make the move."

"I see, and why do you want to go to London? Do you have any family there that you can stay with?"

I shook my head. "No, I've just heard so much about it, and I've never been anywhere except for Oxford. I feel like I've been stuck here in Abingdon all my life, and it's time I left and saw how other people live. I'm going to help my parents out until the end of next summer and save as much as I can, and then I'm going to apply for a course at the London College of Fashion."

Pandora clapped her hands. "Oh, I know where that is. It's right in the heart of London, close to Hyde Park. What will you be studying exactly?"

I grinned at her enthusiasm. "I want to study all the phases of dress and costume design."

Pandora frowned. "Won't it be very expensive just for the courses alone and have you any idea how much it costs to live in London?"

"Well, Mum and Dad put a lot aside for my education so that should take care of most of the cost for college. As for room and board, well, I haven't got that far yet, but I'm sure I can find one or two people to share with and then I'll get a job somewhere. I know it won't be easy, but I don't want to stay here forever."

"And what about your brother, he's older than you, isn't he?"

"No, actually he's a year younger. Luke hasn't decided what he wants to do yet. Mum would like him to stay here and take over running the inn in a few years, but I don't think that will happen. He's really smart and gets really good grades, but I think he likes English best, and he loves participating in the drama class."

I noticed Pandora's face light up. "You mean he might like to be an actor?"

"Oh yes, and I know Mum would love that even if it meant him leaving Abingdon. He was in a play last year, and he was really good. He played Demetrius in *A Midsummer Night's Dream*."

"What a wonderful role to play. I played Helena when I was about your age. She was in love with Demetrius. Perhaps I could help once he finishes school. I'd like to talk to him about it before we finish filming here."

I could hardly believe my ears. "That would be wonderful. He'll be thrilled. If he comes to London, we could get a flat together. We've always been close, and I'd love having him around."

Pandora laughed. "Whoa, slow down, Ariel. Things aren't always that simple."

We talked for almost an hour, and I learned that Martin, who Pandora had referred to earlier, was Martin Cameron, the director of *Moll Flanders*. He was staying at the inn, along with Ms. Teasdale and two other members of the cast. I could hardly wait to see what he looked like.

That evening, I was at the reception desk when Pandora came sweeping down the staircase in a short silver frock, with long matching earrings and silver stiletto sandals. She looked absolutely stunning, and I was wishing that Luke could have seen her, but he had been missing all afternoon. A rather overweight man, of medium height, with thinning hair and a rather boyish face, followed her, and I could only assume this was her director. She strode up to the desk and smiled at me. "Good evening, Ariel, this is Mr. Cameron, and we're just going for supper. Perhaps you can give me directions to the Garden restaurant. You mother told Claire it was in Oxford."

I nodded at Martin Cameron, and he nodded back. "Yes, it's on Plantation Road. It's only about twenty minutes by car and easy to get to, but I can give you a map. It has really good food, all vegetarian and lots of variety, Indian, Greek and even Mexican."

I took a map from under the counter; and as she took it, she turned to her companion. "I know you would rather have a steak, Martin, but please indulge me."

"Don't I always?" he replied with a grin.

I watched them leave and climb into the back of the Rolls, which had just pulled up into the driveway. I was thinking how wonderful it would be to have my own chauffeur when Luke came up behind me. "Who was that guy, sis?" he asked.

"That was the director, Martin Cameron," I answered. "Did you get a look at Pandora? She looked fabulous."

When Luke didn't answer, I turned around to see if he was still there. He was gazing in the direction of the front door with a vacant look on his face. "Oh my goodness," I couldn't help teasing, "you're mooning. I knew this would happen."

He looked a little startled and then frowned. "I certainly am not," he said. "I was just wondering where they were going, that's all."

"They were going to the Garden for dinner. Pandora's a vegetarian, and Mum recommended it to her."

"And how do you know so much about her?"

I gave him my most superior expression. "Because I had lunch in her room. I took up some special sandwiches Mum made for her, and she invited me to stay. I'm surprised your ears weren't burning because we were talking about you."

"Oh? What were you saying about me, and why didn't you tell me about this before?"

"Well, for one thing, I've been helping Mum all afternoon and you haven't been here. You didn't even show up for supper. Where were you?"

Luke shook his head. "Never mind that. What were you saying about me to Pandora?"

"I told her about you acting in the play at school and how good you were, and guess what? She said she wanted to talk to you about it before they finish filming here."

Luke's eyes lit up. "Are you serious? She really said that? Wow, maybe she can help me get started on an acting career."

I smiled at how his demeanour had changed. "Actually I think she's probably going to help you get enrolled in one of the actors studios in London. Just think of it, Luke, if I go to London next year, we could room together. You always said you would rather go to London with me than anyone else."

"Yes, and I meant it at the time, but you're grown-up now, sis. Would you really want to share a place with me? I would have thought that you'd prefer to room with a couple of girls. That way, you can natter on about clothes and makeup and boys."

Arms akimbo, I shook my head. "Is that what you really think of me, that I'm some bimbo that can't have an intelligent conversation?"

Luke laughed. "Just teasing," he said. "I could never think of you as a bimbo. In fact, I think it would be a great idea if we got a flat together, but that's a long way off, and who knows what might happen before then."

Chapter Seven

I was up at seven o'clock the next morning as I'd heard that filming was to begin early, but I wasn't sure where. When I got downstairs, I found Mum alone in the kitchen, making breakfast. I knew Dad was chopping wood behind the inn, but Luke was nowhere to be seen. I assumed that he was still in bed. I walked over to the counter and looked over Mum's shoulder. She was heating some butter in a pan and whisking some eggs in a small bowl. "Morning," I said, cheerfully kissing her on the cheek. "Where's Marcy? Isn't she helping you with breakfast for the guests?"

Mum turned and smiled. "Ariel, honey," she answered, "all of our guests were up at the crack of dawn. They needed to start filming early, so they've already eaten and left. It had something to do with taking advantage of the daylight."

I was really disappointed to have missed everyone. "Oh no," I moaned. "Do you know where they went?"

"Yes, they're filming at Milton Manor, and your brother was tagging along. Now why don't you run out and get your father, and I'll whip up some eggs for you too."

I wasn't too interested in eating at that point. "You mean Luke was up before me and went with them. How did he know what time they were leaving?"

Mum sighed, "I'm not sure, but he was talking to Adrian Evans last night. I saw them sitting outside in the garden near the gazebo."

"Who's Adrian Evans?" I asked frowning.

"He's in the film. I think he's playing the part of one of Ms. James's husbands."

I racked my brains trying to remember the story. "Maybe he's the rich one that owns a plantation in Virginia. I think she meets him in the country, and maybe that's why they're filming here. I was wondering about that because most of the story takes place in London."

Mum grinned. "Well, I'm pleased that you know something about it because I tried to read the book, and I just couldn't get through it."

"I know because I had trouble too. Most of the books written back then are difficult to read. Look, Mum, I'd prefer to skip breakfast and go and see what's going on. Do you need me around here this morning?"

"No, it's fine for you to go, but first you need to get your dad, and I insist you take at least a couple of slices of toast with you. You can't leave here on an empty stomach."

"Okay, Mum," I called out as I raced out the door to fetch my father.

I took my bike and cycled as fast as I could over to the manor. I had been there many times before but not in the last year or two. It was set on beautiful parkland with two lakes; and when I was younger, I would enjoy the pony rides and the animals, including rare pigs, sheep and even a llama. The house itself was open to the public on a daily basis, and I assumed that during the filming, no outsiders would be allowed on the premises.

As I got to the road leading to the manor, I could see four or five trailers up ahead and several brilliant lights even though the sun was already up. Then as I got closer, I could see cables snaking all along the road and a crowd of people on the south end of the park. I decided to get off my bike and walk, and that's when I spotted Luke at the edge of the crowd. I called out to him, but he didn't hear me until I got within a couple of feet of him and called to him again. He smiled when he saw me and beckoned. "Hi, sis, I wondered when you'd show up."

I leaned my bike against a tree and tried to peer over the heads of the crowd. "Thanks for telling me you were coming here," I said with sarcasm.

He looked a little sheepish. "Sorry, I just found out late last night, and you'd already gone to bed."

"You could have woken me when you got up this morning."

Luke smirked. "You're kidding, right? You know how grumpy you are when you first wake up, and anyway, I knew as soon as you found out where I was, you'd follow me."

"That's no excuse," I countered. "I could have missed something. What's happening? Have you seen any action yet? Have you seen Pandora?"

"Haven't seen anything yet. They're shooting inside the manor at the moment, although I did catch a glimpse of Pandora coming out of one of the trailers."

"Oh, what did she look like? Was she in costume? I bet you didn't even notice."

"As a matter of fact, I did notice. Her hair looked the same, only a bit curlier, and she was wearing a long pale blue frock that had a lot of lace over it."

"I bet her boobies were hanging out of the top too," I said giggling.

Luke shook his head at me and then grinned, "As a matter of fact . . ."

I cut him off, "Trust you to see that, you're a typical male."

Just then there was quite a commotion and we noticed a figure exiting one of the manor doors. It was a man in black breeches and a brocade vest over a white shirt with loose-fitting sleeves. He looked to be in his midtwenties and was quite handsome with long dark hair pulled back into a ponytail. "Look," I cried out," I wonder who that is?"

Luke shaded his eyes as one of the lights swung in our direction, "That's Adrian Evans," he said.

"The guy you were talking to last night?"

"Yes, that's him. He's a really nice chap. We talked a lot about acting, and this is only his second film role. It's not a very big part but he's going to be auditioning for the lead in a play in the West End."

I craned my neck to get a better look at Adrian, but he had already gone into one of the trailers. "Did he say anything about Pandora?"

"Just that she's a really cool person, and he's enjoying working with her."

"Did you see her come back from supper last night?"

"No, apparently she was invited to a private party afterwards at the mayor's house. That's why she was all dressed up, and I think they came in really late."

I thought this over for a moment. "I wonder if she's got a thing going on with Martin Cameron."

Luke frowned. "I would hardly think so. He's years older than her."

"Yes, and you're years younger," I said poking him in the ribs.

"Oh, we're on to that again, are we? Just because I obviously find her attractive doesn't mean I've got a crush on her."

I paused as I noticed the crowd disperse and someone walking towards us. "Oh well, I think she may have a crush on you," I said.

It was Pandora coming towards us, and people were standing back to let her through. She was still wearing her costume, and she looked beautiful. The blue frock was covered, from the waist up, with a delicate lace, and she was obviously wearing a push-up bra that showed her breasts to their best advantage. It was even hard for me to keep my eyes on her face, let alone any young man with raging hormones. She smiled at me and then held out her gloved hand to Luke. "Hello, Lucius," she said in her wonderfully melodious voice, "I'm so happy to see you here."

I almost giggled out loud as I watched Luke struggling to concentrate above the level of Pandora's neck. "It's nnnnice to be here, Ms. James, "he stammered.

"Please," she said, "I insist that you call me Pandora."

I wondered if I'd suddenly become invisible, but then she glanced over at me, nodded and said, "Good morning, Ariel,

I'm surprised to see you here. It must be a lot of work for your mother with just that little mouse, Marcy, to help."

I was a little taken aback and was about to respond; but before I got the chance, she looked back at Luke and smiled. "Lucius, why don't you join me in my trailer while I'm on my break. I'm sure you'll enjoy the refreshments." Then she turned on her heel, grabbed onto Luke's hand and walked away.

I stared after them; and although Luke was being pulled along and almost stumbling, he managed to turn his head to look back at me and shrug his shoulders. I was dumbfounded when I realised that Pandora had dismissed me just as she had dismissed Ms. Teasdale the day before. It appeared that whatever Pandora wanted, Pandora got, and I knew she was not to be trusted.

I cycled home at a furious pace, getting angrier by the minute; and when Dad saw me ride up and park my bike against the wall at the back of the inn, he knew immediately that I was not in my best mood. "What's the problem, sweet girl? You look like you could murder someone."

I snorted and shook my head. "That Pandora James is a right cow."

My dad chuckled. "Whoa, nice talk. What did she do to you?"

"She dragged Luke off to her trailer like he was some little kid. She wanted him to sample her refreshments. Huh, I can just imagine what kind of refreshments she was talking about, and she suggested in a smarmy sort of way that I should come back home to help Mum."

Dad roared with laughter. "Oh, honey, that's priceless."

"How can you laugh, Dad? It's not amusing. She's a witch. She even called Marcy a mouse, and she's after Luke even though she's old enough to be his mother."

Dad put his hand over his mouth in an effort to stop smiling. "She's not even thirty, so she can hardly be old enough to be his mother, and I'm sure Luke can look after himself."

"No, he can't," I protested. "He's only eighteen, and he doesn't know very much about women."

Dad came over and, taking my hand, sat me down on one of the benches at the edge of the lawn. "Come, my dear," he said. "Just calm yourself down, and don't worry about your brother. I'm sure he knows a lot more about women than he's letting on."

"But he's never had a steady girlfriend, and I don't think he's ever . . ." I dropped my gaze and looked at my hands resting in my lap. "You know, Dad."

"If he has or he hasn't isn't your business, honey. You're his sister, and I know you two are very close, but there are some things brothers and sisters don't share."

"I know, you're right, Dad," I said, resting my head on his shoulder. "I just don't want to see him taken advantage of."

Dad put his arm around me. "Look, so he has a fling with some film star. It's no big deal, and she'll soon be gone and forgotten. Luke's a smart lad, and I'm sure he can take care of himself."

I sat for a minute, feeling comforted by my father's arm around me. "Thanks, Dad, I feel better now. I think I'll go and see if there's anything Mum wants me to do."

Chapter Eight

By midafternoon, Luke had still not come home, and I was getting a little anxious, so I decided to make myself some tea and relax in the back garden. Minutes later, I walked through the hallway, cup and saucer in hand, and noticed the *Oxford Times* sitting on the hall table. I picked it up and made my way out to the bench where I had been with Dad earlier and just sat for a while, sipping my tea and watching the birds flying in and out of the trees. It seemed so peaceful, and I was beginning to unwind when I opened the newspaper and immediately felt the tension come flooding back. There, on the second page, was a photo of Pandora in her silver frock, with her arms around Martin Cameron's neck and her head thrown back, looking like she was in a moment of ecstasy. At least, that's the way I saw it, and then I noticed the headline, 'Hanky Panky at the Mayor's Party?' I could hardly wait to read the caption beneath the photo, but it didn't say too much other than imply that something was going on between Pandora and her director. I could hardly believe my eyes, wondering how low she could stoop, but then again, maybe that's how she got to be a film star.

I was dying to show Luke the picture and kept glancing at my watch, willing him to walk out through the back door;

but when I heard a footstep behind me, I saw that it was Mum carrying a tray with a pitcher of lemonade and a plate of cookies. "Hi, honey," she said, placing the tray on the bench beside me. "I thought you might like something cold to drink. It's pretty hot out here today, and I don't want you getting sunburn."

"Thanks, Mum," I said, picking up a cookie and pushing the newspaper to one side.

Mum stood for a minute, gazing around the garden and then sat down beside me and took my hand. "Your dad told me all about your conversation, Ariel. I know you're older than Lucius and want to protect him, but he's a grown-up now and he's ready to make his own decisions, right or wrong. Dad and I aren't going to interfere, and I don't think you should either. Maybe you're getting the wrong picture, and I expect Ms. James probably just wants to help him with his career."

I shook my head vehemently. "No, Mum. You didn't see the way she dragged him off and the way she ignored me." I picked up the paper and put it on her lap. "Take a look at this. I think she likes anything in trousers no matter what their age."

Mum read the caption and then looked at me and smiled. "Oh, Ariel, you are taking this much too seriously. She looks like she's just having fun to me, and you should know by now that British papers are notorious for gossip. You're being much too hard on Ms. James, and I hope you won't show any negative feelings towards her. I expect you to be polite. After all, she is a guest here."

I pressed my lips together in a sulk. "I'll try but it won't be easy."

"Good girl, now have some lemonade and cool off. I don't want you worrying about your brother anymore."

"But where is he? He's been gone for ages."

"Who knows, honey?" Mum said, getting up and walking towards the back door. "We don't keep tabs on him, and I expect he'll be home for supper. Now don't you stay out here much longer in this sun."

Mum was right, Luke showed up for supper, looking pretty pleased with himself. I was helping Mum dish the chicken casserole out of the oven when he waltzed through the door and sat down beside Dad at the table. "Hi, Dad," he said. "Sorry

I'm a bit late." Then without pausing for a breath, he looked over his shoulder and asked, "What's for supper, Mum? I didn't even have lunch, and now I'm starving."

I shook my head as I carried the casserole to the table. "I thought Pandora was treating you to some refreshments," I remarked sarcastically.

The innuendo appeared to go right over Luke's head. "Oh, she did. You should have seen the amount of food. There were bagels, donuts, muffins and all kinds of fruit, but it was pretty early. I haven't had a chance to eat since then."

Both Dad and Luke were already spooning some of the chicken onto their plates before Mum and I got the chance to bring the dish of green beans and baby carrots to the table. "You're supposed to wait until we're all sitting down," I said, addressing Luke.

He looked at me with a puzzled expression on his face, but Dad put down his knife and fork and said, "Sorry, honey, I was feeling a little peckish too."

Mum sat down and patted Dad's hand. "It's all right, dear, you go right ahead."

Luke looked at Mum and said, "What's wrong with her?"

Mum didn't get a chance to answer because I cut right in, "There's nothing wrong with me except that I don't like being brushed off like I'm not important."

Dad stopped eating, rolled his eyes at my mother and said, "Ariel, can we have a nice peaceful supper, please? I don't want any arguments at the table."

"Well, what did she mean by that, Dad? I didn't brush her off."

Dad sighed, "Apparently your Ms. James wasn't very sociable this morning. She suggested that your sister should be at home helping your mother."

"Yes, and she called Marcy a mouse, and she doesn't even know her," I said angrily.

Dad waved his hand at me. "Okay, that's enough. Whatever happened, your brother wasn't disrespectful to you, so I think you should just drop it."

Luke reached over and grabbed my arm. "Sorry, sis," he said, "I don't think she really meant to be mean to you."

I shook his hand off. "So where were you all day?"

Luke's face lit up. "I was watching the shoot. Pandora invited me to watch inside the mansion, and I got to talk to all kinds of neat people. It was so exciting, and the more I learn about the film business, the more I want to become an actor."

Now it was Mum's turn to intervene. "But I thought you wanted to be a stage actor, Lucius?"

"I want to do everything, Mum, stage, films and even TV if the opportunity comes along. Pandora has a lot of contacts, and she can get me into one of the actors studios in London. She's even going to ask Martin if I can be an extra in one of the crowd scenes on Saturday."

I pushed my supper plate away from me in disgust. "So it's Pandora and Martin now. Boy, aren't we getting chummy."

"What is your problem, sis? You can come along and watch if you like, and I can even ask Pandora if you can be an extra too."

"Over my dead body," I said, getting up and walking towards the door.

"Ariel, come back here," my father called out, but I just kept on walking.

Chapter Nine

I don't know where Luke went that evening; and by seven o'clock, I was still feeling unsettled, so I decided to take a walk along the riverbank with Sammy. I knew I was being unreasonable, but I couldn't seem to forget about the way Pandora had treated me. I had just reached the entrance to the bridge when I saw a figure leaning over the ledge and staring down into the water. It was still fairly light out; and as I grew closer, I recognised the young man I had seen dressed in costume earlier that day. He turned when he heard my footsteps and started to walk towards me. He was wearing jeans and a black tee shirt, which accentuated his muscular arms and shoulders. In his costume, he had looked almost slight in build, and his hair had been sleeked back. Now his hair was an unruly black mop falling over his forehead, but his face gave him away. It was the same face that I had observed before, handsome with a dark complexion and all sharp angles. I stood still as he approached; and when he got to within a couple of yards, he smiled. "Good evening," he said in the most refined accent I had ever heard. "It's Ariel, isn't it? You're Luke's sister."

I nodded. "Yes, and you're Adrian. Luke told me he'd been talking to you, and I saw you over at the manor this morning."

He took a step closer and then bent down to pat Sammy's head. "And who do we have here?" he asked.

"This is Sammy, and don't worry, his bark's worse than his bite."

He continued to stroke Sammy's head. "He's a great-looking dog. He reminds me of the dog I had growing up."

Sammy was pulling at the leash. "Oh oh," I said, "I think this one's getting impatient. He loves to walk especially at this time of night when it's cooler."

"Do you mind if I walk with you?" Adrian asked.

"I would like that," I replied, and we started to stroll farther along the riverbank.

We walked side by side for a while, with Sammy ambling on in front of us, happily wagging his tail, but I felt just a little uncomfortable. It wasn't because I was nervous about being alone with a stranger, knowing it would soon be getting dark, but ironically because it felt so natural as though we had taken this same walk many times before. It only took me a few moments to realise that I was very attracted to him, and I was anxious to know more about him. I was just about to ask what he thought of Abingdon when he looked up at the sky and said, "What a beautiful evening. Look at the sky, Ariel, it's still a little light out, but you can already see some stars."

I stopped and followed his gaze. "Yes, it's very clear. There's not a cloud anywhere."

Adrian turned to look at me. "Have you lived here all your life?" he asked.

I nodded and started walking again as Sammy strained on his leash. "Yes, and I can't wait to leave. Don't get me wrong," I hastened to add. "I've had a very happy life here, and my Mum and Dad are the best, but I want to see other places."

Just then we came upon one of the many benches along the bank where people liked to sit and watch the boats going down the river. "Why don't we sit for a while?" Adrian suggested.

"Of course, that would be lovely," I replied, tying Sammy's leash to one of the bench's iron legs.

After we were both seated, Adrian stretched out his legs and sighed, "This is so relaxing. I could spend a lot of time here." Then he turned to me and asked, "So have you been to many other places?"

"No, absolutely nowhere except for Oxford, and that's just up the road. I want to go to London. In fact, I'm going next year and not just for a visit."

"You mean you're actually thinking of moving there?"

"Oh, not just thinking about it. I'm really going to do it. I'm saving up to go to the London College of Fashion, and I can hardly wait."

"Do you know just how expensive it is to live in London? Where are you planning to stay. Do you have relatives there?"

I shook my head. "No relatives, but I hope to be sharing a flat with Luke. You know, he's keen on becoming an actor."

"Yes, he mentioned that when I spoke to him yesterday, but I had to warn him it's a tough life and really hard to get a break. Usually you have to know someone to get into the business."

I knew this was my chance to bring up Pandora. "Well, according to Luke, Pandora's going to help him get into one of the actors studios."

Adrian paused for a moment. "Is that what she told him? I'm not sure he should take that too seriously."

I knew I was onto something and was dying to hear more. "What do you mean? Do you think she's leading him on?"

"Well, Pandora's got quite a reputation. She tends to pick up men and then just spit them out when she gets bored. Not that I can blame any man for falling under her spell. She's not only a beautiful woman but she's smart too and a damn fine actress."

I suddenly felt very superior. "I knew it. I just knew it. She isn't to be trusted, and I tried to warn Luke, but he just wasn't listening."

Adrian leaned down and stroked Sammy behind the ear. "You know, Ariel, when you're really attracted to someone, all logic goes out the window."

I glanced over at him and wondered what he was really thinking at that moment. The more I studied his face the more handsome I found him; in fact, he reminded me of a very young Gregory Peck. I hesitated and then found the courage to ask, "Don't tell me you've fallen under her spell too."

Adrian started to laugh, and I felt a little stupid. "Did I say something funny?"

He put his hand on his chest. "Oh, that's priceless," he said. "You mean you haven't guessed?"

"Guessed what? I don't understand."

"I'm gay, Ariel, that's the only reason Pandora hasn't hit on me."

I felt so embarrassed, and yet disappointed at the same time. I had already fantasised about going out with Adrian while he was in Abingdon and maybe even seeing him again after that. "Now I feel really dumb," I said, hanging my head.

Adrian reached over and tipped my chin up. "No need. I guess there's no way you could have known. I live in such a tight-knit community most of the time, and I tend to think that we all know everything there is to know about each other. I guess you're pretty isolated out here and don't get to meet too many of us."

"Actually, I don't think I've ever met a gay person before. I suppose I thought you'd all look like those I've seen on television."

"You mean like a drag queen?"

I couldn't help giggling. "Yes, I guess that's what I meant."

"It's okay," Adrian said, smiling. "Most of us look just like everyone else."

"And do you have someone special in your life? I mean someone who's really important to you?"

"Yes, as a matter of fact I do. His name's Joel, and he's a doctor at the London Clinic. That's not too far from Regent Park. Oh, I forgot you wouldn't know where that is."

"What kind of a doctor is he, and how long have you known him?" I asked, suddenly full of curiosity.

"He's an ENT doctor—that's ear, nose and throat—and we've been together almost four years. We have a garden flat in Kensington and a Maltese named Ziggy. Joel's a few years older than me, but we just connected right away and we share a lot of the same interests even though we're in completely different professions. Of course, I'm away quite a bit, so he has most of the burden of looking after the flat and Ziggy. Fortunately, we have a wonderful neighbour, Mrs. Stokes, who looks after

Ziggy during the day, and her niece, Patty, will always come and dogsit if we need her. I consider myself extremely lucky to have found someone to share my life with, and now I'm hoping to get the lead in a play in the West End, and then I won't have to be away from home for a while."

"You sound like you're really happy, and I hope you get the lead in the play."

Adrian smiled. "I am happy, but enough about me. Tell me more about yourself. You mentioned a fashion school. Do you want to become a model?"

I laughed. "Me, a model? That's really funny. No, I make a lot of my own clothes, and I'd like to go into dress design. Up to now, Mum's helped me a lot, and she has a really good fashion sense, but I know I have a lot more to learn, so I want to go to the best school in London."

Adrian stared at me. "First of all, don't sell yourself short. You could be a model. You're not only tall and slim but you're also a very attractive woman."

I could feel myself blushing, although I was hoping it was dark enough by then so that he wouldn't notice. "It sounds like you really have some serious plans," he continued, "but I'm still a little concerned about you being in London all alone. That is, if Luke changes his mind about sharing a flat with you."

"I don't think he will," I said. "We've talked about it a couple of times, and I know he wants to study there too."

"Nevertheless, things don't always turn out the way you expect, so I just want you to know that you have a friend you can call on for help when you're there. You'll have to come visit Joel and me, and we can point you in the right direction, whether it's the best place to live or to eat or whatever you need."

I was really touched by his generosity. "That's so kind of you, Adrian. I would feel much more comfortable knowing I had a contact there."

"Not just a contact—a friend—and I could even introduce you to my sister, Erica. She's about your age and a lot of fun. I think you two would get along well together."

I started to untie Sammy's leash. "It would be really nice to have another girl to chum around with. I miss my friend, Becky, now that she's so involved with her boyfriend."

Adrian took the leash from my hand and stood up. "Do you mind if I walk him?" he asked.

I nodded and we set off back along the riverbank towards the inn, walking mostly in silence, but I felt comfortable in his company. After we said good night and I refilled Sammy's water bowl, I went looking for Mum to tell her that I'd made a wonderful new friend, and now I was more determined than ever to go to London.

Chapter Ten

I didn't see Luke until the next morning. I'd gone to bed fairly early the night before after having a lovely conversation with Mum about Adrian. We both sat in the kitchen, enjoying a bedtime snack of ice-cold milk and peanut butter cookies, and then Dad came looking for Sammy to take him for his last run before bedtime, and I decided to go on up to my room.

Luke was already sitting at the table, digging into a plate of scrambled eggs and bacon, when I came downstairs for breakfast. He looked up at me as I came through the door. "Hello, sis," he said. "Where did you get to last night?"

I glanced over at Mum, who was washing dishes at the counter. "I was here. Where were you?"

"I was out watching a night shoot, but I came in just after ten. Were you out somewhere?"

I went over to the counter to get some coffee and put some bread in the toaster. "I must have just missed you. I went to bed around that time."

Luke looked at Mum. "You didn't tell me she was in bed."

Mum sighed, "You didn't ask," she replied. "As I recall, you were too excited talking about where you'd been all day. I wish you would let me know if you aren't coming home for lunch or supper."

I sat down at the table opposite Luke, waiting for my toast. "So what was so interesting that you stayed out since early morning, and when did you get to eat?"

Just as Luke was about to reply, Mum came over and put her hand on my shoulder. "Ariel," she said, "what else would you like besides toast? I can make you some eggs too, but I need to get finished here. Marcy and I have already taken care of all of the guests, and now we have to get started on the rooms. Actually I wouldn't mind your help for a couple of hours this morning."

I smiled up at her. "It's okay, Mum, I don't want any eggs, and I'll be glad to help as soon as I've finished my coffee."

At that moment, I heard the toaster pop up, but Mum was there in a flash and bringing it to the table along with the butter dish and a pot of raspberry jam. "Are you sure that's all you want, dear?" she asked.

"Yes, I'm sure, Mum. Thanks," I answered, and she started to walk away but then turned back. "Don't forget, Lucius," she said, "if you're not coming home, I need to know."

"Okay, Mum," Luke replied, nodding his head.

As soon as she had gone, I asked again, "What was so interesting about the shoot?"

"Well, during the day, it got a bit boring because there's an awful lot of just standing around and waiting, but then Martin told me I could stand in for one of the extras who'd come down with a case of stomach flu."

"Are you serious? You mean you're actually in the picture? Did you have to get all dressed up?"

"Yes, but it's no different than getting in costume for a school play, except they didn't have to plaster on the makeup because I was near the back. They may even cut out that scene, who knows."

"So what happened last night?" I asked, trying to find out where Pandora fit into the picture.

"Actually nothing much happened at the actual shoot, but I got invited out to supper with Pandora and Martin and one of the actors, Jamie Levy."

"Why would they invite you? And why didn't they invite Adrian?"

I noticed Luke blush slightly. "I guess they like me—I don't know. As for Adrian, he wasn't filming at all yesterday, and I didn't see him."

"He was out with me," I said proudly.

Luke frowned. "What do you mean, out with you?"

"I was walking Sammy, and I ran into him, so we took a stroll together, and then we sat on one of those benches on the riverbank and we had a nice long chat."

Luke grinned. "He's gay, you know. Too bad for you."

"I know, but he's really nice, and when we get to London, he's going to help us."

"He said that?"

"Well, he said he would help me find my way around, and I could go and visit him and his boyfriend, Joel. I told him that we'd be getting a flat together."

Luke looked pensive. "That's still a long way off, sis, for you at least. I may decide to go to London earlier."

I felt a small wave of anxiety. "You can't do that. You're still only eighteen, and Mum and Dad won't let you go."

"They can't stop me. I'm old enough to leave home. Anyway, that doesn't mean you can't come and stay with me when you get there. I have the chance to go to the actors studio, and I don't want to pass it up."

"And how are you going to pay for all this, or is Pandora footing the bill?" I said sarcastically.

"Now your acting like you're jealous. What have you got against her?"

"I'm not jealous. I just don't trust her, that's all, and she treated me like I was a nobody."

"I think you've misjudged her. She's been really nice to me, and she's a lot of fun."

I got up from the table as I felt myself getting cross. "Maybe you should speak to Adrian," I said, my voice starting to rise.

"Don't run off, Ariel. What did Adrian say?"

"Ask him yourself," I said as I flounced out the door.

After I'd helped Marcy make up the guest rooms, assist with the laundry and finish a pile of ironing, it was lunchtime. I had no idea where Luke had gone, but he didn't show up for lunch and he didn't ring. It was a beautiful day and not as hot as it had been lately, so I decided to take my notepad out into the garden and sketch some designs. There were already indications in the media of what styles were coming for the fall season, and I wanted to create something for myself that would be fashionable but practical. I had only been sketching for about five minutes when I heard the back door open, and Adrian stepped out with a cigarette in his hand.

"Hello, Adrian," I called out. "I didn't know you smoked."

He wandered over to me, smiling. "Hi, Ariel, I know. It's a filthy habit, but somehow I can't seem to give it up. Joel's been after me forever to quit, especially as he's seen what harm it can cause."

I patted the bench beside me. "Have a seat," I said. "Luke and I have never smoked and neither have my parents. I've been tempted on several occasions, but I really wouldn't want to start now."

"You're a wise young lady, and I hope you stay that way. I suppose growing up in a household where there were no cigarettes must have made it a lot easier. It wasn't the same for me, I'm afraid. My father not only chain smoked but he drank like a fish too. In fact, he died from alcohol poisoning when I was fifteen."

"I'm so sorry. That must have been really tough on you."

Adrian shook his head. "Not really. I never liked my father. He was abusive, both verbally and physically. He used to beat up on my mother and call her the most horrific names, and then when he found out I was gay, he decided it was my turn."

I was astounded, unable to understand how anyone would have to endure being treated that way. "What about your sister?"

"Erica?" Adrian chuckled. "She had my father wrapped around her little finger. He never so much as raised his voice to her."

"Really, how did she react when he died?"

"That's the interesting part. She actually celebrated. She hated him, but she never allowed him to see that. I guess you'd call her a master manipulator."

"That's amazing, and I'm dying to meet her one of these days. What about your mother, where is she?"

Adrian grinned. "She's living in Devon now with her cousin, Harold. I'm not sure what the living arrangements are, but she's happy. They have a bungalow in Torquay, just a short distance from the sea, and an Irish wolfhound who's almost as big as my Mum. Joel and I visited last summer when we took a road trip to Cornwall. We only stayed for a few hours, but it was easy to see how content Mum is now."

I closed my notepad and looked out across the garden, trying to imagine living so close to the ocean, but Adrian leaned across and touched me on the arm. "May I?" he asked, looking down at the pad in my lap.

"Oh, I'm not very good," I said as I reluctantly handed it over.

Adrian flipped through the pages slowly until he came to the design I had been working on that afternoon. "These are wonderful," he said. "You're really talented, and you've got some unique ideas here."

"Not too unique, I hope?" I commented. "I don't want my designs to look like costumes. I want the clothes to be wearable."

Adrian closed the notepad and handed it back to me. "Well, I think you're going to be very successful, and I hope you'll still stay in touch when you become famous."

I giggled. "I don't think I'll make it that far, but I'd like to make a living in the fashion business. Maybe my brother will turn out to be the famous one in our family."

Adrian stood up. "Speaking of Luke, I saw him earlier at the manor. He was in one of the crowd scenes."

I stared up at Adrian, marvelling at his chiselled features and warm brown eyes. "I figured that's where he got to. Did you speak to him at all?"

"No, but I do know that Pandora invited him to some club tonight in Oxford. I think it's called the Zodiac. I'm going too. In fact, there's a whole crowd of us going. Why don't you come with us?"

I could feel my body tense up. There was no way that I wanted to be around Pandora James, especially in a place like the Zodiac, which was one of the most popular clubs in town. "No, thank you. I think I'll pass, but I'd really appreciate it if you would do me a favour."

Adrian frowned. "Of course, what would you like me to do?"

"Keep an eye on Luke. I don't think he's used to drinking, and I want to be sure he gets home safely. There's been some talk about raising the drinking age to twenty-one, and it's too bad it isn't in effect already."

Adrian paused for a moment. "It probably wouldn't make much difference. I've seen guys, and girls for that matter, much younger than Luke get into bars and clubs. I even did it myself. Most of these places don't care. They just want to sell liquor and make money. Anyway, don't worry, I'll watch out for him and see that he gets home in one piece."

I stood up and placed my hand on Adrian's arm. "Thank you so much. I'm really concerned about Luke."

Adrian gave me a hug. "You're a great sister, and Luke's a very lucky guy."

Chapter Eleven

By evening, we had still not seen Luke, and my mother was annoyed that he hadn't rung. I noticed Ms. Teasdale come in at just after seven o'clock; but before I had the chance to ask her if she had seen Luke, she swept right past me and retired to her room. On most nights, my father would be at the front desk, waiting for all the guests to be accounted for before locking the front door. It was rare for him to have to stay in the reception area after ten o'clock, as Abingdon wasn't a place where one could partake in any form of nightlife and most of our guests chose the inn because they wanted to enjoy the countryside and experience some peace and quiet. Occasionally, one or two people would sit and chat in the cosy lounge and savour a complimentary cup of tea or coffee, or they would take advantage of a clear night and sit out on the back porch. Somehow, I knew this night would be different. I didn't expect Pandora and company to be back until the wee small hours, and I offered to keep Dad company. "You don't have to do that, sweet girl," he said. "I'll be working on the accounts, and I'm halfway through a Dean Koontz novel, so that should keep me occupied."

"But Dad, I'd like to stay up with you. I'm worried about Luke. He's gone to the Zodiac with the film crowd, and he'll probably have too much to drink. I'll stay out of your way. I have my own book to read, so I'll just sit in the corner."

My father shook his head. "It's not necessary, and I don't want you worrying about your brother. I can take care of him."

"Please, Dad," I protested. "I promise I'll be quiet. You won't even know I'm here."

Dad sighed, "All right, but if you start getting tired, I want you to get on up to your bed. Is that understood?"

"Uh huh," I answered as I made my way to the wing chair in the corner of the reception area with a clear view of the front door. I tried to concentrate on the book I was reading, but my mind was too occupied with thoughts of Luke. I glanced up at my father several times, but he seemed to be thoroughly engrossed in whatever he was doing behind the desk. I did notice Ms. Teasdale come down the stairs at one point and go into the lounge. I assumed she was getting a nightcap and decided not to bother her. Other than that, it was deathly quiet, except for the ancient wall clock, which we were told came from a fourteenth century cathedral. It seemed to dominate the silence with its loud ticking.

At midnight, Dad looked over at me and said, "Ariel, I think you should go to bed. There's no point in you sitting there. It could be a while before they get here."

"I don't want to go, Dad. Please let me stay a bit longer. If they're not here by one, I'll go, I promise."

At that very moment, we heard the sound of a car approaching and the glare of headlights through the large bay window. My dad stepped out from behind the desk and motioned at me to stay where I was. He had just got to the front steps when I heard the sound of the car door close and Adrian's voice. "Good evening, Mr. Regan," he said. "I hope we didn't keep you up."

I stood up and approached the doorway as my father answered, "It's quite all right, Mr. Evans, but have you seen my son, by any chance?"

"He's with Martin and Pandora, and I hope you'll go a bit easy on him, sir. He's had a little too much to drink."

I burst through the doorway. "I knew it. I knew it. I thought you were going to keep an eye on him, Adrian. Where is he?" I cried in frustration.

My father put his hand on my arm. "Now now, my girl. Let's not be disrespectful. Mr. Evans is our guest, and he's not responsible for your brother."

Adrian stepped forward. "It's quite all right, sir. I did promise Ariel that I would watch out for Luke, and I did my best, but the place was so crowded, I couldn't keep up with him. He's fine and he really enjoyed himself, but he'll probably have a headache in the morning."

"Is he on his way back now?" my father asked.

"Yes, they should be here any minute. Pandora's a little the worse for wear too, but Martin doesn't drink so he had no problem driving. You have nothing to worry about."

I breathed a sigh of relief as I saw the Rolls Royce pull into the driveway just seconds later. Adrian walked over and opened the passenger door, and I expected Luke to step out, but it was Pandora who exited in a rather unlady-like manner, wearing a short flame red frock covered in sequins and five-inch red sandals. I hate to admit it, even to myself, but even in her inebriated state, she looked astounding. When she finally straightened up and saw my father, she held out both arms and said, "Why, Mr. Regan, how lovely of you to wait for me." Then she took a few paces forward and threw her arms around his neck.

My father looked at me helplessly, but Adrian came to the rescue. "Come on, Pandora," he said, gently pulling her away, "you need a cup of coffee."

In the meantime, Martin had stepped out of the car and was reaching into the backseat in an attempt to pull Luke out onto the driveway. When he seemed to be having difficulty, both Dad and I rushed forward to help, and I was appalled when I saw Luke slumped over and dishevelled, with eyes closed and bright red lipstick on the side of his mouth. I looked at Dad in horror, but he just shook his head, and between the two of us, we managed to pull him out. Martin got back in the Rolls and drove to the parking area while I helped my father take Luke up the stairs to his room. I assumed that Adrian was still in the lounge, feeding coffee to Pandora, and I was grateful that I didn't have the opportunity to confront her. I'm not sure what I would have said, but I was disgusted. I had never seen my brother in that state before, and something had gone on in the back of that car.

My father didn't even bother to help Luke out of his clothes. He was a dead weight, and it was difficult enough just getting him to his room. We just laid him on his bed and quietly left the room. Fortunately, we didn't wake Mum; and as we tiptoed back along the hall, Dad put his arm around my shoulder and whispered, "I think it would be a good idea if you didn't tell your mother about any of this."

"She'll probably know anyway when she sees how hungover he is in the morning," I whispered back.

Dad nodded. "Maybe and maybe not. I'm usually up first, so I'll make sure he's in reasonable shape before he shows his face."

"What are we going to do about this Pandora thing?" I asked.

Dad sighed as he steered me towards my room, "We're not doing anything. Your brother is old enough to figure things out for himself. He's just sowing his wild oats, that's all. Most young men go through this stage, and you have to remember that he's never been exposed to this kind of lifestyle before. He's bound to be caught up in it."

"Then why aren't I caught up in it too?"

"Because you're my sweet sensible girl, and I want you to stop worrying about your brother. Now go on and get some sleep. Morning will be here soon enough."

I gave my dad a hug and kissed him on the cheek. "Night, night, Dad. See you tomorrow."

Dad grinned. "I think you mean today," he said.

Chapter Twelve

The next morning, I was helping Marcy change the bedding in the guest rooms and didn't see Luke leave the inn. According to Dad, he had woken him just before seven and fed him coffee and aspirin before he left him to get washed and dressed and presentable for breakfast. My mother saw him very briefly when he went into the kitchen and put two bran muffins in a paper bag, but then he was gone. She obviously didn't notice anything different about his appearance, so I could only conclude that Dad had done a good job with the coffee and aspirin; and when she asked Luke why he was in such a hurry, he just mumbled that they had an early shoot. Mum was rather amused at Luke's preoccupation with the picture and had no idea that his real interest was in the film's star, Pandora James. I was a little surprised that both she and Dad let him get away with taking off every day and not helping out with the chores. When I questioned Mum about it, she merely said, "I think, during the summer, you young people should have some time to enjoy yourselves. Marcy and I can manage without you if there's something special you want to do. Why don't you go over to the mansion and watch with your brother."

"Thanks, Mum, but I think I'll pass," I said.

That evening, I was surprised when Luke showed up for supper. Mum was really pleased, especially as she had made his favourite rhubarb pie. Dad gave me a warning look when we sat down, and I interpreted it to mean that I wasn't to say one word about the night before. It was a typical family meal, with Sammy waiting for scraps, just like the hundreds of others we had shared before, but I couldn't help thinking that I needed to talk to Luke. I was determined to catch him before he went off again, no matter where it was. I knew I had to help Mum with the dishes, but Dad offered to do it. He seemed to sense that I needed time with Luke and suggested that we take our tea out to the back porch. Luke looked apprehensive as he carried the tea tray out of the back door and placed it on one of the tables. "How about here, is this okay, sis?" he asked.

"It's perfect," I answered, "and it's such a nice evening. I love it out here at this time of the day. It's always a little cooler especially here in the shade."

Luke sat down and poured tea from the pot into both cups. Then without looking up, he said, "I suppose you want to talk to me about last night."

I had been wondering how to broach the subject without getting into a fight; and surprisingly, Luke had brought it up himself. I added some milk to my tea and then stirred it slowly while I thought about how to answer. "Well, I was a little shocked when I saw what state you were in," I said. "I've never seen you drunk before. In fact, I've never even seen you drink. What happened to you?"

Luke shrugged his shoulders. "I don't know. I was having a great time at the Zodiac, and one of the guys got me some drink called a Zombie. Then I remember having another one and being on the dance floor, doing the 'Macarena,' but after that it's all just a complete blur."

"Do you remember coming home last night?" I asked.

"Luke frowned and shook his head. "No, I don't recall anything. I asked Dad if he knew how I got here, when he woke me up this morning, but he just said that Martin brought me back. Why, did something happen?"

"Considering you were in the backseat with Pandora and you had lipstick all over your face, plus the fact that you looked like you'd slept in your clothes, I would say something happened."

Luke blushed. "I honestly don't remember. Anyway, it may not have been her lipstick. Maybe some other girl came on to me at the Zodiac."

"Fat chance," I said. "It had to have been her. Look, I'm not trying to be a party pooper, and I'm not a prude, but I'm concerned that you're getting too involved with Pandora. You're going to get hurt, Luke, and I don't want to see that."

"Pandora wouldn't hurt me. She's a really great person, and when I get to London, she's definitely going to help me with my career. I want to go soon, sis. I don't want to wait anymore. Soon the whole film crew will be heading back to film the scenes for the Newgate Prison sequence. They've built a huge set to look exactly like the old prison, and I don't want to miss that."

"Oh, Luke," I cried, reaching out to touch his hand, "please don't get your hopes up. I want you to wait so that we can go to London together. Then if she lets you down, I'll be there for you."

Luke got up. "I can't wait, sis. I want to go now."

"But where will you stay? How are you going to be able to afford to live anywhere?" I asked, feeling my heart begin to race.

"Pandora said I could stay at her townhouse," he answered.

I jumped up and grabbed Luke's arm. "No, you mustn't do that. She doesn't mean it. She's not a sincere person."

Luke looked cross. "You don't know her. You've hardly even spoken to her. I know you mean well, sis, but stop interfering in my life. I'm going to London whether you like it or not."

He pulled away and marched off through the back door as I yelled after him, "Mum and Dad won't let you do this." But I knew all my pleading just fell on deaf ears.

I sat down again and sipped my tea, wondering what I could do to stop Luke from making the biggest mistake of his life. Both of us had been brought up in a sheltered environment, and I couldn't imagine him being exposed to a completely different life in London. Even if Pandora meant what she said and let him stay with her, from what Adrian had told me, I knew she would soon tire of him and then what would he do all alone with nobody to support him. I knew in my heart that if he left when the filming in Abingdon was over, I would have to follow him. Luke had always been my hero, and I couldn't let him down.

Gazing out across the garden with its vibrant green grass and myriads of colourful flowers, I noticed that the sun was going down, and there appeared to be some rather ominous-looking clouds in the distance. I was just considering going indoors when I heard a footstep, and Dad poked his head around the door. "How about coming for a walk, Ariel," he suggested. "Sammy needs to go out, and we need to go now before it starts to rain."

I picked up the tray and followed my father into the house. "I'd love to come, Dad," I answered. "I need to get out myself for a while."

A few minutes later, we were strolling along beside the river, and Sammy was running on ahead. He loved to be off the leash; and as long as we were able to keep an eye on him, we let him have his freedom.

"Did you have a good talk with your brother?" Dad asked.

I sighed, "Not really, he's bound and determined to go to London when the filming is over. He claims that Pandora is going to let him stay at her townhouse. Can't you do something to stop him?"

Dad put his arm around my shoulder. "My dear girl, I'm afraid he's eighteen, and he can leave anytime he wants. I don't want to see him go, and when your mother finds out, she's going to be devastated. Luke's never had a serious girlfriend, and now he's met someone he's totally smitten with. It won't be long before he comes to realise that this isn't going to last. I bet he'll tire of her before she tires of him, and then he'll be back home in a flash."

"I hope you're right," I said and instantly decided I wouldn't mention that I was seriously considering following Luke to London. I thought I would just wait and pray that something happened to make Luke change his mind.

By the time we got back to the inn, a very light rain had started to fall. We were just turning into the driveway when I noticed the Mercedes parked near the front door; and a moment later, Martin and Pandora came outside. They were both casually dressed, Martin in jeans and a pale blue blazer, while Pandora wore camouflage pants and a green tee shirt. I grabbed Dad's arm and made him hang back until they got into the car and drove off. "What is it, Ariel?" Dad asked.

"I just don't want to be in a position where I have to be polite to her," I replied. "I might say something I'll regret."

"Wise thinking," Dad said grinning. "Come on, let's get inside before we get wet, and your mother won't be happy if Sammy leaves footprints all over the hallway."

Later that evening, I had just left the kitchen carrying a glass of lemonade when I ran into Adrian on the stairs. "Good evening, Ariel," he said smiling. "How are you?"

"I'm fine. I'm just going up to my room to watch *Doctor Zhivago* on the telly."

"Mmmm . . . that's a great picture. I saw it at a festival last year. They were playing all the top films of the sixties."

"You know it's raining," I said, noticing that he wasn't wearing a raincoat.

"Ah, but I have my brolly," he remarked, revealing a large black umbrella which had been concealed behind his back.

"Are you going somewhere nice?" I asked lamely, dying to know what he was really up to.

"I'm off to the Cherry Tree pub for a couple of pints. This will be my last night here."

I was shocked to hear this. "You mean you're leaving tomorrow? Is everyone else leaving too?"

Adrian shook his head. "No, just me. I've finished with all my scenes, and I could have driven back tonight, but Martin wanted me to join them for a drink so I decided to stay over."

"So Martin and Pandora went to the Cherry Tree? What about Luke, did he go there too?"

"Sorry, I have no idea where Luke is tonight. He may be with them. Why don't you come with me?"

"Thank you, but I want to watch the film. I just hope that, if Luke is there, he doesn't get drunk again. He's got some crazy idea that he's going to London and staying with Pandora. I'm so worried about him. I don't know what to do."

Adrian put his hand on my arm. "Ariel, if anything happens, I want you to get hold of me. Here, I'll give you my phone number." He put his umbrella down on the stairs while he fished in his pocket for a scrap of paper and a pen. After scribbling down the number and his address, he tucked it into my hand and said, "Remember, anytime you need help, you just ring. Now you'd better get along or you'll miss the beginning of the picture."

I gave him a hug, and he hugged me back. "I can't thank you enough," I said. "And even if I don't need your help, I'd like to keep in touch."

"I'd like that too," he replied and then added, "and maybe I'll see you before I leave in the morning."

I felt sad as I watched Adrian go down the stairs. We had spent very little time together, but I already thought of him as a friend and someone I could rely on if I ever needed help when I moved to London.

Chapter Thirteen

I missed seeing Adrian leave the next morning. I was helping Mum in the kitchen; and when I took Sammy out for a run at ten o'clock, I noticed his car was no longer in the parking area. I decided, at that moment, that I couldn't go on worrying about Luke and what I perceived was his obsession with Pandora. If he really meant what he said about going to London when the filming ended, I would deal with it then; but for now, I had to get on with my own life. Mum had reminded me earlier that I needed to go out and enjoy myself rather than hanging around the inn all the time. I realised that I had isolated myself from most of my friends, and Becky spent most of her time with Jordan, so I hardly got to see her anymore. I had actually run into her a couple of weeks before the film crew arrived, and we had spent the evening at the Cherry Tree. It was great to see her, but we didn't get much time to catch up because a couple of the local boys joined us at our table. I had known one of the boys, Terry Butler, since the time we were about eleven years old. We had been in the same class, and although I had never really been attracted to him, Becky had told me, on several occasions, that she suspected he was interested in me.

After a couple of gin and tonics, I was feeling a little giddy; and while Becky was busy telling Donny Baker all about her trip to Cambridge with Jordan, I was giggling at Terry's story about his mother's cat being trapped in a tree for two days. It was a good thing that he persuaded me to eat some of the pub's famous pot pie and mushy peas; otherwise, I don't think I could have found my way home. Terry offered to walk me back, but I lied and told him I was going with Becky. Then when he asked if he could ring me, I suggested that he give me his phone number and I would ring him. Now it was about four weeks later, and I still hadn't made the phone call even though Mum told me he'd telephoned and left me a message. Thinking back on what a good time I had at the Cherry Tree and anxious to distract myself from thinking about Luke, I waited until midafternoon and then finally picked up the phone.

Terry sounded genuinely pleased when he heard my voice. "Ariel," he said, "how nice. I was hoping you'd ring. Did your mother give you my message?"

I hesitated. "Um . . . yes, she did, but it's been really busy here. We have some of the cast and crew from *Moll Flanders* staying here, so things have been a bit hectic."

"It's okay, I understand. How about now, have things settled down a bit?"

"Yes," I answered, "and I hoped I could take you up on your offer to go out. I feel like I've been stuck here at the inn for days on end."

"How about on Saturday? We could go and see *Forest Gump* at the Odeon? My dad will let me borrow his car to drive into Oxford, and maybe we can have a bite to eat afterwards."

"That sounds wonderful," I replied. "What time will you pick me up?"

After my date with Terry, I was feeling much more content with life. We had both loved the picture, and afterwards we went to Café Coco for pizza and coffee. The more we talked, I began to see a side of Terry that I hadn't seen before. Not only was he amusing, but he was also intelligent and knew a great deal about the theatre and various forms of art. I was beginning to notice that he was really quite attractive. He was of average height with a slim build, light brown hair and brown eyes, and I couldn't help noticing that he had a good dress sense. When he picked me up, he was wearing grey slacks with a crisp white shirt and a navy blazer and had obviously made an effort to look presentable even though we were only going to the pictures and for a light meal afterwards. Later, he complimented me on my frock, a scoop neck floral sheath with cap sleeves, and was surprised when he learned that I had made it myself. That led to a discussion about my dream of going to London and studying fashion design; and then to my astonishment, I discovered that Terry was planning on moving to London in October. He had already lined up a job as a graduate trainee with a pharmaceutical company. Fortunately for him, he had an aunt who lived just a short distance from his workplace, and she had offered to let him stay with her until he got on his feet.

"How does your family feel about you leaving?" I asked.

"I've only got my mum at home," he said rather sadly, "and she's not too happy about it, but she understands why I want to get out of Abingdon."

"What happened to your dad?"

"My father left when I was four. He just walked out the door and never came back."

I put my hand on his arm. "I'm so sorry. Do you remember him at all?"

Terry shook his head. "Not really. About the only thing I do remember is him picking me up one day and telling me what a good boy I was. Of course, Mum has lots of photos of him, and I used to look at them and wish he'd come back, but now I don't really care if I ever see him again."

"That's so sad. What about brothers or sisters?"

"Nope, I'm the only one. Mum always said she wanted more children, but she never met anyone she wanted to settle down with after my father left. What about you, Ariel? How does your family feel about you leaving home?"

I thought about it for a moment. "I don't think they're crazy about the idea, but they'd never stand in my way. My parents are great, and I know I'm really lucky. They care for each other a lot, and it shows."

"What about Luke, what's he up to these days? I haven't seen him around for a while."

"Do we have to talk about Luke?" I asked. "He's not exactly in my good books these days."

Luckily for me, Terry agreed to drop the subject, and we spent the rest of our time fantasising about what it would be like living in London. It was after eleven by the time he dropped me back at the inn and kissed me very lightly on the lips. I was praying that he wouldn't come on too strong, and I breathed a sigh of relief as I walked into the reception area and found Dad at the front desk. "Hello, Dad," I called out as I came towards him. "Am I the last one in?"

Dad laughed. "I hardly think so, my dear girl. The only one of our guests upstairs is Ms. Teasdale, and your brother's still out on the town somewhere."

"Probably with Pandora and her crowd. I don't know how they do it, gallivanting every night and having to get up so early each morning."

"I wish I had their stamina, but I'm too old for burning the midnight oil. You, however, sweet girl, might try it yourself. You need to get out and enjoy yourself a lot more. By the way, how was the picture, and did that young whippersnapper behave himself?"

I chuckled. "Don't worry, Dad. The picture was really good, and Terry was a perfect gentleman."

"Well, I'm very glad to hear it. Now you'd better get off to your bed before that lot gets here. I don't want you tangling with any of them, especially if Luke's had a couple too many again."

"You're far too lenient with him," I said as I walked away and climbed the stairs.

"Good night, sweet girl," Dad called after me.

"Night, night, Dad," I replied, shaking my head.

Chapter Fourteen

When I saw Luke the next morning, I decided not to ask him where he had been the night before. He seemed in a really good mood, and he obviously knew about my date with Terry.

"How did the date go, sis?" he asked.

I looked across at Mum, who was standing at the kitchen counter with a smile on her face. "It was really nice," I answered. "We went to see *Forest Gump*, and then we went to Café Coco."

"Are you seeing him again?"

"Yes, he said he'd ring me at the beginning of next week."

Luke smiled. "He's a nice chap. Of course, I don't know him that well, but from what I've seen of him, he seems really decent. I believe he went out with Jeanie Graham for a while, but then she moved to Cambridge."

"Really, I didn't know that. I remember her though. She was really pretty, with long blond hair and very tiny."

I began to realise we were having a normal conversation, and it seemed just like old times, but then suddenly, Luke got up from the table and announced he was late, and minutes later he was gone.

Dad had some heavy chores to do that morning, and Mum and Marcy were busy upstairs, so Dad asked if I could stay at the reception desk, as he was expecting a couple of guests to check into Adrian's old room. It was about eleven o'clock when I noticed Ms. Teasdale descending the stairs. She looked a little flustered as she walked towards me, so I came out from behind the desk and asked, "Is everything all right. You look upset?"

"I'm fine, my dear," she replied, "but I'm afraid I have some bad news. Is your father here?"

"He just went into town to pick up some tools, and my mother's busy upstairs. Can I help?"

"Well, I'm afraid that we'll all be leaving tomorrow. There have been some problems with the shooting schedule, and we have to get back to London. I was asked to tell your father that we would meet our obligation as far as paying for the days we originally reserved, and I hope this doesn't cause you too much of a problem."

As she was speaking, my mind was racing ahead, wondering what would happen with Luke after Pandora left, but I managed to gather my thoughts and said, "Thank you so much for letting me know and also for your generosity. We've really enjoyed having you here."

"And we've enjoyed being here. Your parents are lovely people, and we haven't had a single complaint." Then leaning forward, she whispered, "Between the two of us, Ms. James can be rather demanding, but she has had nothing but good things to say about staying here."

"Really, she's demanding? I would never have thought that," I replied while crossing my fingers behind my back.

When Mum came downstairs a little later and I told her what was going on, she seemed somewhat relieved. "Maybe we'll have some empty rooms for a few days, and that will give your dad and me a chance to relax."

I could see she was looking a little weary. "Why don't you and Dad take off for a few days? You could drive down to Brighton. It's only a couple of hours away."

"We can't leave you here on your own. We've never spent a single night away from the inn since we took it over."

I placed both my hands on her arms. "Mum," I said, "Luke and I aren't children anymore, and Marcy's here too. We can manage, and if anything happens, we'll ring you, and you can be back here in no time."

Mum shook her head. "I don't know, Ariel. I don't feel comfortable about this, but I promise I'll talk to your father when he comes back. I have to admit I really do need a break."

"Okay, Mum, now you promise you'll talk to Dad?"

"Yes, I promise," she replied.

I had just checked our new guests in when Dad arrived back from town. I didn't let him get past me. "Mum needs to speak to you," I called out.

He looked surprised. "What about?"

"She'll tell you. She's in the kitchen having a cup of tea."

"Just what I need," he said as he wandered off. "Hope there's enough left in the pot for me."

As I was no longer needed at the desk, I waited for about ten minutes and then went to see what was going on. Mum and Dad were sitting at the kitchen table, holding hands and smiling. They both looked up as I walked in. "We're going to Brighton," Dad said with a big smile on his face.

"Really?" I remarked. "That's fabulous."

"Yes, my sweet girl, and we have you to thank for the suggestion. I know you can look after the place while we're gone for a couple of days, and I'll make sure that Luke knows he has to help."

"So when are you leaving?"

"After all those film folks check out. I'm sure they'll be gone early in the morning, and then we'll just pack a suitcase, and we'll be off."

"Have you thought about where you'll stay?" I asked. "I can go on the Internet and look up some hotels or B&Bs if you like."

"That would be a wonderful idea. Just make sure we're right at the ocean, and it's not too expensive. We'll stay for two nights, but that's all."

"Okay, but you know the beach at Brighton is all pebbles?"

"We don't care, do we, Jane?" he said, grinning at my mother.

Mum just shook her head and grinned right back.

Mum decided to make something special that evening to celebrate their first vacation in years, even though they would only be gone for a couple of days. Dad's favourite was fish and chips, but only fresh halibut would do. That meant I had to race over to the local fishmonger on my bike and then pick up a tub of ice cream to go with the raspberry pie Mum was baking. We were hoping that Luke would be with us for supper, but I was concerned about how he may have reacted to the news of the film crew leaving.

At six o'clock, I was just bringing Sammy in from his walk when I heard a car drive up and, a few minutes later, saw Martin and Pandora going up the stairs, but there was no sign of Luke. I considered calling out to them and asking where he was, but seeing they were deep in conversation, I decided not to bother them.

Just after seven o'clock, we were enjoying a glass of ice-cold wine when Luke burst through the door. "Sorry, I'm late," he said, sitting down at the table. "Anything left to eat, Mum?"

My mother got up, took a plate from the cupboard, and piled it with what was left of the halibut and chips. "Here," she said, "eat this, and when you've finished, there's raspberry pie."

"Thanks, Mum," he mumbled.

Dad looked at me and shrugged his shoulders. "Anything new, son?" he asked.

Luke hesitated. "No, same old thing," he replied nonchalantly.

I got up and started clearing the table. "Mum and Dad are going away for a couple of days."

Luke looked up at me in surprise and then glanced over at Mum. "You've never been away before. What's going on?"

"You mean you haven't heard?" Dad said.

"Heard what?"

Dad looked at me helplessly. "The film crew's leaving early. They'll be gone by tomorrow afternoon, and your mother and I are taking a couple of days off. There are only two guests occupying one of the rooms, and your sister insists she can manage, but I want to make sure you'll be here to help out."

I knew just looking at Luke's face that he had stopped listening after Dad's first sentence. "You really didn't know, did you?" I asked.

Luke put down his knife and fork and sighed, "I expect that's why Pandora wants to see me later. I'm meeting her at the Cherry Tree at nine o'clock."

"Sorry, we had to spring it on you," Dad said, "but you knew they'd be leaving sooner or later. Don't worry, son, you'll soon forget all about them and find other things to do. I just want your word that you'll help Ariel while we're away."

Luke nodded. "Don't worry, Dad, I'll be here," he said, but I knew from the look on his face that he had other plans.

Chapter Fifteen

Early the next morning, I watched from the doorway of the lounge while my father and a uniformed chauffeur carried several pieces of luggage out to the Rolls Royce parked in the driveway. He then returned to talk to Ms. Teasdale, who was at the front desk, checking out. They seemed to be having a very amiable conversation, and the woman I had considered to be rather stuffy and always serious was actually looking rather coy and even blushing. I had to smile to myself; my dad could charm the birds out of the trees, and it was easy to understand why my mother had fallen in love with him. A noise above me suddenly alerted me; and when I looked up, I saw Pandora and Martin coming down the stairs. They were both dressed casually in jeans and black tee shirts, but Pandora had four or five ropes of multicoloured beads draped around her neck and knee-high black leather boots. With her bright-red hair and flawless makeup, she looked like the consummate film star or super model. They were obviously in an upbeat mood; and when Pandora saw my father, she quickly walked forward, sidestepping Ms. Teasdale and held out both arms. "Mr. Regan," she said, smiling, "It's been a pleasure. Thank you so much for your hospitality."

Dad ignored the outstretched arms but extended his hand. "It was my pleasure, Ms. James. I trust everything was to your satisfaction."

Martin stepped forward and shook Dad's hand. "Everything was perfect, and we'll certainly recommend the Trout River Inn to anyone who might be travelling in this part of the country."

"That's very kind of you, sir," Dad replied. "All your luggage is in the car, and I hope you have a safe journey back to London."

"I'm sure we will," Pandora said. "Now come along, Claire, we need to get going before the traffic gets heavy on the M40."

Moments later, the car was pulling out of the driveway, and it suddenly seemed very quiet. I couldn't help wondering where Luke was and what had happened at the Cherry Tree the night before. I decided to peek into his room and was surprised to see that he was still sound asleep. I was sure he would have been there to say good-bye to Pandora.

At eleven o'clock, Luke finally showed up in the kitchen, where Marcy and I were making sandwiches for Mum and Dad to take on their trip. I didn't want to discuss anything in front of Marcy, so I suggested that Luke waited to eat until lunchtime and, in the meantime, see if Dad needed any help. He seemed very nonchalant and went off without a word. I could hardly wait to find out what was going on.

Mum was excited about going away but worried about leaving us alone. At noon, when Dad finally climbed into the car and Mum slipped in beside him, she had already given me dozens of instructions, and I breathed a sigh of relief when they drove away. Luke had been with me on the front steps, saying good-bye, and he looked rather sad. "Why are you sad?" I asked as we walked back to the kitchen. "You should be happy that they're finally getting some time off."

Luke's face suddenly brightened. "I am happy for them," he said. "Now can we have lunch because I'm starving?"

It seemed strange with just Luke and myself sitting at the kitchen table. I had made him a club sandwich, and I didn't want to spoil his appetite, so I decided to wait until he was almost finished before I mentioned Pandora. It was difficult making small talk, but I managed to keep on the subject of Mum and Dad's holiday until he was taking his last mouthful, and then I said, "I saw Pandora and Martin leaving this morning." He looked across at me and shrugged his shoulders. "So?" he asked. "What about it?"

I was surprised by his attitude. "I thought you'd want to see them off. What happened last night at the Cherry Tree?"

Luke stood up and walked over to the counter to pour a glass of milk. "Nothing happened," he replied with his back to me.

"I thought you'd be all cut up about her leaving. What's going on?"

He turned and smiled. "Absolutely nothing. She's gone and that's it."

I frowned. "I'm sorry, Luke. I guess I was right. She led you on, and all those promises she made meant nothing to her."

Luke came and sat down. "It doesn't matter, sis. It's all over, and I'm not going to get too upset about it. Easy come, easy go."

I wasn't really convinced that he was telling me the truth or just trying to be brave, but I thought the wisest thing to do was change the subject. "If you're not busy tonight, Terry wants me to go to the candlelight concert at the Oxford Castle. Why don't you come with us?"

"Thanks, sis, but I think I'll just stick around here tonight. Someone has to keep an eye on things."

My hand flew to my mouth, realising there wouldn't be anyone left behind to take care of the inn. What if our guests had needed something? I was particularly horrified because these were two elderly sisters, and they may have needed medical attention. It wouldn't have been the first time Dad had to ring for an ambulance. A man in his sixties had spent two whole weeks with us the previous summer; and on the last night, he suffered a heart attack. Thank goodness, he survived but it was pretty scary at the time. "Oh my goodness, Luke," I said, "I forgot about that. Are you sure you'll be all right on your own?"

"Positive, sis," he said. "You just go and enjoy yourself."

That evening, although it was a beautiful night and the candlelight display in front of the castle was so romantic, I couldn't stop thinking about Luke. I had almost convinced myself that he had resigned himself to the fact that Pandora had gone, but I was worried in case something happened at the inn while I was away. Mum and Dad would never forgive me.

Terry and I sat on a blanket on the grass, listening to the music; and after an hour, I was aware of him shuffling closer and putting his arm around my shoulder. It felt comfortable, and I enjoyed his company, but I was glad I didn't have to talk because I had other things on my mind. On the way home, Terry mentioned that I seemed a bit distracted, but he understood when I told him I was concerned about Luke. "Don't worry," he said, "we'll have you home in no time, and then you'll see you had nothing to worry about."

"Thanks, Terry," I said, reaching over and touching his arm. "You don't mind me cutting our date short when we get there then?"

Terry shook his head. "Of course not. We'll go out again at the end of the week if that's okay with you?"

"I'd love that," I replied, "and thanks for being so considerate."

We didn't arrive back at the inn until well after eleven o'clock. I was a little panicked by then and gave Terry a peck on the cheek and then ran up the steps to the front door. It was locked, and that made me feel a lot better; so after using my key, I locked it again from the inside and tiptoed along the hall and up the stairs. It was deathly quiet and almost creepy knowing that Mum and Dad weren't there, but once I got to my room and finally slipped into bed, it didn't take me long to fall asleep.

The next morning, I was up just after sunrise to let Sammy out, and I was well aware that our guests preferred to eat breakfast by seven o'clock. The Newman sisters were both spinsters from Manchester, well into their eighties, and touring southeast England for the first time. I had a pot of fresh coffee already prepared when I heard them coming down the stairs. I waited for them to get settled in the dining room and then popped my head in. "Good morning. I'll be right in with your coffee, ladies. Did you have a good night?"

Gladys, who I discovered was the elder of the two, grinned up at me. "Slept like a baby," she replied in her fascinating northern accent. "Your brother kindly allowed us to take Sammy for a walk. He's a wonderful dog, but we were quite exhausted by the time we got back."

I couldn't help chuckling imagining Sammy pulling the two of them along while they tried to keep up. "Yes, he can be quite a handful. Where did you walk to?"

"All along the riverbank to the old bridge. It really is a lovely area."

"Well, I'm glad you enjoyed it. I'll go and get the coffee now, and I promise to have your breakfast on the table in five minutes."

The younger sister—I didn't know her name—said, "No rush, my dear. We are quite content to sit for a while. It looks like it's going to be a lovely day, and we enjoy just gazing out through the windows. The grounds are so well kept, and we see so many birds. We even thought we saw a skylark yesterday."

"I can hardly tell one bird from another," I remarked as I carried the empty tray back out to the kitchen.

It was just after eight when Marcy arrived. She helped me clear away the breakfast dishes and then left me to make up the Newman's room and vacuum the upstairs hallway. She was concerned the noise would wake up Luke; but when I assured her that he could sleep through a rock concert, she just gave a coy little smile and went on her way.

I was still in the kitchen, having a bite to eat myself when the telephone rang. I knew it had to be my parents calling that early, and I jumped up from the table and grabbed the receiver off of the wall. "Trout River Inn, may I help you?" I asked, for the benefit of whoever was calling, especially if it was my father. He was lenient in so many ways but always believed in being professional and respectful.

The chuckle was unmistakable. "Dad," I cried out, "how are you? Where are you?"

"Never mind about us. Your mother and I want to know how things are at that end and if Luke's been helping out?"

"Everything's fine, Dad," I replied. "I actually went to a concert last night at the castle with Terry, but Luke stayed behind and took charge. He even let the old ladies take Sammy out for a walk."

Dad roared with laughter. "Oh, that's priceless. I can just see him dragging them along."

"I know, but apparently they really enjoyed it."

I heard a muttering in the background, and then Dad came back on the line. "Here, your mother wants to speak to you."

There was a shuffling noise, and then Mum said, "Hello, Ariel, where's Lucius?"

"He's still asleep, Mum. You know how he likes to lie in. Look we're both fine, and Marcy is here, so you have nothing to worry about. Now are you going to tell me what you've been up to?"

I heard Mum sigh, "Oh, Ariel, it's been so lovely to get away. We had a nice drive down, and we managed to get a room at the Lanes Hotel. It's right on the seafront, and our room faces the ocean. Right after we checked in, we went for a walk on the beach, and you were right, lots of pebbles, but we loved it. Then we went on the pier, and it was amazing. There are rides and arcades and all sorts of fun things to do. Your father even won a giant teddy bear. After that, we had the best fish and chips we've ever tasted and then took another walk. The sea air made us so exhausted. We were in bed by nine o'clock. It was wonderful, and I'm so happy you suggested it."

I was excited just listening to Mum and glad they were having such a great time. "So what are you planning for tomorrow?" I asked.

"We're going to tour the Royal Pavilion. We saw it from the outside, and it looks like an oriental palace. I can't wait to see the inside. After that, we might do a little sunbathing or take a drive along the coast. We'll be back here at the hotel by suppertime, and you can always leave a message for us if you need us. I'll give you the phone number if you'll get a pencil."

"Okay, hold on," I called out as I put the receiver down, ran to the reception desk and picked up the other telephone. "Hi, Mum, are you there?"

I wrote down the number and slipped it under a paperweight. "What time do you think you'll be home tomorrow?" I asked. I heard Mum checking with my father, and then she came back on the line. "Probably around two. We're just going to take our time. We'll have a nice brunch here before we leave." "I can't wait to see you," I said. "Tell Dad bye. Love you, Mum."

Mum said good-bye, and I heard Dad call out, "See you soon, sweet girl," and then they were gone.

Chapter Sixteen

I had been so busy with various chores that I lost all concept of time; and when I finally glanced at the clock, I was surprised to see that it was just after twelve. I was irritated when I realised that Luke was probably still asleep and had left Marcy and me to take care of everything. With a feather duster in hand, I climbed the stairs and knocked loudly on his door and then waited impatiently for him to answer. When there was no reply, I knocked again, even louder, but again no answer. I was even more annoyed that he was ignoring me and decided to give him a piece of my mind. I turned the knob and opened the door with such a flourish that it swung back and crashed against the wall, creating a loud bang. I heard Marcy come running along the hall, crying out, "Is everything okay, miss?" I was too stunned to answer because I could see that the bed was empty and looked like it hadn't been slept in. I started into the room, with Marcy trailing behind me, and then just stood there looking down at the bed as though I expected Luke to miraculously appear. Then I walked over to the wardrobe and pulled open the doors. It looked like half of Luke's clothes were missing, and I began to panic. I turned to Marcy, and her eyes were as big as saucers. "It looks like he's done a bunk, miss," she said. It was then, as I looked over her shoulder, that

I saw the letter propped up on the bedside table. "You can carry on with the chores please, Marcy," I said, and I watched as she slowly left the room before I picked up the envelope and sank down on the edge of the bed. It was addressed to me and simply said, "Sis."

My heart was hammering in my chest as I pulled out the single sheet of paper and unfolded it. His words were not what I wanted to hear or see.

Dear Sis,

I know you're going to be awfully mad at me, but please try to understand. I couldn't tell you I was leaving yesterday because you would have tried to stop me. The truth is, I'm in love with Pandora, and I'm going to London to be with her. She's going to help me get into acting school just like she said she would. I know you don't trust her, but I believe her, and so I have to grasp this opportunity while I can. Please explain why I've gone to Mum and Dad and tell them not to worry. Once I get settled, I promise I'll be in touch and let you know where I am. You're the greatest sister anyone can have, and I love you. Tell Mum and Dad I love them too.

Your brother, Luke xxx

It was just a brief note; but by the time I finished reading it, the tears were running down my cheeks. How could he have left just like that? Did he leave last night? Was he already gone when I came home? All these questions were racing through my head, and I didn't know what to do. I folded up the letter, put it back in the envelope and wandered out to the hall where Marcy was hovering and trying to look like she was dusting the banisters. She looked at me and saw the tears. "Has he really gone, miss?" she whispered.

"Yes, he's really gone," I answered and walked slowly past her and down the stairs. Sammy was sitting at the bottom with his head cocked on one side, looking lost. I suppose he was wondering where everyone was. He was so used to having my father around, and I decided it might be a good time to take him for a walk and give myself time to think things through. I told Marcy I'd only be gone for a half hour and to listen for the phone or anyone coming into the reception area. It wouldn't be the first time that a tourist would just drop in asking if we had any vacant rooms. I put on Sammy's leash, and we took a slow walk along the river while I tried to decide whether to ring my father, but the last thing I wanted to do was spoil their little holiday. By the time I got back to the inn, I had made up my mind to wait until suppertime when I knew they'd be back at their hotel and then maybe I would ring.

Meanwhile, Marcy and I finished all of the chores; and after she left, I sat in the lounge, close to the front door, and tried to read a magazine, but my mind was elsewhere. I hadn't even had lunch, and I was getting hungry, so I helped myself to some of Mum's chicken casserole, heated it up in the microwave and took it back to the lounge. I thought this might kill some time, but it was still only four o'clock when I finished eating. The clock seemed to be at a standstill; and then suddenly, I heard the telephone ringing. I ran out to the desk and picked up the receiver. "Luke, is that you?" I said breathlessly, all thoughts of professionalism out of the window.

"Ariel, are you okay?"

It was Terry, and for a second I was disappointed but then relieved that I had someone I could talk to. I told him everything that had happened and ended up sobbing. "What am I going to do?" I moaned.

"I'm coming right over," he said and then hung up.

I stood staring at the phone in my hand and then slowly put the receiver back and buried my head in my hands. Marcy had gone, and the Newman sisters had taken a bus ride into Oxford by the time Terry arrived. Except for Sammy, I had been alone with nothing to distract me from my thoughts of Luke and whether or not I should call my parents. Terry rode over on his bicycle, and I never thought I'd be so happy to see him. When he walked through the front door, I almost ran into his arms and obviously caught him by surprise. "Whoa," he said, "perhaps we should have a crisis every day."

I stepped back but took hold of his hand and sighed, "I just don't know what to do for the best."

He led me over to the small love seat in the reception area and sat me down. "Okay, let's be rational about this. We know Luke's gone to London, and we know he's gone to be with this actress, so he's not exactly missing. Also, he's not a minor and can make his own decisions as to where he wants to live. I think you should wait until your parents get home tomorrow before you tell them. If you ring them now, they're just going to pack up and race home. You told me this was the first time they'd had a holiday, if you can call it that. Why spoil it for them now?"

I shook my head. "But Luke's never even been to London before. He's lived here all his life, just like me, and who knows what he'll get into. As for Mum and Dad, well, I know my Mum will be mad at me for not calling them."

"Luke's not on his own, so he has someone to watch out for him, and your mum will get over it. Listen, Ariel," he said, squeezing my hand, "don't get annoyed, but I think you're being overly protective. You're his sister, not his mother."

I sat there for a moment with my head bowed. "I suppose you're right, Terry. I just don't know what ulterior motive that woman has for luring him to London. She's years older than him, and I heard these stories about her. I know he's going to get his heart broken."

"So he gets his heart broken, and I don't expect it will be the first time. He'll probably be involved in a few more relationships before he settles down."

I looked up into his eyes. "And how about you? Do you expect the same thing to happen to you?"

Terry grinned. "I'm only nineteen, Ariel, the same age as you. I'm not the type of guy who likes to play the field, but I'm a little too young to be thinking about a wife and kids and a house with a white picket fence."

I nodded. "I know. It's just that I haven't really gone steady with anyone or really even cared for anyone until now. I guess I'm being a little naïve to think any relationship can last forever."

"Not at all, Ariel. Look at your mum and dad, they've been married for a long time, and from what you tell me, they're really happy together."

"Yes, they love each other a lot. They were so lucky to have found each other, and I'm so lucky to have them as parents."

I sensed that Terry wanted to change the subject when he stood up rather abruptly and said, "Look, why don't I take you out for a bite to eat and take your mind off this whole Luke business for now?"

I looked up at him and shook my head. "I can't leave here. I have no idea when our guests will arrive back, and I can't just lock up in case they show up. How about we order something in, maybe a pizza?"

"Sounds like a great idea," Terry answered as he walked over to the reception desk. "I'll phone the Pizza Express right now. I hope you like pepperoni."

Chapter Seventeen

It was eight o'clock when the Newman sisters arrived back at the inn. The tour bus had dropped them off right at the front door just as I was saying good-bye to Terry. The moment they saw me on the steps, they almost ran towards me. I couldn't help smiling because they both looked so excited. "Hello." I asked, "How did you enjoy Oxford?"

Gladys was grinning from ear to ear. "It was wonderful. We went to Blenheim Palace and Christ Church College and the botanical gardens."

"Yes," her sister intervened, "and we had supper at this lovely seafood restaurant. Gladys had crab, and I had scallops. It was delicious and all the people on the tour were really nice. They were quite a bit younger than us but really good company." Suddenly, she stopped chattering and glanced at Terry, "Who's your friend, Ariel?"

Terry stepped forward and introduced himself. "I'm Terry Butler. I'm very pleased to meet you."

Gladys looked from me to Terry and back at me again. "Is this your young man?" she asked.

"Terry's a good friend," I replied, "and he's just on his way home."

"Oh, I see," Gladys remarked, looking a little disappointed. "Well, I guess we'll be off to bed. We're just about worn out with all the walking." With that, the two of them toddled off through the hall, and then Gladys called out, "Be good, you two. See you tomorrow."

Terry and I started to laugh. "What a pair," he said. "Now are you sure you'll be all right with just those two in the house?"

"Yes, I'm sure, and Mum and Dad will be home tomorrow. Thanks for coming over and convincing me not to ring them."

"You're welcome," he said, kissing me lightly on the lips.

When I finally got to bed myself, knowing for sure that Luke wasn't in his room, I felt a little nervous. Then Sammy jumped up and snuggled down beside me, and I felt much more secure. Nevertheless, it took me a long time to get to sleep because I couldn't help wondering where Luke was and what he was doing.

I was up again early the next morning and went through the usual routine of serving breakfast and doing various chores with Marcy. Right after lunch, I went into the garden to pick some fresh flowers to put in the reception and lounge areas, and then I sat by the large bay windows, waiting for my parents to come home. I was longing to see them but dreading Mum's reaction when she discovered that Luke had gone.

At exactly two o'clock, I saw Dad's car pull into the driveway and immediately ran out to greet them, but Sammy was well ahead of me, barking like crazy and jumping all over, waiting for my dad. When he stepped out, I threw my arms around his neck with such force that he nearly toppled over. "Hey, what is it?" he asked, hugging me back. I didn't want him to see the tears in my eyes so I just hung on for a few more seconds. "Nothing, just glad to see you, Dad. I missed you," I said.

Mum had stepped out of the car by then and had walked around so that she was standing behind me. Finally, I let Dad go and then turned and gave her a hug. "Hello, Mum. I'm so glad you're home."

Dad got between both of us and put his arms around our shoulders. "Come on, we'll unpack later. I need a cup of tea, and I can't think of better company than my two girls."

When we got to the kitchen, I made them sit down while I put the kettle on, and Sammy settled under Dad's chair. "Okay," I said, "tell me all about your holiday."

"Later," Mum said, giving me a strange look. "Where's Lucius?"

I turned my back on her to get the teacups out of the cupboard. "He had to go out," I lied.

"Ariel?" my mother said. "Where is he?"

I took the kettle off the burner before it started to whistle and walked over to the table. Mum and Dad looked at me expectantly as I took Luke's letter out of my pocket and handed it to my mother. Then I sat down as I watched her unfold the paper and start to read. When she had finished, she slowly passed it to my father, and I saw her face crumple as she burst into tears. Dad hesitated for a moment before beginning to read. "When did he leave?" he asked when he got to the end.

"I found the letter in his room yesterday morning," I said.

Mum stopped crying and looked up at me in surprise. "You mean you knew yesterday and didn't ring us?"

I shook my head. "No, Mum. I didn't want to spoil your holiday."

Mum looked annoyed. "You should have rung us, and we would have come straight home."

Dad reached over and took her hand. "It's okay, Jane," he said gently. "There wasn't anything we could have done."

"But she was here alone," she protested.

"I was fine, Mum," I said. "Marcy was here all day, then Terry came over for a while, and the two old ladies were still here."

Mum got up. "I think I'll go and lie down for a while," she said. "I'm really tired."

I went to stop her, but Dad shook his head at me; and after she left, he got up and put the kettle back on the burner. "Let's have that cup of tea," he said.

I sat quietly while Dad made the tea and then brought two cups to the table. He sat down next to me and reached for my hand. "I know you're worried about your brother, but you need to let it go," he said quietly.

"But, Dad," I said, "what if he gets into some kind of trouble? Why can't we go and look for him?"

"No, Ariel," my father replied rather emphatically, "we're not going to do that. If he gets into trouble, he knows where we are and he can always come home. I'm sure we'll hear from him again in a few days, and then you can put your mind at rest. As for your mother, I'll talk to her later after she's had some rest. I don't want her fretting over Luke."

"Okay," I said reluctantly. "I guess we'll just wait until he gets in touch, but if he doesn't contact us soon, can we please see if we can find him."

My dad sighed, "Yes, we'll try and track him down, and then you and your mother can stop worrying."

I took a sip of my tea. "You haven't even told me about the rest of your holiday."

"It was the best thing we could have done and was long overdue. We went to the Royal Pavilion and walked through a part of town called the Lanes. The streets were really narrow, and they had all kinds of unique little shops. In fact, I had trouble keeping your mother out of them. The best part, though, was when we took a drive along the coast to Shoreham Beach. That's where we came across the mudflats where they had a huge collection of houseboats converted from barges and tugs, and even minesweepers. It was much more interesting than a bunch of shops."

"Don't let Mum hear you say that," I said, grinning.

Dad chuckled and then looked serious. "Actually, your mother and I made a decision while we were away, but I'd rather tell you about it later when she's here."

I immediately felt a little anxious. "What kind of decision?"

Dad shook his head. "I'm afraid you'll have to wait." He looked at his watch. "Why don't we let your mother have a rest, and in an hour or so, I'll help you make some supper, then we can talk."

"Okay, how about a nice shepherd's pie?"

He stood up and took his cup over to the sink. "Lovely idea, sweet girl. I'll be back at about four, but while I'm gone, I don't want you bothering your mother."

"Where are you going?" I asked.

"Taking Sammy for a run," he said. Of course, as soon as Sammy heard his name, he was up from under the chair and ready to go.

Dad was true to his word and back in time to help me with supper. We even managed to put together a rhubarb pie, although we cheated by using ready-made pastry. Mum came down to the kitchen just before we were ready to serve the shepherd's pie. She looked rested and even had a smile on her face. "Are you feeling better, Mum?" I asked.

"Yes, honey," she answered. "I'm sorry if I was cross with you. I know you meant well. As for Lucius, well, he's made his bed, and he'll have to lie on it."

I was surprised at my mother's attitude about Luke but pleased she was no longer annoyed with me. "Why don't you sit down," I said. "Dad and I made supper."

She walked over and put her arm around my father's waist. "I know, I could smell the cooking all the way upstairs. That was really sweet of you both."

Once we sat down, I looked at Dad expectantly, but he gave a slight shake of the head, so I knew he didn't want to talk about any decision they'd made until after we had eaten. Once we had cleared our plates and were all on our second cup of tea, my father turned to me and said, "Your mother and I have something to tell you."

I looked from him to my mother and again felt anxiety creeping in. "What is it?"

"We've decided to sell the inn."

I stared at him in shock and was about to speak, but he held his hand up to silence me. "The last two days made us realise that we're letting our lives pass us by. We've spent nearly all our adult years running this place, and we're tired. Once we sell, we'll probably buy a bungalow in High Wycombe or St. Albans, and I can keep on selling my furniture. We'll have enough to keep us comfortable for the rest of our lives, and we'll be able to afford to go on trips, maybe even to France or Spain. It's time your mother and I saw something of the world instead of being cooped up here every day."

I could hardly believe my ears. "But what about me, Dad? Where will I live?"

"I thought you were moving to London to go to that fashion school, and now that your brother's gone, it will make things a lot easier."

"But what if he wants to come back?" I cried. "You won't be here!"

"Your being melodramatic, Ariel," my mother said. "We're not selling up right away. We'll put the inn on the market next spring, and we'll probably move out in about a year. This wasn't your father's idea. It was mine, but he's all for it. It's not like we're falling off the face of the earth. Once we move, you can visit us anytime you like."

"Why can't you get a house here in Abingdon?"

My mother sighed, "We want a change of scenery. We don't know exactly where we want to go yet, but it won't be far away. It will probably be closer to London so that we can come and visit you all the time too."

"Now I almost wish I hadn't suggested you went away for a couple of days," I said.

Dad smiled. "You did a good thing," he said. "You helped your mother and me to really take a look at our lives. We've been happy here, but it's been a lot of hard work with not too much to show for it."

"I'm going to miss this place," I said, sadly reaching down and stroking Sammy's head.

"We will too," Mum and Dad said almost in unison.

Chapter Eighteen

Almost a week later, when we hadn't heard a word from Luke, I was getting very anxious and had trouble sleeping. Day-to-day life at the inn appeared to be almost normal and there was no more talk of selling up or moving, but that didn't mean my parents had changed their minds. It was just too soon to put the property on the market and I knew they wouldn't do anything until I was ready to move away the following summer. I had tried not to think about Luke; but even on the night when Terry took me out to supper at one of the most upscale restaurants in Oxford, my mind was elsewhere. At one point, he knew I wasn't really paying attention to what he was saying and got annoyed. "Ariel," he said, "you're not listening to a word I'm saying. What are you thinking about?"

I was embarrassed but didn't want to admit the truth. "I'm sorry, I was thinking how much I'd miss living in Abingdon once I move and my parents sell the inn."

"Well, from what you tell me, that's almost a year away. You'll get used to the idea, and in the meantime, can you try to have a good time?"

After that, I did my best to look as though I was enjoying myself, but I could hardly wait to get home to see if Luke had telephoned. When we pulled up at the far end of the driveway, out of sight of the windows at the front of the inn, and Terry put his arm around me, I wasn't very responsive. And when he pulled me roughly towards him and kissed me with surprising force, I squirmed and wrenched myself away from him. "What on earth are you doing?" I cried.

He shrugged and put both hands on the steering well. "Go home, Ariel," he said. "I don't have time to play games."

He didn't have to ask me twice. "I'm out of here," I said scowling. "Good night and thanks for supper."

He didn't even answer me as I opened the door, slipped out and then shut the door with a bang. Then he stepped on the gas and roared out of the driveway.

When I walked into the reception area, Dad was at the desk, "Hello, sweet girl, what's with Terry? He drove off in a mighty hurry. Did you two have a fight?"

"Something like that, Dad," I replied, walking over to the desk.

"Ah the joys of young love," he said, placing his hand on his heart.

I had no interest in discussing Terry with my father at that point. "Did Luke ring?" I asked.

"No, and will you stop asking me every day. If he rings, you'll know soon enough."

"You said we'd go look for him if we didn't hear from him."

"It's barely been a week, and we have to give him a little more time. Now you run on off to bed because your mother tells me that Marcy can't come in tomorrow and she needs you up at the crack of dawn to help out."

"Okay," I said grudgingly, "night, Dad." And I trudged on up the stairs to my room.

It was after midnight and I was still awake when I thought I heard a phone ringing in the distance. Both of my parents were heavy sleepers and Dad snored, so it was doubtful they could hear the telephone. I jumped out of bed and ran out to the hall where, sure enough, I heard the ringing coming from the reception area. I considered sliding down the banisters but decided it might be safer to just run down the stairs as fast as

I could and hope whoever was ringing wouldn't hang up. Of course, I was praying it was Luke.

I was out of breath by the time I picked up the receiver and could hardly get the words out. "Hello, who's there?" I whispered.

"Sis, it's Luke."

"Oh my god," I answered. Luke, how are you? Where are you? I've been so worried about you."

"I'm okay, sis. Sorry I'm ringing so late, but I wanted to be sure and talk to you before I rang Mum and Dad. How did they react when they found out I left?"

"Honestly? They didn't get too upset. They both think you're old enough to know what you're doing, and they said if things don't work out, there's always a place for you here. That is until . . ."

I hesitated and Luke cut in. "Until what?"

"They've decided to sell up next year and get a bungalow in another town, and it's all my fault."

"What do you mean, it's your fault?"

"They realised while they were away that they were missing out on a lot of things and they wanted to make a change."

"I think it's a fabulous idea, and you'll be leaving anyway, so why should you be upset?"

"I'm not upset," I said testily, "but everything's going to be so different."

"Different can be good, sis. Wait till you come to London. You're going to love it. It's so exciting. There are so many interesting people here, and so many things to do. Pandora had three days off, and she took me all over. We went to the Tower and St. Paul's, and you should see the shops."

"So you're still with Pandora?"

"Yes, of course. I told you I was coming here to be with her. Didn't you believe me? She has this fabulous house in Mayfair, and she bought me a whole slew of new clothes."

I felt so helpless at that moment. "Oh, Luke, are you sure you're doing the right thing taking up with her."

"I'm not taking up with her," he said angrily. "I'm in love with her, and you're going to have to get used to the idea."

"And what am I supposed to tell Mum and Dad?"

"The truth, of course. Look, I'll be in touch again soon, and next time, I'll talk to them myself."

"Wait!" I called out. "Give me your phone number so I can ring you."

"Later, gotta go," he said abruptly. "Bye, sis."

I hung up the phone but rather than feeling relieved, I felt more despondent than ever. I had a problem getting to sleep at all that night; and when I finally dropped off, I must have been exhausted because the next thing I knew, Mum was shaking me awake. "Ariel," she said, "it's after nine o'clock. You were supposed to be up early to help me today."

I rolled over, glanced at the clock, rubbed my eyes and then struggled to sit up. My mother looked concerned. "Are you okay? Aren't you feeling well?"

I let out a huge sigh. "I'm fine, Mum, but I was awake for hours last night."

Mum sat down on the side of my bed. "You're not worrying about what your father and I told you, are you?"

"Well, I was thinking about it, but I was also thinking about Luke, and then he rang me."

"What do you mean he rang you?"

I told my mother exactly what Luke had told me and tried to reassure her that he would ring again soon. I was a little surprised at her reaction when she said, "You've always had that special connection with your brother. I suppose that's why he felt he had to talk to you first."

I reached out and took her hand. "Don't be upset, Mum."

She patted my hand and got up. "I'm not upset. I'm just glad to know that Lucius is all right. Now hurry up and get dressed because the Newman sisters are leaving soon, and they want to say good-bye. After that, we're going to the market while your Dad stays here to look after things."

She started to walk towards the door but stopped when I called out, "Mum, does that mean we won't have any guests after they leave?"

She shook her head. "Yes, but just for today. There's a large family coming in tomorrow for a week, and they've booked all the rooms, so we'll be busy again. Now come along, Ariel, and don't be too long."

Later, after I'd seen the Newmans off in a taxi, Mum and I took the car into town. Dad was busy finishing off a table he was making. He was always worried that Sammy would get into the varnish he used for finishing, so we took him with us. I actually enjoyed having him in the car because he took great delight in hanging out the window and feeling the wind in his face. It was a lovely day, so after we had visited the market, we decided to stay in town and have some lunch. We stopped at the Spread Eagle pub, where they had outdoor seating, and we were able to tether Sammy to the railing that ran around the property. We both ordered a prawn salad and a glass of Reisling; and as soon as the waitress left, Mum looked over at me, smiled and said, "This is really pleasant. We should do it more often."

"Yes, it is nice, but I wish Dad could have come with us."

"Well, that's the problem. Someone always has to be at the inn no matter what time of day or night it is. That's why we decided we had to make a change."

"I know, Mum. I understand, I really do. It's just hard for me to imagine not living here. After all, I've been here my whole life."

"Yes, but you've already made plans to go to London next year, and I know you've made the right choice. There's no future for you here, Ariel."

I hesitated while the waitress placed two glasses of wine on the table and then announced lunch was on its way. "I know you're right, but I'm going to miss you both. In fact, I'm going to visit you so often you'll get sick of me."

Mum chuckled. "No chance of that. There'll always be a place for you to stay and that goes for Lucius too."

"You haven't said too much about him, Mum. What do you really think about him taking off like that?"

Mum shrugged her shoulders. "I don't agree with the way he did it, but he's obviously smitten with Pandora. When one falls in love, all reason goes out the window and nothing else seems to matter. You haven't experienced that yet, but I hope one day you do. I just pray that he doesn't get hurt too much."

"You sound like you expect him to get hurt."

"I think it's inevitable. She's years older and a lot wiser. Your brother is smart, but he's naïve in so many ways. I think it's just a matter of time before she gets tired of him, and then he might just come home."

Our salads arrived and we ate in silence for a while, and then Mum asked, "How about Terry? How's that relationship going?"

I pursed my lips and took a sip of wine. "Not very well. I won't be surprised if I don't hear from him again."

"Why? Did you have a fight?"

"Not exactly. I guess it's all my fault. I was so preoccupied thinking about you moving and about Luke that I didn't pay him much attention last time we went out."

"That's too bad, honey. He seems like a nice young man, and maybe you should give it another chance."

"I don't think it's up to me, Mum," I said.

When we got back to the inn, Dad told me that there was a message for me at the reception desk. You can imagine my surprise when I saw that it was from Terry and he wanted me to ring him back that day. I procrastinated for about an hour and then finally picked up the phone. I listened to it ring three times before I started to put the receiver down. Suddenly, I heard a breathless "Hello?"

"Terry? You rang me?" I asked even though I knew the answer.

"Ariel, sorry, I was just coming in when I heard the phone. I hope you weren't hanging on too long."

"No, I just came home myself," I lied. "Mum and I went to lunch in town."

"How nice, where did you go?"

"Just to the Spread Eagle. Was there something you wanted, Terry?"

He hesitated and then said, "Look, Ariel, I'm sorry I took off on you like that the other night. I know you're worried about Luke and your folks. I just thought we could start over, and if so, I'd love for you to go to the theatre with me. I have tickets for *Phantom of the Opera*."

"You do? Where's it playing, in Oxford?"

Terry paused, and then I heard him clearing his throat. "No, it's playing in London, at Her Majesty's Theatre."

I sank down into a chair behind the reception desk. "London? You mean you really want to take me to London?"

"You've never been there, have you, Ariel?"

I felt almost ashamed to answer. "No, I've never been anywhere except Oxford. I know it's ridiculous because it's only about ninety minutes away. Mum and Dad could never get away to take me, and when they had a school trip three years ago, I was sick in bed with the flu. I feel like such a country bumpkin."

Terry laughed. "Don't feel badly. I bet most of the people living around here haven't travelled more than a few miles from home. I promise you'll love it, and if you can stay over, I can take you to see some of the sights."

"Stay over? You mean in a hotel?"

Terry laughed again. "Well, I'm not taking my tent. Of course, in a hotel, and if sharing a room is bothering you, we'll get two rooms."

"But isn't that awfully expensive?"

"Don't worry about the cost. My mother gave me money for my birthday this year, and I've been saving it up for something special."

"When would we go?" I asked.

"This coming Saturday. Please say yes."

I felt my heart start to beat a little faster with excitement. "Yes, yes," I cried out, "I'd love to come with you. I've been wanting to go to London for a zillion years, and I can't believe we're going to the theatre too."

Terry sighed, "Fabulous. So should I book one room or two?"

I paused for what seemed like the longest time. "Just book one," I whispered.

When I told Mum and Dad that night about Terry's invitation, I saw Dad steal at a glance at my mother, and then he put his arm around me and said, "You go and have a great time, sweet girl. You deserve it."

Mum nodded her head very slowly and smiled.

Chapter Nineteen

By the time Friday night came around, I was a nervous wreck. I had several reasons to be anxious. I was going to London where there would be crowds of people, I didn't have a clue what to wear or what to take with me and I had agreed to stay in the same room with Terry. Fortunately, there was one thing Mum was able to help me with, what to wear to the theatre and what I should pack in my suitcase. About a year earlier, Mum had made me a green silk frock with a V-neck, dropped waistline and capped sleeves. I had only worn it once before, when I went to a dance at the Preston Road Community Centre, and Mum assured me it was perfect for attending the theatre. She also suggested that for the rest of my visit, I should just dress comfortably in jeans, flats and tees. I didn't ask her whether I should take my pyjamas or the only frilly nightgown I possessed. I guess the answer was pretty obvious.

Terry picked me up midafternoon on Saturday; and as I climbed into the passenger seat, I began to feel excited. It was as though all my anxiety had been in anticipation of the trip; but once I knew we were on our way, I felt more relaxed. I know I was chattering on aimlessly until we got onto the M40, and then I became engrossed in looking out the window and waiting with bated breath for my first sight of London. Just over an hour later, we were already driving through a residential area, but it wasn't very impressive and looked rather run-down in places. Then suddenly we were in the midst of heavy traffic and a built-up area of tall buildings, swarms of people bustling along the sidewalks and the famous red double-decker buses that I had only seen in the pictures or on the telly. Terry kept glancing over at me to see my reaction and finally spoke. "Well, what do you think, Ariel?"

"It's awfully crowded," I said, "and the traffic's hardly moving."

Terry chuckled. "That's London for you. It's always like this even on a Sunday. There are always thousands of tourists in town, and sometimes it takes forever to get around."

"How many times have you been here?" I asked.

"Lots, my uncle Phil lives just south of here, and we usually visit him two or three times a year. He recommended the hotel we're staying at."

"Which hotel is it?"

"It's the Haymarket, and it's a stone's throw from Piccadilly and from Her Majesty's Theatre."

"You mean it's right in the centre of town? Doesn't that cost a fortune?"

"Well, it's a bit pricey, but it's only for one night, so we might as well do it right."

I wasn't sure what he meant by that, so I didn't say any more; and fifteen minutes later, we were pulling into an underground parking area beside the hotel and then entering the lobby. I didn't even get a chance to look around because I felt really embarrassed checking in as though we were a married couple, and I kept my eyes glued to the floor. Even as we took the elevator to the fourth floor, I avoided eye contact with the bellboy who was accompanying us. It was only when he'd shown us the room and finally walked out the door that I felt I could breathe again. The room itself was actually quite plain with a grey carpet, a queen-size bed with a grey padded headboard and a white comforter. There was also a blue velvet chair, blue drapes and a dresser with six large drawers. It was the bathroom that really impressed me, and it had obviously recently been renovated with all new fixtures including a very deep Jacuzzi-style tub.

"Well, it's not exactly what I expected," Terry said, looking a little disappointed.

I tried to reassure him. "It's nice and the bathroom is fabulous."

"You're just saying that to be kind. It's not like the inn, is it?"

"No, it's not, but the inn is in the country and a lot of the furnishings are handcrafted. My dad made most of the furniture, and Mum sewed most of the curtains and bed covers. You can't expect to find that here."

"Well, as long as you're happy with it, it's okay. Why don't we put our clothes away, and then I'll take you to Piccadilly Circus and we can find a place to eat."

After only a short walk, I was sitting on the steps of the Statue of Eros, surrounded by dozens of people and traffic passing by in all directions. There were the famous London taxi cabs and double-decker buses, and the noise was almost deafening. Terry stood at the edge of the crowd, milling about on the pavement with his camera. He had already taken at least three or four photos of me and was now taking pictures of the statue itself. I felt like I was on a different planet; it was so exciting, and I couldn't believe I would actually be moving to the city one day. That's when my thoughts turned to Luke, and I searched the faces around me half expecting to see him. I was so busy concentrating that it took a few moments before I noticed Terry making his way through the crowd towards me. He smiled as he got closer. "So what do you think now, Ariel?"

"I think it's wonderful. There are so many people. I've never seen anything like it."

Terry reached down to help me up. "Well, there's a lot more to see, but we'd better get something to eat. We still have to go back and change for the theatre afterwards, and we don't have that much time."

We walked a couple of blocks to Leicester Square. There were so many restaurants in one small area, and I had no idea which one to pick, but Terry suggested we go to Bella Italia. We sat outside, and both ordered the Spaghetti Carbonara, along with a glass of Cabernet each. I figured that spaghetti would be a safe bet because I wasn't too familiar with a lot of the other items on the menu, but this spaghetti wasn't like the type with meatballs I was used to. It was made with pancetta, smoked Italian bacon, egg, pecorino cheese and cream, and it was delicious. By the time I had finished, I was full, but Terry persuaded me to try the cheesecake with blackcurrant sauce, and I wasn't disappointed.

On the walk back to the hotel, I started to conjure up a plan, but I wasn't sure if I could pull it off. We had less than an hour before we were to be at the theatre, and Terry suggested that I get changed first, insinuating that it would take me a long time to get ready. I took my frock into the bathroom along with my cosmetic bag; and after a very quick shower, avoiding getting my face or hair wet, I touched up my makeup, ran a comb through my hair and emerged with a grin on my face. Terry was lounging on the bed, reading a magazine, and looked up in surprise. "Wow, that was quick, and may I say you look terrific."

I twirled around and did a little bob. "Thank you, kind sir. Now you can take all the time you want in the shower."

Little did he know that I had an ulterior motive, but it all depended on just how long he would be occupied in the bathroom. As soon as the door closed, I rang information and asked if they had a listing for Pandora or P. James in Mayfair. It only took a few seconds before I was informed that it was unlisted, so then I asked for the number for Adrian Evans in Kensington. While I inwardly chided myself for not bringing Adrian's number with me, I kept my fingers crossed so that when the operator came back on the line and gave me the number, I was elated but not sure if I had time to ring before Terry was finished in the shower. I put the phone down and then listened at the bathroom door, and I could hear the water running and what sounded like Terry singing, so I rushed back and dialled Adrian's number. After the third ring, I was so nervous that I was about to put the phone down when I heard someone pick up. "Hello," said a male voice, but it didn't sound like Adrian.

"Hello, is this Adrian?" I asked.

"No, this is Joel, but Adrian's here if you'll hang on a minute. May I tell him who's ringing?"

"It's Ariel, I met him in Abingdon."

"Hold on, I'll get him for you."

I heard some muttering as I waited for what seemed like an eternity, and I was tapping my foot wondering what to do if Terry came out, and then suddenly, "Hello, Ariel, what a surprise. How are you?"

"Adrian, I'm so glad I got hold of you. Look, I'm sorry but I only have a few seconds. I'm in London, and I need Pandora's address. Do you have it?"

"Is something wrong, Ariel? Is there something I can do to help?"

No," I answered in a panic. "I'm just looking for Luke, and I know he's with her. I can't tell you any more right now because I have to get off this phone, but I promise I'll ring you when I get back to Abingdon and explain."

Adrian hesitated for a moment. "Well, all right, if you promise to let me know what's going on later. I don't have her actual address, but I do know the house she lives in. It's on Brooke Street right at Grosvenor Square. You can't miss it. It's the only one with a red door. You're not planning on just showing up there, are you?"

"I don't know yet. I've got to go, Adrian. I'll ring you, I promise." I rang off just as Terry came out of the bathroom.

"Who were you talking to?" he asked.

"Mmmm . . . oh, I rang Mum just to tell her everything was fine. Did you have a nice shower? You look really dapper. I like your jacket."

Terry walked over and looked in the mirror and tucked a green silk square into the pocket of his navy blazer. "I match your frock now," he said, grinning, and then turned and took my hand. "I think we look pretty good together."

I looked back at our reflection and smiled. "Yes, we do, don't we?"

We walked over to the theatre, and I was grateful it was close by because I wasn't used to wearing heels; in fact, it had been a long time since I had dressed up for any occasion. The theatre itself took my breath away. I was used to old buildings having lived in Abingdon all my life, but this was magnificent. After seeing the exterior, I couldn't wait to go inside, and I was even more impressed. It was immense and so elaborate. I only wished Mum could have seen it. She had always loved the theatre, and I vowed right then that I would bring her there one day. As for the performance, it was like nothing I had ever seen before, and I was transfixed by the music and the costumes. At intermission, I didn't even want to leave my seat; I just wanted to take it all in. It was a night I would never forget for more reasons than one.

Chapter Twenty

As the performance came to a close I began to get nervous. I was twenty years old and had never slept with a man. Becky had filled me in on what to expect over a year before, but I knew I wasn't prepared. I don't know why I ever agreed to share a room with Terry, and I struggled in my mind to think of a way to avoid the whole situation. I even considered feigning being sick, but I didn't know if I could pull it off. I was so grateful when Terry suggested that we have a nightcap; and when we ended up in a cosy bar near the hotel, I decided a couple of stiff drinks wouldn't hurt. Maybe then I could face what I was sure was about to come. I ordered a gin and tonic and swallowed it down within ten minutes and then ordered another one. Terry looked at me a little suspiciously. "Are you okay?" he asked. "You knocked that back pretty quickly?"

"I'm thirsty," I answered, well aware that I was already feeling the effects of the gin.

"Maybe you should have some coffee," he suggested.

"Why? Do you think I'm going to get drunk?" I said with what I knew was a silly smile on my face.

Terry took the glass out of my hand and signalled for the waiter. "You're already halfway there," he remarked.

A few moments later, a cup of very black coffee appeared in front of me. "I need milk," I said rather sullenly. "No, you need it black, and then I think we should go back to the hotel." I took as long as I could drinking the coffee, but I knew I couldn't delay the inevitable much longer. The short walk back to the hotel really seemed to clear my head, and I was starting to get anxious. In the elevator going up to our room, Terry put his arm around me and asked if I was feeling better. I mumbled that I was fine but really tired, and he just nodded his head. Once inside the room, I quickly retrieved my nightgown, which I had stuffed under a pillow, and announced that I was going to the bathroom to take off my makeup. Terry just nodded again, switched on the television and sank down on the end of the bed. I took my time washing up and changing out of my frock; and when I looked in the mirror, I saw this rather pale, frightened young woman staring back at me. I had to ask myself again, what was I doing alone in this hotel room with Terry? When I finally emerged, Terry was no longer at the end of the bed. He had changed into a pair of pyjamas bottoms and a tank top and was lying with his head propped up against the headboard. He glanced at me as I walked over to turn off the lamp on the dresser and whistled, "Wow, you look amazing," he said. "Blue really suits you."

I looked down at my nightgown, feeling rather self-conscious knowing just how frilly and feminine it was. I was also aware that it was semitransparent, and I automatically crossed my arms over my chest. "Thank you," I whispered.

Terry patted the bed beside him. "Why don't you come over here?" he suggested.

I pretended not to hear him and turned to look at the television screen. "What are you watching?" I asked.

"Nothing interesting. Please turn it off, Ariel, and come and lie down beside me. I'm not going to bite you."

Slowly and reluctantly, I did as he asked; and as I lowered myself onto the bed, I could feel myself start to shake. I stared up at the ceiling; and a moment later, I was aware that Terry was reaching over to turn off the bedside lamp. Suddenly, the room was almost in darkness, and I was holding my breath then, without warning, he was on top of me and kissing me with such force that I started to panic. I began to struggle, but he was so heavy that I couldn't move out from under him; and when he thrust his tongue into my mouth, I knew I had to do something. In desperation, I drew both arms up; and using my hands, I grabbed him on both sides of his face and pushed with all my might. I know that surprised him because he drew back for a moment, and that's when I screamed at the top of my lungs. "Get off me, get off. I don't want to do this." He rolled away; and as he did so, I jumped off and ran into the bathroom and slammed the door. I had no idea what he must have been thinking or what he intended to do next, but I knew I couldn't go through with it. I stood gripping the edge of the sink and tried to calm down; and a few moments later, Terry was knocking gently on the door. "Please, Ariel," he said. "Come out. I won't hurt you, I promise."

I waited a few more minutes and then slowly opened the door. Terry was about two feet away, leaning against the wall and looking dejected. "Come here," he said, stepping forward and putting his arm around my shoulders. I shuddered and he released his hold a little. "Let's just sit on the edge of the bed and talk."

I sat down, and he sat beside me, holding my hand. "You're still a virgin, aren't you?" he asked.

I nodded and felt a deep sense of shame, although I knew I had nothing to be ashamed of. "I'm sorry," I whispered. "I've never been with anybody, and I don't think I'm ready."

"Listen, I wouldn't want you to do anything you didn't feel comfortable with. I care about you, Ariel, and I think you care about me. I also think you're going to have to be in love with a man before you're ready to sleep with him."

I looked at him with a frown. "What about you? Don't you feel the same way?"

Terry laughed. "Hardly. I'm not saying I'd take just anyone to bed. There has to be some attraction there. But love? No, I don't have to be in love with them."

"So you're not cross with me?"

He squeezed my hand. "No, of course not. I'm just a bit disappointed." He stood up and then pulled me up too and put both arms around me. "Why don't we just get some sleep. We have a full day tomorrow. I absolutely promise I won't lay a finger on you, scout's honour."

I giggled and poked him in the ribs. "You were never a Boy Scout."

True to his word, Terry made no effort to touch me again even though we were only inches apart all night. We both woke at the crack of dawn, and his first words to me were, "Are we all okay now, Ariel?"

"Yes, we're all okay," I answered giving him a peck on the cheek.

Chapter Twenty-One

Two hours later, after a leisurely breakfast in the hotel coffee shop, Terry took me on a tour of London. We went to the Tower, St Paul's and Westminster Abbey, and I was totally in awe of everything I saw and amazed at the crowds everywhere. Always, though, at the back of my mind, were thoughts of Luke, and I was constantly searching amongst the hundreds of faces for a glimpse of him. Terry was enjoying showing me the city, and I was sure he had no idea of the thoughts going through my head and especially my obsession with seeing where Pandora lived. When we stopped for lunch at a pub in Kensington, I came up with an idea but knew I had to tread cautiously. "Adrian lives around here somewhere," I said nonchalantly.

Terry frowned. "Who's Adrian?"

"Adrian Evans, he's an actor. He has a role in *Moll Flanders*, and he stayed at the inn."

Terry frowned. "What about him?" I reached across the table and touched his hand. "You don't have to be jealous. He's gay and a really nice chap. He told me he lived here in a garden flat with his partner, but I don't know where exactly."

Terry nodded. "This is a nice area and a great place to live."

My idea was starting to work. "He told me that there were some fabulous houses in Mayfair. I'd love to see them. Do you think we could take a drive there?"

"Well, I'm not sure about fabulous houses, but we can take a look if you want to. It's really close by, so not a problem. I just don't want to be starting back to Abingdon too late. Otherwise, we might get into some heavy traffic."

"Oh, I really would like to go," I said enthusiastically. "Can we go right after lunch?"

It was all I could do not to gobble down my cottage pie and swallow my beer in one gulp. I was so anxious for us to be on our way, but Terry was in no mood to hurry. Eventually, we were back on the road, and I could hardly contain my excitement, but how was I going to find the street I was looking for? Somehow, an angel must have been guiding us because as we drove alongside Green Park, I suddenly saw the sign Brooke Street coming up on our right. "Oh, look," I cried out, "let's go down here."

Terry turned the corner, but he was going too fast, and I knew I'd miss the house. "Can't you slow down?" I asked. "I want to look at the houses."

Terry put his foot on the brake and came to a crawl, and I noticed he was smiling, but I had no idea why. I was just about to ask what was so amusing when suddenly I saw the red door, and I only had a second to react. I put one hand to my throat and reached out with the other to grab Terry's arm. "Stop, please stop. I think I'm going to be sick."

The car came to a complete halt, and I jumped out before Terry could speak. Then I crouched down so that he couldn't see me but I could still get a good view of the house. It looked really elegant. There was an arch above the doorway, French windows, steps with a wrought iron railing and a small front garden. I was tempted to just go up and knock and demand to see Luke; but when I thought I saw a movement behind one of the curtains, I ducked down even farther. I wasn't ready to face Pandora; and when I climbed back into the car, wiping my mouth with a tissue and clearing my throat, Terry just glanced at me and said, "You'd better fasten your seat belt." Then as he drove off, he started to laugh and not just a giggle but the kind of laugh that makes your tummy ache.

I glared at him and shook my head. "Thanks for being so sympathetic. Do you always find it funny when someone's sick?"

At that, he started to laugh even more, and I was getting annoyed. "What's wrong with you?" I asked, raising my voice.

He finally stopped laughing but was still grinning from ear to ear. "Oh, Ariel, you're so transparent. Do you think I didn't guess what you were up to?"

"I don't know what you mean," I said indignantly.

"That's the house where Luke is living now with Pandora. Don't try and deny it."

I blushed and hung my head. "How did you guess?" I whispered.

"Well, when I checked out of the hotel this morning, it was obvious that the phone call you made last night wasn't long distance. Otherwise, the charge would have been on the bill. I assumed you must have rung this Adam fellow, looking for Luke."

"It's Adrian."

"What?"

"His name's Adrian, not Adam."

"Adam, Adrian, what's the difference?" Terry responded impatiently. "I'm right, aren't I? That's who you were ringing."

"Yes, I wanted to see where Luke was staying. I guess you're pretty mad at me now?"

"No, I just don't see why you couldn't tell me what you were up to. It's not as though I didn't expect you to be looking for him. I only had to watch your face every time we were amongst a crowd of people. You were hoping to spot him, weren't you?"

"Yes, I was, but at the same time I knew it was hopeless. I'm sorry I deceived you, Terry. I know you were anxious to show me London, and here I was distracted, looking for my brother."

Terry reached over and took my hand. "It's okay. I understand, but what are you going to do now?"

"I'm not sure. Mum and Dad keep telling me not to interfere, and this whole thing with Pandora will probably run its course, but I have a bad feeling about it."

"Well, I've told you the same thing. If it doesn't work out, he'll get over it."

"I guess you're right, but I can't help worrying about him."

Terry squeezed my hand. "Cheer up. It's a beautiful day. We had a great time, and we're on our way home before traffic starts piling up on the M40."

I looked over at Terry and smiled. "Thank you, it really has been lovely and I can't wait to tell my parents about it."

By the time Terry dropped me off at home, I had decided that I needed to get on with my life and not worry about Luke. Not that my life was particularly exciting. I hardly ever saw Becky anymore, and I wasn't sure how much longer Terry would continue to go out with me now that he knew I didn't want to sleep with him. Actually, I was very conflicted about it because part of me believed that maybe my feelings for him would change; and if they did, then who knows what could happen. Thank goodness, Mum put everything in perspective for me later that night when Dad was busy in his workshop. At supper, I had told them about all the places we had visited in London and about the theatre, but I didn't mention our side trip to Brooke Street. They asked me dozens of questions, and Mum was especially interested in *Phantom of the Opera* and wished she had been with us. She had never given up her love of the theatre. Later, when we were alone, she reminisced about her childhood and reminded me of why she had named Luke and me after Shakespearean characters. Then suddenly, out of the blue, she asked, "Did you look for Lucius while you were in London?"

I dropped my gaze. I couldn't lie to my mother. "Yes, Mum, we drove down the street where Pandora lives and stopped outside the house."

Mum frowned. "How did you know where to go?"

"I phoned Adrian, and he gave me the address, at least he tried to. He wasn't sure of the exact number, but he said it had a red door, so it was pretty easy to pick out."

"So obviously you didn't try to see him."

"No, I didn't want to take the chance of meeting up with Pandora, and Luke would probably have been mad at me for surprising him anyway."

Mum nodded, "I think you were wise, and I think you should stop worrying about your brother."

"I know and I've already decided to concentrate on other things."

Mum smiled. "Like Terry, for instance? How's that relationship going?"

"I don't think it's going anywhere. I thought being away with him this weekend might have been really special, but it didn't turn out that way." I leaned over and took my mother's hand. "What's wrong with me, Mum?"

Mum tilted up my chin so that she was looking directly into my eyes. "What are you trying to say, Ariel?"

I could feel myself getting red in the face as I began to answer. "We shared a room. We even shared the same bed, but I just couldn't do it, Mum."

"You mean you didn't want to have sex with him? Is that what you're trying to tell me?"

I bowed my head and nodded. "I've never slept with anyone before, and I thought it was time I did, but when it came right down to it, I couldn't do it. Terry was very sweet, and he didn't try to force me. I wasn't really scared or anything like that. It just didn't feel right."

Mum smiled. "Oh, my precious girl, there's nothing wrong with you. You obviously don't feel deeply enough for Terry, and maybe you never will. Intimacy is not the same for everybody. For some, it's not so big a deal, and they don't have to be in love to fall into bed. Then there are people like you who think of sex as something very sacred and many who even wait until they're married before they consummate their relationship. You'll know when the time is right, honey."

"Were you a virgin when you married Dad?" I asked almost without thinking.

Mum squeezed my hand. "The truth? No, but he's the only man I've ever slept with."

I gave her a hug. "Thanks, Mum. I feel a lot better now."

Chapter Twenty-Two

It was the end of September when Luke finally rang Mum. I wish I'd been at home so that I could have spoken to him, but I was enjoying a rare night out with Becky. Mum said he seemed happy but disappointed that he was too late to begin classes at the actor's studio. Pandora had tried to get him enrolled in classes at the Holborn location, close to the British Museum, but not even her contacts in the film industry helped to find him a place there. This meant that he would have to wait until the new session started in January, and he was getting a little impatient. When Mum asked him how he spent his time, he said he spent most days on the *Moll Flanders* set, either as an observer or an extra, and most of the film was being shot at Pinewood Studios. She also asked him when he was coming home to visit, but he was evasive and she didn't want to push him. Ironically, when she told him that I had been in London with Terry, he had expressed surprise that I didn't try to see him. Mum didn't tell him that I had practically been on his doorstep. She just reminded him that it was hardly likely that I could visit him when I had no idea where he lived, and I silently thanked Mum for telling that little white lie. Before he rang off, he actually gave her his phone number, and I could

hardly wait to ring and talk to him myself, but Mum suggested
I wait a few days.

Terry and I had been out on three or four occasions
since our trip, but it was obvious that our relationship was
not going anywhere, and he now considered me a friend. I
was comfortable with this arrangement and grateful that I
had someone to go out with now and again. We both liked
the pictures and enjoyed fast food, so we'd always end up in
Mick's Café or Pepper's Burgers after the show. It was almost
as though Terry had taken the place of Luke in my life, but he
would never have that special place in my heart.

Almost a week after Mum got the phone call from Luke, I
picked up the phone and dialled the number he had given her.
It must have rung about four times before someone answered,
and I heard a woman's voice with a distinct French accent
on the other end announce, "Hello, how may I help you?" I
should have anticipated that Pandora probably had a maid or
servant to answer her telephone, but I was still a little startled
and hesitated before responding, "Is Luke there, please?"

"You must have the wrong number. There is nobody here
by that name," said the rather authoritative voice on the other
end of the line.

I repeated the number Mum had written on the notepad
and was assured that it was indeed the same number but that I
must have been misinformed.

I then decided to take the bull by the horns. "Is this the
Pandora James residence?" I asked.

There was silence and then, "Who is ringing please, and
what is the nature of your business?"

I sighed in frustration, "I'm actually looking for my brother.
He's staying with Ms. James."

"Ah, so you are looking for Monsieur Regan."

"Yes, Luke Regan."

Again silence and then, "In this house, we refer to Monsieur
Regan as Lucius."

I was getting a little annoyed. "Well, I'm his sister, and I
refer to him as Luke."

"Monsieur Regan is not here. Would you like to leave a
message? I will have him ring you when he gets back."

I knew this person wasn't about to tell me where Luke was or when he would be back at the house. I decided to try a different approach. "What about Ms. Teasdale, is she there, please?"

There was an even longer silence this time. "Mademoiselle Teasdale does not reside here."

I knew then that it was utterly hopeless. "Please ask my brother to ring me. He knows my number." And before she could even respond, I hung up the phone.

Ironically, I didn't have to wait too long to find out where Luke was. The next day, I was in town with Mum, picking up some groceries; and while she was at the checkout, I picked up a copy of the *Sun* and started to leaf through it. The *Sun* was a tabloid newspaper and always full of gossip and pictures of celebrities, but I didn't expect to see a member of my family featured on page five. The photo showed Pandora, stepping out of a limousine, looking amazing in an emerald green mini frock, with five-inch gold sandals, and the man extending his hand to help her was none other than Luke. I gasped when I saw him because this was not the Luke that I knew. His hair was no longer a wonderful chestnut colour but was now jet-black and long enough to curl over the back of his jacket, but I had to admit that he looked like a film star. I could hardly wait to read the caption underneath, and that's when I learned that Luke wasn't even in London when I rang. He was in Paris with Pandora, attending the premier of a film directed by Martin Cameron, but the one sentence that really rattled me was, 'Pandora is shown with her latest conquest, Lucius Regan, a young man she met while filming Cameron's current film, *Moll Flanders*—how long will this one last?'

I looked over at Mum and saw that she was at the front of the queue, so I raced over and added the paper to the pile of groceries. Mum looked at me and frowned. "Don't tell me you're reading the *Sun* now, Ariel?" she said.

"There's something in there I need to show you when we get home," I answered.

On the way back to the inn, I chattered away in an attempt to distract Mum from the paper and any mention of Luke; but once there, I didn't even wait for the groceries to be put away. I called out to Dad as we passed him in the reception area, "Dad. I really need to see you. Can you come into the kitchen?"

He looked up in surprise. "What, right now?"

"Yes, it's important. I have something to show you."

Dad followed Mum; and when we got to the kitchen, he glanced over at her with a puzzled look, but she just shrugged her shoulders. I set the paper on the table and, in a rather dramatic gesture, opened it to page five and stepped back so that they could see the photo. Dad immediately put his arm around Mum's shoulder, and they stood there, staring in absolute silence for a few moments. Then Mum reached out and touched the image of Luke as though he was really there. "What have they done to my sweet boy?" she whispered.

Dad turned and took her in his arms. "It's all right, Jane. He's still your sweet boy." Then he grinned. "To tell the truth, I think he looks pretty handsome with the dark hair. He looks more like me now."

Mum pushed him away. "Stop with your blarney, Casey Regan. Now help me put all this stuff away."

I looked at them in amazement. "Is that all both of you have to say?"

Dad threw up his hands. "What do you want us to say? Your brother's taken up with some film star, and now he's in the tabloids. There's not much we can do about it."

I folded up the paper in disgust. "Well, I think it's sickening, and I hope nobody around here sees it."

"Oh, I'm sure the phone will be ringing off the hook real soon," Dad replied.

Dad was right. That afternoon, we had several phone calls. Most were from neighbours, friends and people I had gone to school with, including Becky; but when both the *Oxford Mail* and the *Oxford Times* rang for an interview, Dad got annoyed and told them we had no comment and didn't want to talk to the press. It really didn't make much impact because the very next day, both papers had pictures of Luke with Pandora in Paris. The *Mail* even went so far as to add a short article about the young local boy who, at the age of eleven, saved his sister from drowning and was now dating a film star.

Three days later, Luke rang home but once again, I wasn't there to talk to him. Mum told me he was excited about his trip to Paris and the glamour of being at the premier and walking the red carpet. He hadn't seen the photo in the *Sun*, so he didn't know about the caption, and Mum wasn't about to tell him. She did ask him about changing his appearance and discovered that he had never really liked his chestnut hair and was happy to get rid of it. Mum said it made her sad to hear that because he'd always reminded her of Nana. Then Mum asked him when he was coming for a visit; but again, he was evasive and said he was really busy and would stay in touch. After that, Mum heard a woman's voice in the background, and Luke said he had to go. He hurriedly sent Dad and me his love, and then he was gone.

I was so upset that I'd missed his phone call and decided to take Sammy for a long walk. The weather was already getting a little cooler, and I figured some fresh air might help clear my head. Rather than taking our usual path along the riverbank, I headed for Abbey Gardens, where the ruins of the first monastery ever built in England stood. It was a popular meeting place for many dog owners in the area, and Sammy was in his element after he encountered several other dogs out for their early-evening stroll. I got such a kick out of seeing him running around that by the time we finally made our way home in the fading light, I was no longer upset. For what seemed like the umpteenth time, I told myself that I needed to focus on my own life and stop obsessing about Luke.

Chapter Twenty-Three

Just over three weeks later, on Mum's birthday, Dad took her to the Apollo Theatre to see a performance of *Guys and Dolls*. This was a rare night out for them, and Mum was nervous leaving me in charge of the inn as all of the rooms were occupied. This was unusual for the time of year, but I assured her that nothing could possibly happen. All of the guests were either in their rooms or out for the evening, and the only thing I needed to do was to make sure there was a fresh pot of coffee, hot water for tea and a plate of biscuits in the lounge. Mum was really excited despite her misgivings; and when she finally came downstairs, Dad let out a loud wolf whistle. She had on a pale blue chiffon frock, which highlighted her eyes and set off her hair, and she was wearing the silver necklace I had given to her earlier. I have to admit, she had never looked lovelier. This was a happy day for her; not only was she going to the theatre but also she had received two dozen red roses from Dad and a beautiful potted orchid from Luke. I had been worrying that he wouldn't remember her birthday, but he had rung Mum and they had chatted for quite a while. This time, I managed to have a short conversation with him and asked him if he would be coming home for Christmas, but he said he didn't know what Pandora was planning and when he found out, he would ring me.

The very next day, I was surprised when Adrian telephoned to ask what happened when I was in London. He had expected to hear from me and kept putting off ringing to find out; but finally, his curiosity had got the better of him. I asked him if he had seen Luke's photo in the *Sun* and that's when I discovered that it was in two other tabloids as well. Again, he voiced his opinion of Pandora and the probable outcome of Luke's affair with her; but when I told him I was done worrying about my brother, he agreed it was a good idea. I got my second surprise when he invited me to a party at his flat, the following Saturday, to celebrate the fourth anniversary of his relationship with Joel. I was excited about the idea of going back to London and asked if I could bring a friend. Adrian said he'd be happy to meet any friend of mine and if I couldn't get a ride and had to take the train; he would pick me up at Victoria Station. He also offered to put us up for the night as we couldn't possibly go all the way back to Abingdon in the wee small hours.

When I got off the phone, my first impulse was to ring Terry and ask him if he wanted to go with me. That way, I knew I would get a ride and not have to bother with the train. On second thought, I realised that if we stayed at Adrian's, we would probably be sharing a room, and I didn't want to go through that again. I decided to ask Mum what to do, and she suggested I had better go on my own rather than give Terry any encouragement, but she was not thrilled about me staying at a stranger's flat. "He's not a stranger, Mum. You met him when he was here, and besides that, he's gay and lives with his partner. That's what this party is all about—they're celebrating four years together."

Mum was still sceptical, but Dad convinced her that it would be good for me to do something completely on my own, and so it was settled. That afternoon, I rang Adrian back and told him I would be coming by myself and taking the train to Victoria.

For the next few days, I fussed over what I was going to wear to the party. I kept going through my wardrobe, but nothing seemed right, except for the green silk frock I had worn to the theatre, but I wanted something new. Mum finally came up with a solution when she suggested I try on the blue frock that she had looked so lovely in on her birthday. We had never exchanged clothes before, mainly because I was taller than Mum and while she was so blond, I took after Dad and had inherited his dark hair. When I mentioned that I was too tall, she insisted I at least try it on especially as I was young and would look fabulous in a shorter skirt. Reluctantly, I pulled the frock over my head; and when I turned towards the mirror, I was amazed at how I looked. The colour really suited me, and the style was youthful and showed off my legs, which were one of my best assets. "See," Mum said with a smile, "I told you it would be perfect. Now all you need is the necklace you gave me and your sandals and you're all set."

"Oh, Mum," I said, giving her a hug, "what would I do without you?"

Terry rang me the next day, asking if I wanted to go to the pictures that weekend. I considered making up some story about being too busy, but I just couldn't bring myself to lie. When I told him I was going to London to a party, he had a dozen questions, and I got the feeling that he didn't really believe Adrian was gay even though I reminded him that he lived with his partner and they were celebrating an anniversary. When he eventually rang off, I know he felt rejected, and I was somewhat puzzled because I thought we had agreed to just be friends. Later, after I'd gone to bed and had time to think about it, I realised that even friends could be jealous just as I was of Becky's relationship with Jordan and, even more telling, Pandora's influence over Luke.

On the train ride into London, I was nervous but excited; and when we arrived at Victoria Station, I was overwhelmed by the size of the place and never thought I would find Adrian in the crowds. I walked along the platform, straining my neck to see over the heads of the people in front of me; and just as I exited through the barrier, I saw him. He was talking to a man who looked somewhat older and quite attractive but completely the opposite of Adrian in appearance. Where Adrian had that smouldering dark quality, the man with him was a couple of inches shorter, fair-haired and could have been taken for a college professor. Suddenly, Adrian turned and saw me and then called out, "Ariel, over here."

I waved and quickened my pace; and a moment later, I felt Adrian's arms around me. "Welcome to London," he said and then stepped back and motioned to the other man. "Ariel, I want you to meet Joel. Joel, this is the young lady I've been telling you about."

Joel extended his hand. "I'm so pleased you agreed to come to our celebration. I trust your journey was a pleasant one?"

I was thinking how extraordinarily polite this man was as I shook his hand. "Thank you for inviting me."

The introductions over, Adrian took my bag; and once outside the station, Joel flagged down a taxi. "We left the car at home," Joel explained. "Parking is a problem, and sometimes it's simpler to take a taxi. I believe you're considering living here in the near future, and I think you'll find that the transportation system is one of the best in the world. You really don't need a car at all."

I nodded as a taxi drew up and we piled into the back and I felt rather inadequate about my ability to have a sensible conversation. Joel wasn't condescending in any way, but I had been so sheltered living in Abingdon that I had never been in this type of situation before. There I was riding along with two gay men, one who I hardly knew and one who I had never met before, and I was staying at their flat overnight. I was mulling this over while Joel was talking and then realised that Mum and Dad hadn't disapproved, so it must be okay. However, that didn't really ease my mind, and it was only after we arrived at their home on Richmond Way that I finally managed to relax. We drew up outside a row of Victorian-style houses; and the moment Adrian opened the door, he was greeted by the fluffiest white dog I had ever seen who proceeded to jump up and down with excitement. Adrian bent down and patted the dog's head. "This is Ziggy," he said. "She's thoroughly spoilt."

I looked into a pair of chocolate brown eyes. "I can see why," I remarked. "She's adorable."

After that, Joel showed me around the flat, which took up the entire ground floor of the house and led out to a garden at the back. The living area was spacious with wonderful fat comfy sofas and dark wood, while a separate dining room held a table large enough to seat eight people, and the ultramodern kitchen had black countertops and stainless steel appliances. Joel didn't exactly show me the master bedroom; but as he led me past the open door on the way to the guest room, I couldn't help noticing all the rich shades of brown and the huge king-size bed. I have to admit it made me feel a little uncomfortable thinking about what went on in there. The guest room was quite a surprise. I'm not sure what I expected, but it had dark-blue walls and a rather colourful bedspread with a geometric pattern. Joel grinned when he saw the look on my face. "I had nothing to do with it," he explained. "Adrian let his sister design this room, and because she likes to stay over on a regular basis, he agreed not to change anything." Then he lowered his voice to a whisper. "To tell you the truth, he hates it, but Erica's a free spirit, so he let her have her way. You'll meet her tonight because she'll be at the party."

"I can hardly wait," I replied, trying to sound sincere.

Chapter Twenty-Four

After I got settled in my room, I went back to the kitchen, where Adrian and Joel were busy getting ready for the party. I was used to helping Mum around the inn; and even though not a great cook, I enjoyed preparing meals for the family. When I asked if I could help, I was pleased when Adrian let me assist him with making the appetisers, while Joel was engrossed in putting together an enormous spicy sausage and rice casserole that looked big enough to feed at least twenty people. It was fascinating watching him, and I must have had my mouth open because suddenly Adrian nudged me and whispered, "He thinks he's the next Jamie Oliver."

"You mean Jamie Oliver, the Naked Chef?" I whispered back.

"Yes, but don't worry, he won't take his clothes off," Adrian answered, and then we both started to giggle.

Joel looked over at us with a frown. "What are you two up to?"

We didn't get a chance to answer because we heard Ziggy barking from out in the hall, and then this extraordinary-looking girl almost leapt through the kitchen door. "Hi, guys," she called out, skipping towards Adrian and giving him a hug. "How goes it?"

"Great," Adrian replied, turning her around so that she could get a good look at me. "I want you to meet Ariel. Ariel, this is my sister, Erica."

I noticed Erica look me up and down as she stepped forward to take my hand; but then with a smile, she said, "Hello. You're from Abingdon, right? That's where Adrian was filming *Moll Flanders.*"

"That's right," I answered automatically because I was totally captivated by her appearance. She was my height but very slight; and from what I could see, she was dressed entirely in black from head to toe in a long sleeveless frock with at least half a dozen strands of scarlet beads draped around her neck and matching earrings that were long enough to brush her shoulders. Her hair, styled in a short bob, was jet-black like her brother's, but her skin was so pale it almost seemed translucent and her makeup was startling. Not only were her eyes ringed in black, her lashes coated in thick mascara and her lips painted a bright vermilion but also her upper right arm was covered in a giant tattoo picturing a leopard ready to pounce.

Erica must have seen me glance down at her arm and grinned. "That's Panar. He killed and ate about four hundred people."

I was dumbstruck for a moment and then managed to utter, "What happened to him?"

"He was shot by a big game hunter."

I had no idea what to say next and was grateful when Adrian came over and asked Erica if she could start blowing up some balloons. She immediately turned away from me and said, "Sure, let's get this show on the road."

I mostly listened for the next half hour while Adrian and his sister bantered back and forth. They obviously got on really well even though on the surface they appeared to be so different. Then out of the blue, Adrian was telling Erica that I was planning on moving to London permanently and going to fashion design school. Once again, I got the impression that Erica was looking me up and down before she asked, "Are you really interested in fashion?"

I felt like a country mouse at that moment and wasn't sure if she was secretly laughing at me. "Yes," I replied, "but I haven't had very much experience up until now. My Mum helped me design and make a few things, but my sewing isn't very good." Erica walked over and picked up the hem of the cotton print blouse I was wearing with my blue jeans. "And is this something you made?" I looked down and wondered what she was thinking and then drew myself up to my full height and replied, "As a matter of fact it is."

She nodded and muttered, "Very nice, very nice."

I think I was prepared to hate her at that point, but I didn't have much time to think about it because Joel suddenly suggested that we should both take Ziggy for a walk. "Erica," he said, "we've pretty well finished with all the food preparation, so Adrian and I are just going to put up some lights in the garden. It's five o'clock, so Ziggy needs to go out, and it would be a nice idea if you took her over to the common. Perhaps Ariel would like to go with you but put on a jumper because it's a little cool out now."

Erica looked at me and said, "Would you like to come?"

I really didn't think I had any choice and replied, "Yes, I'd like that. I'd better go and get my jacket."

"Yes, I need one too," she said and followed me into the guest room and started rummaging in the closet. I should have realised that the clothes I had seen there earlier were probably hers, as I had been told that she stayed over on occasion.

She pulled out a short black coat that looked like leather. "I think this will do," she said. "What about you?"

"My jean jacket's hanging at the end," I said rather meekly.

She picked it off of the hanger, handed it to me and then turned away again and took down my blue frock. "Is this what you're wearing to the party?" she asked, holding it at arm's length and looking it up and down.

Suddenly, it seemed that Mum's lovely blue gown had turned into something out of the dark ages. "Well, yes," I stammered, "that's what I was going to wear."

Erica shook her head. "Don't you have anything else?" she asked.

"No, I'm afraid not. Why? Is there something wrong with it?"

Erica gave a big sigh. "It's okay for someone twice your age, like your Mum maybe."

"It is my mum's," I said, feeling a little annoyed.

"Oops! Look, Ariel, you're a really attractive girl, and you've got fabulous colouring. You'd look wonderful in black, and I have the perfect outfit you can borrow."

"But I've never ever worn black, and what would I do about shoes?"

"Are these the ones you brought to wear with the frock?" Erica asked, picking my sandals up from the closet floor.

I nodded, and then she actually smiled. "I think they're rather glam," she said, "and anyway, you'll hardly see them once we get you all gussied up."

"I'm not sure," I protested. "Maybe I should just wear the blue frock."

"No way," Erica insisted. "You're going to look great, I promise. Now we had better get going before Ziggy piddles in the hall and Joel has a conniption fit."

Five minutes later, we were walking towards the common with Ziggy trailing obediently behind us on her leash. "We have a dog at home," I said.

"Do you? What kind of dog?"

"He's a border terrier. His name's Sammy."

"Oh, so he looks like Lassie?"

"No, no, that's a border collie. Sammy's fairly small. He only weighs fourteen pounds, and he's got a very wiry brindle coat."

"I'd like to see him. You'll have to bring him with you the next time you come for a visit," Erica responded, much to my surprise.

After that, we chatted about all kinds of things. She asked me all about my family, and I told her I had a brother, but I didn't tell her about his relationship with Pandora. I didn't think I knew her well enough for that. She was actually easy to talk to; and while her appearance gave the impression that she was unconventional and maybe a little flaky, I soon learned that she was the opposite when it came to the way she lived her day-to-day life. Adrian hadn't told me that when his father had died three years earlier, he'd left him and his sister quite a bit of money. Adrian had purchased the garden flat, and Erica had opened a shop in Covent Garden, selling vintage clothing. When she told me that, it started to become clear to me why she had such a flair for fashion. "What do you call your shop?" I asked.

"Erica's Attic," she replied, "although it's not really in an attic. In fact, it's on the ground floor, but I had it renovated to look like an attic with slanting wood beams and rough wooden floors."

"I'd love to see it," I said.

"What time is your train tomorrow?"

"Not until two o'clock. I was hoping to do a bit of sightseeing."

"Well, why don't I take you? I can borrow my boyfriend Lenny's car, and we can have a drive around, then have lunch and you can come to my shop."

"It sounds wonderful," I said. "That's so generous of you."

"Nonsense," Erica answered, "it will be fun."

By the time we got back to the flat, it was almost six o'clock, and I felt like I had made a friend but now came the ordeal of my transformation for the party. I was a little embarrassed when Erica told me to strip down to my underwear even though I had worn my best white lacy bra and matching panties. She surveyed me for a moment and then said, "You have a really good figure. I was just wondering if the white would show through, but I think it's going to be okay. Here put this on."

I slipped a black camisole over my head and then a black silky scoop neck top with long sheer sleeves. Then she handed me a long black velvet skirt; and when I put it on, I discovered that it was slit to midthigh. When I was fully clothed along with my own silver sandals, I started to put on the silver necklace that I had brought with me, but Erica took it gently out of my hands. "Here," she said, "try this instead."

When I finally stood in front of the mirror, I wasn't quite sure what to think. "Don't worry," Erica said, "we haven't finished with you yet. We need to change your hair and your makeup."

Fifteen minutes later, I was ready for the party, and I have to admit that I was excited when I saw the finished result for the first time. Erica had piled my hair on top of my head but left several tendrils floating around my face, and she had piled on the mascara and eyeliner along with the same vermilion shade of lipstick that she was wearing. With the dozen or so rows of beads draped around my neck and matching earrings, I looked rather striking, and I loved it. I was no longer a country mouse. Erica insisted that I go and show Adrian and Joel my new look while she got ready; and when I walked into the kitchen, they both stopped what they were doing and stood there with their mouths open. Adrian was the first to speak. "Oh my, Ariel, you look fabulous."

I did a mock curtsy. "Thank you, kind sir," I said, grinning.

Chapter Twenty-Five

By just after seven o'clock, there were already at least fifteen guests milling around the living room and kitchen. They seemed to be a mix of all different ages but all rather sophisticated and I felt a little conspicuous. If it wasn't for Erica I think I would have changed into my blue frock but her outfit was even more outrageous than mine. She was wearing a dove grey sleeveless mini frock, white net stockings, grey platform shoes, a rope of knotted pearls and a skullcap with a small white feather. The makeup was even heavier than before, with charcoal eye shadow and a deeper shade of lipstick so that she looked like a character from a film set in the thirties. She appeared to be in her element, and I was fascinated watching her as she worked the room, and then she suddenly turned and came over to me. "You should try mixing a little, Ariel," she said.

"I know," I replied, "but I haven't been to too many social gatherings, so I'm a bit nervous."

Erica glanced at the glass of wine I was holding. "Maybe you should drink something a little stronger," she suggested, passing me her own glass, which contained a clear liquid and an olive.

I took one small sip and grimaced. "It tastes like straight gin."

"It's a dry martini, mostly gin with a dash of vermouth. A couple of these and I guarantee you won't be nervous."

I shook my head. "I think I'll stick with the wine. By the way, do you really know all these people?"

"Uh huh," she replied, lowering her voice. "I've met most of them before, and they're an interesting bunch, all gay, of course."

"Really? Are you gay too?" I blurted out.

She laughed. "Heavens no. I like the opposite sex too much. In fact, my boyfriend should be here at any moment, and he's bringing a friend."

"That's Lenny, the one with the car?"

"Yes, but he's a little late because he just got back in town this afternoon."

"Oh, what does he do?"

"He plays drums in a rock band. They just finished a tour of Scotland and then did a couple of performances in Liverpool and Manchester."

I had a vision of Ringo Starr walking through the door. "You must miss him when he's away. Have you ever gone on tour with him?"

"No, we've only been seeing each other for about six months; and half the time, he's been out of town. He claims it's lonely on the road, but it's hard to believe when there are four other guys in the band, and they have their own bus."

"What's the name of the band?"

Erica laughed. "Measure for Measure, and I bet you've never heard of them."

I grinned back at her. "No, I can't say I have, but then we don't usually play rock at home. Mum likes to listen to show tunes, and Dad likes James Taylor and the Beatles. We aren't too sophisticated where I come from."

"Well, I'd hardly call rock sophisticated."

"What I really meant was I think we're stuck in the dark ages. I'd really love to go to a rock concert."

There was a bit of a commotion from out in the hall, and we both turned to see what was going on as Erica murmured, "Maybe we can arrange that sometime."

Suddenly striding through the doorway was a lanky young man with almost white hair tied back in a ponytail, wearing stonewash jeans, a black sweatshirt and a puka shell necklace. His face looked gaunt, but he was quite good-looking in an odd sort of way; and when he saw Erica, his smile lit up his whole face. He rushed over and threw his arms around her, and I heard him whisper, "Hello, luv, it's great to be home."

She kissed him on the mouth and then reached for my hand. "Ariel," she said, "I want you to meet Lenny. Lenny this is a friend of Adrian's. She came into the city for the party."

Lenny smiled, extended his hand and said, "I'm very pleased to meet you. Where are you from?" I was just about to answer when I became aware that someone else had joined our little group, and I couldn't take my eyes off of him.

Erica must have noticed the look on my face and grinned. "This is Zach. He's the lead singer and plays the guitar. Zach, meet Ariel."

I withdrew my hand from Lenny's and just stood there mesmerised. I'd never met anyone before who had had such an effect on me from the very first moment I saw them. I was staring into a pair of deep green eyes, set in a face that almost took my breath away. This man wasn't just handsome. He was perfect. He had thick brown hair, which fell almost to his shoulders, a slim straight nose, wide mouth and a strong masculine jaw; and as he took a step towards me, I realised he was almost a head taller than me. He was casually dressed in jeans, a black V-necked jumper and black leather jacket. He was exactly what I imagined a rock star would look like. I couldn't stop staring and was relieved when he spoke first because I couldn't even think straight. "Hello, Ariel, what a delightful name. It's from *The Tempest*, isn't it?"

I started to mumble when Lenny cut in. "Lord mate, I didn't know you read Shakespeare."

Zach punched him playfully on the shoulder. "I'm surprised you even know Shakespeare wrote it," he countered. Then turning back to me, he winked and then took hold of my hand and said, "Let's go get a drink and leave these two lovebirds alone."

I followed one step behind to the makeshift bar that Joel had set up and glanced over my shoulder back at Erica. She was grinning like a Cheshire cat, and I got the feeling she knew that Zach had knocked my socks off. He poured me a glass of white wine, took a bottle of beer for himself and guided me through the crowd to a small sofa tucked in a corner of the room, shaking hands with people as we went. Once there, I sat down and was surprised when he put his beer on the side table and said, "Hold tight, I'll be back in a flash," and then he was gone. I felt like a ninny sitting there nursing my wine; and after a couple of minutes, I even thought about getting up and disappearing myself, but then suddenly, there he was again, smiling broadly and holding a plate full of appetisers. "Sorry, luv," he said, sitting down beside me, "had to get something to eat. I'm a bit peckish."

"Erica tells me you just got back from touring. How long were you gone for?"

Zach offered me an appetiser, but I shook my head. "Almost a month, and it's good to be back. The guys are all great, especially Lenny, but sometimes I'd just like to chill out on my own."

I tried to think of something intelligent to say. "I suppose coming to this party as soon as you got home wasn't really your idea then?"

"I couldn't really avoid it. Adrian invited us, and it's good to see he's still with Joel after all this time. Mind you," he continued looking around the room, "I'm a bit out of my element tonight."

"What do you mean?" I asked innocently.

"Well, take a look, it's pretty obvious. Nearly everyone here is gay."

"And you're not," I announced rather than asking a question.

He chuckled. "No, it's not my cuppa tea. How about you?"

I frowned. "No, of course not. Why, do I look like a lesbian?"

He really looked at me then, taking in my clothes and even checking out my shoes. "Hardly, but it looks like Erica had something to do with your wardrobe."

I was embarrassed and could feel myself blushing. "Well, she did help me get ready for the party."

"What were you going to wear," he teased, "one of your mum's old frocks?"

I stood up. "I'll have you know that my mother is very fashionable, and I won't have you insulting her."

He immediately jumped up, took the glass from my hand, setting it on the table and then took me by the shoulders, "You're a feisty one, aren't you?"

I had never ever felt of myself as feisty; and as those green eyes bored into mine, I felt myself melting. "I just don't like anybody making fun of my family," I whispered.

"Forgive me?" he asked in a gentle voice.

I nodded and then before I could take a breath, his lips were on mine, and I felt myself begin to respond. The kiss would probably have gone on longer if Joel's voice hadn't interrupted us. "I want to make a toast," he called out in a loud voice from the other side of the room. I heard the whole place go quiet, and Zach and I broke away from each other; but as Joel and then Adrian talked about their life together and everybody raised their glasses, we weren't really listening. We were just holding hands and gazing into each other's eyes. I felt like Cinderella, and I didn't want the night to ever end.

Once the speeches were over and people were really starting to relax, the dancing began. At first, I was a little uncomfortable watching men dancing with each other; and when I saw two of them actually kiss, I had to turn away. Zach obviously saw the look on my face and remarked, "I can see you're not used to this. How about we get out of here and go over to the local pub? I think there's one right near here."

I was a little surprised at the suggestion. "But wouldn't it be rude of me to leave the party? After all I am a guest, and I'm staying here for the night."

"Nah, it'll be fine. Adrian won't mind. He's too busy having fun. We can go for a couple of drinks, and then I'll walk you back."

"Well, if you're really sure it's okay."

"I'm positive. Come on, we'll just ask Erica exactly where the pub is."

I figured, once we talked to Erica, she might suggest that she and Lenny go with us, but apparently they had other plans and were already heading back to her place for the night. She arranged to ring me early in the morning to let me know what time she would pick me up, and we left them at the bar having one more drink. The Havelock Arms was only five minutes away, so I knew I wouldn't have any problem with Zach walking me back, but I insisted on telling Adrian I was going out for an hour or two. I'm not sure if he took in what I was saying because he looked like he'd had a little too much to drink, but Joel happened to overhear me and called out, "Have fun and keep your knickers on!" I looked around to see if Zach had heard, but thankfully he was busy talking to Lenny.

I learned a lot about Zach that night. He was twenty-five and had been brought up in Maidstone, about an hour southeast of central London. His parents were originally from Greece; and once they arrived in England, they changed their name from Philemon to Phillips. They were told they couldn't have any children, so when his mother turned forty and found out she was pregnant, they were ecstatic; and later, when his father discovered he was having a son, he bragged to everyone in the neighbourhood. I got a kick out of listening to Zach talking about his parents. He obviously loved them very much.

"How did you get into music?" I asked.

"Well, when I was about four, Dad got me a guitar for my birthday and according to him, I was a natural, so a year later, he got me a private tutor. I think he would have preferred if I'd played traditional Greek music, and he doesn't really understand rock, but he'd rather I was happy and did what I loved best."

"How did you get involved with the band?"

"Actually, Lenny and I formed the band when we were in school together. There were only three of us then, and we called ourselves the Three Bees." He threw back his head and started to laugh. "It was a play on the Bee Gees and not very original. Then Buddy joined the group, and that's when we decided to change the name."

"I have to ask you this. How did you decide on the name? I knew right away that it was the name of one of Shakespeare's plays, but obviously Lenny doesn't have a clue."

Zach looked thoughtful and lowered his gaze. "Someone I once knew played the role of Isabella in a performance of the play. It was put on by the drama club she belonged to, and she got rave reviews. She actually suggested the name." I sensed that I had touched on a sensitive subject, so I decided to talk about something else. "I see. So do all of you room together?"

Zach perked up immediately. "Heavens no! Lenny has a place just a few blocks from Erica, and the other three all still live at home."

"What about you?"

"I have a couple of rooms above a coffee shop in Earl's Court. You probably don't know where that is, but it's pretty central and really convenient. I don't even have to make coffee in the morning. I just amble downstairs, and Polly, the owner, usually gives me a mug on the house. Anyway, I feel like all I'm doing is talking about myself and I don't really know anything about you except that you'd probably look even more striking with your hair down," and with that he leaned over and removed the barrettes so that my hair fell down around my shoulders. I automatically reached up to grasp the back of my head, but he took my hand and said, "Leave it, you look beautiful now."

I lowered my eyes and could feel myself blushing as he tipped my chin up and said, "So are you going to tell me about yourself, or are you going to remain a mystery?"

I felt a little strange at first telling him about my life in Abingdon; it seemed so far removed from the life he was living; but oddly enough, he seemed really interested, and I was flattered. When I mentioned that I had a brother and that he was living in London, I was reluctant to give him more details; but when he wanted to know exactly where he lived and what he did for a living, I told him the whole story. He sat quietly, listening intently, but I noticed that when I mentioned Pandora's name, his expression changed. "So it looks like you've heard of her," I said.

He nodded very slowly and then answered, "I've actually met her. She went out with Buddy a few times."

"You mean Buddy from the band?" I asked flabbergasted.

"Yep, that Buddy. That was before anyone knew who she was."

I leaned forward across the table, dying of curiosity. "What happened? How did they meet?"

"Well, Pandora grew up in the east end in a pretty bad area, but she always had visions of seeing her name in lights, so every chance she got, she'd end up at some concert hall. She'd just hang around the stage door trying to make a connection with someone who might take an interest in her. Every entertainer is used to dealing with a lot of groupies, but Pandora had done her homework. She discovered Harry Reynolds was attending an Elton John concert, and she waited for him at the front of the crowd after the show."

"Who's Harry Reynolds?" I asked.

"He's one of the top film producers. He's no spring chicken, but he always had an eye for a pretty girl, and as he walked past, she latched onto his arm. One of the security people stepped forward, but Harry waved him off and invited her to ride in the limo back to his hotel."

"How do you know all this?"

"She told Buddy every detail, including the fact that she slept with Harry that night and he was so enchanted with her, he promised her a small part in his next film."

I gasped. "Oh my god, what kind of person has Luke got himself involved with?"

"I can't blame you for being concerned. Pandora is pretty ruthless when it comes to getting what she wants. She totally reinvented herself. She changed her hair, her makeup and the way she dressed, and she got rid of the cockney accent. Of course, Harry paid for the transformation and even put her up in a flat in Chelsea. I think the affair lasted about a year, and then he got tired of her. He'd already got her a part in one of his films, and that's when Martin Cameron discovered her and decided to groom her to become a big star."

"But when did Buddy come into the picture?"

"When she came to watch our band one day and took a shine to him. He never stood a chance. You haven't met Buddy yet, but he's quite a character and looks a bit like Steven Tyler. He fell for her hook, line and sinker and even talked about them getting hitched, but she had other plans. One day, when he couldn't get hold of her by phone, he went round to the flat and discovered she was playing house with someone else. He didn't actually catch them in bed, but the way they were dressed, it was pretty obvious. He was devastated and begged her to break it off with the other guy. It was humiliating to watch the way he was behaving. She told him she'd lost interest and didn't want to see him again, so that was the end of it."

"I'm surprised she didn't hit on you," I said indignantly.

Zach grinned. "Actually she did, and I took great pleasure in telling her where to go."

I sighed, "What am I going to do about Luke?"

"Nothing you can do. It will run its course, and he'll probably get his heart broken, but he'll get over it."

Zach was telling me exactly what everyone else had been telling me, but now I was even more worried.

At midnight, Zach walked me back to Adrian's and took a taxi home. I had told him that Erica was picking me up the next day in Lenny's car and taking me to see her shop and do some sightseeing. When he suggested that he and Lenny might join us, I was thrilled. I couldn't wait to see him again. It was difficult when he left me at the front door of the flat, especially when he started kissing me and I felt myself getting aroused. I had never felt a sensation like it before. As he started to leave, I couldn't help calling after him, "What if I don't see you tomorrow? When will I see you again?"

He gave a casual wave of his hand and called out, "I'll get your number from Adrian, and I'll ring you," and then he was gone.

Chapter Twenty-Six

The next morning, when I got up after a rather sleepless night, Adrian informed me that Erica had already rung and that she was picking me up at nine o'clock. I didn't like to ask if she mentioned anything about Lenny and Zach coming with her, so I was feeling a little anxious. Joel was the perfect host, serving me a full English breakfast along with a huge mug of coffee while he and Adrian chattered on about the party. I tried to join in the conversation, but my mind was elsewhere; and on one occasion, Joel asked, "Are you feeling all right, Ariel?"

"Mmmmm, what?" I mumbled. "Oh, yes, I'm fine."

"Well, you don't seem fine. Maybe you're a little hungover."

"Maybe, a little," I answered, "but I had a really nice time, and I can't thank you enough for inviting me."

"Nonsense," Adrian remarked, "it was a pleasure, although we didn't see much of you once Zach arrived."

I blushed. "I'm sorry, I didn't mean to take off for so long. We just got talking, and before we knew it, it was midnight."

"It's quite okay. No need to apologise," said Adrian, glancing up at the clock. "Oh oh, I think you're going to have to pack up your things because Erica will be here soon."

I started to rise from the table, picking up my breakfast dishes to take to the sink, but Joel intercepted me, assuring me he would take care of the cleanup. Ten minutes later, I had my bag packed, and I was sitting on the living room floor, playing with Ziggy, when I heard the honking of a car horn. Adrian called out that Erica had arrived, so I ran out to the hall in a rush and collided with him and Joel. Adrian opened the front door and waved to Erica and then gave me a hug as he said good-bye. Joel was a little more reserved and shook my hand; but all the while, I was peering over both of their shoulders, trying to see if Erica was alone or if there was anyone with her. Eventually I was able to break free of my hosts and practically ran out to the car; but as I drew closer, I could see Erica was driving and there were no passengers. I managed to smile, but my heart felt as though it was sinking in my chest.

Erica looked me over as I got into the car. "What have you done to yourself? You look more up-to-date today."

I grinned. "I put all your clothes away, but I kept the camisole to wear under my jacket instead of the print blouse. Then all I did was roll up the sleeves and leave the collar up. Oh, I'll send the camisole back to you as soon as I get home. I hope you don't mind me borrowing it."

"No, that's fine. See what an effect those subtle little changes have," Erica remarked, "and you're even wearing eye makeup. You certainly look a lot more modern."

"Thanks," I answered, feeling rather proud of myself. "Where are we going now?"

Erica decided that we should go to her shop first, and I think I did a good job of showing my enthusiasm, but I was anxious to know why Zach didn't come. Finally, I managed to blurt out, "Zach mentioned that he and Lenny might come with us today."

Erica nodded. "They still might. Lenny said he'd let me know after lunch."

"Oh, but we won't have much time because my train leaves just after three o'clock. Where are they now?"

"Probably sleeping. Musicians don't usually get up that early. Also, Lenny told me they had to go over some of the lyrics they wrote for a new album they're recording. I expect it will take them most of the day, so don't be surprised if we don't see them at all."

I slumped down in my seat, frowning, and it didn't take much for Erica to pick up on my change in mood. "What's the problem? Don't tell me you've got the hots for Zach?"

I sat right up in my seat, feeling a little foolish, "No, of course not. I only just met him."

Erica glanced across at me, and I could see she didn't believe me. "Everybody falls in love with Zach," she said.

"Did you?" I blurted out.

"Not exactly," she answered, "I fell in love with Lenny. He's the sweetest guy, but I have to admit that the first time I saw Zach, I thought he was really dreamy and I did my share of fantasising."

"I've never met anyone like him before. In fact, everything's so new to me lately. I've lived all my life in a small town where nothing ever happened except when I nearly drowned and Luke saved me."

"What? When did this happen?"

"A long time ago. It was all my fault. I was showing off in front of a friend and fell into the river. He dove in after me and held me above water until we were rescued. It was in all the local papers, and Luke got a hero's award. Anyway, we thought that was enough excitement to last a lifetime, and then this summer, the film people arrived, Luke ran off with Pandora James, I got invited to a gay party and then last night, I get to meet this good-looking rock star."

Erica looked at me with her mouth open, and then she said, "Wait a minute. Did you say your brother ran off with Pandora?"

"Yes, and nothing I hear about her makes me too happy. Even when I met her, I didn't like her. She treated me like I didn't exist, but she was all over Luke."

"Did you tell Zach about this last night?"

"Yes, and he told me all about her affair with the film producer and with Buddy. Now she's got Luke in her clutches, and there's nothing I can do about it."

"What's your brother like?" Erica asked as she manoeuvred through the traffic.

"Well, we were always close up until recently. He's kind, generous, intelligent and good-looking too, but I think he's a bit naïve when it comes to women. Girls ran after him all the time, but he hardly seemed to notice until Pandora appeared on the scene."

"That's not too hard to understand. She's an upcoming celebrity and very attractive, although it kills me to say so. I think she's going to be a big star one of these days, and believe me, unless your brother has something amazing going for him, she'll eventually drop him like a hot potato."

I was thinking about what Erica said, although it wasn't as though I hadn't heard it all before; and then suddenly, we pulled onto a side street and parked behind a rather racy-looking black car, which I later discovered was a Jaguar.

"Oh oh," Erica remarked, "Fern Fielding is here."

"Who's she?"

"Just one of my customers. She's a real pain in the butt. I hope she's not giving Darcy a hard time."

As I got out of the car, I glanced up and saw the sign Erica's Attic in crimson letters on a black background. It didn't really give me the impression of an attic; but once inside, I was surprised to see that the whole place was decorated in natural wood just as Erica had described. There were several old oak chests and wooden barrels scattered about, overflowing with clothes of all colours, and huge wooden closets with open doors where more clothes were on display. I was just about to say something to Erica when I noticed she was walking towards the back of the shop, where a very young-looking redhead was talking with a tall middle-aged woman drowning in a white fur coat. I couldn't help overhearing, "Fern, how are you? Are you able to find what you're looking for?"

"No, I certainly am not," she answered, scowling at the young girl, "but now that you're here, maybe that will change."

Erica nodded. "What's the occasion?" she asked.

"It's my anniversary. George is taking me to the Dorchester, and I want something really retro."

Erica turned to the young girl. "It's all right, Darcy," she said gently, "I'll take it from here."

I wasn't quite sure what to do, and then Erica looked over at me and rolled her eyes as Darcy started towards me. "May I help you, miss?" she asked.

I smiled at her and shook my head, "Oh no, I'm waiting for Erica. She wanted to show me around the shop, and then we're doing a little sightseeing and having some lunch."

Darcy appeared to be a sweet girl and told me she'd been working in the shop on a temporary basis for the past six months. While Erica was busy with the formidable Fern Fielding, she showed me several of the clothes on display, and they were not exactly what I expected. Not only were they vintage but also in most cases, classic. There were satin chemises, lace wedding frocks with high necks, huge picture hats and buckled shoes. Now I understood why a sophisticated woman would be shopping there. I could have spent all afternoon picking through all the merchandise, but it took very little time for Erica to find Fern an outfit she couldn't resist, a rose silk flapper frock that she exclaimed would be sure to make her husband drool. Finally, after picking out several accessories to go with the frock and sending a very satisfied customer on her way, we were ready to leave, but Erica wanted to check first to see if Lenny and Zach were going to join us. She went to the back of the shop to use the telephone, so I couldn't hear what she was saying; but moments later, she was on her way back, shaking her head. "Sorry," she said, "they're too busy working and won't be through until supper time."

I'm sure my expression showed how disappointed I was. "Did you speak to Zach? Did he give you a message for me by any chance?"

Erica looked glum. "No, I'm afraid, not but I'm sure he'll ring you sometime. Did you give him your number?"

"He said he'd get it from Adrian."

"Oh well, then I'm sure he'll ring in a day or two," Erica said with a sigh. "There's no sense worrying about it, Ariel, let's just go on our way. There's a lot to see before lunch."

I followed her out to the car with a heavy heart, but she soon had me laughing, telling me about some of the antics she used to get up to before she got involved in her business. We were giggling so much by the time we got to the main doors of the British Museum that the guard on duty looked at us with such disdain, it made us chuckle even more. I found the museum a little boring, except for the Egyptian mummies, and I was glad when we finally came back outside. After that, we went to Trafalgar Square, and I took several photos, suddenly realising that I had stopped looking for Luke in the crowds. Eventually, we ended up at the Sherlock Holmes Pub on Northumberland Street, and I had an enormous lunch of sausages, mashed potatoes and onions, listed on the menu as Dr. Watson's Favourite. Erica tried to persuade me to have the sticky toffee pudding afterwards, but I was completely stuffed and only managed to drink half a pint of ale to wash it all down.

It was during lunch that Erica mentioned she had an idea I might be interested in, and I was completely bowled over when she suggested that I come to work in her shop when Darcy left early in the New Year. I told her I was flattered that she would even think about offering me a job, considering we had only just met, but she said she thought she was a pretty good judge of character and also it would be helpful in advancing my career in fashion design. When I asked her if she minded if I thought about it, she was very gracious and told me to take my time but to let her know by mid-December. When she dropped me off at Victoria Station and I boarded the train for home, my mind was in turmoil. The idea of moving to London in January, working in Erica's shop and seeing Zach again was overwhelming, but then maybe Zach had already forgotten about me.

Chapter Twenty-Seven

Dad picked me up at the station in Abingdon; and on the drive back to the inn, I babbled on about Erica and her offer of a job, but I didn't mention Zach. I wasn't sure that my family would approve of me seeing someone who played guitar in a band. I know they didn't have great ambitions for me like hooking up with a doctor or a lawyer or someone professional with a steady income, but I don't think Zach would have fit their idea of a suitable partner. When Dad asked me if I was considering taking Erica up on her offer, I hesitated because I didn't know what to do. I needed to speak to Mum and get her opinion because deep down, I was scared to death of making the move. I had been brought up in a loving home all my life, and being on my own in a strange city seemed daunting, to say the least. The only people I knew in London were Adrian, Joel and Erica, and I hadn't even considered where I was going to live or even if I could afford it. Then there was my dream of going to design school. What would happen to those plans? There was so much to think about.

It turned out that Mum was going to support me whatever I decided and if I was going to make the move, even help out financially. She thought it would be a wonderful opportunity and actually encouraged me. That was Mum, always putting my welfare first even though she admitted she would miss me terribly.

Two weeks to the day that I got back, I heard from Zach. Dad called me to the phone and handed me the receiver with a puzzled look on his face. "Phone for you," he said. "Said his name was Zach."

My heart jumped into my throat as I took the receiver out of his hand and then waited while he slowly walked away out of earshot. My voice almost gave way as I managed to croak, "Zach? Hello, it's lovely to hear from you."

"Hello, luv," he answered, "sorry I didn't ring you earlier, but we've been up to our ears working on our album. How've you been?"

I could just picture him at the other end of the line with his hair sweeping his shoulders and those wonderful deep green eyes. "I'm fine, how about you?"

"Well, like I said, we've been busy, but now we have a couple of weeks off to relax. I heard that Erica offered you a job in her shop. Are you going to take it?"

The question was so unexpected I wasn't sure how to answer. "I'm not absolutely certain yet. She gave me to the middle of December to give her an answer."

"I think it's a great idea. Erica's a great girl, and she wouldn't just be your boss, she'd be your friend."

I held my breath as I asked, "So you really think I should make the move?"

"Sure," he replied, "what have you got to lose?"

The safety of my family, I thought to myself. "I hardly know anybody there for one thing, and I have no idea where I'd live."

"You already know a couple of people and finding a place to live shouldn't be a problem. Look, Ariel, why don't you come up this weekend? We've got a gig at the Koko Club in Camden on Saturday, and I'd like for you to be there."

I could feel a fluttering in my chest. I could hardly believe that he was asking me to come back on the weekend. "But where will I stay? I don't know London at all?"

"Well, you could stay with me," he replied with a chuckle, "but I guess that's too much to ask. I'll ask Erica if you can room with her for the night."

"Oh no, you can't do that," I said. "That's too much of an imposition."

"Nonsense, she's always putting people up, and I bet she'd be pleased to see you again. Let me ring her and get back to you."

"Are you sure? I just don't know, Zach."

"Yes, I'm sure. Look I'll be in touch, so start packing your bag."

I hesitated. "Er . . . okay. I'll wait to hear from you."

"Good girl. Ciao, luv," and he was gone just as I was whispering good-bye.

It was almost ten o'clock that same night when I got a phone call from Erica. She had no problem putting me up for the night and even suggested that she pick me up from Victoria as the boys would be busy getting ready for their gig. She also suggested that if I didn't have anything suitable to wear for Saturday night, she would lend me something. I couldn't believe her generosity and must have thanked her half a dozen times before she said, "Hey, Ariel, no big deal. I'm looking forward to seeing you. Just ring me when you've booked your ticket to let me know what time you're arriving."

After I got off the phone, I wondered why Zach hadn't rung me himself, but it didn't stop the excitement that was beginning to build. Without any doubt, I was going to see him again. I told Mum and Dad that night, and they were both all for me going back to London for a visit and having a good time. "It's a treat to see you breaking out of your shell," Dad remarked. "You're too much like your mother, always worrying about other people. You deserve to enjoy yourself, my sweet girl."

Mum shook her head and stuck out her tongue at him, but he just grinned and winked at me.

Erica picked me up at the station as promised, late on Saturday afternoon, and we drove back to her flat. I was surprised to learn that the flat was over her shop, as she had never mentioned it when I was there before. There was a side entrance that led us up a flight of stairs to a huge room that looked like a loft, with floor-to-ceiling windows overlooking a back street and some row houses. The whole flat was open concept except for the bathroom. A bamboo screen sectioned off the bedroom area, where I noticed a queen-size futon and an oriental-style dresser and wardrobe. There was a living area with two black leather sofas, a coffee table, an entertainment centre and a small kitchenette with a counter and some stools. It all seemed rather sparse, but the colours everywhere were striking. All of the walls were painted purple, and there were huge posters, some very modern and abstract and some classic like Van Gogh's *Sunflowers* and Monet's *Water Lilies*. The floors were bleached almost white and covered in multicoloured rugs, and there were cushions scattered all over in reds, greens and yellows. I had never seen a room like it before, and I suppose it showed on my face because Erica just grinned and said, "I know it's a little Bohemian but I like it."

After she made us both some tea, she suggested that we go downstairs to the shop and pick something out for me to wear that evening. When I asked what she would be wearing, she pulled a short black frock from her wardrobe with a halter neckline that dipped dangerously at the back. "This is my fallback frock," she said. "When I don't feel like getting too dolled up, I just add some interesting accessories and I'm ready to go."

"Do you have something else like that, only a little more covered up?" I asked.

Erica chuckled. "Oh, Ariel, I'm sure we can find something. In fact, I think I know exactly what will suit you. Let's go downstairs."

In the end, she picked out a white halter neck frock, reminiscent of Marilyn Monroe's frock in *Some Like It Hot*; and although Marilyn was a platinum blonde, the white contrasted with my dark colouring, and I felt rather glamorous. "Wait until Zach sees you," Erica remarked.

I looked down and then back at my image in the mirror. "Do you really think he'll like it?" I asked.

Erica nodded. "I think he'll love it. You look fabulous, and I suggest we leave your hair just the way it is and just add a little more makeup especially on the lips. If you want to look retro, you need a bright red lipstick."

"You know so much about fashion, Erica," I said rather enviously.

"Well, if you come and work for me, you'll learn a lot too. Did you decide to take me up on my offer yet?"

"I haven't quite made up my mind, but I promise I'll let you know by the middle of December."

Chapter Twenty-Eight

Erica suggested that we go out to eat before going to Koko's, so we drove to La Porchetta's on Chalk Farm Road in Camden, where there were so many pizza and pasta dishes to choose from that I had trouble deciding what I wanted. Eventually I settled on a simple pizza with Italian sausage and mozzarella, but I was too excited to eat. Erica was telling me about Lenny and his family; but when it was obvious that my thoughts were elsewhere, she reached across the table and tapped me on the back of my hand. "Ariel, have you heard a word I've said?"

I had been looking down at my plate, and her touch startled me. I jerked my head up and stared at her for a moment. "What? Oh, I'm sorry, Erica, forgive me for being rude."

Erica just grinned. "No problem, I know exactly what you were thinking about, or should I say, who you were thinking about."

"It's that obvious, eh?"

Erica looked serious. "I'm going to give you a piece of advice, and I don't want you to get upset, but I wouldn't get too involved with Zach if I were you."

I frowned. "Why do you say that?"

"Because he's on the road a lot, and he's not only talented but he's very hot. There are groupies hanging around all the time, and the temptation is always there. If you get too serious, you may just get your heart broken."

"What about you and Lenny? He's on the road a lot too, but you two seem to be pretty serious?"

"Lenny and I take it one day at a time. I love him and he loves me, but I have no illusions about what could happen in the future."

"And you're prepared to live like that, knowing that your relationship could end at any minute."

Erica sighed, "That applies to any relationship. Nothing lasts forever."

I shook my head vehemently. "That's not true. My mum and dad have been together since the day they met, and I know they'll never ever be apart."

"Then they're very fortunate, and I hope you're right, but when it comes to someone like Zach, you have to be realistic."

I could feel tears starting to form, and I was embarrassed to realise just how emotional I had become, "Can we please not talk about this anymore?" I asked.

"Of course," Erica replied. "Anyway, we'd better get a move on or we'll miss the start of the show."

When we arrived at Koko's, I was shocked when I first caught sight of the building. It was huge, and I learned from Erica that it used to be a theatre and could hold about fourteen hundred people. We already had tickets, but that didn't allow us to walk right in, so we stood in line with dozens of others waiting to check our coats and go through the main doors. When we eventually stepped inside, I literally gasped. It looked like a real Shakespearian-style theatre with individual boxes tiered along the side walls and decorated in dark red with gold accents, but there the comparison ended. Hanging from the ceiling was a massive crystal ball, and the audience bore no resemblance to any that I could imagine. Everywhere I looked, there were young people, some dressed in jeans and tee shirts and some in party clothes like Erica and me, and the noise level was chaotic.

I followed Erica down the centre aisle, wondering where we would be seated; and when she led me to the very front row, just a few seats to the left, I could feel dozens of pairs of eyes on me. I sat down and Erica leaned over and whispered, "It's okay, this always happens. Anyone with a front-row seat usually knows someone in the group, or associated with it, so people tend to stare and wonder who you are. That reminds me, I think I saw Buddy's new girlfriend as we came down the aisle. I'll just nip over and say hello."

Erica quickly got up and walked towards the right side of the theatre, and I just sat there trying to take it all in and getting more excited by the minute. Suddenly, without warning, the lights went down, the audience went deadly quiet and Erica came bounding back into her seat. A lone figure entered from stage left, and you could almost hear a pin drop. Erica whispered in my ear, "That's the MC, Danny Stein."

Danny Stein was a middle-aged, short, stocky man, almost entirely bald and dressed in an impeccable grey suit. He hesitated for about ten seconds before speaking, but the audience remained silent. Then in a booming voice, which startled me, he said, "Are you ready for the stars of the show?" and pandemonium broke out. Again he waited; and when the noise finally died down, he said, "Tonight, we are pleased to present five young men who are taking the music world by storm." Then in an even louder voice that mounted to a crescendo, he continued, "Give it up for Measure for Measure," and the crowd erupted as the group exploded onto the stage.

I heard the screaming, and I heard the music; but at that moment, it was Zach who captivated my attention. He was front and centre with his guitar, dressed in black jeans and a sleeveless leather vest that exposed his chest and a large tattoo on his right arm. I watched mesmerised as he walked back and forth, playing with such intensity that within minutes, I could already see the perspiration starting to form on his upper lip; and then suddenly, without warning, the music slowed, and he stood like a statue at the microphone and began to sing. I didn't recognise the song, but it was haunting. His voice was deep and raspy and not what I expected, but every word was clear. The crowd had become deathly quiet; and when I looked around, I could see that everyone was swaying gently from side to side with their arms in the air. When it was over, there was thunderous applause, and that's when I saw Zach turn in my direction and very slowly, blow me a kiss. Erica immediately grabbed my arm and was whispering something in my ear, but the band was already starting into their second number and the noise was deafening.

During the rest of the performance I tried to pay attention to the other musicians. Lenny, on drums, stood out because of his startling white hair, and I finally got to see Buddy, who played bass. I was curious because it was Buddy who had his heart broken by Pandora, and I felt sorry for him, but then I remembered his new girlfriend was in the audience, so he had obviously moved on. That's when I thought about Luke and wondered where he was and what he was doing.

The music was ear-splitting; the lights were blinding, changing from one colour to another; dry ice created an artificial fog and, during the final number, there were flashes of fire. It was almost like a dream; and when it was over, I thought the applause would go on forever. That's when Erica nudged me and yelled, "Come on, let's get out of here."

I didn't want to go, but I followed her up the aisle where a few people were already beginning to line up to exit the theatre. "Where are we going?" I called after her, but she didn't hear me.

When we got to the lobby, we got our coats and were outside on the street when I asked her again, "Where are we going, Erica?"

She grabbed my arm and hustled me along to a side street, where she had parked her car. "We're all meeting up at the Alley Cat. It's a bar and not too far from where I live."

I ran along beside her, trying to catch my breath. "Will the whole band be there?"

"Yes, that's why I want to get there as fast as I can so that we can get a good table. Lenny's a friend of the owner, so it shouldn't be a problem."

We soon found the car and were on our way swerving through the late-night traffic. The city was still wide awake, and despite the chilly night and the hour, there were crowds of people everywhere. "What did you think of the show?" Erica asked.

"It was unbelievable," I answered. "It's the first time I've ever been to a concert like that. I thought my eardrums were going to burst."

Erica chuckled. "Welcome to the world of rock."

When we got close to our destination, we parked the car about a block away and walked to the Alley Cat. Once there, we went down a flight of carpeted stairs and stepped into a long narrow space with lots of wood accents and red banquettes. The place was packed with young people. Most of them were standing with drinks in their hands, and I was beginning to wonder how we would manage to find a place to sit when Erica waved at a tall man, with a rather prominent moustache, standing behind the bar. "Hello, Mike," she called out. "Any free tables?"

Mike leaned over and beckoned to her. "Hi there, Erica, good to see you. How many will be joining you?"

Erica sighed, "Well, there'll probably be nine of us altogether, ten at the most."

Mike looked at his watch and nodded. "Half an hour tops. There's a table of ten at the back right now, but they're leaving at midnight."

"Fabulous," Erica remarked. "We'll have a drink while we're waiting."

Mike handed her two dry martinis. He obviously knew exactly what Erica liked to drink, but he had no idea that martinis were not my favourite, and the first time I had ever tried one was at Adrian's party. I took my first sip and looked around me, wishing with all my heart that Zach would come through the door. Erica was chatting with a girl who was perched on one of the barstools and didn't notice a rather short and sinister-looking individual with jet-black greasy hair and a goatee come within inches of me and say, "Well, hello there, baby. I'm Angelo. What's your name?"

I wasn't used to anybody being that forward, and I had no idea what to say. I reached out and touched Erica's arm, and when she turned around, she seemed to sense what was going on and frowned. "Get lost, Angelo," she said.

Angelo smirked. "Why, Erica, good to see you too. Who's your friend?"

"She's my cousin from Sweden, and she can't speak English, so get lost."

Just then, I saw Lenny quickly making his way through the crowd. He glanced at Erica and then at Angelo. "Is there a problem here?" he asked in a quiet but somewhat menacing voice.

Angelo, who was at least four inches shorter than Lenny, looked up. "No problem, Lenny, I was just leaving." He scurried away like a mouse.

"Thank you," I said rather humbly. "I wasn't sure what to do."

Lenny smiled. "Don't worry, he's always hitting on pretty girls, but he's all talk."

"I still think we're going to have to teach you how to handle yourself if you come to London," Erica remarked.

"You must think I'm awfully naïve?" I said, looking down at my feet.

"Who's naïve?" asked a voice from behind my left shoulder. I whipped around, and there was Zach, looking absolutely gorgeous. He'd discarded his leather vest for a black tee shirt with a Grateful Dead logo, and his hair was tied back in a ponytail. My hand flew to my throat, and I could hardly get any words out, but I finally managed a whispered, "Hello, Zach, you were amazing tonight."

"Thanks, luv," he said. "Did you really enjoy the show?"

"Oh yes, it was incredible. Thank you so much for inviting me."

He put his arm around my shoulder. "I told you I'd ring you, didn't I?"

I was about to answer when Mike came over and told us that he had the table ready. We walked with Erica and Lenny to the far end of the room, and just as we got settled at the table, Buddy arrived with the two other band members and two pretty girls who looked too young to be drinking. Lenny made the introductions; and when I met Buddy's new girlfriend, Donna, I couldn't help comparing her to Pandora. There was no doubt that she was pretty, but she had mousy brown hair and a sallow complexion, and she paled against my memory of Pandora, with her bright red curls and brilliant green eyes.

The other girl, Hazel, was with Paddy, an Irish lad with red hair and freckles, who played keyboard, leaving the last member of the group, Brian, a tall lanky chap with wire-framed glasses, who also played guitar. When I asked Erica if his girlfriend was coming, she said they'd broken up a week before, but she'd been hoping that they'd got back together.

There was a small stage at the other end of the room and a trio began to play some really mellow jazz. Now and again, someone would come up and ask for an autograph or want their photo taken with the group, and all of the band members were obliging. In fact, everyone seemed to be in an upbeat mood, except for Brian, who said he felt like a fifth wheel without his girl. Zach tried to reassure him that he wouldn't be alone for long; but after about half an hour, he said his good night and disappeared. Paddy was obviously the joker and kept everybody laughing with his silly one-liners; but by the time two o'clock rolled around, we were all getting a little weary. Buddy and Donna were the next couple to leave and then Paddy and Hazel. That left just the four of us, and I wasn't sure what was going on when Erica and Lenny rose from the table and excused themselves. I was about to ask them if they were leaving, but they didn't say good night, and I didn't want to appear foolish. I watched them wander into the dwindling crowd and suddenly felt anxious. I was just about to ask Zach if they were going when he squeezed my hand and said, "It's just you and me now, luv."

Chapter Twenty-Nine

I was completely lost for words for a few moments. I couldn't believe that Erica had just left me there. "Isn't Erica coming back?" I whispered, almost on the verge of tears.

Zach put his arm around me. "Don't worry, luv," he said. "They've probably gone back to Lenny's for the night, but you won't have to sleep on the street. My place isn't too far from here."

I started to get up from my chair, but Zach pulled me back down again. "Hey, where are you going?"

I slumped back down and gripped the edge of the table. "I don't know. I thought I'd be staying at Erica's."

Zach tipped my chin up and looked me straight in the eyes. "You're not scared of me, are you?"

I shook my head as I stared back into his deep green eyes. "No, I'm just a bit upset. I didn't expect this."

Zach took both of my hands in his and said, "Look, you'll be fine tonight, and tomorrow we can go and get your stuff from Erica's. What time is your train?"

"It leaves Victoria at noon, so I have to be there before that."

"Well, we'd better get a move on," Zach said, looking at his watch, "or you won't get any sleep tonight."

We got our coats and headed outside. By that time, the club was almost empty and there were very few people on the street. We walked about a block before Zach was able to wave down a taxi and travel the fifteen minutes it took to get to his place in Earls Court. There was a door to the left of a coffee shop, which led up to two rooms that Zach called home. One large room with a small kitchenette was decorated mostly in neutral shades, with two huge sofas, a giant entertainment centre on one wall and a bookcase filled from floor to ceiling with books that all looked to be bound in red leather. I was fascinated when I saw the bookcase, "Do you read a lot?" I asked as I walked over to look at the titles.

Zach came and stood beside me. "Here, let me take your coat," he said as he lifted it from my shoulders. "Not as much as I would like," he continued. "I've only read about one-quarter of the books here."

"These are mostly all classics," I remarked, noticing works by Hemingway, Faulkner and Steinbeck.

"Are you surprised?" Zach asked as he laid my coat over the arm of a chair.

I turned to look at him, and he had an amused look on his face. "Yes, I think I am," I replied.

"Never judge a book by its cover," he said, grinning.

"I'm sorry, I hope you're not insulted," I said, bowing my head.

"Not at all. Let me find you something to wear, and you can take the bed while I'll take the sofa."

I shook my head. "No, I'll sleep out here."

"No way," he mumbled as he disappeared into what I assumed was the bedroom. A moment later, he was back, handing me a pale grey tee shirt. "Here, go through and get changed. The loo's off of the bedroom, and you can wash up there if you like."

My mind was flitting from one thought to another. I'd been over the moon with the idea of seeing Zach again and I had even imagined us as a real couple and now I was actually in his home and sleeping alone in his bed. How many girls had he brought here before me, and how many had he actually slept with? What was wrong with me? Wasn't I attractive enough? I think he must have sensed that something was bothering me. "If you're not comfortable, you can lock the door. I promise I won't break it down."

"That isn't what I was thinking," I said, staring at him directly.

"Then what is it?" he asked

I hesitated for a moment. "How come you haven't made a pass at me?"

He frowned. "Is that what you want?"

I sank down onto one of the sofas. "I don't know. I've never done this before."

Zach sat down beside me and took my hand. "Ariel, look at me. The minute I met you, I knew you were different. You're like a breath of fresh air. I won't lie to you because I've been with dozens of girls. In my line of business, there are always groupies hanging around, but most of them just want to be able to brag to their friends."

"You mean, you've never had a serious relationship?"

"I'm not saying that. I actually had a very serious relationship with a girl I first met in high school. We hadn't seen each other for about three years, and then we ran into each other at a party. We were together for just over eighteen months, and we even talked about getting married."

"What happened?"

Zach hung his head. "She was killed in a car accident. She was on her way to her parent's home in Southampton when a drunk driver forced her off the M3, and she went over an embankment. I was told she died instantly."

"Oh my god," I said, grasping his arm, "I'm so sorry. You must have been devastated."

Zach straightened up and took in a deep breath, "Well, that was a while ago, and I don't like to dwell on the past."

"She was the one who suggested the name for the band, wasn't she?"

"Yes, but do you mind if we don't talk about it anymore? What about you? No serious boyfriends?"

"Not really. I thought I might be getting into something serious in the summer, but now we're just friends."

"Why didn't it work out?"

I paused before answering, "I don't think we wanted the same things."

"What kind of things?"

I began to feel anxious. "Just things, that's all," I said rather abruptly.

Zach reached over and turned me to face him. "What are you afraid of, luv?"

I just shook my head and pressed my lips together, trying to avoid his eyes.

"Tell me the truth, you're a virgin, aren't you?" he said.

I nodded very slowly and felt the blood rushing to my head. "Don't be embarrassed, you have nothing to be ashamed of," Zach whispered.

I looked up at him. "I want to do it. I want to know what it's like."

Zach sat there for what seemed like the longest time, and then he gently helped me up and led me into the bedroom. Once in the bedroom, there was no turning back. One moment, I was standing face-to-face with him, holding onto both of his hands, and the next I was lying flat on my back on his enormous bed and he was looking down at me. Very slowly he knelt down beside me and began touching my cheek with featherlike strokes, and then he kissed me tenderly on the lips. I reached up to put my arms around his neck, but he gently pushed my arms back against my sides and started to undress me. All the time that he was peeling my clothes away from my body, his eyes hardly ever left mine, and I had no feeling of shame or embarrassment. It was only when I was completely naked that he sat back on his heels and said, "Now I'm seeing the real Ariel. Do you know how lovely you are?"

I shook my head and reached out to him again, and this time he stretched out beside me and took me in his arms. He kissed me again, first on my lips, then on my neck and then slowly he continued to kiss me on my breasts and my stomach. I began to feel a stirring in my body that I had never felt before; and for some reason, I felt a compulsion to draw up my knees and spread my legs apart. What happened next, I could never have imagined in my wildest dreams. Zach's head was between my legs, and he was doing things with his mouth that made me gasp. Within moments, this wonderful sensation came over me, and I screamed out Zach's name and grasped at his hair. My body was throbbing, and I never wanted it to stop; but gradually, as Zach crawled back up beside me, the feeling began to subside. He stroked my forehead and whispered, "I'll be right back. Don't go anywhere."

I was still panting as I watched him get up and walk over to a small dresser at the other end of the room. He started to take off his clothes. First, his tee shirt, revealing muscular arms and a smooth chest tapering down to a small waist, and then his jeans, leaving him naked except for a pair of black briefs. I couldn't take my eyes off of him as he opened the top drawer of the dresser, took something out and then walked slowly back to the bed. He stood there for a moment, staring down at me, and then he slowly slipped off his briefs. I gasped as I saw how aroused he was and shocked when he slipped on a condom right in front of me. That's when he said, "Don't worry, I'll try not to hurt you."

I closed my eyes as I felt him get onto the bed and then crawl up and push my legs apart. I clenched my fists and felt my body tighten up, but Zach started to stroke my inner thighs and kept repeating, "Relax, relax."

Gradually I began to unwind, and when I opened my eyes, Zach was on his knees and his face was directly over mine. He was supporting himself on one arm, and I wasn't sure what he was doing with the other until I suddenly felt his hand between my legs and he was guiding himself inside me. There was no resistance. He had prepared me well, and it felt wonderful. I arched my back so that I could take him all in; I couldn't get enough of him. I never wanted it to stop; but after a few moments, he suddenly went very still, and then he shuddered and collapsed on top of me. He stayed there for a while, breathing heavily, while I stroked his back. He then rolled over onto his side and gathered me into his arms. "Are you okay, luv?" he whispered.

"Oh yes, it was amazing. I had no idea it would feel so wonderful."

"You're trembling," he said. "Are you cold?"

I snuggled up against him. "Yes, a little but I really need to go to the loo."

He took his arms from around me and swung over to sit on the edge of the bed. "Me first if you don't mind, luv. I'm about to burst."

I looked up at him and giggled. "I think I can wait, but don't take too long."

He bounced up; and as he passed the dresser, he took another tee shirt from one of the drawers and threw it at me. "Here," he said, "put this on."

I pulled the tee shirt over my head and curled up in a foetal position, watching the bathroom door and reliving what had just happened. All kinds of thoughts ran through my head. Did this make me a real woman now? What would it be like with someone else? What would it have been like with Terry? Would Zach want to make love to me again? Soon I felt like I was beginning to drift off to sleep despite the pressure on my bladder when suddenly I heard the bathroom door open and Zach came out wearing his briefs. "It's all yours," he said as he made his way back to the bed.

I crawled out from under the covers, rather reluctantly, and headed for the bathroom where, after relieving myself, I spent a few moments just staring in the mirror to see if I looked any different. When I came back out, Zach was lying on his back and already asleep. Not wanting to disturb him, I climbed quietly into bed and very gently turned on my side and laid one arm across his chest. There was some light coming through the window from some street lamps, and I could clearly see his profile. I stared at him for the longest time, admiring his face and wondering what he saw in me, and then gradually my eyelids got really heavy and I drifted off.

When I woke up, it was daylight; and for a moment, I didn't know where I was. Then when everything came back to me, I saw that I was alone and the bedroom door was wide open. I wondered where Zach was until I smelled coffee and realised he must already be up and dressed. I crawled out of bed and made my way to the other room, but Zach wasn't there either. I knew he had to be somewhere close by and would probably be back soon, so I got washed up, combed my hair, put on a little makeup and slipped into the white frock. I was just coming out of the bathroom when Zach appeared in the bedroom doorway. "Oh, there you are," he said, smiling, "and you're already dressed."

"Yes," I said glumly, looking down at my frock. "I feel a little silly in this so early in the morning. What time is it anyway?"

"It's just after nine, and I just popped downstairs for a couple of minutes. Polly gave me two freshly baked croissants on the house, so if you will come this way, madame, I will serve you a delightful continental breakfast."

I grinned at him as he stepped aside to let me through, and then he grabbed me, swung me around and kissed me with such passion that it took my breath away. When he finally let go, I looked up into his eyes and whispered, "I could go without breakfast."

He shook his head at me and then wagged his finger. "Oh no, missy. So now you're going to turn into a wanton woman, and I thought I had finally found a sweet and innocent young thing."

I pressed up against him and put my arms around his neck. "Well, it's your entire fault. I can't help myself."

He pulled my arms down to my sides. "I refuse to take the blame, and what's even more important, if you want to pick up your stuff from Erica's and catch that train, we had better start eating and then be on our way."

Chapter Thirty

After Zach rang Erica to make sure she was home, he asked me to wait downstairs for a moment, as it was a chilly morning and there were a lot of grey clouds overhead. I was shocked, to say the least, when a few minutes later, a man on a very large motorbike came tearing around the corner and stopped at the curb right in front of me. Zach whipped off his helmet and goggles and grinned. "Here," he said, getting off the bike and handing me a heavy down coat and helmet, "you'd better put this on or you'll freeze."

I looked at him in disbelief. "I can't get on that thing."

He glanced from me to the bike and back again. "What do you mean? This is my pride and joy. It's not everybody that gets to ride on it."

"But it's a monster," I protested," and I've never ridden a motorbike before."

"Well, there's a first time for everything," he responded with a wink.

I shook my head. "There's been too many firsts this weekend. I'm not sure I'm going to survive it."

"Come on," he insisted, grabbing my arm and placing the helmet on my head.

Reluctantly, I put the coat on over my own thin woolly one and climbed onto the backseat. "What about my legs?" I asked, looking down and realising that I only had my open sandals and no stockings or socks.

Zach, who had already jumped onto the front seat, glanced around and down at my feet, "Sorry, luv," he said. "There's not much I can do about that. Don't worry, I'll get you to Erica's in no time, and then you can change."

I was just about to protest when suddenly, with a roar, we were on our way and racing through the streets. At first, I was terrified but after a few minutes, despite the fact that my legs felt like ice, I found it exhilarating, and I didn't want it to end, but in no time, we were pulling up outside Erica's shop.

Zach opted to wait while I went up to get my things; and when I walked into the flat, I was embarrassed to find Lenny lounging about, watching the telly in his boxer shorts and not much else. "Don't mind him," Erica said, "that's his Sunday outfit. Unless we decide to go out, he'll be stuck in that position all day."

"Well, I just came for my stuff," I replied. "I'll just go and change out of this frock, and thank you so much for lending it to me."

"No problem, did you have a good time last night?"

I felt myself go beet red and turned away, but Erica stepped forward and caught my hand. "Let's go in here," she said, taking me behind the bamboo screen.

"I can't really talk," I murmured, keeping my back to her and reaching for my bag.

"You slept with Zach, didn't you?" she whispered.

I turned and looked at her. "Yes, he took me home with him because you went off with Lenny and I had nowhere else to go."

"I thought that was what you wanted."

I nodded. "Yes, I guess it was, but I was scared, Erica."

"He didn't hurt you or force himself on you, did he?" she asked, frowning.

I got very emotional then and despite the tears in my eyes, I smiled. "No, he was wonderful."

"Oh oh," she remarked, "looks like you've caught the love bug. I told you to be careful."

I didn't want Erica to make me feel foolish or guilty, and I needed to get away from her, so I turned my back again, pulled her frock off over my head and took the jeans and jumper, that I had travelled down in out of my bag.

Erica tapped me on the shoulder. "Ariel?"

"Please," I said, tugging on my jeans, "I need to go. Zach's waiting for me downstairs, and I don't want to miss my train."

Erica stepped back and then very quietly said, "Okay, but it's your funeral. Just ring me when you decide if you're going to take the job, okay?"

I nodded as I heard her slowly go back into the living room; and when I was dressed, I carried my bag out to the front door and called out, "Bye, Erica. Bye, Lenny."

I heard Lenny mutter something, but Erica didn't seem to hear me, so I quietly crept out and down the stairs.

On the ride to Victoria Station, I clung to Zach, just wanting to remember this moment and the feel of his body against mine. I had no idea when I would see him again, and I didn't want to go home, but I had no choice. We had only spent one night together, and who knows if he cared for me at all. Maybe I was just another girl that he'd talked into his bed. He didn't come into the station with me because he didn't want to park his precious bike, so we said our good-byes on the pavement outside the main entrance where buses and taxis were pulling up every few seconds and the noise level made it hard to talk without shouting. I reached up and put my arms around his neck. "You will ring me, won't you?" I asked.

"Course I will, luv," he answered, wrapping his arms around my waist.

"Promise?"

"I said I would, didn't I? Now you'd better hop to it or you'll be late."

I buried my head in his neck, and he released his arms, took my face in his hands and kissed me, gently at first and then growing more passionate.

When he broke away, I wanted to cling onto him, but I turned in the other direction so that he wouldn't see my tears. "Bye," I whispered as I took a step forward.

"Bye, luv," he whispered back; and then a moment later, I heard the roar of the engine and turned to see him pulling away from the curb and possibly out of my life.

On the ride home, the train was crowded, and the last thing I wanted was to be surrounded by a lot of strangers determined to engage me in conversation and small children running uncontrollably up and down the aisles. I just wanted to think about what had happened on the weekend, and Zach. With each mile that separated me from him, I got the feeling that I might not see him again. Then again, if I moved to London to work with Erica and she remained in a relationship with Lenny, Zach would always be somewhere in the picture. I'm not sure why I felt so insecure. I wasn't unattractive, and we seemed to enjoy a lot of the same things, especially literature. I knew I was getting ahead of myself. After all, I had only seen Zach twice and although we had slept together and it had been a turning point for me, he had probably been with dozens of girls. Erica had warned me not to get involved with him, but my heart told me otherwise.

As the train pulled into Abingdon, I made a decision—I was going to move to London in January. Dad was waiting for me and honked his horn as I stepped out onto the street. I ran over to open the door, and Sammy bounded out, obviously happy to see me. "Hello, boy," I said, bending down and stroking his head as he tried to wind himself around my legs.

"Sammy, get back in here," Dad called out.

I opened the back door and Sammy immediately jumped up on the seat and I climbed in next to Dad and then leaned over to kiss him on the cheek. "Hello, Dad, thanks for picking me up."

"No problem, sweet girl," he said as he pulled away from the curb. "Did you have a nice time?"

"Oh yes," I answered, full of enthusiasm, and went on to tell him all about the concert and the visit to the Alley Cat afterwards; but of all the people I had been with or met, I only mentioned Erica by name.

Dad listened while I babbled on; and then when I'd finished, he glanced over at me and said, "What about that chap that rang you, Zach, wasn't it? Did you see him while you were there?"

I must have hesitated a little too long before I replied, "Yes, he was there," because Dad looked over at me again and frowned. "And what happened?" he asked.

I was beginning to feel uncomfortable. "What do you mean?"

"Well, was he just part of a group of people, or did you spend some time with him alone?"

"Dad," I moaned, "why are you asking me?"

"Just curious, that's all. This chap rings you, and you go off for the weekend, but then you don't even mention him. I'm beginning to think something's afoot here."

I chuckled. "Now you sound like someone out of the seventeenth century."

Dad roared with laughter. "Okay, so is he your boyfriend, or isn't he?"

I shook my head but couldn't help smiling. "Maybe," I answered.

There was silence for a few minutes, and then he remarked, "Well, your mother will get it out of you, that's for sure, even if I can't."

It didn't take Mum long to figure out that I had spent the night with Zach. When we were alone, clearing away the supper dishes, she asked me what else I had been up to while I was in London. I had already given both Mum and Dad a detailed account of the concert, our visit to the bar afterwards and Erica's flat, but she sensed that I was leaving something out. "Tell me about the time you spent with this Zach," she said. "What does he do for a living?"

I hesitated for quite a while before I answered, and I could feel Mum frowning at me. "He plays guitar in a band," I replied, busying myself with drying the supper plates.

"What kind of band?"

Again I paused and then answered, "It's a rock band, that's who was playing at the concert."

Mum reached over and, grabbing my elbow, turned me to face her. "Ariel, why didn't you mention this before?"

I lowered my eyes. "I'm not really sure, Mum, but perhaps I didn't think you'd approve."

"Why wouldn't I? I've never even met this young man, but I've always trusted your opinion of others. I suppose what I really want to know is just how much you like him and if you're going to see him again."

I started to turn away as I felt the blood rushing to my head, but Mum pulled me back and forced me to look at her. "You slept with him, didn't you?" she whispered.

I nodded very slowly, and she immediately gathered me in her arms. "Oh, honey," she murmured, "I always wondered when this day would come, but I didn't expect it to be with someone you just met."

I pulled away and looked her in the eyes. "But it was so natural, Mum. Honestly, I'm not sorry it happened, and now I can't stop thinking about him. I can't wait to see him again. That's why I've made up my mind to take Erica up on her offer and move to London in the New Year."

Mum took my hand and led me over to the kitchen table. "Why don't we sit down for a minute and talk?" she said quietly.

After we settled in our chairs, she smiled at me and then reached over and stroked my hair. "You know, Ariel, I still think of you as my little girl and it's hard for a parent to let go, but you're old enough to make your own decisions now. I said the same thing to you about Luke, and maybe now you'll be a little less judgmental about what he did."

I started to interrupt her. "But Pandora isn't a good person—" But she cut me off with a wave of her hand.

"Your brother is listening to his heart, and I have to assume that's what you're doing too. You've only just started seeing this young man, and you really don't know what he's like. It's obvious that he must live a very different lifestyle than the one you're accustomed to, and I'm sure it's all very exciting, but I hope you'll be careful and I hope you'll take precautions."

"I will, Mum, but seriously, Zach isn't like Pandora. I haven't heard anyone say a single bad word about him, and even though he plays in a rock band, he likes all kinds of music and loves to read. You should see all the books he has and all of them are classics. I really hope you get to meet him one day."

"I hope so too, but he might find Abingdon a little quiet for his tastes. Maybe after you move to London, we can come and visit and we can meet him then."

I grasped my mother's hand. "Oh, Mum, so you don't mind me leaving and going to work for Erica?"

"I told you before, it's your decision. Of course, we'll miss you, but we would never stand in your way."

"You're the best, Mum, but I hope you won't tell Dad everything I've told you."

Mum shook her head. "Don't worry, your secret is safe with me, but if you keep on seeing this Zach, at some point, you'll have to tell your father."

"I will, Mum. I will, I promise."

Chapter Thirty-One

Four days after that conversation with Mum, I still hadn't heard from Zach, and I was beginning to get desperate. All kinds of questions were running through my mind. Had he already forgotten about me? Was I just another notch on his bedpost? What would I do if he didn't ring me? I knew I had to do something, so despite the cool evening, I decided to take Sammy for a walk along the riverbank, clear my head and then decide whether I should ring him.

When I got back home an hour later and walked into the reception area, Dad was behind the desk on the telephone. He glanced across at me as I came through the door, and then I heard him say, "Hang on, she just came in."

My heart leapt into my throat as I let Sammy off the leash and then walked towards the desk. Dad was holding the receiver out to me. "Here," he said smiling, "someone wants to speak to you."

I took the receiver from him and held it to my ear for a moment before whispering, "Hello?"

"Hello there, sis."

It was Luke and for a second or two, I felt disappointment and then great joy to finally be hearing from my brother.

"Luke," I called out, "how great to hear from you. How have you been, and where are you?"

"I've been pretty good, although it's hard killing time before my classes begin in January. The filming just wrapped up on *Moll Flanders*, so Pandora and I may go to Spain for a couple of weeks just to get out of this miserable cold. How about you, what have you been up to?"

"Well, I was in London last weekend, and I went to a rock concert."

"What?" Luke asked. "You at a rock concert. Who did you go with? Was it Terry? I assume you're still seeing him?"

"No, it wasn't Terry. We're just friends now, and I only see him occasionally. You remember Adrian? Well, he invited me to his anniversary party. He lives with this chap, Joel, in Kensington. Anyway, I met his sister, and she invited me back again last week. She has this amazing shop that sells vintage clothes, and she wants me to come and work for her."

"Are you serious, sis? You mean you might move here to work in a shop. What happened to design school?"

"I still want to go to school but later. Erica has a great fashion sense, and I think I can learn a lot from her."

"So you've made up your mind already. When do you expect to move here?"

"Sometime early in the New Year. Mum and Dad are okay with it, and maybe when I get settled, I can get to see you all the time. I really miss you, Luke."

"I miss you too, sis. I wish I had known that you were here last weekend. We could have had lunch or something."

"Yes, that would have been nice. I should be back there soon, and then we can get together. Ring again next week because I tried getting hold of you once, and whoever that person was who answered the phone, she wasn't too co-operative."

Luke let my remark slide by and then surprised me when he said, "By the way, I think I'm going to be home for the holidays. I was talking to Mum about it, and she said that Christmas wouldn't be the same without me, so she's hoping I'll be there."

I hesitated for a moment before asking, "Would Pandora be coming with you?"

"No way, she's already arranged to visit her mother."

"Why aren't you going with her?"

"She wants to spend some time alone with her mum, or so she says. That means I'll be stuck here on my own, so I thought it would be a good time to come home."

"I'm glad you still think of this place as home," I said softly.

"You know what I mean, sis. Okay, listen, I gotta go. I'll ring again soon, I promise."

Reluctantly I said good-bye and rang off. I thought that hearing from Luke would really lift my spirits; but for some unknown reason, I felt more depressed than before. I went to bed that night with my mind still in turmoil and had trouble sleeping, so it was not surprising that when I got up the next morning, I wasn't in a happy frame of mind. Dad tried to cheer me up at breakfast by telling me stupid stories about Nana and her cat; but from the look on my face, he knew he wasn't having much affect. "What's your problem this morning?" he asked. I was just about to answer him when Mum came rushing through the kitchen door. "Phone for you, Ariel," she said.

I started to get up. "Who is it?"

"She didn't say. Go and take it in the reception area."

When I realised the caller was a female, my heart sank. I had no idea who would be calling me so early in the morning. I ran out to the front desk and picked up the receiver. "Hello?" I said tentatively.

"Oh, hello, Ariel, it's Erica. Sorry to bother you so early. I meant to ring you last night, and then it slipped my mind."

Hearing Erica's voice gave me a glimmer of hope. "Erica, it's okay. How are you? Is everything all right?"

"Yes, everything's fine with me, but Zach asked me to give you a message. Paddy's father passed away on Tuesday, so all the guys went to Belfast for the funeral. They decided to stay for a few more days, and that's why he hasn't been in touch."

I didn't know whether to laugh or cry. I felt so badly for Paddy, but at least I knew that Zach had been thinking about me. "I'm so sorry to hear that. Was his father sick for a long time?" I asked, attempting to make conversation, even though I had other things on my mind.

"Yes, I'm afraid so. He had a heart problem, and he was quite elderly. Paddy's mum is having a really hard time, and that's why they want to stay for a bit longer."

"I really appreciate you ringing me, Erica. Please tell Paddy how sorry I am when you speak to him, and I guess I'll hear from Zach when he gets back."

"Sorry again that I didn't ring last night, but we had a sale on at the shop and I was worn out by the time I came upstairs."

"Oh, that reminds me, Erica, I've made up my mind to accept your offer of a job. I'll be moving to London in January."

I heard Erica give a whoop. "Fabulous! I'm so pleased. We'll talk some more about it later, but right now I have to run, as Darcy is stuck in traffic and I've got to get the store open."

After she rang off, my mood had changed considerably, and Dad couldn't help remarking, "Well, I'm glad to see my sweet girl is back."

The following day, Terry rang and asked if I wanted to go for a bite to eat. I figured that anything was better than mooning around at home, so I agreed. I also thought it was time I told him that I had decided to go to London, but I wasn't prepared to tell him about Zach. He picked me up at six o'clock, and we drove to the Cherwell Boathouse in Oxford. It's a charming restaurant, almost one hundred years old, on the banks of the Cherwell River. We had this wonderful pan-fried bream with croquette potatoes and cucumber sauce; and then despite, already feeling full, we couldn't resist the apple tart with brandy ice cream. After I ate my last mouthful, I sank back in my chair and sighed and said, "When you said a bite to eat, I didn't expect to come here."

Terry chuckled. "Well, actually it's a bit of a special occasion."

I was puzzled. "What do you mean?"

Terry reached across the table and grasped my hand. "I guess you could call it a farewell dinner."

I shook my head. "Are you telling me I won't be seeing you again? I thought we'd agreed to be friends."

"We are friends, Ariel, but I'll not be going to London now. My uncle Tom offered me a position in his investment company, and I just couldn't refuse. The only thing is it's in Manchester, and I'm leaving next week."

I was taken by surprise and a bit disappointed; but for Terry's sake, I wanted to sound happy for him. "That's amazing. What a great opportunity for you, and I know you'll do well. If I recall, you were pretty brilliant at maths."

"Yes, well, I'm not sure if that will help me too much, but if it works out, I'll have a good career ahead of me."

"And here I was going to tell you some news of my own."

"What is it? Tell me."

"I'm going to London much sooner than I originally planned. I can't remember whether I told you about Adrian's sister, Erica. Anyway, she owns her own shop, and she wants me to work for her."

"Really? What kind of shop?"

"She sells vintage clothes, and I think I can learn a lot from her."

Terry frowned. "You mean more than going to a proper design school?"

I withdrew my hand and put it in my lap. "I think so, but in any case, I can always go to school later."

"You know that won't happen, don't you? Once you start earning your own money, you won't want to give it up."

I suddenly felt very defensive. "That's not necessarily true. In any case, I've made up my mind, and I'm moving in January.

Terry shook his head. "So what do your parents think of this idea?"

I sat upright in my chair and replied rather smugly, "They are supporting me. They think I'm old enough to make my own decisions."

"And your own mistakes," Terry muttered in a very low voice.

After that, things were a little strained between us, and the drive home was difficult. I was relieved when we arrived back at the inn, but then Terry reached over and put his arm around me. "I'm sorry, Ariel. You know I wish you all the luck in the world, and I want us to stay in touch."

I looked up into his face and knew that I didn't want to lose his friendship. "I'd like that," I whispered.

He leaned over and kissed me very gently on the lips, and I suddenly felt really sad knowing that I probably wouldn't see him again for a long time. "When you get settled, ring me and let me know how things are going," I said.

"I will for sure," he replied, taking his arm from around my shoulders.

I turned and opened the car door, ready to get out, when he said, "Ariel, just one more thing. I wish things could have been different between us, but I guess it wasn't meant to be. I just hope that one day really soon, you meet someone you can really care about."

"You too," I answered as I stepped onto the driveway and shut the door quietly behind me; but at that moment, the only person I had on my mind was Zach.

Chapter Thirty-Two

Four days later, I got the phone call I had been waiting for. It was almost eleven o'clock at night and I was just about to go to bed when Dad came looking for me. "That young fella's on the line again asking for you," he said, frowning. "Isn't it a bit late to be ringing here?"

I figured it had to be Zach. "He works late," I replied defensively as I ran to the reception desk.

Dad shook his head as he passed by me on his way to lock the front door. I had no intention of letting him hear what I was saying, so I turned by back and whispered, "Hello, is that you, Zach?"

"Yes, luv," came the response, and I felt my heart flutter in my chest.

"How are you, and how's Paddy? I was so sorry to hear about his father."

"It was rough for a while. His mum took it real hard, but his sister decided to stay on for a while longer, so we were able to leave. We'll be busy for the next few days recording, so it will take Paddy's mind off his troubles. By the way, it's Buddy's birthday, and I think we all need cheering up, especially Paddy, so we're having a party. I'd like you to be there."

My breath caught in my throat. "Really? I'd love to come. When is it?"

"Well, his birthday's on Thursday, but we're celebrating on Saturday. We're having it at his parent's house in Croydon. It's only about an hour from here, and you'll like his mum and dad. They're great people."

"I've never been to Croydon. How will I get there?"

"Just take the train to Victoria, and I'll pick you up. We can drive straight to the party from there."

I had a vision of the two of us on his motorcycle again, with me in my party clothes and an overnight bag. "I hope we're going by car," I said.

Zach laughed. "Yes, of course, and don't worry about getting all gussied up. It's going to be very casual, and I expect everyone will be in jeans."

"And where will I stay?" I asked holding my breath.

"With me of course, luv," he replied. "And then on Sunday, I'll drop you back at the station. It will have to be no later than noon, though, because I have things I need to take care of later."

At first, I was excited knowing that I would be spending another night alone with Zach, but then I felt disappointed that I would have to leave so early to come back home. I hesitated for a moment, and then Zach said, "Ariel, are you still there?"

I quickly pulled myself together. "Yes, yes, I'm still here. I was just thinking about making arrangements for the trip."

"Look, if you need money for fare, luv, I can pay you back when you get here."

I was shocked that he thought I was worrying about money. "Oh no, I don't need any money. What time will you pick me up?"

"Let's say around six. Ring me when you know what time your train arrives."

"Okay, I will. I'm really looking forward to seeing you, Zach."

"Me too, luv. I'll talk to you later. Take care of yourself."

"Bye," I whispered, but he had already rung off.

I could hardly wait for Saturday to arrive. I rang Zach the next morning with my arrival time at Victoria, but he wasn't at home, so I left a message. Then I spent some anxious moments trying to decide what to wear and what to get Buddy for his birthday. In the end, Mum loaned me a midnight blue cowl-neck jumper scattered with black bugle beads, which she had in the back of her wardrobe; and for Buddy, Dad gave me a bottle of good Scotch that he had stored away.

When I saw Zach again, I was on cloud nine. He showed up in a bright red 1960 Austin Healey, which he told me was his first gift to himself when they started to be successful. He looked amazing; and all the way to Croydon, I could hardly take my eyes off of him.

Buddy's parents turned out to be much older than I expected, but they were full of life and mixed right in with the young crowd. The house was bursting with people, and I was relieved when I saw that Erica was already there. Nevertheless, I found the evening a little overwhelming, and I guess that's why I ended up drinking a little too much. By eleven o'clock, I was feeling a bit tipsy, and that's when Erica came up to me and said, "How about a smoke, Ariel?"

I shook my head. "I don't smoke. I never have."

She chuckled. "It's just a joint. Come on have a little fun."

I was horrified. "You mean marijuana?" I looked around the room. "Is that what all those people are smoking?"

Erica grinned. "Sure, can't you smell it?"

"Yes," I replied rather indignantly, "but I didn't know what it was. What about Buddy's parents, do they approve of this?"

"Approve? They're flower children at heart. They never stopped smoking, so they're fine with it. You really should try it."

I shook my head again vehemently. "No, leave me alone please, Erica. I don't want it."

"Okay, okay, keep your shirt on," Erica remarked, and then she took off across the room, and I saw her go up to Zach and whisper something in his ear.

I stood there scowling as he approached me and then put his arm around me. "It's okay, luv," he said gently. "Don't let anyone make you do anything you're not comfortable with."

I sagged against his chest and started to cry and realised that I really had had way too much to drink. He led me over to a sofa in the corner of the room and sat me down. "Stay here and just relax for a few minutes, and then we'll leave," he said.

I reached up and grabbed his arm. "Oh no, please don't leave the party on my account."

"Not to worry, I've had enough for one night. I'll just say good-bye, and then I'll come and get you."

I was so relieved when we walked out of the front door a few minutes later. When the cold air hit my face, I felt better almost immediately, but I spent the next little while apologising for my behaviour. Zach tried to assure me that he wasn't upset, but I couldn't help feeling guilty about leaving the party so early. I knew then, more than ever, just how naïve I was. Growing up in Abingdon, I had never been exposed to smoking pot. I had heard of some of my school chums hiding out in the loo one day and trying it, but they got caught and were suspended, so most of us were pretty cautious. Zach seemed to understand, as he had been brought up in Maidstone, which was only twice the size of Abingdon, and his parents, being Greek, were old school and frowned on drugs of any kind.

By the time we got back to his flat, he had convinced me that I had nothing to be embarrassed or guilty about and if I was worried about Erica, I needn't be.

We spent a good half hour just cuddling and listening to music, but then he started kissing me; and before I knew it, we were back in the bedroom and frantically ripping off our clothes. What followed was another night like the first one I had experienced with Zach, except that we had many more hours to spend together and very little was wasted on sleep. Every time I looked into his eyes, I was on the verge of telling him I loved him because that's the way I really felt, but I bit my tongue. We had known each other for such a short time, and I had no idea how he really felt about me. I was terrified that if I told him I loved him, he would push me away. Becky always told me I should play hard to get, but it really wasn't in my nature, and I struggled to control my emotions.

Early in the morning, just as it was beginning to get light, my thoughts turned to Luke. Is this what happened when he met Pandora? Did he just fall madly in love with her, or was it just infatuation? I had been so judgmental, and I knew then that I needed to reach out to my brother and tell him that I understood. That's when I decided to ask Zach if he could help.

We eventually managed to crawl out from under the covers at nine o'clock; and when Zach suggested that I hop in the shower with him, I couldn't resist. It was a lot of fun and rather erotic, but then the hot water started to run out, and we were forced to jump out and wrap ourselves in thick fluffy towels. I didn't feel particularly attractive with my hair dripping wet and no makeup, so I pushed Zach out into the bedroom so that I could make myself presentable. "Out," I said, "I feel like a drowned rat."

He grinned. "Maybe I should call you Willard from now on."

I stuck out my tongue and closed the door and then looked in the mirror. It looked like I had some work to do.

When I finally emerged, I felt like a whole new person. I had managed to dry my hair with a rather ancient hair dryer, apply some makeup and put on my jeans and jumper. Zach was standing at the kitchen counter when he glanced over at me and whistled, "Wow, Willard, you clean up real good," he said.

I walked over and put my arms around his waist. "If that's a compliment, I'll take it," I whispered.

He tilted my head up and brushed my hair away from my forehead. "Seriously, luv, you look gorgeous."

I realised, at that moment, that it was the first time he had really commented on my appearance. That made me happy because I was certain that most of the girls he had dated must have been beautiful. I thought I had been out of his league, but now I wasn't so sure. I know I was a little embarrassed, and so I stepped away from him and looked to see what he had been doing. I noticed a bowl of what looked like batter and some oil beginning to sizzle in a frying pan on the stove. "Are you making pancakes?" I asked.

"Yes, and I've got some of those precooked sausages that I'm going to stick in the microwave. Will that be enough for breakfast?"

"I thought you always picked up breakfast from Polly downstairs."

"Not always, and if I have a guest, I usually like to cook."

I hesitated for a moment but couldn't help asking, "Do you have guests often?"

Zach looked at me and wagged his finger. "Now you're prying, luv."

I felt as though I'd been reprimanded, so I decided to change the subject. "Can I help you do anything?"

"Yes, you can make some coffee," he said as he began pouring the batter into the pan.

There was silence while we both attended to what we were doing, and I even felt some tension between us. By the time we sat down at the table, I was feeling really uncomfortable and was determined to clear the air. "I'm sorry about before," I said, reaching over and grasping Zach's hand. "I hope you're not upset with me."

He shook his head. "I'm not upset, but you need to know that whatever's happened in the past has nothing to do with our relationship."

"I know that," I said, feeling ashamed. "Can we forget I ever said anything, please?"

"Yes, of course," he replied. "Now eat your pancakes before they get cold."

I started toying with my food, not because I was still worried that I had upset him but because I didn't know how to approach the subject of Luke. It didn't take him long to notice. "Do they taste that bad?" he asked.

"No, they're really good, but I'm not very hungry and I'm worried about Luke."

"Why, has something happened?"

"No, I just feel that I need to speak to him."

"Then why don't you just pick up the phone and ring him?"

"Because when I called there last time, it was like Pandora was having the phone monitored. I know if I ring, they'll say he isn't there or make some excuse so I can't talk to him."

Zach frowned. "Don't you think you're being a little paranoid? Why wouldn't Pandora want him to speak to his own sister?"

"Because I'm sure she doesn't like me. That's why I want to ask you for a big favour."

"Oh, what is it?"

"Will you ring and ask to speak to Luke? You can say you're an old friend of his. You can say your name is Jimmy. Luke used to chum around with him at home. If they believe you, I'm sure they'll bring him to the phone."

"And what if he's not there?"

"Tell them you'll call back. Please, Zach, can you do it now? I'd really like to talk to him."

"Can I finish my breakfast first?

I pressed my lips together and just stared at him until he got up abruptly from the table and walked over to the telephone. "Okay, what's the number? Let's get this over with."

I ran into the bedroom to rummage through my handbag for the number and ran back again, handing the slip of paper to Zach. While he dialled, I perched on the arm of the sofa and waited nervously. After a moment or two, I heard him say, "May I speak to Luke, please?" Then there was a pause before he looked across at me with a puzzled look. "Yes, that's right, I mean Lucius."

I took in a breath and nodded back at him and then waited again. There was another pause before he said, "My name's Jimmy, I'm a friend of his."

A minute passed while Zach stood there tapping his foot and looking at the floor. Then suddenly he looked up. "Luke? Hold on, will you? Someone wants to speak to you."

My hand went to my throat as I took the receiver from him. "Luke, it's Ariel," I whispered.

It didn't take me long to realise that Luke wasn't too pleased with the way I had pretended that it was Jimmy on the phone. "What an earth are you up to, sis? Why didn't you just ask for me yourself?"

"Because Pandora's screening your calls," I said indignantly.

"That's nonsense," he replied. "Anyway, what are you calling for?"

I was a little taken aback. "Can't I even call my own brother?" I asked. "I happen to be here in London this weekend, and I was hoping to see you. I have a train booked back to Abingdon at noon, but I can always take a later train."

Luke paused. "Sorry, sis, I'm busy this afternoon. You should have rung me yesterday or during the week when you knew you were coming here. Anyway, what are you doing here again so soon?"

"I was invited to a party, a friend of Erica's," I said, shaking my head at Zach.

"Sounds cool," Luke remarked. "Look, sis, I have to run. Pandora and I are having brunch with some friends, and I still have to get ready."

I was beginning to get annoyed. "When do you think we'll have time to talk, Luke? You're always in a hurry."

"Probably at Christmas, that's when I'll be coming home, and we'll have plenty of time then."

"Okay. Well, I'd better let you go, but try and call Mum a bit more often. Take care of yourself. I love you, Luke."

"Love you too, sis," he said softly, and I waited until I heard the click before I hung up the phone.

I looked at Zach, who had been listening to every word. "He's too busy to see me and doesn't even have time to talk," I said as I felt the tears start to form.

Zach walked over and put his arms around me. "I'm sorry, luv. Is there anything I can do?"

I laid my head on his shoulder. "There's nothing you can do. We used to be so close, but now I feel like I'm losing him. Pandora seems to be all he thinks about now."

Zach gently stroked my hair. "He's in love with her. Either that or he's totally infatuated. He can't help himself, and it isn't because he doesn't care about you. Once the romance wears off a bit, he'll pay more attention to you just like he used to."

"You really think so?"

"I know so. Now if you want to take a later train, I can run you over to Erica's. Why don't you call her and see if she's free?"

"No, I think I'd just like to go home."

Chapter Thirty-Three

I went back to London one more time before the Christmas holidays and stayed with Zach for the whole weekend. There wasn't any doubt in my mind that I was in love with him, but I had no idea how he felt about me. When I wasn't with him or talking to him on the telephone, I thought about him all the time, and I could hardly wait to leave Abingdon for good and be closer to him. One day, I was feeling really low, and Dad suggested that I call Becky and go out to the pictures or take a walk, anything to stop me from mooning around the house. I really wasn't in the mood for company, so I decided to spend some time with the only one who could make me smile, Sammy.

Despite being the middle of December, it was a beautiful day. There was a blanket of fresh snow on the ground, and the sun made the ice on the trees glisten. Sammy loved the snow; and when I took his leash down from the peg behind the kitchen door, he was already, jumping up and down with excitement. Once we were close to the river, I let him run free, and he was in his element. He was a great dog, and I knew that once I left, I'd really miss him. I didn't know how much longer we would have him, as he was getting old, although one would never know it to see him racing around and rolling over and over in a snow bank.

By the time I got home, I felt better, but I hadn't got any thoughts of Zach out of my head, so I decided to ring him. I think he was surprised to hear from me because he had always been the one to initiate any contact. "Ariel?" he said, "Hello, luv. What's up?"

Just hearing his voice made my heart beat a little faster. "Oh, I was just out for a walk with Sammy, and it's such a beautiful day here. I was thinking about you and wondering what you were doing."

"Yes, it's a great day here too. I'm just getting ready to go shopping with Buddy and Donna. I've got no idea what to buy my folks. They've pretty well got everything."

"I know what you mean. I have the same problem. What day are you going back home for the holiday?"

Zach hesitated. "Not absolutely sure yet but probably Christmas Eve. I'll only stay for about three or four days. By the way, Adrian's having a New Year party at their place. Would you like to come?"

"Oh, I'd love that," I replied excitedly. "Will all the boys be there?"

"Yes, except for Paddy. He'll still be in Ireland with his mum."

"It sounds great. Thanks for inviting me. I'll look forward to seeing Adrian and Joel again."

We chatted some more, and then he had to go because Buddy and Donna had arrived to pick him up. I didn't even mind when he finally rang off because I was so excited about the party and couldn't wait to tell Mum and Dad.

"When are we going to meet this young man?" Dad asked with a rather stern look on his face.

"Maybe after I move to London and you come to visit me," I answered.

On Christmas Eve, at noon, Luke arrived with a suitcase full of presents and a big smile on his face. Mum was so pleased to see him that she couldn't stop hugging him; and when she finally stepped back to get a good look at him she said, "Lucius, what have you done to yourself? Your hair's so dark, and you've lost some weight."

Luke patted his midriff and grinned. "Been working out, Mum."

"I think you look great," I said as I threw my arms around his neck.

He gently took my arms down and looked over at Dad. "It's good to be home," he said.

Dad shook his head and then stepped forward to give him a hug. "Good to see you, son."

That evening, after a lovely meal Mum had prepared especially for Luke, he suggested that we all go down to the Cherry Tree for a drink. Dad reminded him that someone had to stay behind at the inn, and he tried to persuade Mum to go without him, but she didn't want to leave Dad behind. So it turned out that Luke and I were able to spend some time together, and I was able to learn more about his life with Pandora. At first, he was not very forthcoming; but after two beers, he became more relaxed and confessed that living with a film star was not easy, but it was exciting, and he was in love with her. When I asked him if they had any plans for the future, he hesitated and then replied in a whisper, "I asked her to marry me, but she turned me down."

I gasped in surprise. "Why?"

"She said I was too young to get married and not mature enough to know my own mind," he answered dejectedly.

"Then why does she stay with you?" I said indignantly.

Luke threw back his shoulders and grinned. "Great sex."

I'm sure my eyes grew as big as saucers. "I don't think I want to hear this," I said, covering my ears. "Too much information."

"Come on, sis," he remarked, "you're not that naïve. Don't tell me you're still a virgin."

I felt the blood rush to my face. "None of your business."

He reached over and tipped up my chin, looking directly into my eyes. "Who is he? Not that Terry fellow, I hope."

"I told you, it's none of your business."

"Okay, fair enough, but I'll find out sooner or later. I just hope he's a good guy, sis."

We bantered back and forth, and I felt like I had my brother back again. We were comfortable with each other even though there were things we didn't want to talk about. We stayed until the pub closed, joining in with some of the locals, singing carols and some of the old favourites. By the time we got back home, we were tired but happy and glad to be together.

Christmas Day was much like all the previous holidays we had spent together as a family. Dad had strung up streamers in the reception area and brought in an enormous spruce tree that took forever to decorate. We were actually quite busy that year and had only one vacancy. I know the guests appreciated the effort Dad put into making the inn look as festive as possible. Luke bought Mum and Dad several gifts, including a lovely miniature print of a painting by Monet, which he picked up in Paris. While there, he also bought a beautiful Hermes scarf for me and a wonderful CD of Edith Piaf. I had always found Luke difficult to buy for, but he seemed delighted with the two tickets for a David Bowie concert at the Rainbow Theatre.

It was only after we had finished opening our gifts that I thought about the fact that I hadn't received anything from Zach. Exchanging presents had crossed my mind when he had mentioned shopping for his folks, but I didn't want to make him feel obligated. Looking back, I regretted not asking him what he would have liked or what he really needed, and now I was beginning to question if he had been thinking the same thing. I was longing to talk to him but knew he was spending the day in Maidstone, so I tried to concentrate on helping Mum with preparing the turkey dinner, which she planned to serve midafternoon. We sent Dad and Luke off to the Cherry Tree for a pint so they would be out of our hair, and Mum and I spent a pleasant few hours in the kitchen.

After dinner, Dad entertained us, singing some Irish songs while we sipped on white wine and tried to digest all the food we had eaten. We didn't even have the energy to clear away the dishes until it had grown really dark outside; and for those few hours, I felt really content. We were anxious to know when Luke would be going back to London and were surprised to learn that he was staying in Abingdon for another three days. "So is Pandora staying at her mother's all that time?" I asked.

"So she tells me," Luke replied.

"Where does her mother live?"

Luke seemed distracted. "What? Oh, in the east end somewhere. I think she lives in Stepney."

"And you've never met her after all this time?"

"No, apparently she's not very well and can't get around too easily."

"Then why haven't you been to visit her?" I asked, becoming more and more curious.

"Gee, sis, you ask a lot of questions," Luke replied, looking rather annoyed.

I decided to drop the subject, not wanting to spoil the lovely day we had all spent together. "Why don't we go for a walk?" I suggested. "Sammy loves to go out in the snow."

Sammy, who had been reclining under Luke's chair reacted immediately on hearing his name and bounded out, wagging his tail. Luke reached down and tickled him behind the ear. "Hello, boy, did you miss me?"

Sammy began to lick Luke's face and soon had him laughing. "Come on, sis," he said, "let's get his leash and get out of here."

We spent the next three days just enjoying each other's company, except when Luke tried to pry information from Mum and Dad about the mysterious new man in my life, but they were quick to tell him that they knew just about as much as he did. I found it all rather amusing and decided to go on with the charade until I felt really comfortable about my relationship with Zach. On the evening before Luke left to go back to London, Dad invited our paying guests to join us in an early New Year's celebration, and Mum set up a table in the lounge with sausage rolls, mini pizzas, nachos and mince tarts. Luke got a little drunk but managed to behave himself, and I could see the joy on Mum's face from just having him back home again, even if only for a short time. The next morning, he left, just after breakfast. It was a tearful time for all of us, although he promised he would visit Mum and Dad again in a couple of months and get together with me often after I moved to London permanently. We watched him drive away in the green Aston Martin that Pandora had loaned him for his trip to Abingdon, and I put my arm around Mum as she whispered, "Bye, Lucius, take care of yourself."

Waiting for the next few days to go by was excruciating. Mum knew I was all wound up about going to the party at Adrian's, so she decided to take me shopping in Oxford to help me find a frock for the occasion. After trying on several outfits, we finally found a plum-coloured velvet frock with long sleeves and a scoop neck that seemed to cling to my body in all the right places. Mum and I both wore the same size shoes, and she had a perfect pair of black suede heels to go with the frock and some long drop earrings made of onyx that just brushed my shoulders. When we got back home, I tried on the whole outfit to see if Dad approved, and he let out a very loud wolf whistle as I descended the stairs to the reception area. "What do you think, Dad?" I asked.

"I think you're going to knock everyone dead, sweet girl," he replied.

Chapter Thirty-Four

I will never forget that New Year's Eve because that was the night I learned that my brother had been made a fool of, and I vowed to do something about it. It wasn't until the party ended, just after midnight, while a few of us were mellowing out in Adrian's living room when Joel asked me if I'd had a good Christmas with my family. I told him that it had been especially enjoyable, as Luke had been home for the first time in a number of months. Adrian chimed in, wanting to know if Pandora had come with him, and I was very quick to tell him that he had come alone and that according to Luke, Pandora was visiting her mother. I immediately saw a look on his face which told me something wasn't quite right; and at the same time, I noticed Erica look over at him and give a slight shake of her head. I looked from one to the other and asked, "What's going on? Is there something I should know?"

I was sitting on Zach's lap, and he put his arm around me and said, "Best leave it alone, luv."

I got up and faced Adrian. "If this involves my brother, then I need to hear it."

Adrian shrugged and glanced at Erica, who sighed and said, "Pandora's mother has been dead for years."

I didn't realise the significance for a few seconds, and then it dawned on me that Pandora had obviously lied in order to cover up whatever devious thing she had been up to over the holidays. "I knew it," I said. "It was only a matter of time before she broke my brother's heart. She was probably off shacking up with someone else."

Zach got up and, standing behind me, put his hands on my shoulders. "You don't know that's what she was doing."

I turned towards him with eyes blazing. "Do you want to bet?" I spat out. "That woman is a witch, and Luke needs to know the truth about her."

Zach shook his head. "You need to calm down, luv. If you start interfering, you're just going to get Luke upset with you. Surely you don't want that?"

"What am I supposed to do, just forget that she's a liar and a cheat? I can't do that. I care too much for Luke to let him be treated like a fool."

Zach looked a little put out. "I think we should finish this discussion at my place and let everyone go on enjoying themselves," he said solemnly.

Everyone was sitting, staring at me, and I felt so conflicted. I was furious with Pandora, worried about Luke and embarrassed that I had spoiled the party. "I'm sorry," I said in almost a whisper. "I think Zach's right, and we should leave. Thank you so much, Adrian, and you too, Joel."

They both got up, along with Erica, and each of them gave me a hug. "Don't do anything too hasty," Erica warned, "and call me next week so that we can talk about when you'll be back to start working."

"I will," I said; and taking Zach's hand, we walked out onto the snow-covered street, where all seemed peaceful, but my mind was in turmoil.

We drove back in silence to Zach's place, and I couldn't help wondering if he was really annoyed with me. By the time I changed out of my clothes and put on a terry towel bathrobe of Zach's, I found him in the kitchen, making coffee. He was reaching up into a cupboard to retrieve a tin of shortcakes when I walked over and put my arms around his waist. "You're mad at me, aren't you?" I asked.

He turned around and took both my hands in his. "I'm not mad, Ariel, I'm just a bit disappointed that we had to leave the way we did. Those are my closest friends, and it would have been nice to have spent a little more time with them."

I pulled away and looked down at the floor. "I said I was sorry, but you can't blame me for being upset. I thought you would understand."

Zach took a step towards me and tipped my chin up so that I couldn't avoid his eyes. "Truthfully, I'm not sure I do understand. I know you've been close to your brother, but he's an adult and responsible for his own actions. It's obvious to me that you intend to get involved with what may or may not be going on, and frankly, I don't want any part of it. I suggest you go home tomorrow and forget all about it. Luke won't appreciate you interfering with his life, and you might just be barking up the wrong tree. Pandora could have a legitimate reason for not wanting to be with him during the holiday, and it's really none of your business."

I felt my blood pressure start to rise. "You're wrong," I shouted. "It is my business. This is my brother you're talking about, and I can't let him be hurt. I'm not going home tomorrow. I'm going round to Pandora's house to see what's going on."

Zach threw up his hands and sighed, "Have it your way, but I think you're making a big mistake. Just don't come crying to me when Luke tells you to keep your nose out."

I started to respond, but Zach turned his back on me. "Enough," he said, "I'm going to bed. If you're coming, fine. If not, then you can stay out here and worry about your brother."

"What about the coffee?" I asked meekly. Luke just shook his head and disappeared into the bedroom. I must have sat for at least thirty minutes thinking about what I should do. Eventually, I decided that I needed to go to bed and try to get some rest; and when I went into the other room, Zach was sound asleep. I crawled quietly into bed and turned my back on him. I was cross that he wouldn't support me; and at that moment, I felt really alone.

The next morning, I slept in until after nine and when I got up, Zach wasn't in the flat. I knew he couldn't be downstairs at the coffee shop because it was New Year's Day and they would be closed. I decided to go ahead and get dressed and make myself some breakfast, but I wasn't really hungry and ended up with a bowl of shredded wheat and a glass of orange juice. I was sitting at the table, contemplating, making a fresh pot of coffee, when Zach walked in the door. "Hello, luv," he said, walking over and kissing me on the cheek. "I see you found some breakfast."

"Good morning," I answered. "Where were you?"

"Just out to get some air," he answered. "I had a bit of a headache from all the drinking last night."

"It was probably me that gave you the headache."

He shrugged. "Let's not get into that again, luv. Now what time does your train leave?"

I got up from the table and took my dishes over to the sink. "It doesn't matter what time it leaves because I'm not going home until later today."

"Well, you're welcome to stay here until you're ready to go, but I have to take off soon. You don't have to worry about locking up because the front door automatically latches when you go out."

"Where do you have to go today? It's a holiday, and I thought you'd be here all day."

"No, I'm actually driving to Southampton because there are some people I want to see."

My mind started to tick over, and then it came back to me. "Southampton? Isn't that where the parents of your ex-girlfriend lives?"

"Yes, it is. They invited me to stay with them for a couple of days, and I told them I'd be there later today."

"I see, I didn't realise you were still in touch with them," I said, quietly feeling a little resentful.

Zach sat down at the table opposite me. "I talk to them fairly often, but I haven't seen them for quite a while."

"Doesn't it make them sad when they see you?"

"On the contrary, they get to talk about Celeste and that makes them happy."

"Celeste? That's a very pretty name. Do you have a photo of her?"

Zach frowned. "Are you sure you really want to do this?"

I nodded. "Yes, of course. I'm surprised you don't have any on your dresser or anywhere else in the flat."

"Let's just say that sometimes memories can be a little painful," Zach said as he got up and went into the bedroom.

While I waited, I tried to convince myself that I was just curious; but deep down, I knew that I was jealous. I was jealous of a young woman who had lost her life and no longer a threat to me. I was deep in thought when Zach suddenly appeared at my side, holding a framed photograph. "Here's one of the last photos taken of Celeste," he said.

I took it from him and studied the picture which was taken from the waist up against a plain dark background. Celeste had the face of an angel and hair the colour of wheat, and I could see that she was very slight. I couldn't tell if she was wearing a frock or blouse, but it was a small floral print with a square neck and cap sleeves, the only adornment being a simple silver pendant in the shape of a heart. "She was lovely," I said, suddenly feeling a little ashamed.

"Yes, she was," Zach said, taking the photo out of my hand and starting to walk away.

I reached out and grabbed his arm. "Wait. Don't go off like that. Why don't you sit here and tell me all about her."

He stopped and turned to face me. "There's no point, luv."

"You'll talk to her parents but not to me?"

He shook his head. "That's different. You never met her."

"She still means a lot to you, doesn't she?"

I watched while he hesitated and then looked irritated, "Yes, she still means a lot to me and probably always will, and that's why I'm not ready for another long-term relationship. Look, Ariel, I don't want to mislead you. I think you're a great girl and I enjoy your company, but I can't think about the future. Right now, all I can concentrate on is my music and my career. In fact, I've been meaning to tell you, we're going on tour again next month and we'll be gone for quite a while."

I was stunned into silence. I hadn't expected or wanted to hear what Zach had just told me. I sat there staring at him, and I could feel the tears starting to form. He stared back at me for a moment and then came over and sat beside me and took my hand. "I'm sorry, luv. I didn't mean to spring all that on you. We can go on seeing each other, but I can't make any commitment."

I nodded very slowly. "It's all right," I said, although nothing felt right at that moment. "How long will you actually be gone?"

"At least ten weeks. We'll be in Scotland and then in Manchester, Liverpool, and quite a few other cities."

"Why didn't you tell me this before?" I said softly.

"Because I didn't want to spoil your Christmas knowing that I would be going away soon."

"It seems like I'm the one that spoiled everything," I whispered.

Zach put his arm around me. "That's not true, luv."

We sat like that for a few moments while he gently rubbed my back, and then he got up and said, "I really have to get going. You stay here as long as you like, and I'll call you tomorrow. Just make sure you don't do anything rash today."

I got up, put my arms around his neck and kissed him very lightly on the lips. "I do love you," I said. "I can't help it."

He kissed me back and then, without saying a word, took Celeste's photo back to the bedroom and then quietly left through the front door.

After Zach left, I decided to call Mum and Dad to let them know that I was catching a later train and wouldn't be home until early evening. Mum wanted to know all about the party and what I was going to be doing all day, but I stalled and said that Erica was waiting for me and I'd fill them in when I got home. After that, I rang information to get the number for Victoria Station and then had to endure the monotony of listening to a robot voice listing the departure schedules from Victoria to dozens of destinations. I figured that taking the five o'clock train would give me enough time to see Luke and try and make him see some sense. I considered ringing him but believing that any calls were being screened and not having

Zach to cover for me this time, I knew that I had no alternative but to go to the house on Brooke Street.

I had another cup of coffee and tried to get my thoughts together, and then I packed up my overnight bag and left the flat, making sure that the door was firmly closed behind me. I wasn't sure how easy it would be to get a taxi on New Year's Day, but I assumed that if I walked out to the main street, there might be one passing by. It was bitterly cold out, and the pavement was icy, but I was lucky because as soon as I turned the corner onto Earl's Court Road, I saw the familiar sight of a London taxi coming towards me. I flagged him down and then suddenly realised that I didn't know the actual address. I felt rather stupid telling him I needed to go to a house on Brooke Street with a red door, but he just laughed and in one of the broadest cockney accents I had ever heard, said, "Been partying too much last night, 'ave yer?" He then assured me that we would find the right house; and as he started pulling away from the curb, I began to wonder if I was really doing the right thing.

I was still feeling unsure of myself when the driver called out, "Well, we're on the street, so just keep your eye out for a red door," and he started to chuckle.

I felt like he was making fun of me but didn't have time to respond because he was suddenly pulling up to the curb. "'Ere it is, miss."

I paid him and slowly got out of the taxi onto the pavement, which had already been covered with a layer of salt to melt the ice. There was no one else on the street except for a solitary man walking a large English sheepdog; and as the taxi drove away, I felt very lonely and rather conspicuous. I stood for a moment, staring up at the red door, and then with all the courage I could muster, I climbed the steps and rang the bell.

Chapter Thirty-Five

I stood on the top step, straining to hear if anybody was inside the house, but it remained eerily silent. I felt my resolve start to slip and considered walking away, but then suddenly, the door opened, and a very diminutive woman with short coal black hair and an elfin face appeared. The moment she opened her mouth and spoke just one word, "Oui?" I knew it was the same person with the distinct French accent I had spoken to on the telephone. Remembering her rather authoritative attitude, I decided to take the gentle approach. "Good morning," I said, smiling. "I'm Ariel Regan, Luke's sister—oh, excuse me, I mean Lucius. I'm sorry to bother you, but is he in by any chance?"

The woman looked me up and down and then muttered, "Monsieur Regan does not live here."

I stared at her for a moment, trying to take in what she had just said, "What do you mean he doesn't live here? He lives with Pandora, he must be here."

With a motion that looked like she was about to close the door in my face, the woman shook her head and repeated, "I 'ave told you, Monsieur Regan is not here."

I slammed my hand against the door to prevent her from closing it. "Please," I begged, "I need to see him. If he isn't here, then tell me where he's gone."

"That," she answered angrily, "is not my business."

"But . . . but . . . ," I stammered, "what about Pandora? Is she here? I need to speak to her."

"Mademoiselle James is not at home. Now if you would please take your hand off of the door."

I dropped my hand, and she immediately slammed the door, leaving me standing helpless on the top step. I don't know how long I stood there, but I could sense someone peering at me from behind one of the lace curtains at an upstairs window. I looked around at the empty street and felt utterly hopeless. Where was Luke?

After waiting for a few more moments, I descended the stairs and started walking. I had only gone a short distance when I saw a woman pushing a large black pram, and I stopped her to ask where I could find a telephone. She wasn't sure but suggested I walk to Green Park tube station, which was just a few blocks away. I thanked her and proceeded along Piccadilly and then made my way into the station. It wasn't a long walk, but I wasn't really dressed for the icy weather; and by the time I got there, my hands and feet were frozen. I decided I needed something to warm me up, so I went into the coffee shop and ordered a hot chocolate but was too anxious to drink it. I spied a telephone close to the entrance and rang Erica's number, hoping I could visit with her until my train left, but she wasn't at home. Not bothering to leave a message, I had no alternative but to ring Mum and Dad and tell them what had happened, at the same time, praying that they had heard from Luke. Dad answered the phone; and when I told him I had discovered that Luke was no longer living at Pandora's, he didn't seem very surprised. "Well, sweet girl, I expected that little affair to run its course. How did you find out?"

I hesitated for a few seconds. "I went to the house and knocked on the door. I was told he didn't live there, and they didn't know where he'd gone. I don't know what to do now, Dad."

"You do nothing. When your brother's ready, he'll ring us. You don't know if Pandora kicked him out or if he left of his own accord so until you find out what happened, I suggest you stop worrying."

"I can't stop worrying, Dad. He told me he was in love with her, and he must be really upset. I can't imagine where he can be."

I heard Dad sigh, "Oh dear, come home, Ariel. You can't wander around London looking for him, and you'll miss his call if you're not here."

I looked around me at all the people bustling through the station and knew that I didn't have a hope of finding Luke. "Okay, Dad, I'm going to ring Victoria and see when the next train leaves and if I can catch it. I'll see you soon."

"All right, hurry back."

"I will," I whispered and gently hung up the receiver.

I managed to get to Victoria and change my ticket about five minutes before the next train was scheduled to leave for Abingdon. The journey seemed endless; and even though I had a book to read, I just couldn't concentrate. I almost regretted going back home and even considered getting off at the next stop and returning to London, but I had no place to stay and no idea what I would do when I got there. I could only hope and pray that Luke would ring Mum and Dad and let them know where he was and if he was okay.

I took a taxi from Abingdon Station, and Dad came out onto the front steps as we pulled into the driveway. He came forward and opened the door to help me out. "I'll get this," he said, handing the driver some money. "You'd better get on inside. It's pretty cold out here."

I went on ahead through the reception area and into the kitchen, where Mum was sitting at the table, shelling peas. She got up when she saw me and put her arms around me. "Oh, Ariel," she said, "I'm so glad you're here. Take off your coat and sit down and I'll make you a nice cup of tea."

"Thanks, Mum," I responded, dropping my overnight bag onto the floor, shrugging off my coat and sitting down.

While we waited for the teakettle to boil, I told Mum why I had gone to Pandora's house to see Luke. She felt that there must have been some plausible explanation for why she had told him she was visiting with her mother at Christmas when apparently her mother was no longer alive. "What possible explanation can there be?" I asked. "She was obviously involved with something she didn't want him to know about. My bet is she was with someone else and he must have found out and they had a big fight."

"That doesn't answer the question as to why you went round there. Why didn't you just ring him?"

"Because this person who lives there, a secretary or maid or whatever, screens all the calls. I figured if I went there and knocked on the door, I'd stand a better chance of seeing him. I was determined to prove to him what a liar Pandora is, but it looks like he already found out."

I hadn't notice Dad walk in into the kitchen while I was talking and was startled when he said in a very commanding voice, "I think that's quite enough interfering, young lady. I'm getting a little tired of all this. You are not your brother's keeper, and I want you to leave him alone."

I got up and faced my father, who had never used that tone with me before. "Why can't you understand?" I answered back angrily. "Nobody seems to care. Even Zach doesn't want to hear about Luke."

"I assume this Zach is the new boyfriend. Well, I can hardly blame him because it's all you seem to talk about."

"That's not true," I yelled, starting to cry and heading towards the door.

Mum called out, "Come back, Ariel, please don't upset yourself."

I heard Dad say, "Let her go. She'll get over it. I'll take her bag upstairs once she's settled down."

I was on the way up to my room when Sammy came bounding up the stairs, wagging his tail. The sight of him made me cry even more, and I sat down on one of the steps and just held him in my arms while he gently licked my face. "You understand, don't you, Sammy?" I whispered.

I suppose the stress of it all finally got to me because shortly after I got to my room and lay down on my bed, I fell asleep. About an hour later, I heard someone knocking on my door; and after calling out, "It's open," Mum came in carrying my bag. By this time, I was sitting up and perched on the edge of the bed. "Sorry, dear," she said. "I hope I'm not disturbing you."

"It's okay, Mum. I guess I fell asleep for a while. I felt really tired for some reason."

Mum sat down beside me and took my hand. "I'm not surprised after all the worrying you've been doing. Your dad thought it would be best if I talked to you. What can I do to help?"

I shook my head. "I don't know, but somehow we have to find Luke. I know I can't go back to London and just start looking for him amongst all those millions of people. I can't get to Pandora, and I don't know where else to turn."

"I'm sure your brother will ring us when he's ready, Ariel. We have no idea what happened between him and Pandora, and there's no use trying to speculate."

"You're right, Mum, but I want to be here when he rings. If I leave here now, he won't know where to find me."

Mum frowned. "That's not true, your dad and I can give him your phone number if he rings. I assume you'll be starting your job with Erica soon, and we'll be able to find you there during the day until you find someplace to stay. Do you have any idea where that will be yet?"

I stood up, walked towards the window overlooking the snow-covered grounds and then turned to face my mother. "I'm not going back to London until we hear from Luke."

"But what about the job Erica offered you? If you don't go soon, perhaps she won't be able to wait for you."

I shrugged my shoulders. "I can't help it. Anyway, maybe Luke will ring in the next day or two, and then I can still go."

Mum got up and came over to me. "I think you should call Erica and tell her what's going on. If she tells you, you have to be there by a certain date to start work, you have to be realistic and tell her you're not sure you can make it. She can then decide whether she's willing to wait or if she needs to start looking for someone else."

"I guess you're right," I agreed with a sigh. "I'll phone her later after I get my thoughts together. Right now I'd like to take Sammy out."

"That's a good idea, but bundle up because it's pretty cold and I hear it's going to start snowing quite heavily by this evening."

We both left my room and walked down the stairs together, where Sammy was sitting patiently on the bottom step, almost as if he knew it was time to go out. I bent down and patted his head. "Okay, boy, I'll just get my coat and boots, and we'll be on our way."

Chapter Thirty-Six

After supper, I rang Erica, but she still wasn't home. I considered getting in touch with Zach but had no idea what I would say to him. I thought if I mentioned Luke, he might even get annoyed with me, and I didn't want that to happen. I was still in love with Zach, but I wasn't obsessed with him the way I was in the beginning and it didn't look like there was any future for us. On top of that, he was going off on tour for a long time, and he probably had dozens of women chasing after him. It would be stupid of me to think that he wouldn't take advantage of the situation.

Mum suggested that Dad and I should go to the Cherry Tree for a drink while she stayed behind and took care of the inn. Dad said he'd go on one condition that any issue concerning Luke was off limits. I was irritated at first but I really needed some distraction, so I agreed to go. We actually had a really enjoyable time. One of the locals played a few popular tunes on the old upright piano, and we got into a game of darts with our neighbour, Jerry Barnes, and his wife. By the time we got home, it was close to ten o'clock, and I thought it might be a good time to try and ring Erica again. I took Sammy for a quick five-minute walk, said good night to my folks and then went to the reception desk to make the call. After the fourth ring, I was about to hang up, and then I heard Erica's voice. "Hello, hello," she said, breathing heavily.

"Erica, it's me, Ariel. Sorry to bother you so late."

"Oh, Ariel, it's okay. Lenny and I just got in. We just saw this really weird foreign film. I loved it but he hated it. He says he can't keep up with reading the subtitles."

I heard Lenny muttering in the background and chuckled. "I know exactly how he feels. I have trouble keeping up with them too. Look, I called to let you know I have a bit of a problem making a commitment about coming to work for you. Luke seems to have gone missing, and I don't want to leave home until we hear from him."

"What do you mean by gone missing?"

"Well, he's not at Pandora's anymore, and I can't find out where he is."

"How do you know he's not at Pandora's?"

I proceeded to tell Erica what happened when I went to the house. "I'm just really worried that she kicked him out, and he's really upset and done something stupid."

There was a pause, and then Erica said, "Well, I hardly think anything bad has happened to him, and in any case if he rings home, your parents will know where to get hold of you."

"I know, but I'm just not comfortable about it, and I want to be here when he rings."

There was another even longer pause. "I have to be honest, Ariel, I do think you're overreacting a bit, and I really do need you here by the end of next week. I'm sorry, but if you're not sure you can commit, then I'll have to start looking for someone else."

I felt really let down, but I wasn't going to tell Erica that. "I understand," I replied, "and I think you should go ahead and start looking. I'm grateful that you even offered me the job in the first place."

"Yes, it's too bad because I thought you'd really fit in well at the shop. I hope we can stay in touch though. You'll have to come and see me when you come into town again."

"Oh, I'll definitely be back," I said. "I'm still seeing Zach, you know."

"Then you must know the band is going on tour, and they'll be away for some time."

"Yes, Zach told me." I hesitated for a moment. "Erica, has he ever said anything to you about me?"

There was silence at the other end of the line. "Erica, are you still there?" I asked.

"Oh yes, I'm here. What was it you asked me?"

"I asked if Zach ever talked about me."

"Well, he said he thought you were a great girl and he liked you a lot."

"Just liked, that's all?"

"Look, Ariel, Zach's just not ready to get really serious with anyone right now."

"Is that because of his music or because of Celeste," I spat out angrily.

"Both," Erica answered immediately. "His career is very important to him, and I know he's not over losing Celeste. She was the love of his life, and they were going to get married."

"What was she like?"

"I know you don't really want to hear this, but she was a lovely person and very attractive too. I really liked her."

By then I felt totally rejected. "I guess I don't stand a chance with him then," I said.

"Truthfully, I think you should give up on the idea of a long-term relationship with Zach, and if you can't deal with it, then maybe you should cut and run now."

"Maybe I will," I whispered.

For the next day or two, I began to wonder if I had made the right decision telling Erica to look for someone else. I could be waiting for Luke to ring for weeks, but then again there was no way I would be able to just sit back and do nothing. I even wondered about going to the police; but when I mentioned it to Dad, he thought I was joking and told me to forget all about it. I tried to keep busy helping Mum around the inn; and then all of a sudden, both Marcy and Mum got sick with the flu, and I was forced to take over most of the chores, including cooking breakfast for six guests who were visiting from Edinburgh. Dad did his best by helping out, but he had committed to making a large maple hutch for the community centre by the weekend, so spare time was at a minimum. By evening, after tending to Mum, who was laid up in bed, cooking supper for Dad and myself and taking Sammy for a walk, I was exhausted. Thankfully, I fell asleep soon after my head touched the pillow and Luke existed only in my subconscious mind.

It took almost a week for Mum to recover; and even then, she was not her usual cheery self. She insisted that Marcy stay home for a few more days until she felt well enough to return to work, so I was still needed to clean the rooms, do the laundry and make sure all the common areas were spotless. It was hardly what I expected to be doing. Here, I was still living in Abingdon, and I would probably have to revert to my original plan of moving to London in the fall and taking the course in fashion design. That would mean I needed to apply right away to be sure there would be a place for me, but I just couldn't pick up the telephone and make that call.

Almost ten days had gone by, and I hadn't heard a word from Zach. I was beginning to wonder if Dad was right and he was sick of hearing me talk about Luke; then on Tuesday, I received a card from him, inviting me to a party for the band before they went on tour. My emotions ranged from excitement, anger and disappointment. I couldn't really understand why Zach would send me a formal invitation; it all seemed so impersonal. I talked to Mum about it, and she thought it was a little odd but suggested that I ring him and then maybe I would get a better idea of how he really felt about our relationship. I didn't have too much time to mull it over because the party was on Friday, so that same evening, I picked up the phone and rang his number. It must have rung about eight times before the answering machine came on, and I left a very brief message asking him to ring me back. It was Thursday when I finally heard from him; and by that time, I had pretty well given up on any idea of attending the party. Dad told me it was Zach on the phone, so I was prepared when I picked up the receiver and with little emotion in my voice said, "Hello, Zach, I expected you to get back to me before this."

There was silence for a moment, and then he replied, "Sorry about that, luv, but I've been pretty busy."

I decided not to comment but in the same tone of voice asked, "Why did you send me an invitation instead of ringing me?"

Again there was a moment of silence and then, "As I said, Ariel, I've been busy, and if you really want the truth, Erica sent out all of the invitations and even signed my name on some of them."

I felt my throat start to close up and couldn't even speak until I heard Zach say, "Are you there?"

"Yes, I'm here," I whispered, "but maybe I'd better not come to the party. It doesn't sound like you'll miss me if I'm not there."

"Look, I'm sorry you feel that way, and I'm sorry if I hurt your feelings. I'd really like you to come and for us to stay friends."

"Is that how you think of me, as a friend?"

"Yes, it is. I know you want there to be something more but that's not possible. I have too much going on with the tour and everything else."

"It didn't feel like just a friendship when you slept with me," I snapped back.

It went really quiet at the other end of the line, and then in a really low voice, Zach said, "I think it would be better if we talked about this some other time."

"Good idea," I replied and hung up the phone.

I tried very hard to hold back the tears as I raced up to my room, but Mum caught me at the top of the stairs, and I just fell into her arms. "Oh dear," she murmured in my ear, "I guess the conversation with Zach didn't go too well."

"I thought he really cared about me, Mum," I responded, leaning my head on her shoulder.

She led me into my room and sat down on the edge of the bed next to me. "I'm sure he does care about you, Ariel, but not in the way you want him to. I know you don't want to hear this right now, but you're still young and you'll meet someone else one day and forget all about Zach."

I shook my head vehemently. "He just wants us to be friends, but I don't know how we can be. I slept with him, Mum, so how can I just be a friend?"

Mum put her arm around my shoulders. "Oh, honey, sometimes the best friendships of all can develop after two people have been intimate with each other, so I wouldn't just brush him off. When you move to London, you're going to need some support from Erica and Zach and the other young people you've met. Your father and I would be much more comfortable knowing you weren't all alone there."

"I don't think he'll even talk to me anymore. I hung up the phone on him."

Mum sighed, "Well, maybe that was a bit hasty, but I'm sure he'll get over it. Why don't you call him back and apologise?"

I got up and reached for a tissue from my bedside table to dry my eyes. "Maybe I will but not right now. I need to think about what I'll say to him. Maybe I'll write him a letter instead."

Mum nodded. "That might be a good idea. So obviously you're not going to the party."

"No, I'll just stay home and mope," I replied, managing a grin.

"That's my girl. Now come on downstairs, and we'll have a nice cup of tea."

Chapter Thirty-Seven

On Saturday evening, I couldn't help thinking about the party
and wondering who was there. I heard the telephone ring a
couple of times, and Dad answered; but when I asked him who
it was, he said they just hung up without speaking. I fantasised
that it was Zach calling me and trying to avoid talking to my
parents; so when I heard it ring for the third time, I rushed to
the phone in the lounge and yelled out, "I'll get it."

I picked up the receiver rather tentatively and whispered,
"Hello, Trout River Inn, how may I help you?"

"Ariel? Thank God."

He sounded so different, but it was Luke. I could hardly
believe it. "Luke, oh my goodness, it's really you. Where are
you? We've been so worried about you."

"Don't tell Mum and Dad it's me," he said.

"Why? Was that you who rang before and hung up on Dad?

"Yes, I don't want to talk to them now. I need to see you,
Ariel. Can you come to London?"

"Of course, but what's going on? Why aren't you with
Pandora anymore?"

"I don't want to talk on the phone. Can you take the train to
Victoria tomorrow? There's one that arrives at eleven o'clock. I
can meet you there, and then I'll tell you everything."

I hesitated, trying to figure out how I would explain taking off to London to Mum and Dad, but there was no way I would let Luke down. "I'll be there," I said, "but can't you tell me anything? You sound strange. I hardly recognised your voice at first."

"I've got a bit of a cold," Luke answered, although I suspected that he wasn't telling the truth. "Look, sis," he continued, "I need you to bring me some money."

I was a little taken aback. "What, how much money?"

"At least a hundred pounds, maybe more if you have it."

"Where am I supposed to get more on a weekend? I only have about twenty pounds on me."

"Can you go to the bank machine and take some out? I'll pay you back, I promise, sis."

He sounded so pathetic that I couldn't say no to him. "Okay, I'll meet you at Victoria at eleven. Make sure you're there, Luke. Otherwise, I'll really be worried about you."

"I'll be there, just don't tell Mum and Dad."

After he rang off, I ran up to my room to avoid Dad who was just coming in the front door. I had to think up a story to tell him and Mum. They didn't really need to know that I was planning on going to London. I could pretend I was spending the day with Becky. I hadn't seen her for a long time, so I didn't think they would question it. I decided to ring her and tell her what I was up to just in case she happened to try and get in touch with me on Sunday. It was highly unlikely, but I couldn't take the chance. She was just as curious as I was as to what was going on with Luke, and we arranged to meet the following week for supper at the Garden restaurant in Oxford. I felt crummy lying to my parents, but they accepted the story that I was seeing Becky and pleased because I'd finally be spending some time with my closest friend. Later, I took Sammy for a walk and stopped at Barclays Bank to draw some money out of the machine. I was only allowed to withdraw two hundred pounds at a time, and I had a feeling that Luke might need that much so I slipped in my card and watched as the notes tumbled out. I tucked them away in my coat pocket; and as I led Sammy back home, I felt as though I had done something illegal, but it was just my guilty conscience. I wasn't used to lying to my folks.

I was up early on Sunday morning and anxious to be on my way. I helped Mum make breakfast for our guests and then had a bite to eat with Dad, who offered to drop me off at Becky's. I hadn't expected him to give me a ride and quickly made up the excuse that I needed some exercise and preferred to walk. Thankfully, he didn't push me and just after nine, I was on my way to Abingdon Station.

The journey to London, as always, was relatively short; but this time, it felt like it was taking forever. And then to make matters worse, there was a delay at one of the stations on route. I was so worried that I would be late and Luke would give up on me but hoped he'd have sense enough to check the arrival board. Finally, we were pulling into Victoria, and I assumed that he'd be waiting at the main entrance, but I had just arrived at the main concourse when I heard him calling out from somewhere behind me. "Sis, over here."

I turned and scanned the crowds of people swarming through the station, but I couldn't see Luke. Suddenly, I felt a hand grasp my right elbow and looked up to see someone I hardly recognised. He looked like he'd lost a lot of weight, and his face was pale and gaunt. His hair, now coal black, was long and almost reached his shoulders. I stared at him for a moment and then looked down at his clothes, which looked like they'd been slept in and had a musty odour about them. I shook my head slowly in disbelief. "What's happened to you?"

"Don't I even get a hug?" he answered, looking puzzled.

"Yes, of course," I said as I reached up to put my arms around his neck and kiss him on the cheek.

He hugged me back and then held me at arm's length. "You're looking good, sis."

"Well, I can't say the same for you. Have you been ill?"

"Let's not talk here," he responded, grabbing my hand. "We'll go to my place. Do you have money for a cab?"

I ran along beside him as he exited the station out onto the main street where a line of taxi cabs were waiting. "It depends on how far it is."

"Not far," he answered; and before I could say another word, I found myself in the back of a cab and Luke was telling the driver to go to an address on Camden High Street. Then he looked at me and put a finger to his lips. Obviously, he didn't want to have a conversation with me until we got to his place, and I sat in silence on the edge of my seat while we travelled through a maze of streets with traffic running in every direction. Twenty minutes and fifteen pounds later, we pulled up outside the Laundry Locker, a dry cleaning store with a side entrance which I assumed was where we were going. It reminded me of Zach's place above the bakery, and I was curious to know what it was like inside. By the state of the stairwell, I began to prepare myself for the worst. The walls were a putrid shade of mustard, and the stairs themselves were covered in dark brown linoleum which had been worn through in several places.

As we reached the second floor, Luke said, "Don't expect a palace," and I grew even more apprehensive. When Luke opened the door at the top of the stairs and I walked through, I could hardly believe what I was seeing. The room was almost devoid of furniture, except for a tattered beige sofa, a scarred wooden coffee table, a small telly sitting on top of a narrow bookcase and a kitchen table with an Arborite top and two metal chairs. At the far end of the room, there was an open kitchenette; and to my left, I could see another door.

"What's through there?" I asked.

"That's the bedroom," Luke answered heading for the kitchen area. "I wouldn't go in there if I were you because it's a bit of a mess."

I looked around for another door. "Where's the bathroom?"

Luke picked up a kettle and started to fill it with water. "It's down the hall. I share it with one other tenant."

I sank down onto the sofa and shook my head. "This is horrible, Luke. How on earth did you end up here?"

Luke plugged in the kettle and then came over to sit beside me. "She threw me out, and I had nowhere else to go, sis. I didn't have any money, so this was all I could afford. That's why I rang you. Did you bring the money with you?"

I looked at him incredulously. "You've got to be kidding. You have a perfectly good home to go to. I'm not giving you money so that you can wallow in a dump like this."

Luke got up and stamped his foot. "I'm not going back to Abingdon. You don't understand. I need to stay in London, and then maybe Pandora and I can get back together."

I could feel myself getting cross and stood up to face him as the kettle started whistling on the stove. "Are you crazy?" I yelled. "Take a look in the mirror. You look like a bum. I hardly recognised you at the station. Why would any woman want to be with you?"

I watched as his shoulders slumped, and he brought up his hands to cover his face. Then he started to sob, great gulping sobs that just broke my heart. I ran over to shut off the kettle and then ran back to take him in my arms. "I'm so sorry, Luke. I didn't mean to say that. Sit down here with me, and we'll talk some more."

Slowly he began to recover from crying and sat down beside me again. "I don't know what to do, sis. I love her, and I'd do anything for her. I even asked her to marry me again."

"What did she say this time? Tell me what happened. Why did she ask you to leave?"

"We had a fight after I found out that she lied to me at Christmas. She told me she was visiting her mother, but I found out that her mother was dead."

I decided not to mention that I already knew about Pandora's deception. "Where was she really?" I asked.

"She wouldn't tell me at first, and then I saw a photo of her in one of those tabloids. She was in Monte Carlo, coming out of a casino on the arm of Garrett Blake."

"Who's Garrett Blake? I've never heard of him."

"He was one of the actors in *Moll Flanders*. I never met him because he was never in Abingdon, but I knew he'd been cast for some scenes with her later on."

"What did Pandora do when you confronted her?"

Luke hung his head, and I thought he was going to break down again. "She admitted it, but she swore he was gay and just a friend. She said she had to get away for a while and she couldn't commit to one person, she had her career to think about and if I didn't like it, I should leave."

I had a feeling of déjà vu; it was like listening to Zach all over again. "So I assumed you just walked out after that."

"No, when I asked her to marry me, she laughed in my face. That's when I got cross and slapped her."

I gasped, unable to imagine my brother hurting anyone. "Oh no, Luke. What happened next?"

"She ran into the bedroom, grabbed some of my clothes and threw them out onto the front steps. Then she yelled for that witch of a housekeeper of hers to call the police. I didn't know what to do, so I just left with the clothes on my back and the few she threw out."

"Where did you go after that?"

"I went to a hostel, but I only stayed one night. Angus, the old chap who runs the place, told me about this flat, and here I am."

"But why didn't you come home? We've been so worried about you."

Luke stood up and threw his hands in the air. "I told you, sis, if I'm going to get back with Pandora, I have to stay here."

I looked up at him, frowning. "What makes you think she'll take you back?"

"I called her, and she said she'd meet me for lunch on Tuesday, but I can't go looking like this. That's why I need some money, sis. I need to get a haircut, get my clothes cleaned and my shoes shined."

"You don't seriously expect me to give you money for that, do you?"

To my dismay, Luke actually got down on one knee and reached for both of my hands. "Please, sis, you've got to help me. I'll never ask you for anything again as long as I live."

I pushed him away and stood up. "I can't believe you've let yourself get into such a state, especially over someone like Pandora. How on earth would you want to marry her when she treats you this way? Anyway, you're far too young to get married. You need to come home with me now, Luke."

Luke got up off of his knees and slumped down onto the sofa. "You really don't understand, do you?" he said, covering his face with his hands again. "I love her, and she means everything to me. You've never even been in love, so you don't know what it feels like, sis."

"I think I do know," I replied, thinking of Zach, "but what good is it if she doesn't love you back?" I sat down beside him and put my arm around his shoulders. "Give it up please, Luke. Come home with me this afternoon, and I promise you'll soon forget all about her."

He shook his head and then looked at me with tears in his eyes. "I can't as long as there's a chance that she'll take me back."

"And what if she doesn't? If I give you this money to get cleaned up, and then she still rejects you, will you promise me you'll come home?"

Luke hesitated and then slowly nodded. "I promise, sis," he whispered, but somehow I had trouble believing him.

Chapter Thirty-Eight

On the following Tuesday afternoon, I waited to hear from Luke. I had finished helping Mum and Marcy with some chores in the morning and was at loose ends. Dad tried to encourage me to go for a walk with Sammy, but I didn't want to leave home in case I missed Luke's call. I didn't even want to go to my room in case I missed hearing the telephone, and I was afraid that if Dad picked it up, Luke would just ring off. I sat in the lounge for a while, trying to read, but I was having a hard time concentrating; and by four o'clock, I began to get anxious. At five o'clock, I decided to ring Pandora's house, but nobody answered, and I became even more desperate and even considered telling Mum what had transpired in London. Then fifteen minutes later, just as I was about to go and help Mum with supper, I heard the phone ring in the reception area, and I raced to answer it. I could hardly make out the person on the other end of the line because it sounded as though they were choking. "Luke, is that you?" I asked.

There were more muffled sounds, and then I heard Luke's voice, although it was barely recognisable. "Sis, it's me."

I breathed a sigh of relief. "Luke, are you all right? What happened? Did you see Pandora?"

"It's over, sis," he said, and I heard his voice start to quiver. "She said she doesn't want to see me ever again."

"Oh, I'm so sorry, but why couldn't she tell you that on the telephone?"

"Because she brought the rest of my things with her, and when I walked into the restaurant, she was already sitting there with my suitcase. I knew then that she wasn't going to take me back."

"Then you'll come home now, Luke? I hope you're going to keep your promise."

He didn't answer me but whispered, "There's more, sis."

"What do you mean?"

"She just didn't go off with Garrett for a vacation. She went away because she needed some time to recover."

"Recover from what? I don't understand."

"She had an abortion on Christmas Eve, and that's not all, sis."

I drew in a breath. "What else, Luke?"

He hesitated and then in a voice that began to quiver again, he said, "It was my baby. She killed my baby."

I felt as though my heart had leapt into my throat. "Oh my god, how awful, but are you sure she was telling you the truth?"

"Why would she lie?"

"Maybe she was just trying to hurt you. You can't trust her."

"She wasn't lying. She showed me the report from the clinic."

"But you don't know if the baby was yours."

"It was mine. I know it was mine, and now it's gone and there's nothing I can do about it."

That's when I heard him start to break down, and I called out to him. "Luke, it's okay. You'll be okay. Please come home now."

There was silence for a moment, and then he said, "I'm sorry, sis, but I'm going away for a while and I don't want you coming looking for me."

"No, you can't do that," I cried out. "Please, you're not thinking straight. You need to come back to your family."

"It's too late for that. Tell Mum and Dad I love them and not to worry. I have to go now, sis."

"No." I called out. "Don't ring off, Luke. Talk to me some more. We'll work something out."

"Good-bye, sis," he whispered. "I love you." Then I heard the line go dead.

I slowly hung up the receiver. "I love you too," I whispered back.

I sat for a while, trying to digest what Luke had told me; and when I realised what he must be going through, I just broke down. At that very moment, Dad came through the front door with Sammy and stopped in his tracks when he saw me. "What on earth is the matter?" he called out, but I shook my head, unable to answer him. He slipped Sammy's leash off and then rushed behind the reception desk to take me in his arms. "What is it, my sweet girl?" he murmured, gently rubbing my back. "Is that boyfriend of yours giving you a hard time?"

I shook my head again. "No, it's Luke."

"Luke? Why, what's happened?"

Just then Mum came out of the lounge and saw us huddled together. She started to walk towards us and called out, "Casey, what's going on?"

Dad released me and, turning to face Mum, shrugging his shoulders, said, "It seems that something's happened to Luke."

Mum put her hand to her throat. "Oh my goodness, is he all right? Ariel, tell me, where's your brother."

I stood up, brushing the tears from my cheeks. "I don't know, but I need to tell you what's been going on. Can we go to the kitchen? I don't want to talk out here."

Mum nodded and Dad started to walk away. "I'll go and put the kettle on," he said.

It wasn't easy telling my parents that I had lied to them about going to London and seeing Luke in such a state, and it was even harder telling them how Pandora had aborted Luke's child. Dad was very philosophical about it all and suggested that, in the long run, it was better for everyone concerned. Mum reacted quite differently and, contrary to her usual quiet demeanour, raised her voice. "How can you say such a thing? You're talking about our grandchild. May God forgive that woman for what she's gone and done. As for Lucius, he must be absolutely devastated, and he'll need a lot of support from us when he gets here."

I looked at Mum and gently shook my head. "He's not coming home, Mum."

"What do you mean? Of course he's coming home. Where else would he go?"

I got up and put my hand on her shoulder. "Sorry, Mum, but he told me he was going away for a while and not to look for him."

"What about his phone, can't you ring him?"

"He told me that he never got his phone back from Pandora."

Mum shrugged off my hand and stood up. "But he has no money and no job. Where on earth can he go to? We have to go and look for him."

Dad looked up at her and frowned. "Where do you suggest we start. London only has a few million people?"

"I want to go back," I answered. "I'll go to the flat in Camden, and if he's not there, I'll go and see Pandora and demand that she tell me where he is."

Dad threw up his hands. "Just a minute, young lady, you're not going anywhere by yourself, and what makes you think Pandora knows where he is? It sounds like she's washed her hands of him."

I reached over and grabbed his hand. "Then come with me, Dad," I replied.

Chapter Thirty-Nine

The very next morning, we were on the M40 heading for London. Mum wanted to go too, but somebody had to stay behind to look after the guests and Marcy just wasn't capable. Mum insisted that we take Sammy with us, and he was happily sitting bolt upright on the backseat of the car with his nose stuck out of the window. When we finally arrived at Camden High Street, we drove up and down, and then suddenly, I saw the Laundry Locker. Dad managed to park just a few yards away, and we approached the side door and rang the bell. There was a great deal of traffic on the street, and we couldn't hear if anyone was coming down the stairs; and so after a about a minute, we rang again. Just then, the door to the shop opened, and a very small and very ancient Chinese man came out and waved his hand at us. "What you want?" he asked, looking us up and down and paying particular attention to Sammy, who took one look at him and then barked aggressively.

"Stop, Sammy," Dad commanded in a loud voice. Then in a gentle tone, he said, "Good morning, I'm looking for my son, Luke Regan. I believe he lives above your shop."

The little man shook his head vehemently. "He no live here anymore. He no pay rent, so he go."

"When did he leave?" I asked.

"He go in the night."

"Last night?"

"Yes, yes," he replied, nodding his head up and down.

"Could we possibly go up to his flat to see if he left anything there? It may help us to find out where he's gone."

"No, no, nothing in flat. I go there this morning."

Dad hesitated for a moment and then reached into his pocket and pulled out a handful of notes. "Thank you, sir. Please take this for your trouble and have a nice day."

The old man grinned, showing uneven yellow teeth. "Thank you, thank you," he said, bowing from the waist and almost touching Sammy's nose with the top of his head.

Dad looked at me and rolled his eyes as we slowly walked back to the car. "What are we going to do now?" I asked.

"We're going to see Pandora, and I hope you've got the proper address."

I felt a little sheepish as I settled into the passenger seat. "Well, I don't know the exact address, but I know the name of the street and the house has a red door. I'll look up the street on the map and give you directions."

Dad finished settling Sammy in the back and climbed in beside me. "Sounds to me like you've been roaming around London half the time not having a clue where you're going," he remarked.

I didn't answer; I just busied myself looking up Brooke Street on the map and feeling grateful that the London taxicab drivers always knew their way around.

Later, as we were driving, I asked Dad what he intended to do when we got to Pandora's. "Well, for one thing," he said, "you're staying in the car."

I looked over at him and frowned. "Why? I want to know what she has to say."

"Look, the housekeeper, or whoever she is, doesn't know me. You said she was a problem, so it's best you stay out of sight."

I felt a little indignant. "Hmm . . . so what are you going to do, turn on the charm?"

Dad grinned. "A little bit of sweet talk doesn't hurt. She's French, you said?"

I shook my head at him, but he kept his eyes on the road. "Yes, she's French, and if you're expecting some attractive young thing in a maid's uniform, you're going to be sadly disappointed."

At that, he started to roar with laughter. "Chance would be a fine thing," he said.

I knew the house was near the end of the street, so it didn't take me long to recognise the red door. Dad parked a few yards away and ignored my moaning as he stepped out of the car and told me to stay where I was. I watched as he climbed the steps and knocked, and I was about to jump out and yell out to him that he should ring the bell when I saw the door open. It was hard to tell from where I was sitting but it looked like a small figure in black was standing there, and I assumed it was the housekeeper. It seemed like forever that Dad was talking to her, and I could feel my blood pressure rising just waiting to hear what was going on. Meanwhile Sammy had fallen asleep and was oblivious to the drama. Finally, I saw Dad shake the woman's hand and then tip his cap and walk slowly down the steps as the door closed behind him. After he climbed into the driver's seat, he turned to me and said, "Pandora isn't there. According to the housekeeper, she's in Glasgow, promoting the film which is coming out in June. From there she's going on to Dublin and Belfast, and she won't be home until the end of next week."

"Wow, she wouldn't even give me the time of day. How did you manage to get her to tell you so much?"

Dad chuckled. "Simple, sweet girl, I told her Pandora had stayed at our inn when she was in Abingdon, and then I turned on the charm. After I threw in a couple of French words, she was putty in my hands and even asked me if I'd like to come in for a cup of tea."

"You're lying," I said abruptly.

"Now is that any way to speak to your father?"

"Well, I just can't imagine it, that's all."

"Anyway, I declined very gracefully and then asked about Luke. She said she didn't know any Luke, but she did know Monsieur Lucius."

"I should have warned you about that."

"It doesn't really matter because she told me that Monsieur Lucius was no longer there, and she had no idea where he went. I don't think we're going to get any further trying to trace him through Pandora, and maybe we should just go home and wait for him to ring us."

"No, Dad, we can't do that," I protested. "We have to find him. He could be in trouble."

"And what do you propose we do? Shall we just keep driving all over London, looking for him?"

"We have to think of something," I replied as we pulled away from the curb. I racked my brains, trying to come up with an answer; then just as we were heading out towards the M40, I yelled for Dad to stop. He pulled over onto a side street and asked, "Okay, what grandiose idea have you come up with?"

"Luke told me he stayed in a hostel one night. Maybe he's gone back there."

Dad sighed, "And how many hostels are there in London?"

"I don't know, but we could go to one of those Internet places and look them up."

"And then what, we go racing all over, visiting every one of them, hoping he's there or that someone's seen him?"

"Yes, something like that," I answered enthusiastically.

"Do you have a photo of Luke with you?"

I pulled my wallet out of my coat pocket and flipped it open, revealing a photo of Luke taken with Sammy about a year before. "Voila!" I cried out triumphantly.

Dad glanced over at it then took the wallet out of my hand and studied the photo. "Didn't you say his hair was black now and he was thinner and his clothes were a mess?"

I felt defeated for a moment, but then I remembered why he needed money. "Yes, but he was going to get cleaned up, have a haircut and get his clothes fixed."

Dad handed me back the wallet. "Okay, let's go find one of those Internet places, but we aren't staying around after dark."

I grabbed his arm as he started to drive off. "Thanks, Dad," I whispered.

We had only gone a few blocks when Sammy started whining, and we realised he needed a comfort break. Now we had to find a suitable place to let him out and do his business. Not expecting to find any hostels in an upscale neighbourhood like Mayfair, we decided to head a little farther north and look for a green space. Fortunately and in the nick of time, we came upon a small park, and it didn't take much to coax Sammy out of the warmth of the backseat onto the snow-covered grass. A little farther ahead, we stopped a young couple to ask if there was an Internet café close by; and luckily, we discovered that we were only a block away from the Matrix, a small café where the couple usually hung out and spent many hours playing video games. "Let's get a bite to eat and a pot of tea," Dad said as he parked the car. "We'll have to leave Sammy here, but we'll bring him a treat and some water. He should be all right for a half hour or so."

We ordered three hamburgers, the extra one being for Sammy, and sat down at one of the small tables to eat, but we were both anxious and gobbled down our food so that we could continue our search for Luke. "I'm glad you know how to use these things," Dad said, looking around helplessly at all of the computers lining one wall of the café.

I laughed. "It's okay, Dad, I just have to Google."

He shook his head. "All these weird words, Google, Twitter, texting. I don't know how you keep up with it all. If you ask me, I think you young people are murdering the English language."

"Yes, Dad," I said patronisingly as I started surfing the Internet and he stood peering over my shoulder.

"I think I should just look for hostels for men only," I suggested and could hardly believe my eyes when one of the first names to come up was a place called Cambria House in Camden. I turned to my dad. "This could be it," I said, pointing to the screen. "Let's look at the map and get directions."

"Why don't we phone them?" Dad suggested.

"No, we need to show them the photograph," I replied as I typed in the address of Cambria House. It was then that I realised that I didn't have a clue where we were, so I leaned over towards a young man who was perched on a stool beside us and asked him if he knew the street address of the café. He looked at me as though I was completely stupid and then shook his head. "You'll have to ask the bloke over there," he said in a broad cockney accent, glancing over his shoulder towards the door.

Dad was just about to head for the man behind the cash register when I grabbed his arm. "It's okay, I can look it up online," I said.

I got the address on Pratt Street and proceeded to get directions, and it only took a moment to discover that we were only a few blocks from the hostel. I looked at my dad. "Are you ready?" I asked.

He nodded and followed me out of the café to the car, where we found Sammy patiently waiting for his treat. I unwrapped the hamburger and placed it on an old towel on the backseat and then poured some bottled water into the small bowl we always took with us when we took Sammy for a drive. "There's a good boy," I said, patting his head and then climbing into the passenger seat.

"I think we should just sit for a minute and let him eat," Dad suggested. "At the same time, we need to think about what we're going to say when we get to this place. There's only a remote chance that this is the same hostel."

I sat for a moment, racking my brains, trying to remember the conversation I had with Luke; and then out of the blue, I recalled him telling me that the man who ran the hostel had told him about the flat over the dry cleaners. I know he'd mentioned the man's name, but it was stuck somewhere in the back of my brain. Dad glanced over at me, and I could see he was about to say something, but I shook my head because right then it came to me that the man had a Scottish name like Andy or Alastair. Now I was really anxious for us to be on our way, and I turned around, hoping to see that Sammy had wolfed down his food, and I wasn't disappointed. "Let's go, Dad," I said.

Dad looked back and started up the car; and with me giving directions, we arrived at Cambria House just a few minutes later. As we pulled up, I noticed the building was much larger than I expected, and I felt a little nervous as we parked, got out and then approached the front door. Dad put his hand on my shoulder and whispered, "Don't get your hopes up, Ariel."

I held my breath as we entered what appeared to be a reception area which was surprisingly bright and clean. The walls looked like they had just been freshly painted, and there was a long counter of highly polished wood to our left and five grey upholstered chairs to our right. A young man with dark brown skin and short curly hair, wearing a light blue cotton coat, looked up as we walked in. He smiled, showing gleaming white teeth, and said, "Good afternoon. How can I help you?"

My father smiled back and responded, "Good afternoon. I was wondering if we could talk to the gentleman who runs this place?"

The man looked at his watch. "Well, Major Campbell is still at lunch. He's running a bit late today. He should be back in about fifteen minutes, and I'm sure he'll be able to see you then. Please take a seat."

I started towards the other side of the room and then turned back. "Excuse me, but is Major Campbell's first name Andrew?"

"No, it's Angus," the man replied.

I could hardly contain my excitement. "Thank you so much," I responded as I ran back to my father, who had already sat down and was frowning at me.

I plopped myself down beside him. "This is the right place," I said excitedly. "This Major Campbell, his first name is Angus. That's the name Luke mentioned."

"I thought you said it was Andy or Alastair?"

"No, I said it was something like that. Oh, Dad, can you believe it. Perhaps he came back here when he left the flat, and he's still here. Maybe I should show that chap behind the desk his photograph."

"No, I think we should wait. I don't think we should tell him our business."

"Okay, I guess we'll wait," I said, slumping down in my seat and tapping my foot impatiently.

Dad put up with my fidgeting for about five minutes and then suggested that I go and check on Sammy just to give me something to do. I got up rather reluctantly, but I had only gone two steps when an elderly man dressed in a Salvation Army uniform came through the front door. He glanced over at us and then walked over to the counter. "Now we know why they call him Major Campbell," Dad whispered in my ear.

I sat back down again, and almost immediately the Major came over to us, stuck out his hand and introduced himself. Dad gave him our names and asked if we could speak with him privately, at which point he asked that we follow him to his office, which was on the same floor down a short hallway. Just before we reached his office, we passed an open door, and I could see several men sitting in a row of metal chairs, facing a middle-aged woman who appeared to be teaching or lecturing them. I strained to see if I could pick out Luke amongst them. If he had been there, I have no doubt I would have broken away and caused quite a scene, but none of the men looked like Luke. Major Campbell invited us to sit down and even offered us a cup of tea, but we declined. We were anxious to tell him the reason we were there; and the minute I mentioned Luke's name and passed his photo across the desk, he started slowly nodding his head. "He was here last night," he said.

"Oh my god," I blurted out, "he was here? Is he still here? Has he gone? Is he coming back?"

Dad placed his hand on my arm. "Steady on, sweet girl, let the Major talk."

Major Campbell leaned forward and looked directly at me. "I'm afraid he's gone, Ms. Regan. He left with one of the other men. They became acquainted the last time your brother was here. I'm afraid I don't know where they went. I only wish I could be of more help."

"Can you tell us this person's name or anything else about him?" Dad asked.

"I'm afraid not because of the confidentiality rules. I'm very sorry, but my hands are tied."

Dad got up and shook hands with the Major. "Thank you for taking the time to see us." He then nodded at me, indicating it was time to go.

As we left the office, the Major patted me on the shoulder and whispered, "May the Lord be with you."

I was well out of earshot when I whispered back, "Fat lot of good the Lord can do."

I felt very despondent as we walked back to the car. "What are we going to do now?"

Dad took me by the elbow and guided me towards the passenger door. "You get in and check on Sammy. I'll be back in a few minutes."

"Why? Where are you going?" I asked as I watched him walk back towards the hostel without stopping to answer me.

I climbed into the car and looked around at Sammy, who was sleeping peacefully on the backseat, and then I waited. It seemed like fifteen minutes had gone by, and I was getting impatient, but it was actually only five minutes before Dad came back and hopped in beside me. I couldn't help noticing the grin on his face. "Where have you been?"

"Ah, there's nothing a few bob won't help. Most people can be bought for a price."

"What are you talking about?" I demanded, getting more impatient.

"Well, the little man behind the counter was only too willing to talk after I suggested that it might be worth his while. He told me that the man with Luke was Bert Sparrow."

"Sounds like a character from a Dickens novel," I interjected.

"Anyway, he'd been at the hostel for almost three months and was a bit of a troublemaker. Yesterday they found drugs in his room and had no choice but to ask him to leave. A middle-aged woman picked him up in a beat-up old minivan, possibly his mother, and Luke went with them. That's all he knows, but at least it's a start."

"Didn't he know where this Bert Sparrow came from?"

Dad looked at me and shook his head. "He was a homeless man, sweet girl, so I doubt if he had an address to give them."

"What about the van? Did you ask what colour it was?"

Dad scratched his head. "Mmmm, let me think. Yes, now I remember, he said it looked like a Morris, a blue Morris."

"I don't suppose he told you what shade of blue?"

Dad looked at me with exasperation. "Men don't know shades. Blue is blue."

"So now Luke's mixed up with a drug addict or maybe even a dealer. What are we going to do?" I asked, feeling almost hopeless.

"We're going home and then we're going to assume that the woman is his mother and we're going to try tracing her by checking telephone numbers."

"But there could be hundreds of them, and maybe this woman wasn't even his mother. Then again, maybe she was, but she got married again and doesn't have the same name. Maybe she doesn't even live in London."

Dad sighed, "That's a lot of maybes. I don't know what else to suggest. We have to start somewhere."

"Why can't we stay here a little longer?" I said as we started to drive away.

"No," Dad answered decidedly. "There's nothing more we can do here, and I want to get home before it starts getting dark. Your mother is probably expecting us for supper."

"Mum won't mind if we're a bit late," I protested.

"I mind," Dad said in a stern voice. "We need to get Sammy home, and I promise I'll help you keep looking for your brother. Perhaps we can pick up a copy of the phone book somewhere."

"Oh, Dad," I replied, "there are about four volumes of the London phone book, and it's probably a lot easier to look on the Internet."

"You mean you can look up people's numbers on a computer."

I glanced over at him and shook my head. "Yes, you can actually do that amongst a lot of other things."

Dad stared straight ahead. "I guess I'm in the dark ages," he mumbled.

Chapter Forty

We arrived home well before supper, just as it was beginning to get dark, but Mum was already feeling anxious about where we were and whether we had found any trace of Luke. During the drive home, Dad and I discussed just how much we should tell her; and in the end, we agreed that she deserved to know everything including the fact that Luke had befriended a man who was obviously involved with drugs. After we finished telling her everything we'd discovered that afternoon, Dad said, "That's as far as we got, Jane. Now we have to start looking for this chap, Bert Sparrow."

Mum started to weep. "But why was he in a homeless shelter. Why didn't he just come home? Oh, my poor Lucius, where are you?"

We tried our best to console her; but realising just how upset she was, Dad insisted that she went upstairs and had a rest while we made something special for supper.

"I already made a casserole for supper," she wailed. "I just have to boil some rice and cut up some of that apple cake."

"Well, Ariel and I will take care of that. You just take a half hour or so and have a catnap."

Mum started to walk towards the kitchen door and then turned to me. "You have to heat up the casserole," she said.

"Yes, Mum," I answered, stepping forward and pushing her gently out into the hallway.

Dad shrugged his shoulders. "I knew she'd be upset. Let's hope she feels better by the time we get supper on the table."

I nodded. "When are we going to start searching the Internet?"

"You can start right after supper while I'm catching up on a couple of chores. If you manage to find some phone numbers, write them down, and we can start ringing people in the morning."

"Okay," I replied, "but why don't you start catching up on your chores now? I'll finish preparing supper, and I'll fill up Sammy's bowl. Perhaps you can take him for a walk later while I keep looking for numbers."

Dad bent down and patted Sammy's head. "Sounds good to me," he said.

I discovered that there were over one hundred people with the surname Sparrow in the Greater London area, but they weren't all listed in the phone book. By noon the next day, Dad and I had rung about thirty numbers; and while some people were co-operative, others were downright rude or suspicious. Nobody who answered knew of an Albert or a Bert Sparrow and our hopes were beginning to dwindle. We still had a lot of numbers left on my list, so we decided to take a break, have lunch and then start back at it again, not knowing that the very next call we made, we would hit the jackpot. When I dialled a number which appeared to be in East London, after about five rings, a woman with a gravelly voice and a strong cockney accent answered, "Ullo, who's this?" she asked rather abruptly.

I glanced over at Dad and rolled my eyes. "I'm looking for Bert Sparrow."

"He ain't 'ere. Who wants 'im?"

"You mean he's not there at the moment?"

"That's what I said, didn't I?"

I looked at Dad again and pointed to the receiver, nodding my head at the same time. "Is this Mrs. Sparrow?"

"Yeah, Doreen Sparrow, that's me."

"Mrs. Sparrow, I'm sorry to bother you but are you his mother?"

"Last time I looked I was. Whadya want him for?"

"My name's Ariel Regan. I'm looking for my brother, Luke. I believe he was with your son yesterday."

"S'right, some chap Luke was 'ere, but they've both gone now. You missed 'em."

I was holding my breath as I asked, "Do you know where he went please, Mrs. Sparrow? It's very important."

"'Both of 'em went to Southampton yesterday. Took my van they did, and I'm bloody mad. Said they'd pay someone to bring it back, but I don't believe 'em?

"Do you know why they went to Southampton?"

"Sure do. They got 'emselves a job on some boat."

"What kind of boat? Didn't they tell you anything else? Did they tell you where they were going on this boat and when they were coming back?"

"It was one of those big boats, 'ang on I got a scrap of paper 'ere somewhere."

I put the receiver in my lap for a moment and quickly told Dad what I'd just heard. He frowned but didn't say anything, and then I heard Mrs. Sparrow come back on the line. "Some boat called *Artmiss*, not sure that's the way you say's it. It went this morning but can't remember where. Bert said he'd ring me when he got back."

"*Artmiss*? Would you mind spelling that, please?"

"Oh, lordie, it's A-R-T-E-M-I-S," she replied very slowly and deliberately.

"Ah, so it's *Artemis*, like the Greek goddess. Tell me, did your son tell you what kind of work they'd be doing?"

"My, you ask a lot of questions, missie."

"I'm sorry but anything you can tell us will be helpful."

There was a long pause, and then she said, "Something to do with cleaning up cabins after all those rich people."

"And did they say how they managed to get these jobs?"

"That's an easy one. Bert's sister, Lizzie. She's been working on the boats for a donkey's age."

I rolled my eyes again. "Thank you. You've been very kind."

"What's your name again, ducky?"

"It's Ariel, Ariel Regan."

"I'll tell Bert you rang when he comes back," she said.

"Bert doesn't know me, Mrs. Sparrow. I'm the sister of his friend, Luke."

"Oh, that's right, you said that. I gotta go, me kettle's boiling. Ta-ta."

I heard a distinct whistle in the background. "Bye, and thank you again," I whispered and then rang off.

As soon as I got off the phone, I turned to Dad. "Did you get all that?"

He nodded. "I gather he got a job on a ship and it's already sailed."

"Yes, and now I'm going to go look up this ship on the Internet to see where it's headed."

"Okay, I'm coming with you," he said as I got up and headed for the lounge where we kept the computer.

It took me all of one minute to discover that the *Artemis* was a luxury liner and had just left Southampton on a thirty-four-day cruise to South America, with a stop in Madeira, and Barbados and several stops in Brazil, with a final destination of Rio de Janeiro. As I scrolled down the information on the Web site, I felt more and more hopeless and finally slumped back in my chair. "He'll be gone for over two months," I said to my dad who was sitting beside me and shaking his head. "I don't understand how he even managed to get out of the country. He didn't have a passport."

"But he must have had one," Dad said. "He was in Paris with Pandora, don't you remember?"

"You're right," I sighed, "and now I guess there's nothing we can do but wait for him to come back."

Dad nodded. "Maybe he'll send us a postcard."

I threw my hands up in the air. "I just don't know what to make of all this, but I do know one thing, I'm going to be on the dock when that ship sails back into Southampton."

Chapter Forty-One

The next two months seemed to drag by with not a single word from Luke. After we had first discovered that he had left England, I even considered ringing Erica and asking her if the job was still available, but then I had second thoughts. What if working for Erica meant exposing me to Zach all over again? Knowing the true nature of his feelings for me, I didn't think I could deal with seeing him again despite Mum telling me that we could remain friends. Then there was my commitment to finding my brother. What if he suddenly showed up and needed me? How could I just drop everything and leave Erica without any help? It didn't take me long to decide that I had to stay in Abingdon, at least until the fall.

I saw Becky three or four times during the month of February, and then in March, Abingdon held its annual arts festival. There were a lot more tourists in town, and all of the rooms at the inn were booked. I spent a lot of time helping Mum and Marcy, but I grew more and more impatient waiting for Luke to return. I had always taken it for granted that Dad would go with me to Southampton when the time came, but two days before the *Artemis* was due to dock, he suggested that I get myself a train ticket. Mum had convinced him not to take me, as she now felt that Luke needed to accept some responsibility for his own life, and she was annoyed that he had abandoned his family. In fact, she was totally against me going at all and asked Dad to talk me out of it, but he knew I was determined; and after two months of waiting, nothing could deter me.

On the last Saturday in March, I left Abingdon at seven o'clock in the morning and took the short train ride to Southampton's Central Station and then a taxi to the Mayflower Cruise Terminal. The *Artemis* was due in port at eight thirty, but when I arrived, there was no sign of her. Only the *Royal Princess* was in dock, and it was an amazing sight. It had only taken just over an hour to travel from Abingdon, and I realised again just how narrow my life had been. I felt as though I had seen more of the world in the last six months than in all my years growing up. What I didn't know, at that moment, was how much more I was about to experience. After waiting another half hour, I decided to check to see if anyone knew why the ship was delayed. There were a number of people waiting to greet returning passengers, and I soon learned that there had been a severe storm when approaching the Bay of Biscay, and they had to travel several miles off course to avoid it. The *Artemis* was now expected to dock at ten o'clock. I was already a bundle of nerves but decided that waiting around would make me even more anxious; so I found a café in the debarkation lounge, ordered a cup of hot chocolate and a bran muffin, and tried to read the newspaper someone had left sitting on the table. I had always loved doing puzzles, and the crossword kept me occupied for a while, but then I just sat twiddling my thumbs and constantly looking at my watch. When I suddenly noticed a lot of activity in the room and several people making their way towards to windows, I knew something was going on, so I got up and rushed outside just in time to see the *Artemis* pulling into its berth. "Are you waiting for someone, dear?" asked an old gentleman with pure white hair and twinkling blue eyes, who was standing beside me.

"Yes," I said excitedly, "my brother, and how about you?"

"I'm waiting for my daughter. She's visiting from Puerto Rico with her brand-new baby."

I smiled at him. "You must be so excited. Is this your first grandchild?"

"Yes, and it's a boy. She named him Felippe after my father," he replied, grinning with pride from ear to ear.

"How wonderful," I remarked. "I bet you can hardly wait to see them."

He nodded. "Yes, miss, but it will be quite a while before any of the passengers are allowed off the ship."

"What about the crew?"

"Oh, they probably won't get off until the middle of the afternoon."

I let out a deep sigh. "Oh no, my brother's a crew member. You really think it will be hours before I see him?"

"Yes, I believe so. There's no point in you waiting here. Do you live far away?"

"Far enough," I replied despondently. "I came from Abingdon."

"I think I know that place. Isn't it near Oxford?"

"Yes," I said with surprise. "Not many people have heard of it."

"Well, believe it or not, I attended Queen's College. Oxford is a lovely town."

"And where do you live now, if you don't mind me asking?"

"Not at all, my dear. I live in Bishop's Waltham. It's only about thirty minutes from here. It's too bad I don't live a little closer because you could have come home with us while you waited."

I was just about to thank him for his thoughtfulness when there was a commotion, and we saw dozens of people on one of the upper decks of the ship. "I think they're going to be disembarking soon," the old man said. "But it could still be another hour or so."

"I think I'll go inside," I said, wrapping my arms around myself. "It's really cold out here."

"Well, good luck, my dear. I hope you see your brother really soon."

"I hope so too," I whispered as I walked away.

Three hours later, I was feeling emotionally exhausted. I had watched hundreds of passengers disembark, completed three more crossword puzzles and eaten a soggy tuna sandwich washed down with two cups of tea. I had also discovered from a man dressed in what looked like an officer's uniform that the crew members would be leaving the ship by a specially designated gangway, and he directed me to where the gangway was located. It was close to where I was standing that I overheard someone mention there was a boat drill going on, and it would be another half hour or so before anyone would be leaving the ship. At that point, I felt like giving up, but common sense told me I had waited long enough and a few minutes longer was no hardship considering I would soon be seeing Luke again. Finally, there was some activity at the top of the gangplank, and a number of men began to descend, some chattering amongst themselves and some waving to people who were obviously waiting for them. This parade of crew members, mostly men but including several women, continued until I figured that at least five hundred of them had left the ship, but there was still no sign of Luke. Too late, I realised that I should have had a sign with Bert Sparrow's name on it, and then I would have had more chance of finding out if Luke was delayed on board.

When the line started to really thin out, I got very anxious and found myself holding my breath each time a new group appeared at the top of the gangplank. Then when there appeared to be nobody left on board, my heart seemed to sink in my chest, and I could feel my face begin to crumple and the tears started rolling down my cheeks. Slowly I made my way back into the debarkation lounge and tried to find the same officer I had been talking to earlier. I walked through the lounge twice without seeing him, but I spotted another man in a similar uniform and hoped he would be able to help me. I soon learned that he was an officer from the *Royal Princess*, and he told me that a few selected crew members didn't get shore leave and there was a possibility that my brother was still on board and would still be on the *Artemis* when it set sail again. "How do I find out if he's one of the crew selected?" I asked.

"You would have to get in touch with P&O Headquarters here in Southampton," he replied, "but they're closed now until Monday. I suggest you just go home, young lady, and wait for him to get in touch with you."

I thanked him and walked away with no intention of going home. Someone had to know where he was, and I figured if I asked enough people, I'd know how to find him. With this in mind, for the next forty-five minutes, I walked up to dozens of strangers, asking them if they had been on the *Artemis* and if they knew Luke Regan, but nobody had even heard of him. After that, I tried asking if anyone knew Bert Sparrow, and one man, who also turned out to be a cabin steward, said he knew Bert but hadn't heard of Luke. I knew at that point that it was hopeless for me to stay in Southampton, and I should have called home hours before to let my parents know what was going on. Hearing my dad's voice brought me to tears again. "What is it, sweet girl? Did you find your brother?"

"No, Dad," I managed to say, "he didn't come off the ship. I've been waiting for hours and hours and he's not here. He might still be on board if he didn't get shore leave, and that means he'll soon be gone again. I can't get any information until Monday, and then it will be too late."

"Ariel, your mother and I want you to come home. When you get here, we'll figure out what to do next, but you can't stay there."

"I know, "I said, choking back more tears. "I'm going to get the next train back, and I'll take a taxi from the station."

"Okay, we'll have supper when you get here. Your mum's made your favourite shepherd's pie."

"Thanks, Dad, "I replied. "I'll see you soon."

It didn't surprise me to find Dad waiting at Abingdon Station when I got there. He had checked the timetables and worked out which train I would be on. When I saw the car and jumped into the passenger seat, I was so happy to see him. I put my arms around his neck and hugged him. "I thought you'd be pleased to see a friendly face," he said.

"Oh, Dad, it was awful. I waited so long, and then he never showed up. What are we going to do now?"

"Well, right after supper, we're going to ring Mrs. Sparrow and see if she's heard from Bert."

"Perhaps you'd better talk to her this time. She may not be too happy with me bothering her again and asking a lot of questions."

"No problem. I can do that, and I'll be my usual charming self," he said, grinning.

I shook my head. "What on earth am I going to do with you, Dad?"

Despite my sombre mood, I really enjoyed the supper Mum made. Not only did we have shepherd's pie but she had also baked a rhubarb pie, my favourite dessert. It was almost seven o'clock by the time we had finished eating and cleared away the dishes; and after that, Dad made the call to Mrs. Sparrow while I sat close beside him, holding my breath in anticipation.

"Is this Mrs. Sparrow," he asked after dialling and holding on for what seemed like an interminable length of time.

I watched his face as he listened and then said, "This is Casey Regan, and my daughter Ariel rang you in January about her brother Luke. You told us he had a job with your son, Bert, on a cruise ship. I believe the ship came back to Southampton this morning, and I was wondering if you'd heard from Bert."

There was silence as Dad held the receiver and nodded. I started to speak, but he held his finger to his lips. "I see, and so Bert's on his way home now, and I don't suppose he mentioned Luke."

There was more nodding and then, "Yes, it would be appreciated if your son would ring me when he gets there. I'll give you my number, and please feel free to reverse the charges."

He looked at me and whispered, "She's getting a pen and paper," and then he went back on the line, proceeded to give her the number, thanked her for being so kind and wished her good night.

Chapter Forty-Two

By noon on Sunday, we still hadn't heard back from Bert or his mother, and I was practically climbing the walls with impatience. Dad suggested we have lunch and then if we still hadn't heard anything, I should ring Mrs. Sparrow again. Usually, on a Sunday, we would have a heavy meal at midday and then something light later on, but none of us felt like eating, so we each had a small bowl of cauliflower soup and an egg salad sandwich. There wasn't too much talk around the table as we listened for the telephone, but all we could hear was Sammy under the table, fast asleep and breathing heavily after devouring the remains of a meat loaf Mum had made the day before. Finally, after practically scalding my tongue with a cup of lemon tea, I glanced over at Dad, and he just looked back and nodded. That was the only signal I needed. I was hoping when I rang the Sparrow number, Bert would answer, but that wasn't the case. Doreen Sparrow's gravelly voice was unmistakable. "Ullo, who's there?" she asked when she picked up after the fifth ring.

"Good afternoon, it's Ariel Regan again. I'm sorry to bother you, but we haven't heard from Bert."

"'E's not 'ere," she said abruptly.

I paused, not quite sure what to say next, until I heard her repeat, "Ullo, ullo?"

"Oh, I'm sorry. I thought you said Bert was on his way home, and we've been waiting to hear from him. We're really anxious to find out if he knows where my brother is."

"'E's not coming 'ome now. 'E rang me last night from some bloke's 'ouse. Don't know nuffink about yer brother."

"But that doesn't make sense, Mrs. Sparrow. They worked together on the ship."

"Don't ask me, dearie. I'm only telling yer what 'e told me."

"Well, perhaps I could talk to Bert myself. Do you have a phone number where I can reach him?"

"Didn't leave me no phone number. Can't even ring 'im meself."

"Oh my goodness," I sighed. "I don't know what to do now."

"I can't 'elp yer, and me kettle's boiling so I gotta go."

It seemed like the kettle boiling again was a good excuse for her to get off the line; so once again, I thanked her and slowly hung up the phone. I didn't realise it at the time but Dad had been standing behind me; and when I turned around and he saw tears in my eyes, he just gathered me in his arms and whispered, "We'll call the P&O offices tomorrow when they re-open."

The call to the P&O Offices early the next morning left me even more frustrated. I was passed from one individual to another and got the feeling they were being evasive. They couldn't, or wouldn't, even tell me if Luke had been on board the *Artemis* and asked me to ring back on Tuesday once they had gone over all the reports from ship. The next twenty-four hours were agonising, and I vowed that if I didn't get a satisfactory answer when I rang back, I would be on the next train to Southampton and demand to see whoever was in charge. It turned out, I didn't need to make the trip because when I did ring, just after nine o'clock, I was told that according to the report, Luke had been taken on as a cabin steward and had boarded the *Artemis* at Southampton, but after they had left the port of Santarem in Brazil, they discovered that he was no longer on board. Apparently he had gone on shore leave with another crew member who had returned to the ship without him. He claimed he did not realise that Luke had not followed him back until they were well out to sea. He also claimed that Luke had told him he might not come back at all and he'd left him in a bar, not believing for one minute that he may have meant it. I questioned whether the crew member was Bert Sparrow, but they wouldn't divulge his name, and then I asked what they did when they realised Luke was missing. The report indicated they contacted the authorities in Santarem and had even faxed a photograph they had on file, but there had been no sign of him.

I asked about getting hold of the British Consulate, but it was over a thousand miles away in Manaus and would be of little help in attempting to locate any missing person. I was assured they would continue to keep in touch with the authorities in Santarem; but as it appeared that Luke had decided to remain in Brazil and there was no evidence of foul play, they were not responsible for his disappearance. They did add, however, that should he attempt to rejoin the ship when it returned to Brazil on its next cruise, he would be brought up before the Captain's Court and face charges. They would not elaborate on what the charges might be; and at that point, I didn't really care. All I knew was that my brother was somewhere in some place in Brazil that I had never even heard of before.

After I finally got off the phone I told Dad that we couldn't rely on the P&O people to find Luke and we needed to get in touch with the authorities in Santarem ourselves. Dad hesitated, looking very thoughtful, and then said, "But they probably only speak Spanish."

"Actually they speak Portuguese," I responded, "but there's nearly always somebody around who can speak English. We have to try, Dad. I'll ring information and see if they can give me the number of the police there."

Dad sighed, "I just don't understand why your brother didn't go back to the ship. I can't imagine him just deciding to stay in Brazil. He doesn't know a soul there, and he probably has very little money. Something's really fishy about all this."

"I know and I forgot to ask why we weren't notified as soon as they knew he was missing. Usually they know who to contact in an emergency. In fact, I'm going to ring back right now and ask them why they didn't do that. They may claim they aren't responsible for his disappearance, but they should have got in touch with us."

Dad nodded as I picked up the phone and rang the P&O office back. It took a while before I managed to locate the individual I had been talking to before; and after we had finished speaking, I almost wished I hadn't rung back at all. Dad saw the look on my face. "What excuse did they have?" he asked.

"I can't believe it," I answered. "He listed Pandora as his emergency contact, and they tried to reach her but were advised she was out of the country. Her representative informed them they had no evidence she ever knew a Lucius Regan."

"That is unbelievable. Why on earth wouldn't Luke list someone in his family? No, sweet girl, there is definitely something not right about all this."

"Okay, well, I'll try and get the number of the Santarem police now."

Dad went upstairs, where Mum was cleaning up one of the guest rooms, to let her know what was going on, and I got hold of the international operator and finally managed to get the number I needed. After that, I went on the Internet to check the time difference and was surprised to learn that Santarem was only four hours behind us, making it close to six o'clock in the morning there. Next, I checked the Internet again to translate a few words into Portuguese, hoping they would get me through to an individual who could speak English.

Holding my breath and with great trepidation, I dialled the number the operator had given me. It only rang twice, and then there was a crackling noise, but then a man answered, "Santarem policia."

I paused and then said, "Ola. Faz alguém diz o inglês por favor."

The person at the other end of the line must have understood because he said what sounded like "Sim esperum";

and suddenly, while I was murmuring, "Obrigado," I heard a new voice with the same strong accent but speaking English, "Yes, how can I help you?"

I repeated the story the P&O office had told me and that I understood they had been contacted to try and locate Luke. He asked me to wait, and I could hear him in the background speaking to someone else, but I had no idea what he was saying. Then I heard a lot of rustling of papers, and finally, he came back on the line. "Ola, yes, we have all of the information here, and we have been trying to locate Mr. Regan but have had no success. We have talked with several people who saw him on the day the ship docked here, but nobody has seen him since. I am sorry, but there is nothing more we can do."

"His friend said he left him in a bar. Did you talk to the people there?"

"Ah, the Madalena. Sim, he was there until very late, but I'm afraid when he left, he was, shall we say, a little drunk."

"I see, and do you know if he left by himself?"

"We don't know that. I'm sorry, I cannot help you more."

"So are you telling me that you've stopped looking for my brother?"

"Yes, senhorita. You have to understand that this place is not like England. We are no longer able to search for him."

I felt my hand begin to tremble. "Thank you for talking to me, senhor. May I please have your name."

"Sim, it is Policia Sargeant Domingos Alves."

"Obrigado, Sargeant Alves," I whispered and hung up the phone.

Chapter Forty-Three

From the moment my conversation with Sargeant Alves was over, I only had one thought in my mind—I had to go to Santarem to find Luke. Needless to say, the opposition from Mum and Dad was intense, and they didn't even want to discuss the idea. Both of them were appalled to think that I would even consider going off to some remote city over five thousand miles away. The fact that I was female and didn't know a soul there just added to their concerns, and the more I talked about it, the more I could see them just shutting down. By evening, we were all tense, and I was getting irritated to the point where I finally lashed out, "What do you propose to do then?" I asked angrily. "Are you just going to sit around and hope Luke's okay. He could be dead for all we know."

Mum took a step forward and slapped me hard across the face. "Don't you ever say that," she shouted. "I never want to hear that kind of talk from you again."

Dad gently grabbed her arm, and I staggered backwards in shock, with my hand to my cheek. My mother had never hit me before, even as a small child when I sometimes clearly needed to be punished. We all stood there like a frozen tableau for a few moments, and then Dad said very quietly, "I think it might be a good idea if you went upstairs, Ariel."

I left without saying a word, but I felt like a four-year-old being sent to my room, and I was resentful. The question kept running through my mind, "Was I the only one who really cared about finding Luke?"

The next morning, having had a restless night, I was late getting up and just about to leave my room when there was a knock on my door. It was Dad, and he asked if he could come in and talk for a few moments. Still feeling bitter about what had happened, I waved towards the tub chair near my bed and then stood with my hands on my hips. Dad sat down and then, looking up at me, said, "Why don't you sit down, Ariel, instead of standing there, glaring at me?"

I flounced over and flopped down onto the edge of the bed with my arms crossed over my chest. "What else is there to say?" I asked. "You and Mum made yourselves very clear yesterday."

"Are you going to sulk, or are you going to listen?"

"I'll listen," I answered reluctantly, "but don't expect me to change my mind."

Dad sighed, "Never have I met a more stubborn person, and your mother and I both know that we're not going to talk you out of this inane idea. What's more, we can't stop you and if you're hell bent on going ahead, we're willing to help but on one condition."

My hopes had started to rise, but I held my breath, waiting to hear what was coming next. "What's the condition?"

"That you wait for thirty days. This will give us time to do a little more investigating and will give you time to get your passport, if you apply right away. Hopefully, we'll hear from Luke before the thirty days are up, and all of this will be unnecessary."

I started to speak, but Dad held up his hand to silence me. "We're also willing to give you three thousand pounds from the trust fund your grandmother left you so that you'll have money for your return flight and enough left over for expenses. If, and it's a big if, you manage to find Luke and persuade him to come back, all you have to do is telephone and we'll wire you more money."

While my dad was talking, I could feel my heart beginning to race with excitement. "Oh my god," I said, standing up, "you really mean it? I didn't even think about what it would cost, and I forgot all about the trust fund Nana left. What made you change your mind?"

Dad got up and put his arm around me. "I already told you. You're as stubborn as an old mule, and I knew you wouldn't give up so rather than cause even more friction, we decided to support you."

"I'm so grateful, Dad, I really am."

"Yes, well, that doesn't mean we think it's a good idea, and we'll still worry about you every minute that you're gone. I don't know much about this place you're going to, but I know it's not like anywhere you've ever seen before. They don't even speak the same language. We'll be worrying about you from the minute you step on that plane until the moment we see you again."

I slipped out from under Dad's arm and gave him a kiss on the cheek. "Don't worry, Dad, I'm going to find out everything I can about Santarem before I get there."

"So we have a deal then? You'll wait for thirty days?"

"Yes, we have a deal," I whispered.

I had never had a passport; so the very next day, I filled out an application online, had my photo taken at Boots the Chemist on Bury Street and managed to get an appointment with Dad's lawyer, Mr. Iverson, to get him to sign my application. Naturally, he was interested in knowing where I was going; but fearing that he might try to talk me out of it, I just told him that I was thinking of going to Paris with a friend.

After that, I spent nearly every day for the next two weeks learning everything I could about Santarem. I was surprised to learn that the Amazon was the widest river in the world and was so deep that cruise ships could travel as far as Manaus, the river's furthest navigable port, some one thousand miles from the ocean. Santarem was five hundred miles inland and had a rich history, but I needed to educate myself about the weather, which I learned was always between seventy-five and ninety degrees, the accommodation, currency and all the practical details so that I was fully prepared when I finally reached my destination. What I wasn't prepared for was the length of time it would take me to get there; and having never even flown before, my anxiety level started to escalate. I knew there was no way I could back out after all the fuss I had made, but what really kept me going was the fact that Luke might be in trouble.

I received my passport just two weeks after I submitted my application, and that's when Dad suggested I book my flight in case there were no seats left at the time I wanted to leave. I was worried about spending all that money and had two concerns: how long should I stay in Brazil, and what would happen if Luke just showed up on our doorstep. Dad said that was a chance we had to take, and he felt that ten days was long enough for me to find Luke, or at least what had happened to him. I wasn't so sure that this would be long enough, but Dad insisted in case I just hit a complete dead end and had nowhere to go but home. "And what if I'm on his trail, and it's time for me to leave?" I asked.

"We'll cross that bridge when we come to it," he replied. "Nothing is etched in stone, and I expect you to keep us posted. I assume they have those Internet cafés there, so you'll have to teach me how to send an e-mail, or whatever you call them."

I started to giggle. "Oh, Dad, I never thought I'd see the day when you'd be sitting at a computer. Welcome to the modern world."

Just then, Mum came out to the reception area, where we were talking. "You may want to see what's on the telly," she said.

We followed her into the lounge; and when I saw who was on the screen, I felt myself begin to tremble. It was Zach, larger than life and looking more handsome than ever. I just stood there while some blond bimbo type in a low-cut red frock asked him a lot of inane questions about the tour and the groupies who followed the band from city to city. Zach remained serious, and I couldn't help noticing that he looked a little weary. It was inevitable he would be asked if there was a special person in his life, and I held my breath as he paused and then slowly shook his head. "Not right now," he said. "There was somebody special, but the boys and I are too busy these days working on our music."

I hoped in my heart that he was talking about me, but I knew deep down that he was thinking about Celeste. When the interview was over, Dad just nodded, but Mum picked up the remote, turned off the telly and said, "I can see why you fell for that young man, Ariel. He seems very intelligent and very good-looking too."

I sighed, "I know, Mum, but I just don't fit into his world, so I just have to forget all about him."

"Good thing too," Dad said. "We wouldn't want you traipsing all over the country following some rock star."

I shook my head. "Oh, but it's okay if I fly off to some godforsaken place thousands of miles away looking for my brother, who might not even be there?"

"That's different," Dad mumbled as he walked out of the room.

That night, as I was lying in bed, I thought a lot about Zach and realised that I would probably never see him again. I decided that I had to cut all ties with Erica and Adrian if I wanted to completely sever any relationship with him. I didn't think I could bear to hear stories about him or even run into him when I still had such deep feelings. I even considered that I might never go back to London to live, and maybe I was always meant to be a small-town girl. I almost giggled to myself thinking about it considering the journey I was about to take.

Early the next morning, I attempted to find a flight to Santarem on the Internet. Being rather naïve, I expected to board a plane in London and, several hours later, arrive at my destination. I had a rather rude awakening when I discovered that all the flights had two or even three stops, and most of them had very lengthy layovers. Dad suggested I call our local travel agent to get advice. We had dealt with them on many occasions in the past, helping to arrange trips for our guests; but this time, they were just as unsuccessful as I was in finding what I was looking for.

Chapter Forty-Four

At eight-forty-five on a Saturday evening in late April, I boarded a TAM Airlines Boeing 777 at Heathrow Airport. Dad drove me from Abingdon; and when we arrived at check-in almost three hours before departure, we discovered that there were very few people on my flight, and we were through all the formalities within minutes. I only had one piece of baggage, a knapsack stuffed full with shorts, an extra pair of jeans, four tee shirts, a lightweight cardigan, underwear, a pair of Converse trainers and a minimal amount of toiletries. To pass the time, we decided to explore the airport and spent time in several of the shops and then had a gin and tonic in one of the bars. I wasn't really sure if I should drink any alcohol, but Dad thought it might settle my nerves and help me to sleep on the plane. He even suggested that I had another drink once on board, and I just laughed. "You're trying to corrupt me, Dad. What would people think?" but he just grinned, and I couldn't help thinking what a great father he was.

When the boarding call finally came, I felt my heart start to race, but Dad took me in his arms and, with tears in his eyes, said, "It's going to be all right. There's nothing to be afraid of. You just take care of yourself, my dear sweet girl, and remember, the minute you get settled, you let us know you're okay."

I looked at him, trying to hold back my own tears. "I promise, Dad, as soon as I get to the hotel, I'll find a place where I can e-mail you."

I turned back just before I passed through the gate, and he was still standing there watching me. I lifted my hand to wave, and he blew me a kiss, and then I was suddenly in this tunnel, following a group of people I didn't even know. When I walked onto the plane, I was astounded by the size of it. There were rows and rows of seats, two on each side near the windows and five in the middle, and they all seemed to have television screens on the backs of them. I had no idea where to go, but this lovely young lady with jet-black hair, dressed in a navy uniform with bright red trim, directed me to my seat. I was pleased when I found that I was in a window seat but a little concerned about who might be sitting next to me. The first stop was São Paulo, and it would take eleven and a half hours, so I was hoping that my travelling companion would be pleasant and not too talkative.

My thoughts were interrupted by an announcement that we were to follow the video on the screen in front of us. This was to instruct us what to do in case of an emergency, and it didn't help to make me feel any less nervous. By the time we were ready to depart, the seat next to me was still empty, and I noticed that there were several more empty seats close to me, including the five centred directly to my left. I had a feeling of relief; but when I was reminded to fasten my seat belt and realised we were taking off at any moment, I started to panic. The same young lady who had found me my seat must have sensed my distress and bent down to whisper in my ear, "Is this your first flight, dear?" I nodded but couldn't speak. "It's all right, it's perfectly safe and we'll be off the ground very quickly. Just try and relax."

I nodded again and tried to thank her, but the words wouldn't come out; and then suddenly, I felt some movement, and we began to veer away from the airport terminal. It seemed as though it took forever before we were on the runway; and after that, we were picking up speed, and I was gripping the arms of my seat and hardly able to breathe. Somehow I managed to glance out the window, even though I was terrified at what I might see, and then the earth seemed to fall away and we were soaring upwards. It was at that point that my heart rate began to slow down, and I felt my whole body go limp. I could hardly believe that we were actually up in the air, and I didn't feel panicked anymore. I continued to look out of the window, hoping to see London below me, but it was already dark and I could only imagine that I was able to pick out the lights of the bridges over the Thames and the huge Ferris wheel, the London Eye. I continued peering out until I couldn't see anything but blackness, and I realised that we were no longer climbing but had levelled off, and it was eerily quiet, except for the constant noise from the jet engines.

For the next hour, I leafed through the magazine which I found in the pocket of the seat in front of me. After that, I was presented with a pair of earphones by one of the cabin attendants, and I checked out the films playing on the monitor. *Fatal Attraction* was listed, and I started to watch it but got distracted when I noticed people were being served food and beverages. I was fascinated with the new experience of travelling by plane; and after I had selected a ham and cheese croissant and a glass of white wine, I felt very sophisticated. The snack was just what I needed, as I had last eaten several hours before in order to leave home in time to get to the airport. It was now almost ten thirty, and I suspected most of the passengers would soon be trying to get some sleep; but immediately after I'd finished eating, we were offered more drinks, and I couldn't help myself, I had to have that second gin and tonic that Dad had suggested.

Hours later, I woke up with a start, wondering where on earth I was for a moment. It was still dark outside; and when I looked at my watch, it indicated it was five thirty and that meant it would be almost another three hours before we reached Sao Paulo. I didn't remember feeling drowsy, but I did remember the lights being dimmed, being given a blanket and a small pillow and lifting up the armrest so that I could curl up in a foetal position. My legs felt really cramped, and I needed to go to the loo, so I crawled out of my seat and made my way down the aisle. Other people were beginning to stir, and some even wished me good morning or, in Portuguese, *bom-dia*. The loo was really small and made me feel claustrophobic, so I couldn't wait to get out of there, but I stayed long enough to relieve myself, wash my face and hands and rake my fingers through my hair. I knew I should have brought my comb with me; but when nature called, I didn't have any time to waste.

After I returned to my seat, I listened to some music and then decided to read the book I had brought with me. It wasn't a really interesting book and I was getting a little restless. When, an hour later, all of the overhead lights came on, we were served a lovely breakfast of mushroom omelettes with sausages and sliced potatoes followed by yogurt, fresh fruit and coffee. I was very impressed until I remembered just how much this trip was costing.

About a half hour before we were due to arrive at Guarulhos Airport, we were told that we would soon be descending and needed to prepare for landing. Once again, I felt my heart start to beat a little more rapidly; but as we got a little closer to Sao Paulo, I looked out of the window and all my anxiety fell away. It was still very early, only about six thirty, and just beginning to get light, but the sight below me was breathtaking. I had read a little about São Paulo and even seen photos of the city; but to actually see it thousands of feet below me, almost made me gasp. Being the largest city in Brazil, it was densely populated with about eighteen million people. It appeared to cover a large area and was dominated with high rises and expressways.

As we passed over a plateau and the plane dipped lower and lower, I began to notice movement on the ground and realised I was seeing the beginning of what must be a normal work day for many, with hundreds of cars making their way into the centre of the city. I was so intrigued with the view from my window that I had almost no time to brace myself before we landed, with a slight bump, and then the engines roared as we raced down the runway and gradually came to a stop. I was surprised to hear a lot of people clapping, but I had to admit that after almost twelve hours in the air, it was a great feeling to be back on the ground.

When I had booked my flight to Santarem, I had discovered, to my dismay, that there was a thirteen-hour layover in São Paulo before the next flight to Belem. I had been nervous about wandering around such a large city where I couldn't speak the language, even though I would have loved to have explored some of the places I had read about. Instead, I had booked a room at the airport in what was called the Fast Sleep Hotel. Fortunately, our travel agent knew about it and recommended that I stay there while waiting for my connection. The room was like a small cabin with a bunk bed and a communal bathroom in the hallway. The television only had two channels, both in Portuguese, so I had little to keep me occupied. It had now been about four hours since I had last eaten, so I decided to leave the room after a quick nap and visit one of the airport restaurants for a bite and some coffee. I didn't realise just how tired I was after spending the night cramped up on the plane; and when I woke up, it was almost four o'clock in the afternoon. My flight left at just after seven, so I managed to get a quick shower, worrying all the time that someone else might need to use the bathroom, and then I checked out and had supper at the Devassa restaurant where they served some wonderful croquettes stuffed with beef and a glass of pale ale.

After the long flight from London, I felt like a seasoned traveller when I boarded the plane to Belem. This leg of my journey was about three and a half hours with only an hour layover before my ninety-minute flight to Santarem. As we approached my final destination, I thought about what I had learned about this place and what I had passed on to my parents. The one thing I hadn't told them was that Santarem was linked to illegal trafficking of cocaine from Columbia and Peru. Remembering the reason Bert Sparrow was asked to leave Cambria House, I couldn't help wondering if Luke had become involved in some illicit drug dealing. I silently prayed I was wrong and that the brother I knew and loved was here for some other reason; but in my heart, I just knew he was in trouble.

It was just after one o'clock in the morning when I arrived at the Hotel Santo Amaro, and I was exhausted. Thankfully, the young lady on duty at the reception desk spoke perfect English, and I was taken to my room by an elderly gentleman who insisted on carrying my backpack. I had already had some difficulty in counting out the right change for the taxi, and I had no idea what to tip. The Brazilian currency was completely foreign to me, and I realised it was important that I quickly learned the value of the money before I ran out and had to wire my parents for more. I knew Mum and Dad were probably anxious to hear from me, and I had noticed a sign in the lobby offering Internet service; but because it was already very late back in England, I decided to wait until morning to contact them.

I was surprised to find that my room was immaculately clean, decorated in pale cream and deep shades of red with colourful tiffany lamps. The bathroom was modern and equipped with fluffy white towels, all manner of soaps and creams and even a hair dryer. This wasn't what I expected; and in some strange way, I was a little disappointed. I had imagined that Santarem would be rather primitive, despite my research on the Internet; but as I sat on the edge of the bed and looked around me, I felt as though I could have been in any civilised city in the world. I began to question my decision to travel thousands of miles to look for Luke. He could be anywhere, and I might never find him. I felt lonelier that night than at any other time in my life.

Chapter Forty-Five

The next morning, after a rather restless night, I awoke to hear the sound of heavy rain; and when I drew back the curtains, I discovered that my room led out onto a balcony which overlooked an elevated area covered in trees, with a few houses and a tower in the distance. I realised that I had not prepared myself for torrential rain and hoped that by the time I left the hotel, it would have stopped. After soaking in the tub and getting dressed, I left my room and e-mailed my parents using the Internet service the hotel provided. I detailed my trip from Heathrow and told them I'd check back to make sure they got my message later in the day. After that, I had breakfast in the dining room and indulged in a wonderful buffet with all of my favourite foods, scrambled eggs, sausages, home fries and even pancakes. The waiter who served me coffee spoke a little English and told me we were situated in the historic area of the city near the Fatima Basilica and I assumed this must have been the tower that I could see from the balcony. When I asked him where the police station was, he seemed a little nervous but gave me the address and suggested I take a taxi because it would be too far to walk.

The rain had stopped by the time I got to the police station, and I was surprised to see there was only one person on duty.

He looked me up and down as though I was an alien from outer space and then nodded. I smiled and bade him good morning in Portuguese. "Boa manha." He nodded again, and I asked if he spoke English. "Faca voce diz Ingles?" And with that he shook his head and frowned. I wasn't sure what to do next, so I tried a different approach. "Sargeant Alves, está ele aqui?" As soon as the words were out of my mouth, I heard footsteps behind me and turned to see a very tall, heavy-set officer coming towards me with his hand outstretched. "Boa manha, Senhorita," he said.

"Are you Sergeant Alves?" I asked, looking up at him.

"*Sim*, I am," he replied, "and may I ask who you are?"

"I'm Ariel Regan. I spoke to you on the telephone from England about two months ago about my brother. He never returned to the ship he was working on, the *Artemis*."

He looked at me incredulously. "And you've come all this way, Senhorita Regan?"

"Yes, I need to find Luke, and I need your help."

He stood to one side and motioned for me to go ahead of him into an office at the rear of the station. Once inside, he directed me towards a chair placed in front of a desk, and I waited in silence while he searched through a cabinet drawer and pulled out a file which he then placed on the desk in front of him. He looked across at me and then slowly opened the file, sorted through some papers and took out a photograph, which he slid over the surface of the desk towards me. It was Luke, looking exactly as I had last seen him, with the same gaunt features and the same coal black hair, except that it was tied back in a ponytail. "Is this your brother?" the sergeant asked.

I nodded. "I would like this or a copy of it." Sergeant Alves stood up as I continued. "What information do you have that will help me to find him?"

He walked over to a copy machine at the far side of the room. "I'm afraid I have very little news for you," he said when his back was turned. "People go missing all the time in this part of the country."

"May I see the file?" I asked, feeling frustrated by his response.

He returned and sat down, handed me a copy of the photo and then slid the file across the desk. There were only three documents inside, a copy of Luke's application for employment, a report from the *Artemis* on his disappearance and the police report which told me that little had been done to locate Luke, other than a visit to the bar where he was last seen.

I closed the file. "And this is all you've done to try and find him?" I asked, trying to remain calm.

"Sim. You have to understand, Senhorita, this is not England. Many people pass through here, and things happen that we have no control over."

"You mean like the trafficking of cocaine?" I countered.

He looked surprised. "*Sim*, that is part of the problem. This is not the first time that a crew member or a passenger failed to return to their ship. Maybe your brother doesn't want to be found."

"I don't believe that. I think he's in some kind of trouble, and I'm going to find him. Where is this bar, the Madalena, where he was last seen?"

"I don't advise you to go there. It is very dangerous for a woman like you to go to such a place alone. I cannot guarantee your safety, Senhorita Regan."

I stood up and tucked the photo in the pocket of my jeans. "I can't help that. I'm going to find Luke no matter where I have to look for him."

"If you insist, the Madalena is near the Mercado Modelo—that's the main market downtown across from the waterfront. It doesn't open until late afternoon, so I suggest you go back to your hotel and wait."

"Thank you for your time, Sergeant," I said as he walked me out through the front door, but I was just being polite. In my heart, I knew that the Santarem police had made no effort to find Luke, and now it was all up to me.

Rather than chance eating in one of the local restaurants, I decided to have lunch at the hotel and then do a little exploring before going to the Madalena. By early afternoon, I found myself in the museum and learned a great deal about the history of the area, and then I started to wander through the markets downtown, finally ending up at the Mercado Modelo.

It was an amazing place, full of exotic smells and vibrant colours. There were leather goods, wood carvings, basketry, jewellery and all manner of items which were very tempting. I almost bought a wonderful beaded necklace for Mum but common sense prevailed. I knew I had to conserve what money I had. I was so conscious of the time that I kept checking my watch, and I could hardly wait for five o'clock, when I thought I should make my way to the Madalena.

By the time I arrived at the front entrance, I was already beginning to feel anxious. When I saw how seedy it looked, I almost turned back; but after hesitating for a few moments, I was compelled to go in. I walked through the door from the brilliant sunshine into almost complete darkness, or so it seemed. I stood just inside for a moment trying to adjust my eyes and noticed that there were already two people at the bar and a number of others at some small tables. Two of the individuals at one of the tables were women, and they were accompanied by two elderly men with cameras over their shoulders. They were obviously tourists, and I felt a lot more comfortable as I approached the end of the bar and perched on one of the stools. The bartender glanced over at me, nodded and then walked towards me. He started to speak, and I assumed he was asking me what I would like to drink, but I cut him off and asked him if he spoke English, to which he replied, "Sim."

I had Luke's photo in my hand and passed it to him. "Have you seen this man?" I asked, holding my breath.

He looked down at the photo and then passed it back and said, "Um momento." After that, he retreated to the other end of the bar where he motioned to someone who was seated in the far corner of the room. I watched as a tall man emerged from the shadows, walked towards the bartender, engaged in a short conversation and then walked around the bar in my direction. As he approached, for a brief moment, I thought it was Zach. He looked so much like him, with the same black hair, same chiselled features and lean build. It was only when he got closer that I could see he was a little older and a little taller, with a hint of a beard. He was only steps away when he held out his hand. "Ola, Senhorita, I am Carlos Escada. Maybe I can help you."

I jumped down from the stool and shook his hand. "I'm Ariel Regan. I've come all the way from England and I'm looking for this man. He was here, in this bar, about two months ago."

"Why don't we sit down, Senhorita Regan," he suggested, motioning to a table nearby.

Once we were seated, he called over the bartender and ordered me a margarita, so I was obliged to wait patiently even though I had no desire to sit drinking with a man I didn't know and all I wanted was to find out what he knew. Once the bartender had taken the order, the stranger asked, "May I see the photograph?"

I passed it to him, and he studied it carefully and then looked across at me. "Yes, I remember him," he said.

My heart started to hammer in my chest. "You do? Did you speak to him? What did he say? Do you know where he went or where he is?"

He began to grin as I rattled on and then replied, "I did speak to him but not for very long. He was with another man at the bar, and when the other man left, he moved to a table, ordered some food, then asked me if I had a light for his cigarette and that's when we started to talk."

"But he doesn't smoke," I said. "Are you sure it was him?"

He looked down at the photo again, which was still in his hand. "Yes, I am sure. He told me he had just arrived on one of the cruise ships and had to be back on board by midnight. We had a couple of beers together, and then I had to leave. When I came back later, he was gone. Paulo, the bartender, told me he had too much to drink and he wouldn't serve him anymore. He left with one of the local girls and that was the last Paulo saw of him."

"Who was the girl? Do you know her?"

The stranger lowered his gaze and hesitated, so I asked again. "You do know her, don't you?"

"I am sorry, Senhorita, her name is Inez. She is a *mulher das ruas.*"

I searched my brain for a translation, and then it came to me. "You mean a prostitute?"

"*Sim,* a prostitute."

"Do you know this woman?"

"She is here on many evenings. This is one of the places where she solicits the tourists, especially Americans who are known to carry a great deal of money."

I looked directly into his eyes. "And have you ever been solicited by this woman, Mr. Escada?"

He hesitated for just a second and then threw back his head and roared with laughter. "Ha! You are very direct, Senhorita. No I have not been solicited by Inez or any other woman. I assure you, I do not need to pay for my pleasures."

I felt myself begin to blush and lowered my gaze. "I'm sorry," I murmured, "I didn't mean to be rude."

"It is no problem. In fact, I find it rather refreshing, but then you are very young, so I should not be surprised."

"I'm not that young," I replied indignantly.

"Then your appearance is deceiving," he said smiling. "I would not expect to see a young woman like you here alone in Santarem. Tell me about the man you are looking for. I see you are not wearing a wedding ring, so I assume he is your lover."

I shook my head. "No, he is my brother, and I believe he's in some kind of trouble."

"You must be very close to him if you would travel so far to find him."

"I'd like to think we were very close," I answered and then proceeded to tell him all about Luke and my family. I told him about growing up in Abingdon, Luke's relationship with Pandora James and how he ended up being a cabin attendant on the *Artemis*.

He sat there listening intently; and when I had finished, he reached across the table and gently took my hand. "I am so sorry, Senhorita," he said.

He seemed so sincere that I felt a genuine connection with him; and as he withdrew his hand, I said, "Please call me Ariel."

"That is such a pretty name. Isn't it the name of a mermaid in a Disney film?"

I grinned. "Yes, but I was named after a Shakespeare character, and so was my brother. His real name is Lucius."

"I see, well, as we are on the subject of names, I insist you call me Carlos."

"Thank you, I would like that. Tell me, Carlos, are you able to help me find Inez? Maybe she can lead me to Luke."

He nodded. "I would be happy to help, but my stomach is telling me I need to eat. I would be honoured if you would join me for dinner. We could always come back here later in case Inez shows up."

"Why, can't we stay here and eat?" I asked. "If there is a possibility that Inez might come here, we might miss her."

"There is no chance of that. The street girls do not emerge until late in the evening. As for the food here, I would not recommend it. I will take you to the Casa do Saulo, and I can promise you that the food there is not only edible but enjoyable."

"That's very kind of you, but I don't think I'm dressed appropriately," I said, glancing down at my casual denim shirt and jeans.

He threw open his arms and gestured to himself. "We are both very casual and would be welcome at any restaurant in Santarem."

"In that case, I am ready whenever you are," I said, smiling.

Chapter Forty-Six

We arrived at the restaurant perched on a hillside overlooking the Tapajos river. The Tapajos was a tributary of the Amazon, and both rivers ran side by side for miles before merging at Santarem. Because of the acid content of the water, the Tapajos was clear and a deep shade of blue, while the Amazon was muddy and brown. I had learned this from my research before I left England and wanted to know a lot more. I also wanted to know a lot more about the stranger sitting across from me at the table.

Carlos ordered a glass of white wine for me and a beer for himself and then suggested that he explain the many dishes listed on the menu. Of course, I was very familiar with chicken and paella, but I had never heard of *pirarucu* or *tambaqui*, which were two species of fish common to the area. He recommended the *tambaqui*; and while we waited for our meals, I decided to ask him about his life. "Tell me," I said, "how is it you speak such perfect English?"

"Ah well, I grew up with my older sister in São Paulo. My father was a lawyer, and my mother, a schoolteacher, so I learned English very early on. My father wanted me to be a lawyer too, but I had other ideas. I had always liked to paint and fancied becoming a world-famous artist, so at the age of twenty-one, I moved to New York and studied art at the Pratt Institute for two years. Unfortunately, I wasn't talented enough or unique enough to make an impression, and I ended up working for a theatre group painting scenery."

He paused while the waiter returned to place some bread on the table. "But how did you end up here?" I asked.

He sighed, "My father had a fatal heart attack, and my mother became so depressed that I had to return to São Paulo to take care of her. A year later, she took a massive overdose of sleeping pills and was in a coma for three days. Then suddenly, she was gone."

I gasped. "How terrible. You must have been devastated."

"*Sim*, it was a difficult time, and it took almost a year to sort out all of their affairs. They owned a house in the most prestigious area of São Paulo and a villa in São Sebastião, where we used to spend our summer vacations. As well, they had a significant amount of investments, so there was a lot to deal with."

"You mentioned a sister, where was she when this was going on?"

"Christina? Just before I left for New York, she got married to an Australian who had been working in São Paulo for a year on an engineering project. Six months later, he moved back home to Sydney, and she went with him. At the time of my father's death, she was six months pregnant, and when my mother died, the baby was too young to travel so far."

"That's too bad, but is she happy living in Australia? You must miss her."

"I do, but she sends photos all the time and we keep in touch on a regular basis. She seems really happy, and with the money from my parent's estate, she opened a restaurant where they serve a lot of the dishes from this area of Brazil, except that they have to substitute the fish."

Just then, our meals arrived; and when I took a bite of the *tambaqui*, it was delicious, with almost a fruity taste. "This is wonderful," I remarked.

"I thought you would like it. There are so many different kinds of fish in the Amazon, but this is one of my favourites."

"How did you end up here?" I asked again, anxious to hear more about him.

"I took some time off and did quite a bit of travelling. A friend and I went mountain climbing in the Andes, and a month later, I took a trip down the Amazon and fell in love with the river. I know that sounds bizarre, but I knew I couldn't go back to living in a big city. Santarem was just a stop along the way, but there was something about this place that made me want to stay."

"But what do you do all day?"

He grinned. "I fish."

"Really, is that how you make a living?"

"I sell the fish to the local market, but it's more of a hobby than anything else. I was very fortunate because my parents left a sizeable estate and the cost of living here is so low, I'm able to be very comfortable without actually having to work."

His answer made me even more curious. "It's hard to imagine the kind of life you live. Is it really satisfying?"

"I find it so. I not only fish. In the dry season, I help the people on the islands rebuild their homes. Most of them are covered in water from December until June, when the river rises, even though many are on stilts."

I hesitated for a moment and then decided to just plunge right in. "Have you ever been married, Carlos."

"No, but I was once engaged to a girl in New York. She was brought up on a ranch in New Mexico, and we had plans to move there. Then she changed her mind and wanted to stay in New York, and I couldn't cope with that, so I broke it off. Now I don't have to consider anyone but myself."

"But isn't it awfully lonely?"

"Not at all. I am content the way things are. I can come and go as I please and I do. Once or twice a year, I leave here just to see how people in other parts of the world live. Last year, I went on a safari in Africa, and the year before, I was up in Alaska."

"Oh my, it all sounds very exciting. You'd probably be bored to death living in Abingdon, where I come from."

"Is that an invitation?" he asked, grinning.

I felt myself blushing again. "No," I replied, lowering my eyes.

There was silence for a brief moment, and then I noticed him look at his watch. "Let's have some coffee and then go back to the bar and see if Inez shows up."

We waited at the Madalena until about midnight, but there was no sign of Inez. Eventually Carlos suggested that we call it a night and offered to drive me back to my hotel. I wasn't sure that was a good idea, but it was late and I was tired so I agreed. On the way, he proposed that we try again the following evening and during the day, he would take me on his boat down the river. Again, I wasn't totally comfortable with the idea, but the thought of spending a whole day alone didn't appeal to me, so I agreed to meet him in the lobby at ten o'clock the next morning.

When we reached the hotel, he was the perfect gentleman, jumping out of the car to open my door and then shaking my hand and wishing me pleasant dreams. I thanked him for his hospitality and then watched as he drove away. Later, after I was tucked up in bed, I couldn't stop thinking about him even though I tried to steer my thoughts in another direction. Here was my own Indiana Jones, and I got lost in the fantasy.

Chapter Forty-Seven

The next morning, I had intended to get up early so that I could take my time with breakfast and contact my parents, but it was just after eight o'clock when I opened my eyes. I showered and dressed in khaki shorts, a white tee shirt and a pair of Keds and then went downstairs to check the Internet for messages. Dad had replied to my earlier message and was happy to learn I had arrived safely after such a long journey. All was well at the inn, and he hoped to hear from me again soon. I sent back a quick e-mail telling them I had a lead on Luke but couldn't check on it until later and that I was going on a sightseeing trip down the Amazon, but I didn't mention Carlos. After that, I had a light breakfast in the coffee shop; and at ten o'clock, I was standing at the hotel entrance when Carlos pulled up honking his horn. I didn't wait for him to get out. I just ran over and jumped into the passenger seat. "Good morning," I said, noticing that he too was wearing shorts.

"Bom-dia," he replied, "did you sleep well?"

"Yes, how about you?"

"Oh, I always sleep like a baby, especially when beautiful young ladies keep me up until midnight."

I just shook my head at him and grinned. His boat was docked about fifteen minutes from the hotel; and on the way, we passed the museum where I had been the day before and the cathedral. There were no large cruise ships in port, but there were a couple of Amazon cruise boats waiting to take tourists for an excursion down the river. I had no idea what to expect when we finally reached the dock where Carlos's boat was moored. There were numerous vessels tied up, most of which looked rather ancient and weather beaten and Carlos's was no exception except, unlike most of the others, it had a covered section built out of wood resembling a small cabin. He parked close to the dock; and as we got closer, I noticed the name painted on the side, Constancia. He must have read my thoughts. "Constancia was my mother's name," he said.

"That's a very pretty name."

"Yes, I agree. Even though it's supposed to be bad luck to rename a boat, I didn't think I could live with Vinganca.

"What does it mean?"

"It means revenge. The previous owner needed to settle a score."

When we boarded the boat, I was surprised when Carlos took me inside the cabin. There was a long green upholstered bench set against one wall, a small table and a counter for what looked like all kinds of electrical equipment. The wooden walls had been varnished and displayed three colourful seascape paintings, and there was a bright red rug covering the floor so that it all seemed rather cosy. I also noticed a picnic basket on the table and couldn't resist asking, "Did you bring lunch?"

"*Sim*, I thought you might be hungry in a couple of hours. Right now, though, we should get back up on desk and I'll cast off. I heard we are in for more rain this afternoon, so we should get started."

Minutes later, we were moving away from the dock and proceeding down the Tapajos towards where it merged with the Amazon. It was so peaceful, and I saw many small boats tucked under the trees that overhung the river and several small children swimming. Carlos suggested I might like to try fishing; but when he mentioned the piranhas, which were abundant, I wasn't too keen on the idea. Later, I saw several tourists fishing from the deck of one of the cruise boats, and

Carlos told me they liked to catch the piranhas, take photos and then release them back into the river.

After travelling for another two hours, Carlos moored the boat, and we went to the cabin for lunch. The picnic basket was packed with chicken salad sandwiches, cucumbers, chunks of pineapple, a bottle of Riesling and two wine glasses. Carlos deftly uncorked the wine and poured a generous amount into my glass. "Here's to finding your brother," he said.

I immediately realised that I had been so caught up with my adventure with Carlos that Luke had been absent from my thoughts since early morning. I pressed my hand against my forehead. "Oh my god, I feel so guilty."

Carlos reached over and gently pulled my hand away. "What are you feeling guilty about?"

"I haven't thought about Luke once today, except for when I first woke up. How could I just forget all about him, just like that?"

"That's what the river does to you. Maybe you can understand now why I chose to stay here."

"I do understand, but I came here to look for him, and I'm not going to stop until I find him. I didn't come here to have fun or enjoy myself."

Carlos shook his head. "Ariel, we will go back to Madalena tonight, and hopefully Inez will be there. There's nothing you can do until then."

"I know, but what if she doesn't show up again?"

"Then I will find out where she is, and we will go to her. I promised I would help you and I will."

I reached over and put my hand on his arm. "Thank you. I'm really, really grateful."

He covered my hand with his own, looked straight into my eyes and whispered, "O meu prazer," and I felt my heart skip a beat. I quickly withdrew my hand and took a sip of my wine in a desperate attempt to stop him from being aware of what I was feeling.

"Aren't you going to eat?" he asked.

I glanced down at the food he had put on the table and took one of the sandwiches. "These look delicious. I didn't know you were so domesticated."

Carlos chuckled. "I do my best, but it's hardly gourmet."

I was just about to respond when I heard the patter of raindrops on the roof of the cabin. "Oh dear, the rain's started."

"It's likely to get really heavy, so we'll just stay here until it lets up. Hopefully, it won't be too long."

The rain came down in torrents for about an hour and then suddenly stopped, and the sun came out. After that, we started back towards Santarem and arrived at the dock at just after four. Carlos suggested I might like to go back to the hotel and rest, and then we could go to dinner at around eight before going back to the bar. I know he was disappointed when I declined his invitation and made the excuse that I needed to use room service, as I was waiting for my parents to ring me, and I would meet him at ten at Madalena. Of course, it was all a lie; I just didn't trust myself to have dinner alone with him again.

He dropped me off at the hotel, and I decided to soak in the tub and then have a short nap. It was already after seven when I woke up, so I quickly got dressed in a pair of white slacks and a pale yellow tank top and went downstairs to the hotel restaurant. The lobster and asparagus dish I ordered was wonderful, but I would have enjoyed it even more if I had been able to stop fantasising about Carlos. I was becoming infatuated, not only with the man but also with his lifestyle, and I knew it had to stop. Luke had to be my priority, and I kept telling myself over and over again to focus, focus, focus.

I took a taxi to the Madalena and found Carlos was already there waiting for me. He gave a low wolf whistle when he saw me. "You are looking *muito belo* tonight."

"Why, thank you," I said, noticing his tailored beige slacks and a black short sleeved shirt.

Once again, without consulting me, he ordered a margarita for me and a beer for himself, and we just casually chatted, mostly about the trip down the river, but we were distracted several times when the door opened and we expected to see Inez walk in. By midnight, I was getting sleepy again and more than a little frustrated when suddenly Carlos glanced towards the door and whispered, "She's here."

I looked around and saw a petite woman, very pretty, with long black hair, approach the bar. She was wearing a bright red halter top, a multicoloured skirt and five-inch-high red sandals. Except for her hair colour and her height, she reminded me of Pandora. No wonder Luke went off with her.

"Stay here," Carlos ordered as he got up and walked towards her.

I was too far away to hear what they were saying but close enough to know they were talking in Portuguese. At one point, Inez appeared to get cross and her voice rose to the point where I heard her say *bastardo*, and then I saw Carlos pass something to her, and she grew quiet again. A moment later, she glanced in my direction, stared at me with a haughty expression and then turned her back on me while waving Carlo away. I could hardly wait to find out what she had told him and didn't even give him a chance to sit down. "What does she know? Where's Luke?"

Carlos looked rather solemn as he sat down. "It's not very good news, I'm afraid."

My hands started to shake. "I need to know what happened to Luke, and what did you give that woman?"

"She didn't want to talk to me, but a few dollars always loosens people's tongues. Your brother went home with her, but things got a little too cosy and her boyfriend walked in on them."

"Her boyfriend," I exclaimed. "You mean that women like her have boyfriends?"

Carlos shook his head. "Oh, Ariel, you really are naïve, aren't you? Yes, even women like Inez can have someone special in their lives, but in this case, Bruno Mendes is not someone you would ever want to tangle with."

"Go on, so what happened when he found them together? Isn't that what she does for a living?"

"Yes, she mostly makes her money off of tourists. Usually they end up in a back alley, and it's all over in a matter of minutes. This time, she took your brother back to her house, but she didn't expect Bruno to come around. I could still see the bruises on her face and arms, where he had obviously beaten her."

"And Luke, what did he do to him?" I asked as my hands continued to shake.

Carlos had a problem looking me in the eyes. "He forced him out of the house at gunpoint, and that's all she knows."

"Oh my god," I cried out, "so he could have killed him."

I started to get up with the intention of confronting Inez, but Carlos intercepted me. "Don't, Ariel, you'll only make matters worse. If you cause any trouble, you could put yourself in great danger, and if Luke is still alive, you'll have no chance of ever finding him."

"Please, let's get out of here," I said.

Carlos took my arm. "Very well, we will talk in the car. Would you like to go back to the hotel?"

I nodded and he led me out of the bar. My legs felt like lead, and I leaned on him heavily. I couldn't accept the fact that Luke might be dead. I climbed into the passenger seat and sat staring out of the window as we drove back to the Santo Amaro. Carlos was silent for a while, but then he reached over and grasped my hand. "It isn't over. We'll keep looking for him."

"What about the police? They must have known what happened. They knew he was at the Madalena, and Paulo must have told them he left with Inez."

Carlos sighed, "I'm sure that's as far as they wanted to go in investigating his disappearance. They weren't about to confront Bruno."

"Are you saying that he has power over the police?"

"He's a drug dealer, Ariel, and he's got a lot of connections. The last time the police invaded his territory, one of their houses was torched. Luckily, no one was hurt, and they had no proof that he had anything to do with it, but the message was loud and clear."

I felt my face start to crumple, and that's when I began to sob. "So what do I do now? I'm not going to stop looking for Luke even if I have to take him home in a coffin."

Carlos stopped the car by the side of the road and put his arm around me. "You are not alone. I promised to help you, and the promise still holds, but we have to be careful. Tonight, I want you to try and get some sleep, and tomorrow, I want you to stay in your room until I telephone you. Early in the morning, I will take the boat down the river and talk to as many people as I can to find out if they have seen Luke or know anything at all."

"But why can't I come with you?"

"These people don't know you. I know everyone on this part of the river, and they trust me. They'll talk to me if I go alone."

I nodded as Carlos started up the car again; and when we reached the hotel, he leaned across me and pushed open the door. "Go," he said, "it's getting late, and you need to get some rest. Remember, stay in your room until I telephone you."

I got out rather reluctantly and closed the door and then leaned down and stuck my head through the window. "You promise you'll ring me no matter what you find out?" I whispered.

"I promise. Sleep well," he answered.

Chapter Forty-Eight

As I entered the lobby, I thought about contacting Mum and Dad, but I couldn't bring myself to do it. I had no idea what to tell them. I tossed and turned for most of the night and eventually dozed off at around four o'clock. Three hours later, I was wide awake but emotionally exhausted. The thought of staying in my room for hours on end was nerve racking but leaving was too risky in case I missed Carlos's getting in touch with me. I took my time soaking in a hot bath, got dressed and then rang room service. While waiting for my breakfast to arrive, I attempted to read another chapter of my book, but it was hopeless. All I could think about was Luke. The time dragged on interminably, and I paced the floor like a caged animal. By eleven o'clock, I was on the verge of breaking my promise and leaving the room when the shrill ringing of the telephone startled me. I snatched up the receiver, "Carlos, is that you?"

"Yes, it's me. Are you all right?"

"Yes, yes. Did you find out anything?"

"I'm in the lobby. Meet me downstairs, and I'll fill you in."

I practically dropped the phone. I was so anxious to see Carlos; and a minute later, I had bypassed the elevator and taken the stairs to the lobby. When I got there, he was waiting near the reception desk, and I ran up to him, searching his face to see if I could tell what news he had brought me. "Let's go to the coffee shop," he said.

He sat me down and ordered coffee for both of us while I drummed my fingers on the table impatiently. "Tell me," I said. "I've been cooped up in that room for hours. I can't wait any longer."

"I think it's good news, at least I hope it is."

"Why? What did you hear?"

"Two of the old fisherman heard a rumour that one of the locals found a man on the outskirts of the rain forest. He was badly beaten and unconscious, so he put him on the back of his truck and took him to the municipal hospital. That's all they could tell me, and there's no reason to believe it was Luke, but the man was found at about the time Luke was reported missing."

I stood up. "We have to go to the hospital. We have to see if it's him."

Carlos looked up at me. "Sit down and finish your coffee, and then we'll go. If it was Luke, then I doubt that he's still there, but we may be able to find out where he went."

When we walked into the hospital, there were dozens of people in the waiting area, but Carlos motioned for me to stand beside him and then just nonchalantly leaned against a wall as though he was waiting for something. "What are you doing?" I asked.

"You'll see," he answered. "Give me Luke's photo."

I handed it over and listened while numbers were being called out over a public address system. The minutes were ticking by, and I was getting impatient when suddenly, Carlos grabbed my hand and pulled me towards a long counter where several clerks were dealing with the mass of people. It was then that I realised what he had been up to. He had been waiting to speak to the person most likely to be susceptible to his charms. It was an extremely pretty young woman with large brown eyes, long black hair and wearing a rather low-cut peasant-style blouse. "Bom-dia, Senhorita Barreto," he said, checking the name on the tag pinned just over her left breast.

She looked up in surprise and smiled. "Bom-dia."

There was a commotion behind us as a large man in overalls with his arm in a sling started yelling in Portuguese. He was obviously annoyed that we had jumped the queue, but the *senhorita* smiled at him sweetly and said a few words, and he went back to his seat as docile as a lamb. After that, I couldn't make out a single word of the conversation. At one point, Carlos passed Luke's photo across the counter, and the senhorita began to tap into her computer. Finally, she stopped, sighed, looked back at Carlos and then began to speak in a low voice. Once again, I had no idea what was being said, but after she jotted something down on a piece of paper and handed it to Carlos, I heard him say, "Obrigado, Senhorita Barreto," and he guided me towards the elevators.

"Where are we going?" I asked, feeling a little frantic "Luke's here, isn't he?"

Carlos shook his head. "No, the man who was found was brought here, but we still don't know if it was Luke. We need to go up and speak to a nurse on the ward where he was taken, and then we'll be able to learn a lot more."

After we rode up four floors, I followed Carlos out of the elevator in a daze. I couldn't figure out what was going on. Why didn't the hospital know who the man was who was brought in and where he was now? Carlos wasted no time in talking to one of the nurses, and I waited, feeling frustrated and helpless. Again, he pulled out Luke's photo, and I saw the nurse nod, and my heart leapt in my chest. I could hardly breathe, and I was desperate to know what she was saying. Then she walked over to a small table, wrote something on an envelope and passed it to Carlos. "Boa sorte," she said.

Carlos nodded and motioned to me to follow him back to the elevators. Before I could ask him any questions, he said, "After seeing the photograph, she's almost one hundred percent sure it was Luke."

I gasped. "Oh my god, is he still alive? Where did he go?"

We entered the elevator, and Carlos smiled. "Yes, he's alive, and I know where he is."

I felt almost faint with relief and leaned against Carlos for support. He put his arm around me; and as we exited at the ground floor, he glanced at the envelope the nurse had given him. "I have to make a telephone call to a person named Ann Conway, but we need to get out of the hospital first. After I've spoken to her, I'll let you know what I find out."

Once in the parking lot, he pulled a mobile phone from his pocket. Then in English, I heard him say, "Hello, is this Mrs. Conway?"

There was silence for a moment, and then he said, "My name is Carlos Escada. A nurse at the hospital—her name was Ms. Silvano—gave me your number. We believe that the young man living in your home is the brother of Ariel Regan. Ms. Regan is here right now, and she is anxious to find out if it is him. Would you allow us to visit you this morning?"

Again there was silence, and then Carlos continued, "Thank you, Mrs. Conway. Yes, I know the area. We will be there shortly, and thank you again."

He sighed as he rang off and then steered me towards his car. "Let's go," he said.

As we drove away from the hospital, he filled me in on what he had discovered. The man who had been taken to emergency had been badly beaten and still unconscious. He had broken ribs, a fractured right arm and had suffered trauma to the head, which had resulted in a haemorrhage, and he needed immediate surgery to control the bleeding. The operation saved his life, but he had no memory of who he was or anything about his past. Any identification he may have had on him had been taken. The only clue to his identity when he finally awoke after being in a coma for almost two weeks was his accent, which was decidedly British. I learned later that Ann Conway was an American who had married a Brazilian doctor but had retained her first husband's name for the sake of her son. She was a nurse on the intensive care ward at the hospital and was the only person the patient was able to converse with. When he was well enough to leave the hospital but had nowhere to go, she took him into her home, and that's where we were headed.

When we reached the house on Rui Barbosa, I was so nervous I was shaking; but when I saw the woman standing on the porch and she appeared to be waiting for us, I began to calm down. She looked to be in her fifties, only about five feet tall and slightly overweight, but she had the face of an angel. As we drew closer, I noticed her fair hair was sprinkled with grey and she had the softest blue eyes and the gentlest smile. "Hello," she said, stepping forward and extending her hand towards Carlos. "It's so nice to meet you, Mr. Escada, and this must be Ariel—what a lovely name."

Carlos shook her hand. "Thank you for allowing us to come here at such short notice, Mrs. Conway, but Ariel came all the way from England to look for her brother, so I'm sure you can understand how anxious she is."

"I understand perfectly," she responded. "Please call me Ann and do come inside."

We followed her into the house, and she took us to a small living room, where she invited us to sit down while she exited to the kitchen to bring us some tea. I looked around me, desperate to know where Luke was, if indeed it was him, but she was soon back with a tray and, as if reading my thoughts, said, "Thomas is in the garden right now, resting. He doesn't know that you are here to see him, and I thought it would be best if we talked first."

My mind was in a turmoil. "Thomas?"

Ann began pouring from a teapot into two china cups. "That's what I call him. We had no idea what his real name was so we had to come up with something. If this really is your brother, my dear, I would like to hear all about him before I take you to see him."

I proceeded to tell her all about Luke and how much he meant to me. When I got to the part about what we had discovered after he left the ship in Santarem, she shook her head. "These women prey on tourists and the like. Did you contact the police after he disappeared?"

"Yes," I replied, "but Carlos told me they wouldn't get involved because of Bruno Mendes. What about when he was brought to the hospital, didn't you ring the police?"

"We did, as we always do in cases like this, but I suspect they knew a lot more than they made out and were not about to take the investigation any further."

Suddenly, I heard a noise from just outside the room, and I glanced towards the door. "It's only, Bandit, our dog. It's strange because Thomas seemed to have a connection with him right from the start, and now they are almost inseparable."

At that moment, Bandit appeared in the doorway, and I almost dropped my cup, "Oh god, he's the image of our Sammy. He's a border terrier too. Maybe he thinks it's Sammy. Maybe he's remembering something."

Carlos put his hand on my arm. "You may be right, Ariel, but don't get your hopes up just yet."

Ann nodded in agreement. "Carlos is right. This may not be your brother."

I suddenly remembered the photograph. "Oh, the photo, Carlos, show Ann the photo."

Ann looked apprehensive as Carlos took it from his pocket and passed it to her. She took it gently in her hands and studied it for a brief moment. "It's him," she said.

I felt all of the tension drain out of me and burst into tears. My brother was here, just a few yards away. Ann continued, "His hair is very short now because they had to shave his head, but it's the same colour as in the picture. His face is a bit thinner, but there's no doubt it's him."

"Can I see him now, please? Please take me to him," I begged, with tears still streaming down my face.

Ann came and sat beside me and took both of my hands in hers. "I will in a minute, but you have to be prepared for the fact that he won't recognise you. He's still very frail and hasn't fully recovered from all of his injuries. On top of that, he's on medication that makes him drowsy, so besides having no memory, he's in a bit of a fog. You will have to be very patient."

Carlos cut in. "You may be disappointed when you see that he isn't the brother you remember."

I looked at Ann. "Will he ever regain his memory?"

She smiled. "That's the good news, my dear. The doctors are optimistic about his recovery. It could take a long time, but on the other hand, it could be spontaneous and happen tomorrow."

Carlos looked across at Ann. "I think she's ready to see him now."

Ann stood up, and we followed her down a hallway towards an open door that I could see led onto a garden. When we reached the door, she stepped away and said, "We'll just wait here."

I walked tentatively outside into the bright sunlight and looked across a lawn, bordered by a colourful flower bed, and noticed two deck chairs. One was empty; but in the other, I could see that someone was sitting with his back to me and lying close by was a dog. It had to be Bandit. I looked back towards Ann and Carlos, who were framed in the doorway, and they both nodded at me, encouraging me to go on. I stepped onto the grass and got halfway across the lawn and then stopped. I felt my throat constrict as I tried to get the words out; and when they finally came, I wondered if he could even have heard me. "Luke, it's me. It's sis." I waited with arms by my side and fists clenched, and the tension was almost unbearable.

Meanwhile, Bandit got to his feet and stared at me, head cocked to one side. I watched as I saw a hand reach out and stroke the dog's head and then two jean-clad legs swing slowly over the side of the deck chair. It was like seeing a slow motion picture; but when it was over, it was Luke who was standing there with a puzzled expression on his face. I took another step forward and then another, wanting so desperately to run up and wrap my arms around him but too afraid in case he pushed me away. Very slowly, he walked towards me, holding his right arm at an awkward angle; and as he got closer, I noticed a scar on his cheek that extended up to his right eye. Then, when he was just two feet away from me, he looked straight into my eyes, and I thought I saw something change in his expression. He reached out and touched my shoulder, and I just stood there holding my breath. His hand dropped to his side, and he whispered one word, "Sis?"

My hand flew to my mouth, and the tears started to fall again. "Yes, it's me, Ariel. Don't you remember me?"

"Sis?" he repeated, still staring at me.

I had no idea whether he knew me or not; but at that moment, I was determined to get my brother back and take him home, no matter how long it took. Ann came forward and put her arm around Luke's shoulder. "This is your sister. She's come all the way from England to find you, and she's going to help you remember so that you can go home to your family. Your name isn't Thomas, it's Luke and that's what we'll call you from now on."

Chapter Forty-Nine

I spent the next hour alone with Luke, attempting to jog his memory. I described the inn where we grew up together. I talked about Mum and Dad, about school and his best friend, Jimmy, but he just stared at me or shook his head. At one point, he put his hand to his head and closed his eyes and then muttered, "I don't remember any of this. You say my name is Luke Regan, but my mother calls me Lucius. You say you're my sister, but why should I believe you?"

I passed him the photograph. "Why would I be carrying this picture of you? Why have I come here to talk to you? What on earth do I have to gain? You're my brother, and I'm going to help you remember."

Ann, who had been in the garden with Carlos, came into the room. "I think Luke must be getting tired. Maybe you should let him rest."

At that, Luke stood up. "Yes, I think I'll go and lie down. Please excuse me."

I was dumbfounded; it was almost as though he was speaking to a stranger, but I didn't want to upset him. "Of course," I responded. "I'll come back tomorrow if Ann doesn't mind, and we can talk some more."

He merely nodded, touched Ann lightly on the shoulder and left the room. I looked at Ann helplessly. "He really doesn't know who I am. I thought when he first saw me that I noticed something in his eyes. I was sure he recognised me, but obviously I was wrong."

Ann sighed, "It's going to take time and a lot of effort on your part. Let's go into the garden, and I'll bring us some lemonade. We can talk out there, and maybe Carlos will be able to figure out what to do. By the way, he's a very charming man. He told me how the two of you met and that he's been trying to help. You were very fortunate to have made a friend under these circumstances. I know how difficult it is being in a foreign country where one can't speak a word of the language."

"Honestly, I don't know what I would have done without him."

Ann found an extra deck chair, and the three of us settled down in the garden with a pitcher of ice-cold lemonade and some delicious shortbread cookies that Ann had baked herself. "These are wonderful," I remarked, "even better than my favourite Peak Freans."

Ann chuckled. "Why, thank you. I love to bake, but when Miguel is away, I don't usually bother."

"Where is your husband?" Carlos asked.

"He's in Manaus at the moment and likely to be there for a while longer. His mother passed away two weeks ago, and he's in the process of selling her house and sorting out the estate."

"What about his father, is he still alive?"

"No, he died many years ago. We wanted to move his mother here with us, but she didn't want to give up her home."

Carlos spoke up. "I went through the same thing myself when my mother died. It was a nightmare getting everything settled."

"Where are you from, Ann?" I asked.

Ann smiled. "I'm from Phoenix, Arizona. I was working at St. Joseph's Hospital, and Miguel was interning there. I didn't expect to marry him and move to Brazil, but I never regretted it."

"How did you end up in Santarem?"

"We actually lived in Manaus for five years—that's where Miguel was brought up—and then we heard that the hospital here was in dire need of doctors and nurses, so we decided to move. I wasn't too happy at first, but now I love it. The people, for the most part, are warm and friendly, and we've made some good friends. What I cherish most is the pace here. It's so far removed from living in a big city, and I can't ever imagine going back to that kind of life."

"Do you have any family back in Phoenix?"

"Yes, my parents are both dead, but my brother still lives there with his family. We don't see each other very often, but we keep in touch all the time by e-mail, and occasionally, we'll call to have a long chat."

My thoughts turned back to Luke. "What made you take my brother in, Ann?"

She hesitated for a few seconds. "He was like a lost soul with nowhere to go, and I missed having my own son with me, if the truth be told."

"Where is your son?"

"Mario is studying at the University of São Paulo. When he left home last year, it was hard for me to deal with. I have no other children, so he means the world to me. Anyway, Luke is about the same age and he reminded me of Mario, so I decided to bring him home with me."

"What about your husband? How did he feel about you bringing home a complete stranger?"

Ann laughed. "Miguel's used to me picking up strays. Bandit was a stray too. He was only a puppy when I found him lying on the front porch. I had no idea where he came from, but he looked pretty pathetic. That was about six years ago, and our other dog, Sophie, wasn't too thrilled at the time, but they soon became firm friends. Sadly, Sophie died a year later, but she'd already lived a full life, and I think during that last year, she was happier than ever before."

"Where is Bandit?" I asked, looking around me.

"He's probably with your brother, curled up on his bed. He's going to be lost when Luke leaves here."

"When do you think I'll be able to take him home?"

Carlos reached over and squeezed my hand. "I think you're going to have to be patient, Ariel. It may take a lot to persuade Luke to leave here if he has no memory of his past. He's obviously settled here, and his surroundings are becoming familiar to him. Any drastic change might cause him extreme anxiety."

"But how can I make him remember? I have to take him home. I can't just leave him here."

Ann held up her hand to stop me from continuing on. "I'd like to suggest that you stay here, Ariel, at least until Miguel gets back. That way, you can work with Luke every day. You should call your parents, tell them what has happened and ask them to send you as many photographs as possible of your home and your family, especially those that include Luke. Better yet, get them to scan them and send them by e-mail so that you get them right away. We have a computer here at the house, and I can give you the address."

"That's a great idea," Carlos said. "You should call your parents this afternoon, Ariel."

I shook my head. "That's really kind of you, Ann, but I can't stay here. I have a return ticket to London, and I'm almost out of funds."

Carlos looked exasperated. "Heavens, woman, you can change your ticket, and as for lack of funds, I can help out there."

"I couldn't ask you to do that," I protested.

"You didn't ask me, I offered. Also, you have to think about how you're going to get Luke back to England. He has no passport and getting a new one might be difficult. You'll need to get his identification sent here, and I suggest you get a copy of the report from P&O Lines about his disappearance."

"Oh my god, I never thought of that. Where would I go once I get all the papers?"

"Probably Manaus, but let's not get ahead of ourselves."

"Carlos is right," Ann said. "So will you stay, Ariel? You'll have to bunk in with me, but don't worry, Miguel and I have twin beds. We both get a better night's sleep that way, and let's face it, the honeymoon is over for us."

I looked over at Carlos, and he nodded. "Yes, I'll stay, but I'll go back to the hotel for tonight, and this afternoon, I'll ring my folks. Thank you so much, Ann."

Ann stood up. "Good, I'm glad that's settled, now how about some lunch?"

We didn't stay for lunch; I was too anxious to get back to my room and let Mum and Dad know what had happened. But before we left, I had to ask about the cost of all of Luke's medical bills. I was almost afraid to ask because I didn't know how I was going to pay for everything. Both Ann and Carlos assured me that, in Brazil, health care was available for all people free of charge in the many public hospitals and had been since the late eighties. As for Luke, not being a resident or even having a working visa, Miguel pulled a lot of strings, and he was treated like any other Brazilian. I couldn't believe how compassionate Ann and Miguel had been, and I felt that I owed them so much.

Chapter Fifty

Carlos dropped me off at the hotel but not before he had persuaded me to join him for supper again that evening. I was grateful for the invitation as I didn't relish the idea of spending the rest of the day alone, and he arranged to pick me up at seven. When I got to my room, I rang my parents via the hotel operator and had to wait, for what seemed like an eternity, before she rang me back. I was beginning to think she had forgotten all about me and was about to reach for the phone when it began to ring. There were a lot muffled sounds and crackling; and then as clear as a bell, I heard my father's voice. "Ariel, are you there?"

"Yes, Dad," I answered. "It's so lovely to hear your voice. I just had to talk to you. I have some really good news and then not so good news."

I recounted every detail of how, with the help of a friend, I had managed to locate Luke and the fact that he had lost his memory. Dad was shocked, to say the least, but thankful that Luke was alive. Naturally, he wanted to hear all about the friend who had been helping me, and I had to tell him about Carlos. I tried to assure him that he was completely trustworthy and that I couldn't have found Luke without him, but I'm not sure Dad was convinced. He understood why I needed to stay in Brazil until I was able to arrange for Luke's return home and was pleased to hear that I would be staying with Ann.

I didn't have to ask him to send any money; he immediately offered to transfer funds once I had arranged to open an account in Santarem, and then we discussed how we were going to get the necessary documents so that Luke could return home. Dad said he would get in touch with the P&O Office in Southampton and even go there if he had to, as he felt we might need more than just the simple report we had received earlier. He even suggested he should contact the immigration office in London to see if they could help. Finally, we talked about gathering all the photos of the family and how to get them to me quickly. I chuckled when I realised that Dad was becoming quite computer savvy. I gave him Ann's e-mail address and then asked to speak to Mum, but she was out grocery shopping with Marcy. I was disappointed that I had missed her but happy that Dad and I had been able to talk. It made me feel a little closer to home again.

After lunch in the hotel restaurant, I took a walk around town and then decided to sit by the river and read my book. I was actually able to concentrate without a million thoughts going round and round in my head, and I enjoyed the peacefulness of the afternoon in spite of the rainclouds looming menacingly overhead. I returned to my room at four, just as the rain began to fall, took a short nap and then soaked in the tub. I hadn't thought to ask Carlos where we were going for supper and didn't know what to wear, not that I had much choice. I finally threw on a black tank top and my white jeans, and I added a pair of long white coral earrings that I had picked up in the market. Surveying myself in the mirror, I thought I looked pretty good, especially as I had already acquired a slight tan from being out in the sun.

I was in the lobby exactly at seven, and Carlos arrived just a minute or two later. He grinned when he saw me; and after opening the door for me and then settling into the driver's seat, he said, "You are looking *muito bonito* tonight."

"Thank you. You look nice too," I responded, noticing his pristine white shirt and dove grey slacks. He really was a handsome man; and the more time I spent with him, the less

I thought he resembled Zach. He was much more mature and that got me wondering just how old he was.

As he began to drive away, he said, "I would like to invite you to my home for supper. It's only a short-distance drive, and don't worry I didn't prepare any of the food."

I was a little surprised, I hadn't even considered for a moment that we would not be going to a restaurant. When I hesitated, he looked across at me and said, "Have I been too presumptuous, Ariel?"

I looked back at him and smiled. "No, of course not. I just wasn't expecting it. I'd love to have supper at your home, but tell me, did you have it catered?"

Carlos laughed out loud. "No, I have a wonderful lady who comes in two or three times a week to clean and do laundry, and occasionally, if I have guests, she will cook for me. Her name is Renata, and she can make *fijaoda* like nobody else."

"What is that?"

"Ah, you will see. It has beef and pork and black beans and bacon. It is the national dish of Brazil."

"It sounds wonderful. So I gather you do all of your own cooking most of the time?"

"Yes and no. I can fry up some fish, broil a steak and throw some vegetables in the microwave. Often, I'll eat out at a place right around the corner from my house."

"I'm really anxious to see where you live," I said.

When we arrived at the house, I was pleasantly surprised. It was a one-storey structure with white walls and a red-tiled roof and surrounded by trees, and the interior was furnished in an eclectic mix of country and modern and even had some feeling of Africa about it. The floors were dark hardwood; there were mirrored cupboard doors, overstuffed sofas and maple tables and chairs, and the kitchen had all the latest appliances. When I first walked into the living room and began to examine the chairs surrounding the table in the dining area, which was already set up with a tablecloth and silverware, Carlos looked at me with curiosity. "My dad makes furniture like this," I said, "and he's really good at it."

"I thought you said he ran the inn with your mother."

"He does but he also makes custom furniture as a sideline."

"You sound like you're pretty proud of him," Carlos remarked as he gestured to me to have a seat on the sofa.

"I am. He's a great father. In fact, both of my parents are wonderful people."

Carlos took a bottle of white wine out of an ice bucket, opened it and poured the wine into two glasses. He handed one to me and remained standing. "Here's to your family," he said, raising his glass. "I'd like to meet them one day."

I chuckled. "That's not likely to happen."

"One never knows," he responded, putting his glass down and walking away. "I'm just going to heat up our supper, and I'll be right back."

The *fijaoda* was just as delicious as Carlos said it would be, and afterwards he brought out a wonderful dessert of bananas and coconut, also made by Renata. We had finished the bottle of wine and were now onto our second bottle when Carlos suggested that we sit in the garden. Once outside, I discovered he had an oversized hammock strung between two very large trees; and when he asked me to join him in it, I was a little reluctant. Fortunately, the wine had helped rid me of most of my inhibitions, and I climbed in very tentatively while he held it steady. It was a beautiful night with a clear sky, except for dozens of stars, and I couldn't help thinking how romantic it was. After Carlos climbed in beside me, almost tipping me out onto the grass and causing me to giggle uncontrollably, we just lay there quietly for a few minutes. Carlos was the first to break the silence when out of the blue he said, "You know I'm very attracted to you, Ariel."

I turned my head and looked at his profile, but he continued to stare at the sky. "What do you mean?" I asked and then immediately felt like an idiot because what he meant was pretty obvious.

He rolled over onto his side and stared into my eyes. "I think you're an exceptional young woman. You're smart and thoughtful and beautiful, and I'd like to kiss you."

"Are you serious?" I asked and then again felt like an idiot.

"I've never been more serious," he whispered; and then leaning over so that half his body was almost on top of me, he kissed me fully on the lips. Strangely enough, I wasn't even startled; deep down, I had wanted him to kiss me.

When it ended, he said, "You really are lovely, Ariel."

I had never been very good at accepting compliments because I wasn't always sure people were being sincere; but at that moment, Carlos made me feel very special. I stared into his eyes and then reached up to wrap my arm around his neck and gently pulled him closer so that he had no alternative but to kiss me all over again. This time, it lasted a lot longer; and as he pressed against me, I could feel that he was becoming aroused. When he finally pulled away, he flopped over onto his back and gave a deep sigh, "You are really killing me," he said.

Before he could say another word, I turned onto my side, put my arm across his chest and whispered, "You haven't shown me your bedroom yet."

He hesitated for a moment and then sat up abruptly, almost tipping both of us out of the hammock. "Well, that can be arranged. How about right now?"

I nodded and he swung his legs out onto the grass, stood up and then quickly grabbed my hands and helped me out too. He continued to hold one of my hands as he led me back into the house and down a hallway to his bedroom. I was pleasantly surprised when I walked through the door and saw a queen-size cannonball bed covered in a multicoloured quilt, a lovely old pine dresser, a thick sage rug and several framed landscapes on the pale green walls. I looked around, not sure what to do next, and I think Carlos must have sensed my uneasiness. "Are you sure you want to do this?" he asked.

"Yes, I'm sure," I replied, "but I have to be honest, I haven't had a lot of experience."

"Come," he said, putting his arm around me and leading me to sit on the edge of the bed. "You're not a virgin, are you?"

I shook my head. "No, but I've only ever been with two men."

"Forgive me if I am being too inquisitive but were these just casual encounters?"

I shook my head again. "Uh, uh, I had a boyfriend for a while, someone I knew from school, and then not too long ago, when I was in London, I met this musician. I really fell for him, but I think it was my preoccupation with Luke that ended our relationship."

"What are you saying? Didn't he understand how important it was for you to find your brother?"

"I think he did, but I think he got a little tired of hearing about it, and I don't believe he'd ever gotten over the girl he was going to marry. She was killed in a car accident, so it was hard competing with a ghost."

"Are you still in love with him?"

"No, I'm ready to move on," I said, turning to look at him, "but we both know I'll only be here for a short time, and then we'll never see each other again."

He put his hand up and brushed my hair away from my cheek. "Perhaps that's true, Ariel, and if you want me to take you home now, I will. I won't make love to you if you don't want me too."

I took his hand away from my face and laid it against my breast. "I do want you to make love to me," I said.

Chapter Fifty-One

That night was like nothing I had ever experienced before. Carlos was a superb lover. He brought me to the edge again and again until I was almost begging for mercy. There was so much passion between us and, for the first time, I really knew how it felt to please a man. We made love for hours and then fell into a deep sleep brought about by exhaustion and contentment.

When I awoke, just as it was getting light, Carlos was still asleep; and as I watched him, I wondered, is this what love really feels like? Maybe I was kidding myself when I thought I was in love with Zach. I tried to go back to sleep, but the thoughts kept running through my head. I couldn't be in love with Carlos; we had only just met and were from two different worlds. Soon I would be back in England, and he would be gone from my life. I vowed to end it before it went any further; but when Carlos woke up and reached for me, there was no way I could resist him.

When we finally made it out of the bedroom and were sitting at the breakfast table, in a small alcove off the living area, Carlos said, "I hope you don't regret the night we just spent together."

I reached across the table and grasped his hand, "How could I possibly regret it? It was wonderful. I'm just concerned about getting too close to you when I know I'll be leaving soon."

He looked at me rather solemnly and said, "Is it wrong to live in the moment sometimes?"

I sighed, "I'm not sure I can handle that. I guess I'm pretty naïve."

"I don't think you're naïve. You just need to let go and take life as it comes. You are so young. You have plenty of time to settle down."

"Now you're beginning to sound like my father."

Carlos grinned. "I don't think I'm quite old enough for that."

"How old are you?" I asked

"You really want to know? I'm thirty-six and quite a bit older than you, I imagine."

"That's just about how old I thought you were. I'm only twenty-two, so I have quite a bit of catching up to do."

"Well, I can tell you one thing for sure. Last night, you were amazing, and you could satisfy any man. I don't think you need more experience on that score."

I felt myself blush. "I think you had a lot to do with my performance," I whispered.

After breakfast, Carlos drove me to the hotel and waited in the lobby while I gathered together my few belongings and then checked out. We drove to Ann's, and Carlos let me out of the car, promising to call around that evening to see how I was getting along. I felt conflicted watching him drive away; I didn't want him to leave, but I was anxious to see Luke. Ann greeted me with open arms and helped me get settled in her room. She told me that Luke had said very little after I had left the day before, except that he was pleased I was going to be staying for a while. I knew then that he really hadn't accepted the idea that, at some point, I wanted to take him back to England with me. I was a little disappointed when I discovered that he wasn't at home and was out taking Bandit for a walk, but it gave Ann and me a chance to talk.

She had been chatting with a neighbour and found out that, unless one was a resident of Brazil, one couldn't open a bank account. She didn't feel this was a big problem and suggested that, if I felt I could trust her, my father could transfer funds to her account and she would be sure to turn the money over to me immediately. How could I not trust someone who had taken in a complete stranger and asked for nothing in return? I e-mailed Dad right away to give him the information, and he wrote back to tell me he would be sending the photos later that day and also he had news about Luke's passport. He had been in touch with the immigration office in London, and he would be able to get a replacement passport provided that we sent an original passport photo to him. This, along with a signed affidavit documenting the loss and the report from the P&O Line would be sufficient. It meant that I wouldn't have to travel to Manaus, and I was relieved. All I had to do was persuade Luke to get his photo taken and send it off by courier to Dad. I knew this would mean convincing him of where he came from and the need to take him back there. I wasn't sure how he would react because he obviously felt safe with Ann. He was in a familiar place, and now he would have to face the unknown. I just prayed that the family photos would convince him that I really was his sister.

Luke walked in the door just as I was helping Ann prepare lunch. He greeted me formally, and I had to hold myself back from hugging him. Bandit gave me the distraction I needed, and I playfully stroked his head and asked if he'd had a good run. He looked exactly like Sammy, except for a patch of dark fur between his ears. I had decided to wait until after lunch to approach Luke about his passport, but Ann suggested I wait even longer until after he had seen the family photos. It seemed to make sense, but I was impatient, and it would mean another day before I could bring up the subject. During the afternoon, I spent time with Luke in the garden, and I told him a lot more about his life, his likes and dislikes and his dreams, but I couldn't bring myself to tell him about Pandora. The time just didn't seem right.

Early that evening, we got several e-mails from Dad. Each one had three or four attachments, and I was excited. Luke had already gone to his room to rest and to do some reading, so I managed to share my excitement with Ann. She thought Dad looked like a charmer and was amazed when she saw Sammy.

"Oh my," she said, "no wonder you were surprised when you saw Bandit."

I think what impressed Ann the most were the photos of the inn and the surrounding area, "What a lovely place," she remarked. "You are so fortunate to have been brought up there, Ariel."

We decided to wait even longer to show the photos to Luke. I needed to take it very slowly and explain each one and not go rambling on like I had with Ann. However, that didn't stop me from getting excited all over again when Carlos showed up and had to listen to me babbling. He was just as impressed as Ann but had more compliments for Mum than Dad. "Your mother is lovely. She looks like a really sweet person," he said.

Carlos stayed for a glass of wine; and when Luke joined us, he chatted to him about the fish he had caught that afternoon and then said he was leaving to get an early night. When I saw him out, I whispered, "What's the matter? Didn't you get much sleep last night?"

He chuckled. "I could say that, and it's all your fault."

"So when do I see you again?" I asked, reaching up and winding my arms around his neck.

"Tomorrow," he answered. "We'll have supper together. We'll go back to Casa do Saulo, and then maybe we can slip back to my place for an hour or two."

"I grinned and kissed him lightly on the lips. "Sounds wonderful," I said.

He winked at me, kissed me back, only much more passionately, and then as he walked away, called out, "I'll pick you up at seven."

When I returned to the living room, Ann looked up from where she was sitting, knitting, and said, "I really like Carlos. He's such a pleasant man and sexy too."

I laughed. "Why, Ann, I didn't think you'd noticed."

She just chuckled to herself and kept on knitting.

Chapter Fifty-Two

The next three days were spent rather leisurely. Most of the time, I was with Luke going over all of the major events in our lives. He acknowledged that the photos showed he was part of the family, but he didn't recognise our parents or the home we had always lived in. Even though Ann had warned me that it wasn't likely he would remember, I felt so let down, and I was running out of hope but I did persuade him to get his passport photo taken. He accompanied me into town, along with Bandit, and afterwards we went to the market and sat for a short time by the river. Even there, I was hoping it would bring back memories of the Thames, but it was not to be.

I managed to see Carlos every day, even if only for two or three hours, and we spent most of the time in his bed. We just couldn't get enough of each other, and I felt myself getting deeper and deeper into a situation which could only end in heartache.

One afternoon, I was in the kitchen, rolling out some pastry for an apple pie. Ann, Luke and Bandit had just left for the store to pick up some groceries when I heard somebody walk in the front door. I looked towards the hallway and saw the figure of a man half hidden in the shadows. "Que está lá?" I called out in my best Portuguese as my hands began to shake.

The man came out into the light. "Tarde boa," he said. "You must be Ariel."

I'm sure I looked puzzled because he took a step forward and extended his hand. "I am Miguel Caldeira, Ann's husband."

"Oh my goodness," I said, dusting the flour from my hands and then shaking his. "I'm so sorry, I didn't recognise you from your photos."

He threw back his head and laughed. "I am not surprised. Those photos are a little ancient. Believe it or not, I used to be quite handsome."

I couldn't help smiling because he was still a good-looking man, older but with a head of thick brown hair and the most unusual grey eyes. "Was Ann expecting you?" I asked.

He shook his head. "No, I thought I would surprise her. She told me you were staying here for now. I hope I'm not inconveniencing you?"

"Of course not," I replied, although I was wondering what we would do about the sleeping arrangements. I would probably have to go back to the hotel.

Miguel was anxious to see Ann, and I assured him they would be back within the hour. After that, he settled himself at the kitchen table and asked me if I had made any progress with Luke. I enjoyed talking to him; he was obviously a very intelligent man; and being a doctor, he gave me a lot of insight into Luke's condition. Above all, he encouraged me to continue coaching Luke and never to give up; and by the time Ann came back, I felt more hopeful than before.

Ann was shocked when she walked in and saw her husband, but the delight on her face was obvious. It was only after she got over her surprise that she realised we had a dilemma; and when I suggested going back to the hotel, she was genuinely upset. I tried to assure her that it was fine, and I would come back every day to spend time with Luke, and she finally accepted the fact that I had no other choice. Neither of us expected that Carlos would save the day. He dropped by that evening to take me out to supper and saw my belongings packed and sitting in the hallway. He soon found out, after meeting Miguel, what the situation was and, to my astonishment, in front of everyone, suggested that I stay at his house. I noticed

Miguel lift an eyebrow, while Ann grinned and Luke actually smiled. Needless to say, I was a little flustered but only hesitated for a moment before accepting his offer. "I'll be back in the morning," I called out as we left later that evening.

Ann just winked and said, "Have a good night, you two."

The next few weeks, I spent most of my evenings and all of my nights with Carlos; and during the day, I was with Luke. It was idyllic, in a way, because I felt as though my life had been suspended in this remote place yet, at the same time, frustrating because I had no idea what the future would bring. At some point, I knew I would be forced to make a decision. If Luke didn't recover his memory, he might refuse to go back to England with me. Then again, I might not want to go either, but I really didn't have much choice.

During the week, Ann and Miguel were at the hospital; and occasionally, Miguel would be called out on an emergency after he had settled in for the night. Before leaving for work, Ann would spend at least half an hour with Luke. While she was still living in Phoenix, she had taken a physiotherapy course, and it proved to be a godsend because she was able to help Luke try and regain the normal use of his arm. Every day, he seemed to be getting stronger, and he began to resemble the brother I remembered. His skin had lost its pallor, his wonderful chestnut hair had grown longer and he had gained some weight. As his health improved, he took more interest in what was going on around him; and as always, I hoped he would stumble onto something that would jog his memory.

Every other day, I would e-mail Mum and Dad, and I even took some photos to send to them of Luke along with Ann, Miguel and Bandit. I was surprised when, for the first time, I got an e-mail back from Mum. She was overwhelmed after seeing Luke's picture, and she couldn't wait for me to bring him home. She was also happy that I had found such nice people to stay with, and I felt a twinge of guilt because I hadn't told either of my parents that I was now staying with Carlos. After consulting with Ann, I decided to show Mum's e-mail to Luke and even encouraged him to write back to her, but he was reluctant, and I didn't want to push him.

Two or three times, Carlos took Luke out fishing on his boat, and he always came back with quite a catch. This didn't surprise me because he had always been adept at catching fish, but it still didn't help him remember those times when he would sit on the riverbank or fish from the Abingdon bridge.

As the end of the rainy season began to arrive, I could no longer deny my feelings for Carlos. I had fallen in love with him, and I didn't want our relationship to end. Every moment I spent with him was precious to me. When he walked through a door, I felt an adrenaline rush, and whenever I left him each morning to go to Ann's, I couldn't wait to see him again. Living together, I had discovered what a gentle and thoughtful human being he was. He treated all people with the utmost respect, no matter what their station in life. He didn't fish every day to make a living; he was independently wealthy, and so he would always give half of his catch away to the less fortunate people of Santarem who relied on the river to feed their families. So far, I had been able to keep my true feelings to myself. I was almost certain that if I told him I was in love with him, it would change our relationship, and not for the better. I even discussed it with Ann one night, and I know she felt my frustration. The only advice she could give me was to follow my heart but be prepared for the consequences. This left me even more conflicted, and I had no idea what to do.

One weekend, Carlos took me to Alta do Chao, a resort on the Tapajos with pristine white sand beaches and deep blue water. It was still early, so there weren't too many tourists and it was peaceful walking through the town with its quaint architecture. We visited the cathedral, bought some souvenirs, ate at one of the most popular restaurants and even sunbathed on the beach. It was such a glorious day; and that night, once we were back home, I was on the verge of breaking my silence, but Carlos had some news that stopped me in my tracks. We were in the garden, lying in the hammock, when he said, "I didn't want to spoil our day together, but I have some news. I have to go to São Paulo tomorrow, and I'll be gone for a few days, maybe even a week."

I was a little shocked. "Why do you have to go to São Paulo?"

"I think I told you about mountain climbing with a friend. Well, I've been talking to him for the last few months, and he's been trying to recruit a group of six guys to go on a climbing expedition to Mount Aconcagua in Argentina. Now that six of us are committed to go, he needs my help in organising the whole thing, so I'll be flying out in the morning."

"Why didn't you ever mention this before?"

"Honestly, I didn't think he'd pull it off. I didn't want to get my hopes up, so until it was certain, I didn't see any sense in talking about it."

I nodded. "I see. So you're only going away for a few days now, but when will you actually be going on the expedition?"

He slipped his arm underneath me and pulled me towards him. "We're aiming to start out in August from Santiago, Chile, and it should take us about three weeks. Don't worry, it will be long after you leave here to go back home."

I hesitated, trying to take in what he had just said, and then the anger hit me and I got up rather abruptly, almost falling onto the grass while the hammock swung precariously. "Is that it?" I asked, my voice rising in frustration. "I go home and you go off climbing some mountain and we never see each other again?"

Carlos leaned up on one elbow. "Come back here, Ariel."

"No, I'd like to leave now. You can drive me back to Ann's," I responded. I knew I was acting like a petulant schoolgirl, but I couldn't help myself.

Carlos got up and followed me into the house. "You're acting rather childishly," he called out.

That was the last straw. Turning, I pummelled his chest with my fists, and the tears began to fall. That's when he grabbed me by my shoulders and held me so tightly that I couldn't move. He kept on holding me until I started to calm down and then let me go and rested his hands lightly on my shoulders. "Ariel," he said. "I care for you deeply, and I wish we could have met under different circumstances, but my life is here and yours is back in England. Let's not spoil the precious time we have left while you're here."

I brushed the tears away and reached up to hold his face in my hands. "Then please don't go tomorrow. Stay here with me until I have to go home."

He took my hands away from his face and shook his head. "I can't do that. I promised Ben I'd be there. He's been working on this for months, and now he needs help. You have to understand that organising an expedition like this takes time."

"Why can't one of the others help him? Why does it have to be you?"

"Because I'm the only one who's here in Brazil, and I don't have a real job to worry about."

"Where are the others from?"

"Jack and Chris, who I've climbed with before, are from Canada, and the other two, who I've never met, are Australians.

"Isn't it awfully dangerous?" I asked.

"It can be, but we're all experienced climbers, and we'll have all the safety equipment we need."

I turned away and walked towards the window. "I can't bear to think of you on that mountain. I'm glad I won't be here in August because I won't have to sit here wondering if you'll ever come back."

I heard him walk up behind me and then felt his arms wrap around me. "My silly little *ganza*," he said.

"What's that?" I asked, leaning my head back on his shoulder.

"A *ganza*? It's a goose. You're my silly little goose."

I swung around and put my arms around his neck. "You know I'm falling in love with you, don't you?"

He nodded very slowly and then kissed me briefly on the lips. "I know," he said and led me into the bedroom.

Chapter Fifty-Three

After Carlos left the next day, I felt really lost. I had to take a taxi to and from Ann's house because I had never learned to drive. When Ann suggested that Luke could pick me up from Carlos's each morning and drive me back later, I was reluctant. I knew he had driven our car at home but assumed he had forgotten how. Miguel assured me that the type of amnesia Luke was experiencing had not erased all of his memory, and he had already done a couple of practice runs in their car since his health had improved.

During the following week, I spent even more time with Luke, and I felt as though the bond we had shared was beginning to return. He still didn't remember anything about his past life, but we became so comfortable with each other that, by the third day, when we were sitting near the river, I began to talk about my feelings for Carlos. He wasn't in the least surprised but was concerned about how I was going to face the strain of leaving and going back to England.

"I have no choice," I answered. "He's already told me, in so many words, that there is no future for us."

Luke looked worried. "Do you think he might be taking advantage of you? He's obviously quite a bit older, and I expect he's had a number of relationships."

I shook my head. "No, I think he genuinely cares for me, but I don't think he's in love with me. Anyway," I continued, "I know I'll get over it, especially as I'll have you with me when I leave."

Luke turned away for a moment and watched a fisherman steering his boat into the riverbank, and then he turned back. "Was I ever in love with anyone?" he asked.

I sucked in a breath, not sure how to respond, and then decided it was time to tell him the truth. "This is going to be hard for you to believe," I said, reaching for his hand, "but you fell madly in love with a film star."

He looked at me in astonishment. "You're kidding? Who was she?"

"Her name is Pandora James. She's starring in *Moll Flanders*. It's a remake of a film from the sixties that starred Kim Novak. I think it's being released in June."

I went on to tell him how they met and how he had moved to London to live with her, but I couldn't bring myself to tell him about the baby. When he asked why they broke up, I had no choice but to lie and tell him that I wasn't really sure but I assumed her work was more important than their relationship.

I waited for some sign that he remembered, but there was none, and then he asked, "What was she like?"

I sighed, "Well, she was a little older than you but looked really young. She was stunning, with flame red hair and wonderful green eyes, but to be honest with you, I didn't take to her."

Luke looked puzzled. "Oh, why not, you seem like the kind of person who would get along with everybody."

"She talked down to people, including me. I just didn't feel she could be trusted, especially where you were concerned. I was really worried about you at the time, but Dad kept telling me you were old enough to make your own decisions."

"I suppose it was after we broke up when I took the job on the cruise ship?"

"Yes, but there was a short time in between when you were living on your own, and then you met Bert Sparrow, and that's how you got the job."

I had already told him about Bert, but I never told him how they met in a hostel or the circumstances under which he had been living in Camden. I just couldn't see the point in elaborating on all the depressing details. Maybe, one day, he would recall exactly what had happened; and then I would learn even more myself about that period in his life. By the end of that day, I realised that something had changed. We were actually having real conversations, and Luke was asking questions instead of just listening. He appeared to be taking more and more interest in who he was and where he came from, and I felt a ray of hope. I even acknowledged to myself that even if he never regained his memory, I would be able to take him back to Abingdon and he could start over. It wouldn't be an ideal situation, but it was possible, and it gave me something to focus on rather than thinking about Carlos and wondering what he was doing in São Paulo.

It was just over a week before Carlos returned. He had contacted me earlier to tell me they had made a lot of progress but still had a few loose ends to tie up. I was disappointed that he wasn't coming back right away, but just hearing his voice put a smile on my face. After he finally returned, everything fell into the usual routine, and the hours I spent with Carlos were as blissful as ever.

Then two weeks later, Ann approached me about my plan for returning to England. That evening, out of Luke's hearing, I sat down with Ann and Miguel and asked them if they really thought Luke was ready to leave Santarem. Miguel was very straightforward and felt that there was a better chance of Luke recovering his memory at home, especially as that's where he had spent all of his life, except for the last few months. I remembered him telling me earlier that it was unusual for a head trauma victim to lose all of their memory. Although he had seen several patients suffering from amnesia, it usually only covered a period of a few hours prior to the trauma. He had heard about amnesia covering a period for as long as four years, but it was extremely rare. He suspected that something else might be going on with Luke, and it could be a combination of the effect of the trauma and also an emotional issue. He suggested that when we got back to England, we consult with a specialist.

I was expecting Luke's passport to arrive in about a week; and when we received it, I thought it would be the perfect opportunity to begin to prepare him for our journey back home. I was anxious about what his reaction would be, and how I would handle it if he needed more time or, worse still, if he refused to go altogether. Ironically, deep down, I almost wished he would refuse because then I would have an excuse to stay myself. I had never been so conflicted before. The prospect of leaving Carlos was daunting, but Luke had to be my priority. He needed to be with our parents and in a place he was familiar with, if he was ever to revert to the brother I had always known and loved. Ann sensed my frustration and suggested that I tried to take my mind off leaving until we had actually booked our flights. She had a few days off from her job at the hospital and took Luke and me on a visit to the national forest, which was about twenty five miles from Santarem. We spent a glorious day hiking and even took a canoe trip along some of the small rivers, but what impressed us the most was the size of the gigantic samauma trees, which could grow up to almost one hundred feet tall and twenty feet wide. By the time we got home, we were exhausted but ready for more adventures; and when Carlos offered to take Luke and me on a cruise along the Tapajos to the Jari River, we were ready and willing.

Three days later, at five o'clock in the morning, Carlos and I picked up Luke and Bandit, and we drove to where the boat was moored. Ann had suggested that we take Bandit along, and she had generously provided a picnic basket packed full of food for that day and even a bottle of wine. It was a long trip to our destination at Vitoria do Jari, and Carlos insisted that we leave before the sun came up because he wanted to get there before nightfall. I had been curious about how we were going to manage sleeping on the boat, especially with Bandit along, but Carlos had already arranged for an old friend to put us up for the night.

The journey along the Tapajos was relaxing and uneventful; but by eleven o'clock, the temperature had climbed to eighty-six degrees, and I wasn't used to that kind of heat or being out in the sun for too long. I had purchased a swimming costume at the market. It was a modest one-piece, and I was prepared to do some sunbathing, but Carlos suggested that I cover up and spend some time in the cabin rather than suffer the consequences. Meanwhile, Luke appeared to be in his element. He was wearing khaki shorts and had already stripped off his tee shirt, and I couldn't help admiring how good he looked. It was a far cry from the man I encountered when I first arrived. Carlos was showing him how to steer the boat, and he looked like he was really enjoying himself.

It was almost seven in the evening when we finally arrived at our destination, and I was surprised to find that Carlos's friend was there waiting for us. Luis was a much older man whom Carlos had met several years ago at an art gallery in São Paulo. He was born and raised in Vitoria do Jari but educated in São Paulo. He had intended to remain there and pursue a career in physics but had developed a severe respiratory problem and needed to escape from the pollution of the city. Just prior to returning home, he met not only Carlos but also his future wife, a French Canadian girl named Yvette. I found Luis to be absolutely charming and his wife even more so. They had a comfortable two-bedroom home, and Luis, like so many people in the area, made his living from fishing. Yvette made us welcome from the moment we stepped through the front door and insisted on feeding us *tourtiere*, a meat pie with a savoury pork, beef, onion and spice filling, which she had baked herself. I had never heard of it before, but it was delicious.

Meanwhile, Bandit was in his element because he had found a friend, a very large and exquisite Persian cat named Belle. Belle was a wonderful pale golden colour, with amber eyes, and she had a sweet nature. She didn't even take offense when Bandit ate some of her supper even though Luis had already given him a healthy portion of his *tourtiere*. All in all, it was a lovely evening, and I was glad that Carlos had saved the bottle of wine to share with our hosts.

In order to direct attention away from Luke and myself so that his amnesia would not be evident, I asked Luis about the time he was in São Paulo, and I was especially interested in Yvette, who was born in Quebec and was travelling throughout

South America when she met Luis. I found her to be such a warm and caring person, and she reminded me a lot of Ann. I think she sensed that something was going on between Carlos and me, but she didn't pry; and when the evening was over, she discreetly showed me to a small den, off the living room, where she had set up a cot for me. I realised then that Carlos and Luke were expected to share a bedroom, and I had to chuckle to myself because I don't think Carlos envisioned that was how he would be spending the night.

I actually slept really well and was ready for the six o'clock wakeup call and a quick breakfast of croissants and coffee before we were back on the boat and headed for the Jari River. Both Luis and Yvette had seemed reluctant to see us go, and we had difficulty coaxing Bandit to leave his new lady love, but we had no time to waste. We reached the Jari within the hour, and it was all that Carlos had promised it would be. We saw caimans, iguanas, all kinds of birds, freshwater dolphins and, most fascinating of all, huge capybaras, which were semiaquatic rodents that weighed about a hundred pounds. Along the way, we stopped at the Indian village of Arapixuna, where they lived mainly on fish and *manioc*, an edible root. It was a wonderful experience, but the heat of the day was starting to get to me, and I was anxious to get back into the shelter in the cabin for a while.

Chapter Fifty-Four

We were only about an hour from the dock at Santarem when everything changed. The sun had gone down, and it was quite a bit cooler. I had been in the cabin for a good part of the journey and was thankful to be back in the open air. I was perched on the rail at the stern of the boat talking to Luke, who was sitting, lotus style, with Bandit on the deck in front of me while Carlos was busy steering us through one of the narrow areas of the river. Suddenly, it felt as though the boat was rapidly slowing down, and we heard Carlos call out in alarm, "Hold on, hold on." Then without any further warning, there was a tremendous crash and a terrifying grinding noise. At first, I pitched forward, and I grasped the rail, trying to steady myself; but to my horror, my body was then thrown backwards, and I was falling headfirst into the river. The next thing I knew I was underwater and descending quickly towards the bottom of the river. I was terrified because I remembered the caimans we had seen earlier and knew piranhas were common in the area. I had never been a good swimmer, but I frantically struggled to reverse direction and reach the surface; and when I finally emerged, I was gasping for air and thrashing my arms about in desperation. I couldn't see the boat and started screaming for help. I don't think I had ever been more scared than at that moment. Then when I thought I was going to go under again, I felt a pair of strong arms grab me from behind and start to pull me backwards. I didn't know who it was until I heard the voice. It was Luke. "Hang on, sis, I've got you," he said.

I tried to glance back over my shoulder. "Where's the boat?" I called out.

"It's okay. It's right behind us," he answered, and then I heard voices and saw lights reflected in the water. A moment later, a dark shape loomed in front of me, and I gasped and starting kicking out with my feet. As it got closer, I saw that it was Bandit and realised he had come to rescue me too. He came within inches of me and began to push at me, with his nose against my chest. All at once, I had déjà vu; I was twelve years old again, floating down the Thames with Luke and Sammy, and I knew everything was going to be all right.

Moments later, I heard Carlos yelling, "You're nearly there, Luke. There's a rope ladder just below where I'm standing. You'll have to help Ariel up."

It was a struggle getting up that ladder. I was almost sitting on Luke's head as he pushed me upwards, and then he had to get Bandit on board too. Once on deck, I collapsed, and Bandit was doing his best to revive me by licking my face. Carlos pushed him away and knelt down beside me. "Are you okay?"

I attempted to sit up; and as he put his arm around my shoulders to help me, I noticed a man standing a yard or two away. "I think so," I answered. "What happened?"

Carlos nodded towards the man who took a step forward. "This is Angelo Bando. I'm afraid he and his friends were doing a little too much partying, and it interfered with his ability to steer his boat."

Angelo looked down at his feet and began to ramble in Portuguese. I had no idea what he was saying, but he appeared to be apologising. Carlos got up off of his knees, rested his hand gently on Angelo's shoulder and proceeded to talk to him for a few moments. Finally, Angelo raised his head, shook Carlos's hand and walked away towards the bow.

"So he crashed into you?" I asked. "Was there any damage?"

Carlos nodded. "Let's just say he sideswiped me and the only damage is to the surface of the hull, but it was enough to catapult you over the side."

I looked around me. "Where's Luke? Is he all right?"

Carlos looked around too. "He must be in the cabin. I'll go and see if he's okay and bring you a blanket. You're shivering. Are you cold?"

"No, I think I'm still in shock, but I'll be fine. Please go and find Luke. I'm worried about him."

It seemed like quite a while before Carlos came back and handed me a blanket. "Is he in the cabin?" I asked as I wrapped the blanket around me.

Carlos nodded. "Yes, he wanted to be sure you were all right."

I was puzzled. "Then why didn't he stay with me?"

"Why don't you go and ask him?" he replied in almost a whisper as he helped me to my feet.

I made my way slowly to the cabin; and just before I descended the stairs, I looked back at Carlos. He nodded at me, encouraging me to continue; and when I reached the bottom stair, I saw Lucas sitting on the bench with his head in his hands. I sat down beside him, and he turned to look at me with tears in his eyes. "What is it?" I asked. "I'm fine. You don't have to worry about me."

He stared at me for a moment, and then he said, "I remembered."

My heart leapt into my chest, and I grabbed his hand. "What did you remember? Tell me, tell me."

The tears were still there, but he smiled. "I remember riding my bike with Jimmy, and I saw you on top of the bridge. Suddenly, you were falling, and I ran down the bank into the river. I couldn't find you at first, and when I did, we floated down the river. Sammy was there too."

I was ecstatic and wanted him to go on. "Do you remember what happened after that?"

Luke nodded. "You were in the hospital, and they made me out to be a hero. They gave me an award, and my picture was in the paper."

"Yes, that's right, and Mum and Dad were so proud of you."

"Mum and Dad," he repeated slowly as though he was thinking. "Yes, I remember them being there."

"What else?" I asked impatiently.

He shook his head. "That's all."

"You mean you don't remember anything else?"

"No, but it's a start. Maybe now it will all come back to me."

I put my arms around him. "Yes, it's a start, and tomorrow after a good night's sleep, we'll go over the photos again. They might help now. I do hope so, Luke, because it's almost time for us to go home."

He rested his head on my shoulder. "It scares me to leave here even though I know you'll be with me."

"I'll always be with you," I said. "You're my brother."

When we finally arrived back in Santarem, we made our way to Ann's, and even though we were all tired, including Bandit, who fell asleep almost as soon as we got there, Carlos and I decided to stay for a while. I wanted to fill Ann and Miguel in on what had happened; and although they were concerned about my fall into the river, they were elated about Luke's breakthrough. When we eventually left at almost midnight, I gave Luke a hug and whispered, "Sweet dreams." He actually grinned and gave me a thumbs-up, and I rode back to Carlos's with renewed hope.

Later, as Carlos and I lay in bed, with our arms around each other, he said, "You seemed really happy tonight."

I snuggled closer and smiled. "I am happy. I'm getting my brother back. It may be little by little, but I have to believe that one day, he'll remember everything."

Carlos stroked my arm. "I'm so pleased for you, Ariel. Soon you'll be able to make plans to go back to England."

I detected a note of sadness in his voice. "Will you miss me when I'm gone?" I asked.

He rolled onto his side and then leaned over me so that he could look into my eyes. "More than you know," he replied.

I bit my lip to stop myself from tearing up. "I wish I could stay. I have to go back, but I can't bear the thought of not seeing you again."

"One never knows what might happen in the future."

I shook my head in frustration. "You know it's true. Once I leave here, you'll forget all about me, but I'll never forget you, not ever."

"Shush, we'll stay in touch, and maybe one day, I'll even come and visit you."

"You know that will never happen. You'll be too busy with your fishing or your mountain climbing. You might even meet someone else and fall in love with her."

"Ah! Do I detect a hint of jealousy?"

I pushed him away and turned my back on him. "No, I don't want to talk anymore. I'm going to sleep now, so I'll just say good night."

I heard Carlos chuckle; and as he snaked his arm around my waist, he whispered, "Good night, my silly little *ganza*."

Chapter Fifty-Five

The next few days seemed to fly by in a flash. I had already brought Mum and Dad up-to-date on what had happened, although I made light of my fall into the river. Dad immediately gathered together more photos in the hope that it would help Luke to recover more of his memory. By the third day, after spending hours with him and both of us becoming exhausted in the process, I was almost ready to give up; but by the following morning, he had had another breakthrough. He was waiting for me impatiently when I arrived at Ann's a little later than usual. I saw him peeking through the window as we drove up, and a minute later, he was running out to open the car door for me. "Where were you?" he asked. "You're late."

I looked at Carlos and winked as I stepped out onto the driveway. "We slept in," I responded. "What's the hurry?"

"I need to talk to you. Is Carlos coming in with you?"

"No, he'll be back this evening. Just let me say good-bye to him."

Luke waited impatiently, tapping one foot, as I leaned through the car window and blew Carlos a kiss, and then I followed him into the kitchen. I realised that Ann and Miguel had already left for the hospital, and it was eerily quiet, except for the scrabble of Bandit's feet as he ran in from the garden to greet me. I patted his head, and he settled down near my feet as I sat down at the table. "I'd love a coffee," I said to Luke, who was about to sit down opposite me.

I watched as he measured out the coffee, filled the percolator with water, and set out two mugs. He seemed to have calmed down a little. "Okay, what is it?" I asked. "You're obviously excited about something."

He turned and leaned back against the counter. "I had a dream last night."

"Go on, what was it about?"

"I was in a play. I think it was *A Midsummer Night's Dream.* I was all dressed up in this costume, and it was in an auditorium. It must have been at school, and all the parents were there."

I nodded. "Yes, yes. You were playing the role of Demetrius, and the audience loved you."

"It was weird because when I woke up, I knew it wasn't just my imagination. I knew it was something that really happened to me, and I really enjoyed being on stage."

I hesitated for a moment. "Do you remember me telling you about Pandora James, the woman you were in love with?"

Luke nodded and moved away from the counter to sit down. "What about her?"

"Well, when they were filming in Abingdon at Milton Manor, you were an extra on one of the sets. We always thought you'd become an actor one day."

I could see the strain he was under as he struggled to remember, and then suddenly, his face lit up. "Why don't we look Pandora up on the computer?"

"What a brilliant idea," I replied as though I had never considered it before. If the truth be told, I was nervous about exposing Luke to that period in his life. I had brought up the subject of Pandora initially, but every time her name was mentioned, I wondered if he would remember that she had aborted his child. Was that the emotional baggage that Miguel suggested Luke was carrying along with the effects of his trauma? A short time later, we were seated in front of the computer, and I reluctantly turned it on.

"Google Pandora James," Luke instructed, and with a few strokes of the keyboard, several Web sites that included Pandora's name popped up.

Luke didn't hesitate; he reached over to hit "images," and up came dozens of photos of Pandora. They were mostly publicity shots, but there were also some of her in her *Moll Flanders* costume; and in every one of them, she looked amazing. Luke kept scrolling down without saying a word, and when he had seen them all, he slumped back in his chair and said, "Wow, she's beautiful."

"Yes, she is," I agreed rather grudgingly.

"I don't understand it," Luke continued. "Why would she go out with someone like me?"

I reached for his hand. "Maybe because you're a really nice person and pretty good-looking yourself."

"But she's some famous film star, and from what you tell me, I'm just a country boy."

I chuckled. "Hardly a country boy. Anyway, she's not that famous, at least not yet. Maybe after this film is released, she will be."

"Let's look at the Web sites. I want to know more about her."

In the next fifteen minutes, I think Luke learned everything he needed to know about Pandora, including the accounts of her various romances. It was ironic that amongst those accounts was a reference to her mystery companion at a premiere in Paris and the photo I had seen in the *Sun* accompanied it. Luke gasped. "Oh my god, that's me. Look at my hair, it's jet-black. I look so different."

"I know. We saw the picture in the paper. It was quite a shock because we didn't know where you were at the time."

Luke logged off of the computer. "I think I've seen enough," he said and then got up and walked away.

I followed him out into the garden, where he appeared to be deep in thought. "Does any of this come back to you?" I asked.

He shrugged his shoulders and sighed, "No, but maybe when we get back to England, I'll be able to see Pandora, and then I'll remember."

In the following week, Luke began to recall some of his memory, but they were just snippets of events that had happened during his childhood. I was disappointed that he was unable to remember anything that had happened just prior to leaving England or his journey on the *Artemis*, but I had to face facts. Miguel reminded me again that the period prior to the trauma Luke suffered might be lost to him forever. With every conversation Luke and I had, I felt we were becoming closer. He was like a sponge and wanted to know more about our parents, the inn, his friends, and my own hopes and dreams. It was almost as though we were children again when we shared that special bond, and I secretly cursed Pandora for coming into Luke's life and pulling us apart.

When Luke's passport finally arrived, I knew it was time to return home. I contacted Dad, and he made arrangements with the travel agent in Abingdon to get us on a flight out of Santarem just one week later. Somehow, because he had purchased travel insurance, he had managed to get a refund on the return portion of my original ticket, but now the cost of two one-way flights to London seemed outrageous, and I vowed that one day, I would repay him.

I expected the days leading up to our departure to fly by, and I was determined to spend as much time with Carlos as possible. Our hours together were bittersweet, and I cried a lot, but I never let Luke know how torn I was about leaving Carlos behind. He questioned me on two or three occasions about our relationship, but I downplayed it. I really wanted him to believe that I was excited at the prospect of taking him home where he belonged.

On the evening before we were due to fly out, Ann and Miguel threw a going-away party for us. They invited some neighbours who we had come to know quite well, and Ann cooked up a veritable feast of local dishes, while Miguel made certain that nobody's glass was empty for more than a minute. When Carlos and I left at midnight, I realised that I would only see Ann and Miguel briefly in the morning when we picked up Luke to go to the airport. As we stepped out onto the front porch, Ann pressed something into my hand and told me to keep it as a memento. It was a beautiful gold bracelet engraved with flowers, which I had seen her wear often and had admired. "It's lovely," I said, "but I can't accept it. I don't need anything to remind me of you. You've been so amazing, and I can never thank you enough for what you've done for Luke."

"I want you to have it," she insisted, "and I want you to promise me that you'll stay in touch."

I slipped the bracelet onto my wrist and embraced her. "I will. Thank you so much. I'll see you both in the morning, bright and early. Make sure Luke gets to bed soon or he'll never be up in time."

Ann chuckled and waved as we drove off, and I felt really sad. By the time we crawled into bed an hour later, I was even more distraught, and although I had wanted our last night together to be our most memorable, it didn't turn out quite the way I expected. I imagined a night of frenzied lovemaking, but we were both so subdued that we ended up just clinging to each other, and we eventually fell asleep.

Carlos was already up when I opened my eyes the next morning. I called out to him, and he came into the bedroom and sat on the bed. "This is it, Ariel. You're going home today."

I smiled. "I know. I can hardly believe it, by tomorrow night we'll be in London."

He ruffled my hair. "Come on, sleepy head. Get up and get ready or you'll miss your flight. I've already got the coffee on, and I'll scramble some eggs while you're in the shower."

I smiled again. "You're going to miss having someone to cook for when I'm gone."

Carlos stood up and walked away from the bed. "I guess I'll be eating most of my meals out like I used to."

I lay there for a moment, imagining him going back to the life he had led before we met, and I wondered how long it would take for him to forget me.

The final good-byes when we left Ann's house were tearful. Luke had trouble keeping a check on his emotions as he hugged Ann and promised to stay in touch. Even Bandit seemed to sense that we weren't coming back. When we eventually drove away, he chased after us until we were out of sight.

"Will you see Ann and Miguel from time to time?" I asked Carlos.

"Yes, of course. In fact, they've already invited me for supper next Saturday. They're a great couple, and I really enjoy their company."

"I'm so glad," I said. At least I would be able to get news of Carlos through Ann if I never heard from him again.

When we arrived at the airport, we had an hour wait before our flight, and I could see that Luke was getting anxious. I wasn't sure if he was upset about leaving Santarem or if he was nervous about flying. Only a few days earlier, I realised that he had never been on a plane, and I remembered how I felt when I left London. When he suggested that he needed to go and find a magazine, I was concerned that he might run off and not come back, but I decided to take my chances and let him go. While he was gone, I talked to Carlos about whether I would ever see him again, and he made it sound as though it was something he wanted, but he made no commitment. When they called our flight number, it all became a bit of a blur. Luke had returned with his magazine, and we were being herded towards the gate with dozens of others. I tried to hang back; and in a last desperate move, I clung to Carlos, throwing my arms around his neck and whispering, "I love you so much."

I remembered him kissing me very gently on the lips, and he had tears in his eyes when he said, "Eu te amo demasiado."

I understood what he had said immediately and gasped as I tried to hang on to him, but Luke was pulling me away. "Come on, sis, we have to go."

I was dragged through the gate; but all the while, I was looking back at Carlos, who was standing as still as a statue, staring after me. Then suddenly, I was in the Jetway, and he was gone.

Chapter Fifty-Six

I was amazed of how calm Luke was after we were in the air. He was excited by the speed with which we raced down the runway. But once we left the ground, he was transfixed by the sight of Santarem falling away beneath us; and when we levelled off, he sank back into his seat and sighed, "This is really neat," he exclaimed. I nodded in agreement, but my mind was on Carlos.

There was a four-hour layover at Belem; and by the time we arrived in São Paulo that evening, I was ready for bed, but Luke had other ideas. On the descent into the airport, he had seen the glittering lights of the city, and he wasn't about to waste an opportunity to explore some of the nightspots. When I protested, he reminded me that our flight to London didn't leave until ten in the morning and we had plenty of time to sleep. I brought up the fact that we couldn't afford to go out on the town, but he begged me to go with him; and in the end, I couldn't refuse him.

At my suggestion, Dad had booked one room in a hotel for Luke and me. When I told Luke about the arrangement and that Dad was just being economical, he didn't seem to mind and even mumbled something about it reminding him of when we were small. We took a taxi to the hotel, dropped off our bags and walked out onto the streets of São Paulo. I had to admit it was magical, and there was an atmosphere that was hard to explain. All around us, people were talking and laughing; and although we had no idea what they were saying, we got caught up in the gaiety of it all. We needed to find a place for supper, so I looked for someone in the crowds who was likely to speak English. When I spotted a fair-haired man with a camera slung over his shoulder, I approached him and was relieved to find that he was actually Danish but spoke English very well. He recommended a restaurant called Mestico, where we could find all types of food at a reasonable price, and suggested we have a drink at the Liquid Lounge afterwards. We walked the few blocks to Mestico and found the place to be charming and the food exceptionally good; but after my second cup of coffee, I could hardly keep my eyes open. "You can't go to bed yet, Ariel," Luke said. "Come on, one drink, and then we'll go back to the hotel."

I reluctantly agreed and, fifteen minutes later, found myself sitting on a bar stool in the Liquid Lounge, with a margarita in my hand, listening to the beat of bossa nova. Luke seemed to be in his element, and it was easy to see why. Every time I glanced behind me, I noticed one beautiful dark-haired beauty or another smiling at him. I was just about to make a comment when he swung around to face the bar and abruptly turned to his right. I leaned forward to see what had caught his attention and, at the same time, heard a girl's voice speaking English with the hint of an Irish accent. She was talking to another girl seated next to her, and they looked enough alike to be sisters. Luke waited until there was a lull in the conversation and then leaned over and said, "Excuse me, but I couldn't help overhearing you talking. Where are you from?"

The girl closest to him smiled. "We're from England. I know we sound Irish, but we lived in Belfast until I was about twelve, and then we moved to Oxford."

When I heard that, I immediately jumped off of my stool and stood next to Luke with my hand on his shoulder. He was taken by surprise, but I didn't give him a chance to speak. "Hello," I said. "I'm Ariel, and this is my brother Luke. I can't believe you're from Oxford. We're from Abingdon."

The other girl spoke up. "You're kidding? This is unreal. We're so happy to meet some fellow Brits. By the way, my name's Bridget, and this is my sister, Jenny."

We all shook hands and decided to look for a table where we could sit comfortably and chat. It turned out that the sisters had won a prize on a television show when they were on a weekend visit to London. The prize was an all-expense paid trip to Rio de Janeiro and São Paulo. Incredibly, they were due to go home on the same flight as Luke and me. Bridget was the elder and more outgoing of the two, but it was obvious that Jenny had caught Luke's eye. She was very pretty, with wheat-coloured hair like Mum, light blue eyes and a slight boyish figure. Meanwhile, Bridget, though similar in facial features, was not as pretty and quite a bit heavier. The conversation got a little awkward when Bridget asked Luke what places he usually frequented in Oxford; and of course, he couldn't remember. When I was forced to intervene on two occasions, Luke finally said, "You might as well tell them."

"Are you sure?" I asked as both girls stared at Luke apprehensively.

"Yes, I'm sure," he replied.

I didn't go into all the details of what had happened to Luke; I merely explained that he was working on a cruise ship which stopped in Santarem, and he was mugged and suffered a head injury which resulted in memory loss.

"Can't you remember anything?" Bridget asked, obviously intrigued.

"Some things from my childhood are starting to come back but nothing from recent years."

"That's a bummer," Bridget remarked.

Jenny, who had been staring at Luke, glanced over at me. "Did you come all this way to take Luke back home?"

I nodded. "Yes, after I got here, we stayed in Santarem until Luke was well enough to travel and ready to face going back."

She turned back to Luke. "Do you remember your parents?"

Luke frowned. "I recall some things that happened with them when I was younger, and I've seen some photos taken with my parents just before I left England, so it won't be a shock when I see them again."

"By the way," I said, "my dad's Irish too. His name's Casey Regan. You can't get more Irish than that."

Bridget laughed. "That's for sure, and I'd love to meet him someday."

"I'd like for you both to meet him," Luke remarked, looking at Jenny.

It was midnight when we eventually got back to the hotel after agreeing to meet up with the girls at the airport the next morning. It felt strange sharing a room with my brother, but we both gave each other privacy; and a half hour later, we were in our beds with the lights out but both wide awake.

"Thanks for coming out with me, sis," Luke said.

I felt my heart give a little leap. "You called me sis just like you used to."

"I know, it sounds natural to me now somehow."

"I'm so pleased, Luke. Did you enjoy this evening?"

"It was great, and I'm glad you stepped in when you did. It was really awkward until you told them what happened."

"Well, I'm glad you agreed to let me tell them. That Bridget is quite a character, but I really like Jenny. She seems really sweet and thoughtful."

"Yes, that's what I thought about her too. I hope she gives me her phone number. When we get home, I'd like to see her again."

I chuckled. "Don't worry about that, I'm sure you'll be seeing a lot of her."

There was silence for a moment, and then Luke said, "We should get some sleep. Night, sis."

"Night, night," I whispered, but I didn't go right to sleep; I was thinking about Carlos and wondering if he was thinking of me.

The flight from São Paulo took twelve hours; but when we flew over London, it all seemed worthwhile. I had told Luke so much about the city, and he was straining to make out the historical landmarks in the darkness; but all too soon, we were touching down at Heathrow. Bridget and Jenny were on our flight but were seated at least a dozen rows behind us, so we had little chance to talk. Thankfully, we had managed to exchange phone numbers because once we reached the gate and were let out onto the jetway, Luke and I were swallowed up in the crowd. I was excited about seeing Mum and Dad, but I could tell Luke was nervous, and he clutched my hand. "It's going to be okay," I yelled at him over the noise of all the people and the public address system.

The moment we walked out into the arrivals lounge, I heard Dad call out, "Ariel, over here."

I turned in the direction of his voice, and there he was behind the barrier with Mum. I couldn't help it and started to cry. Releasing Luke's hand, I ran around the barrier and threw myself into Dad's arms. "Oh, I'm so happy to see you," I cried.

He kissed me on the cheek and then, holding me at arm's length, looked past me at Luke, who was walking very slowly towards us. "Hello, son," he said.

I watched while Mum took two or three tentative steps forward and then raced towards Luke and took his face in both of her hands. "Lucius," she whispered, "my darling Lucius, welcome home."

Luke looked so bewildered that I touched Mum on the shoulder and said, "I think Luke's a little overwhelmed right now, Mum. It's going to take him some time to get used to everything."

Mum took her hands away from Luke's face and put her arm around him. "It's fine, Lucius. We'll take things very slowly, I promise."

Dad nodded. "I agree with your mother, my boy. We're just grateful that you've come back to us."

We followed Mum and Dad out to the car; and as we drove out of London, there was little conversation, but when we got onto the M40, Luke began to talk. He described our journey all the way from Santarem and even got a little animated when he recounted the experience of meeting Bridget and Jenny. I smiled to myself; and when Mum asked if we were going to see them again, Luke grinned from ear to ear and said, "I certainly hope so."

After we pulled into the driveway of the inn, as we began to step out of the car, I looked back at Luke. "Anything familiar?" But he just shook his head. A moment later, the front door opened and Sammy came bounding down the steps towards us. I bent down, ready to pat him on the head, but he rushed right past me and hurled himself at Luke, barking loudly. Luke was startled but lifted him into the air; and when he began to lick Luke's face, he said, "This feels familiar."

I glanced over at Mum and grinned. "I had a feeling he'd remember Sammy."

When Luke finally got Sammy under control, I noticed that Marcy was waiting at the door. I turned to Luke. "This is Marcy. She helps out with all the day-to-day chores."

"Hello, Marcy," Luke said, shaking her hand.

"Hello, Mr. Luke," she responded, blushing. "It's nice to have you back again."

Dad said he would drive Marcy home, as it was late, and not to wait up if we were tired after our long journey. I gave him a peck on the cheek, and we went into the reception area, where Luke stood and looked around, trying to take it all in. "How about now?" I asked.

He shook his head again. "No, not really. I feel like I've been here before, but it's all really vague."

Mum looked at me and shrugged. "Let's go into the kitchen, and I'll make some coffee. Perhaps you'd like a bite to eat too?"

We didn't feel like eating, as we had already had a late supper on the plane, but we were both desperate for some coffee. We dropped our bags in the hallway and went into the kitchen, where we decided to wait for Dad to come back. Marcy only lived a short distance away, so it was less than twenty minutes later when he walked through the door, and his face lit up when he saw us. We talked long into the night; that is to say, I did most of the talking. I wanted to fill them in on every detail of what had happened in Santarem except, of course, my intimate relationship with Carlos. When I mentioned his name, I tried to sound casual, but I could swear that Mum was studying me closely, and I expected to get the third degree sooner or later. At one point, I noticed Luke starting to get sleepy and suggested it was time to turn in, so after saying good night, I led Luke to his old room and couldn't resist asking him, "How about this room, do you remember being here before?"

He threw his bag onto the bed, looked around and then walked over to the far wall. He stared at the picture framed in cherry wood for a moment and then said, "I remember this picture. This is Nana, isn't it?"

The picture was indeed a photo of Nana, with her chestnut curls, wearing a powder blue dress with a lace collar and holding her beloved cat, Buffy. I was elated, "Yes, yes. It is," I responded, walking over to stand beside Luke, "and that's Buffy."

Luke looked at me and smiled. "She used to tell us stories, didn't she?"

I nodded. "Oh my goodness, Luke, this is wonderful. I think your memory is coming back." As I spoke, I heard a slight noise behind me and turned to see Sammy standing just inside the doorway, motionless except for the wagging of his tail. "I think you're going to have company tonight," I said.

Luke stooped down and patted the floor. "Come on, boy," he said. "You can stay with me as long as you don't hog the bed."

I laughed and gave Luke a hug. "Good night and sleep well."

He hugged me back. "You too, sis. See you in the morning."

"It's already morning," I remarked as I left the room.

Chapter Fifty-Seven

A few days later, after Luke had a chance to settle in, I was a little apprehensive when my parents said they wanted to talk to us about a decision they had made. I helped Mum and Marcy with breakfast for the ten guests who were booked into the inn that week; and after I had something to eat myself, I joined Mum, Dad and Luke in the lounge. Dad looked a little solemn, and I began to wonder if he was ill and was about to give us some catastrophic news; so when he reminded me of their decision to move, I was somewhat relieved.

"So you really mean to sell this place?" Luke asked.

"Not if you and your sister are willing to take it over," he said.

I was shocked for a moment. "Are you really serious, Dad? How can you afford to get a house in St. Albans or somewhere like that without money from the sale of the inn?"

"Well, we have more than enough money saved up for a down payment, and I can still earn more from my furniture-making business. I just can't bear the idea of getting rid of this old place. The problem is, your mother and I don't want to run it anymore."

I stared at Luke, but he wasn't reacting. "What about my plans to go to London and take up fashion design, Dad, and what about Luke's plans?"

"Don't be offended, sweet girl, but I don't think you're really cut out for designing dresses, and as for Luke, I don't imagine he has any plans."

I looked at Luke again, but he just shrugged. "I don't know, Dad. It's something we really need to think about. I didn't expect to stay in Abingdon for the rest of my life."

Mum spoke up. "It doesn't have to be forever, Ariel, but it will give you both an income and something to do for the time being. If you want to give it all up, at some time down the road, whether it's sooner or later, we are willing to accept that. What's more, if the inn is sold, your Dad and I are willing to split the proceeds so you'll both have a little something for the future. Please take a little time to think about it. We don't expect to start looking for a new house for two or three weeks."

During the next two days, Luke and I had several discussions about taking over the running of the inn, and he suggested that we got involved in the day-to-day operation so that we would have a better idea of what we were dealing with. I already had a lot of experience; but in order to understand exactly what Luke and I were in for, we decided to go ahead. I had to persuade Mum and Dad to let us take over, even if only on a temporary basis. At first, they were reluctant; but when I told them it was the only way we would consider running the inn, they relented.

I was so engrossed in the whole concept of Mum and Dad moving away and leaving Luke and me behind that Carlos only crossed my mind occasionally during the day. At night, it was a different story, and I would lie awake for ages, imagining his arms around me. It wasn't surprising that I was thrilled when I received a huge bouquet of red roses with a card that I had to go online to translate. It read, "Thinking of you with love, my little goose." Mum raised her eyebrows when she saw the roses and wanted to know what the card said. I felt myself blushing as I told her, and then she asked me the inevitable question, "Did you fall in love with this man, Ariel?'

I tried to make light of it, but Mum didn't believe me; and in the end, I confessed that I had being staying with Carlos most of the time I was in Santarem and, yes, I had fallen in love with him.

"But surely you knew there couldn't be any future for the two of you?" she asked, frowning.

"You're right, Mum, but I couldn't help myself."

"So now what happens? Are you just going to keep in touch as friends?"

"I guess so, but I don't know for how long. Carlos is going on a mountain climbing expedition in August. Maybe then he'll forget all about me."

"Oh, Ariel," Mum sighed, "I wish you hadn't got so involved with this man."

"Don't worry, Mum, it's all over," I said, but in my heart I prayed that it wasn't.

Later that night, I rang Carlos to thank him, but he wasn't there. Rather than leave a message, I decided to e-mail him, but I deliberately kept it brief in an attempt to keep my emotions in check, and I never once referred to what he had whispered to me at the airport.

The next afternoon, I got a telephone call from Bridget. I was rather surprised because I had expected her to ask for Luke. She wanted to know if we wanted to come to Oxford the following Saturday and join her and Jenny for supper. Naturally, Luke was all for it, but we suddenly realised that we were now fully in charge of the inn and that meant one of us would have to stay behind. When Dad heard about our dilemma, he offered to take over for us but suggested that, if we were planning to become innkeepers, we had better think about how we would handle this kind of situation. Feeling a little humbled, we thanked him; but as soon as he was out of sight, our mood changed to one of excitement. We were actually getting a night off.

The evening with Bridget and Jenny marked the beginning of a new friendship for me and a much deeper relationship for Luke. Bridget and I seemed to share the same sense of humour and really enjoyed each other's company. After that first supper together, we talked often on the phone; and when Luke was available to take care of the inn, we would meet for a bite to eat or go to the pictures. Fortunately for me, Bridget had her own car, and she had no problem driving in from Oxford to pick me up. Meanwhile, Luke fell under Jenny's spell, and they began dating. Even when the inn was completely booked and we both needed to be there, I'd remain alone for an hour while Luke would speed off in Dad's car and bring Jenny back for the evening. I thought she was the perfect match for Luke; and after a month, whenever she was at the inn, she would help out at the reception desk and encourage me to take some time out for myself.

Luke and I were doing our best to prove we were good innkeepers, and Mum and Dad kept their distance but were always available if we needed them to guide us whenever we had an issue we couldn't resolve. Gradually, we realised that we both really enjoyed what we were doing; and at the beginning of August, we approached Mum and Dad and told them we were willing to take over permanently. They were elated, but Dad wanted to know exactly what had made us come to that decision. I looked at Luke before answering, "I can't really speak for Luke, but I like the feeling of independence it gives me and I really enjoy dealing with the guests."

Luke nodded in agreement. "I feel the same way as sis, but we ought to tell you that we've talked about making some changes."

Dad frowned. "What kind of changes?"

"Well, we want to expand the services. Instead of just offering breakfast, we're considering providing supper and also a boxed lunch."

Mum's eyes widened in surprise. "My goodness, that's quite a change. Do you realise how much extra work that would be?"

Luke continued, "Yes, but it will bring in a lot more money, especially if we apply for a license to serve wine and beer with supper, then we'll be able to afford more help, including a proper chef."

"You're really serious about this, aren't you?" Dad remarked.

"Yes, we are," Luke said. I think sis and I can make a good living out of the inn, and we want to be sure that you and Mum reap some of the benefits."

"There's no need for that, Lucius," Mum said, shaking her head.

"Yes, there is," Luke replied. "You've run the inn for a long time, and you can't just give it up without expecting something in return."

Mum hesitated and then said, "Maybe your Dad and I were being a little hasty. I've been thinking about this a lot since we first brought up the subject of you taking over. What if either one of you wants to get married? How are you going to handle that?"

I waited for Luke to answer. "We'll work something out. There's no reason why one of us would have to leave because there's plenty of space."

"But what if you have a family? It's bound to get a bit crowded," Mum persisted.

Luke laughed. "You worry too much, Mum. Nana's room still isn't being used, and we can always add some more living space onto the back of the inn. Anyway, we aren't expecting any rug rats around here in the near future."

Two weeks later, that remark came back to haunt me.

Chapter Fifty-Eight

I couldn't believe how well Luke adjusted to being back at home without having any recollection of the last few years of his life. Even his childhood memories were few and far between, although they were slowly coming back to him. One day, he even mentioned getting in touch with Jimmy again, and I was enthusiastic about it; but when he tried to contact him, he discovered that Jimmy had moved to Glasgow to work in his uncle's auto repair shop. His decision to contact Jimmy encouraged me to ring Becky, but I was shocked to learn that she had married Jordan and disappointed to learn that she too had moved away and was now living in Bournemouth. Now my only close friend was the girl I had just met, and I thanked heaven for Bridget every day because she made me laugh a lot and I enjoyed her stories about the men she was dating. It didn't seem to matter whether they were young, old, rich, poor or ugly, she just liked having a good time. When I asked her if she slept with them all, she just giggled and said it depended how much she'd had to drink. Luke thought she was a bit of a floozy, but he couldn't help liking her all the same, and he didn't dare say anything negative to Jenny about her because she absolutely adored her sister

A week after we told Mum and Dad that we wanted to take over running the inn permanently, they informed us they had found the house they had been looking for in High Wycombe and would be moving there in mid-September. We both knew they had been out house hunting nearly every day, but it was still a shock to learn that we would soon be on our own, and we were nervous, to say the least. Dad decided that he was going to buy a brand-new car and leave his old one behind so that we would have some means of transportation. Luke was elated but suggested that I learn to drive because he had no intention of running all the errands himself.

I was wondering how Marcy was going to react to all the changes going on at the inn and decided to talk to her about it. She was a really hard worker but very shy and hardly ever spoke; so when Luke and I approached her together, I wasn't sure if she would be entirely forthright with us. I was surprised when she appeared to be really pleased that we were taking over, and Mum had already told her about the plans we had for expanding the services, but she was a little anxious about her job and hoped we would keep her on staff. We assured her that we had no intention of letting her go, and when Luke said, "You're very important to us, Marcy. We couldn't run this place without you," she turned scarlet and couldn't look him in the eyes. Luke looked really puzzled until later when I told him that she had always had a crush on him, but he had never believed it.

The very next day, when I accompanied Luke to the store to purchase some provisions, we passed a billboard on the way that caused me to gasp. It was an advertisement for *Moll Flanders*, which had just opened at a theatre in Oxford. I hadn't heard anything about the film by the end of June, when it was originally supposed to be released, and had forgotten all about it, but now here she was, Pandora, ten feet tall, wearing her *Moll Flanders* costume and looking gorgeous. When Luke heard me gasp, he automatically glanced out of the car window and then slowed to a crawl. "Isn't that Pandora James?" he asked.

"Yes," I replied. "Her film just opened in Oxford."

"Wow, she's really something. I can't believe I actually went out with her."

"Now I wish I'd never told you," I said as he sped up again.

"Why? What are you worrying about?"

"Well, you just might get some crazy idea to try and see her, and I hope you don't because she's not good enough for you. Anyway, she's probably forgotten all about you by now. She's had so many men friends."

"Thanks for the vote of confidence, sis."

"Look, you're going out with Jenny now, and I think she's a lovely person. Why do anything to mess up your relationship?"

Luke chuckled. "I have no intention of chasing after any film star even if she is beautiful and probably rich too, but I may just go and see the film. After all, you said I was an extra in it."

I breathed a sigh of relief. "Thank goodness for that," I said, "but as for the film, don't get your hopes up. You're probably on the cutting room floor."

Luke stuck his tongue out at me, but I just grinned back; and later that same day, when I caught him and Jenny making out behind the inn, I knew that Pandora had been buried in the past.

As Mum and Dad started preparing for the move, I became more and more aware of how much I would miss them, and I was dreading the idea of not having Sammy around. "Do you really have to take him with you?" I asked.

"We really do, sweet girl," Dad replied, patting Sammy's head. "He's fifteen and won't be around much longer. We want to make sure that we are there for him all the time, and you'll be too busy for that. There's a huge yard at the back of the house with lots of trees and a park just around the corner. I know he's going to love it there."

I stooped down and put my arms around Sammy's neck. "Maybe we'll get another dog just like him," I said.

Dad shook his head. "There'll never be another dog like Sammy."

Chapter Fifty-Nine

It was the last week in August when it suddenly hit me that I had missed my last period. I had never been regular, so for a moment, I dismissed it as nothing unusual, but later I began to wonder if I was in denial. I began to count backwards to the time when I was with Carlos, and although we had always used protection, I wondered about the one night when we were both really tipsy. Had we been careless? I began to look for other obvious signs and even went on the Internet to find out what symptoms I should be looking for. Relieved that nothing seemed to support my being pregnant, I tried to put it at the back of my mind, but I couldn't help think about a conversation I had with Carlos. I had asked him if he had ever wanted children, and his answer was an emphatic no, and he went on to say that he wasn't cut out to be a father and couldn't imagine raising a child. I hadn't been in touch with Carlos for a month because he was away on his mountain climbing expedition in Argentina, but I still felt connected because I had talked to Ann by telephone, and we had exchanged several e-mails. Just being in touch with someone in Santarem who knew Carlos made me feel that much closer to him, and I longed for the day when I could hear his voice again.

In mid-September, as planned, my parents left for High Wycombe in their brand-new Ford Fiesta, and I cried a river of tears. Even Luke was emotional when we all hugged on the steps of the inn; and when he picked Sammy up in his arms and he licked his face, I thought he was going to lose it. As we watched them drive away, Luke put his arm around me. "It's going to be all right, sis. We're going to make this place into a little gold mine."

"I hope so," I said, still sobbing. "I'm just going to miss them so much."

"Me too," he said. "I'm glad you brought me home. I couldn't have wished for better parents, and if we ever get some time off in the next couple of weeks, we'll go visit them. If not, you can be sure they'll be back here checking up on us, so stop your crying, and let's go inside and have a cup of tea."

Two days after Mum and Dad left, I got the long-awaited telephone call from Carlos. He was excited because the expedition was a great success, and he was anxious to tell me all about it. They had experienced some scary moments, including the time when Ben slipped into a crevasse and had to be rescued, but they had made it to the summit, and they were planning to go climbing again the following year. As I listened to Carlos reliving his adventure on the mountain, I began to feel so far removed from his world that I knew I had to do something about it. Then when he told me he had already spoken to Miguel and was planning to join him and Ann for supper that night, I made a decision. I think Carlos must have sensed my change in mood because he paused and then asked, "What's wrong, Ariel? You're not saying anything."

I sighed, "I just miss everyone there, especially you."

"I miss you too. Surely you know that?"

"I know but you're so far away you might as well be on another planet. I'm not sure if I'll ever see you again, and I have to be honest, it may be better if we just cut all ties with each other."

There was silence for a moment, and then Carlos said, "I don't think you really mean that. I think you're just feeling a little low today. Why don't you tell me what's been going on there? I heard from Miguel that your parents found a house, and they were due to move there around this time. How are you and Luke feeling about that?"

"They already left a couple of days ago, and Luke and I are doing okay. Look, Carlos, what's the point in all this? I just don't think I can handle this long-distance relationship anymore."

There was an edge to Carlos's voice when he spoke. "Did you suddenly decide this, or have you been thinking about it all the time I was away?"

"Believe it or not, I've been longing to hear from you, but when you were telling me about the expedition and your plans to go back again, it just confirmed the fact that I don't fit into your life and never will. I love you, Carlos, but I need to move on."

"Surely we can remain friends, Ariel? You're important to me, and I don't want to lose you."

"You've already lost me," I whispered.

Carlos paused. "I'll call you again in a few days. Maybe you'll feel differently then."

"No, please don't. It just makes it so much harder to let go. I'm sorry, but I have to ring off now, one of my guests needs to speak to me."

"I don't believe you, and I'm still going to phone you again. I hope you take my call."

"Don't count on it," I said and hung up the receiver.

For the next week, I stewed over what I had done and my sombre mood took its toll on Luke and even Marcy. Luke was sympathetic but thought I had done the right thing and did his best to cheer me up. As the days passed and I didn't hear from Carlos again, I was both relieved and saddened; and by the end of the second week, I accepted the fact that he had gone from my life forever. The only way I managed to cope was by throwing myself into the job of running the inn; but when I began to feel exhausted, Luke suggested I should take a few days off. I just couldn't do that because I needed to keep busy. Eventually, I got to the point where I felt really sick; and after speaking to Mum, I decided to pay Dr. Rourke a visit. He had been our family physician for as long as I could remember and was now in his early seventies. I wondered how long he would be able to keep up his practice and didn't look forward to the day he retired. He had always been very thorough; and this time, it was no different. He asked me a lot of questions as he took my vital signs; but when he looked me straight in the eyes and asked, "Do you think you could be pregnant?" I just knew the answer. Every time it had crossed my mind, after the first time I had considered the possibility, I just tossed the thought aside. I just couldn't accept the fact that I could be carrying Carlos's child.

When I nodded at Dr. Rourke with tears in my eyes, he put his hand on my arm and in a very gentle voice said, "We need to make sure, and once we know how far along you are, we can talk about what you want to do."

Tests confirmed that I was fourteen weeks pregnant, and now I had to decide whether I really wanted this baby. I knew Mum would come running back the minute she found out, so I decided not to tell her or Dad. An abortion was still possible, and then my parents need never know, but I couldn't imagine destroying the life that was already growing inside me. I had to talk to someone, and the only person I knew who I could rely on was Luke.

Chapter Sixty

It was just after ten o'clock, and all of the guests had retired for the night when Luke locked the front door and asked me if I'd like some lemonade or milk before we went to bed ourselves. I knew this would be the perfect opportunity to talk to him, so I suggested we take our drinks into the garden. I convinced him it would be a lot pleasanter than sitting in the kitchen, especially as it was an unusually warm and clear evening. If the truth be told, I knew I would feel more comfortable giving him my news when I was sitting in the shadows and not under a bright fluorescent light. When we were settled outside, Luke looked up at the sky and sighed, "Look at the moon and all those stars, sis. I wonder if it's as clear in Santarem today."

"You really miss it, don't you," I asked.

"Yes, in lots of ways I do, but I like it here too. I remember so much now from when I was younger, and we always had a lot of fun. I wouldn't mind going back there one day to see Ann. She was so good to me, and I keep meaning to e-mail her, but I just never seem to get around to it. Incidentally, I know you said you'd broken up with Carlos, but have you heard from him at all?"

I looked down as I answered, "I cut off all contact with him. I told you, it was just too difficult carrying on a long-distance relationship."

Luke started to respond, but I reached out and laid my hand gently on his arm. "That's why what I'm about to tell you has to stay here in Abingdon."

In spite of the lack of light, I could see Luke frown. "What is it? Are you sick? Is that why you've been feeling so tired lately?"

I shook my head. "No, I'm not sick. I'm pregnant."

There was silence for a moment, and then Luke scooted over to sit beside me on the bench and put his arm around me. "Oh, sis, what are you going to do? Obviously this is Carlos's baby. Surely you're going to tell him?"

"No, I'm not going to tell him, and you can't either. He doesn't ever have to know about it."

"Wait a minute, are you telling me you're going to have an abortion?"

I shook my head again. "No, I thought about it, but I can't do it. I'm going to have the baby and bring it up on my own."

"Have you really thought this through? It's not going to be easy. Maybe if Mum was still here, it would make more sense. I think you need to reconsider and tell Carlos. After all, he deserves to know."

I felt myself start to panic. "No, I don't want him to know. There's no future with him. He lives thousands of miles away, and he already told me he isn't cut out to be a father. I absolutely forbid you to tell him, or Ann. You have to promise me you'll do as I ask."

Luke removed his arm from around my shoulder and took my hand. "You have my word, sis, and I'll help you all I can. We can put our plans to expand our services on hold so that you won't have even more work to do. By the way, when is the baby due?"

"The end of February, but I don't want you to delay all the plans we made. We can still hire a cook to take care of supper service, but maybe we can wait before adding more rooms."

Luke nodded. "Okay, we'll talk about it tomorrow. Right now, I think you should drink up and then get to bed. You need to take good care of yourself, especially now that I'm going to be an uncle."

I couldn't help grinning. "Uncle Luke, I never thought I'd see the day. Just imagine, Mum and Dad are going to be grandparents."

"Speaking of Mum and Dad, when are you going to tell them?"

"Well, I'd like to avoid telling them on the telephone. If we can get Marcy to take over on Sunday afternoon, when it's quiet, perhaps we can visit them for an hour or two, then we can see the house and I can tell them my news."

Luke looked thoughtful for a minute. "I don't think asking Marcy to do that would be fair. She's a bit of a mouse, and it's her day off. Obviously you can't go on your own because I'll have to drive you. What if I asked Jenny? She's been here quite a bit, and I'm sure she can take care of any guests and answer the telephone?"

"That sounds like a good idea. I'm sure Jenny will do it if she's available and if not maybe Bridget can do it."

Luke grunted. "Huh, I'll make sure Jenny is available. I like Bridget, but she's a bit of a flake."

I couldn't help laughing. "I have to agree, but she's a lot of fun and I enjoy her company. I haven't been in a very good mood lately, and she always manages to put a smile on my face."

"Well, I know Jenny thinks the world of her sister, and you know what?"

"What?"

"I think the world of mine."

Jenny was more than happy to help out, so we rang my parents to tell them we were coming for a visit on Sunday. They were thrilled, but a little uncertain about leaving Jenny in charge until we managed to convince them that she was more than capable. I had asked Luke not tell a soul about the baby until I told Mum and Dad, and I promised him I'd tell Jenny and Bridget myself after we got back from High Wycombe. I was excited about seeing the new house; but on Sunday, as we got closer to our destination, I grew more and more apprehensive about how Mum and Dad would react to my news. We turned the corner onto Bridle Crescent, and I caught sight of the house. I had expected to see a bungalow, one level without a lot of character, but this house was exactly what Mum had always longed for. It was reminiscent of the Tudor period, with a steeply pitched roof, tall narrow doors and windows with small diamond shaped panes. I could hardly wait to see inside. No wonder Mum had been so secretive about it; she wanted to surprise us. We pulled into the driveway, and Mum came running out of the front door, followed by Sammy, who raced past her and practically bowled me over as I stepped out of the car. There was a lot of hugging and kissing and then Mum said, "Your Dad had to take a chair he just finished making over to a neighbour's house but he'll be back in a few minutes."

I was disappointed that he wasn't there when we arrived, but Mum took this opportunity to show Luke and me through the house, and I was impressed. When they left the inn, they only took their bedroom furniture and a few supplies they would need for the kitchen, but they had already completely furnished the living room with a sofa, wing chairs, tables, plants, lamps and some wonderful landscape paintings. The only thing missing was a large area rug to tie it all together, although the dark wooden floors were prefect in my opinion. I was so proud of what they had accomplished in such a short time. Once we had toured the whole house, as well as the back garden, which was huge and bordered with towering oak trees, Mum settled us at the kitchen table and insisted we have something to eat, even though it was the middle of the afternoon. She set out a traditional English tea with cucumber sandwiches, scones with raspberry jam and Devonshire cream; and just as we were about to tuck in, I heard the front door open, and Sammy ran out of the room. "There's your father," Mum said.

Luke and I looked up expectantly; and a moment later, we were embraced in a group hug. "How's my sweet girl?" Dad asked. "And how are you, my boy? It's so good to see you both. Has your mother shown you the house?"

"Yes," Luke replied as we sat down at the table again. "We really like it and can't believe what you've done with the living room already."

Dad chuckled. "You can credit your mother for that. She had me out every day, shopping for furniture. I thought my legs would give out."

Mum rolled her eyes. "You can stop your blarney, Casey Regan. You enjoyed it as much as I did."

"Oh? What about the arguments we had about colours?" Dad said, winking at me. "Your mother wanted a blue sofa, and I wanted green."

"I see you won," Luke said, giving him a thumbs-up.

We continued talking about the house; and then suddenly, Dad asked how we were progressing with our plans for the inn, and that's when I looked at Luke, and he nodded. "Well, I have some news," I said almost in a whisper, "and now Luke wants to hold off with our plans for a while."

Mum looked at me and frowned. "What is it, Ariel? Aren't you feeling well? You do seem a little pale."

Luke reached over and squeezed my hand. "Go on, sis," he said.

I looked down at the table. "There's no easy way to tell you this, but I'm almost four months pregnant."

There was silence for what seemed like an eternity, and then Mum got up and came to sit beside me. "Is this Carlos's baby?" she asked.

I nodded and glanced at Dad, who hadn't moved or uttered a word. Mum put her arm around me. "Why didn't you tell us about this before?"

"I think I was in denial for quite a while, but then I began to feel so tired that I just had to find out and Dr. Rourke confirmed it."

Finally, Dad spoke up. "What does this Carlos have to say about this?"

"He doesn't know, and I'm not going to tell him."

Dad rose from his chair, and I was surprised to see him looking cross. "Why not? He has to accept responsibility. You can't let him get away with this."

Luke raised his hand to stop Dad from saying any more. "Cool it, Dad. Let Ariel explain."

Dad sat down again, but he perched on the edge of his chair as he waited for me to continue. "This wasn't a casual fling. I fell

in love with Carlos, and we were living together for practically
the whole time I was in Santarem. We both knew it wouldn't
be a permanent relationship, and Carlos never wanted to be a
father. This was purely and simply an accident, and to expect
him to be responsible is out of the question. Not only that, I
don't want to be tied to a man who isn't totally committed to
me. Carlos lives in a different world, thousands of miles away,
and so you're going to have to accept my decision, Dad."

"Have you heard from him since you found out?" Mum
asked.

"Yes, but I had already told him it was over and not to
ring me or e-mail me again. I don't think he believes me at
this point, but if I keep ignoring him, he'll eventually get the
message."

Dad was shaking his head. "I'm not happy with this, my girl.
It isn't right, and now, to make matter worse, your mother and
I aren't there to take care of you."

"I'm there to take care of her, so you have no need to
worry," Luke said.

For the next half hour, we went on discussing the baby
and all of the changes that were about to take place, and I was
beginning to feel exhausted. Eventually, Mum intervened. "I
think Ariel's had enough. Let's just change the subject. Maybe
Luke can tell us about Jenny. We only met her briefly, and I'd
like to know more about her."

Luke was more than happy to oblige, and I relaxed as the
attention was taken off of me, but I couldn't help noticing that
Dad still looked tense and wasn't his usual charming self. At five
o'clock, I suggested we should leave; and as we walked out onto
the driveway, Mum looked me up and down and remarked,
"You're hardly showing at all. I would never have guessed you
were pregnant. You take after me, Ariel. I was the same way
with both you and Luke."

"It's all in the genes," I said, giving her a hug.

As we drove away, Sammy chased after us, and Mum waved
at us like a crazy lady, but Dad just stood there with a strange
expression on his face. I had always been his sweet girl, and
now I wondered if that had suddenly changed.

When we arrived back at the inn, we checked to make sure that Jenny hadn't run into any problems and were surprised to discover that not only had she taken two new bookings for the following month but was already in the process of preparing supper. I had no idea what a good cook she was until I tasted her lasagne, made with roasted peppers, zucchini and mushroom sauce. "This is wonderful," I remarked. "Are you a vegetarian, Jenny?"

She smiled. "No, I'm not actually, but there wasn't any ground beef, so I made do with what I could find."

I looked at Luke and winked. "Maybe we should hire Jenny as our chef."

"Sounds like a plan," he responded nonchalantly.

Jenny didn't comment, and I had only made the remark in jest, so I decided to drop the subject, although I wondered what plans she had for the future.

After we were through eating, I helped with the dishes and then asked Jenny if she would join Luke and me for a glass of wine, as I had some news I wanted to share. I thought I would be nervous confiding in someone who I considered almost a stranger, but I was perfectly calm and surprised at her reaction. The first thing she did was to congratulate me and tell me how fortunate I was. Then she asked me all the normal questions. When was the baby due? Did I know if it was a boy or girl? I got caught up in her enthusiasm; and for the first time, I felt a glimmer of excitement at the thought of becoming a mother. "Thank you for being so thoughtful," I said. "You never asked me who the father is."

"It's none of my business, but I just assumed it was the man you met when you were in Brazil."

"You assume correctly. It's Carlos, but he isn't going to be involved with this child in any way."

Jenny glanced at Luke. "I'm sure whatever you've decided will be best for you and the baby, but you'll need a lot of help in the beginning."

"I'm going to help," Luke said. "Ariel won't be alone."

"I want to help too," Jenny retorted with enthusiasm. "I love babies. I worked as a candy striper at the Children's Hospital in Oxford for two years. It was an amazing experience."

I learned a great deal about Jenny that evening and was especially pleased that Luke had met someone who had a good heart and obviously cared a great deal about others. I couldn't help comparing her to Pandora; and in doing so, it reminded me that I still hadn't seen *Moll Flanders*, and that was one film I had no intention of missing. I decided to ring Bridget and ask her if she wanted to have lunch with me sometime in midweek and also go to the matinee. I wanted to share my news with her, so I asked Jenny to keep it a secret until her sister had been told.

Bridget was eager to see me, so after arranging with Luke to stay behind with Marcy, on the following Wednesday I took the bus into Oxford and met her for lunch at the Grand Café, on the High Street. She was her usual bubbly self, and I was beginning to wonder if I would have the opportunity to tell her about the baby when suddenly there was a scream from a table to the left of us. We observed a child who looked to be about two years old struggling to get out of a high chair and making a big fuss at the same time. "Oh oh, just what we need," Bridget whispered. "Why do people bring their brats into a restaurant like this?"

"Perhaps it's the one time they can get out of the house," I shot back.

Bridget shook her head. "I'm never having any kids. They're too much trouble and messy too. Imagine having to change diapers. Ugh."

"So I guess you won't be around to help me when my baby is born?" I asked, watching her expression closely.

She frowned and then replied, "Well, I hope that day is a long way off so that I can get used to the idea."

"How about five months?" I asked. "Does that give you enough time?"

I watched as Bridget's mouth dropped open, and then she reached across the table and grabbed my hand. "You're kidding, right?"

I just shook my head and grinned, and she released my hand and then slumped down in her chair. "When did this happen?"

"I think that's pretty obvious," I replied.

Bridget wanted to know all the details of my affair with Carlos; and even though she had no desire to be a mother herself, I found her surprisingly supportive. By the time we left the restaurant, I was relaxed and looking forward to seeing *Moll Flanders*. I hadn't told Bridget about Luke's relationship with Pandora because I thought she might slip up and mention it in front of him, and I didn't want him to know I had gone to see the film. Any mention of Pandora now, especially with all the talk of the baby on the way, might have triggered his memory, and he might recall that she had aborted his child. I didn't want him to go through all that pain again.

I had to admit, after seeing the film, that Pandora was amazing as Moll. She was already receiving rave reviews in the press, and there was talk of an Oscar nomination. I was transfixed as I sat watching her because she lit up the screen, not only with her acting ability but also with her beauty. Bridget raved over her performance as she drove me back home, and I had to bite my tongue because I could just imagine her reaction if I told her she had stayed at the inn and actually dated Luke.

The very next day, there was another e-mail from Carlos, but I deleted it without reading it. Then two days later, Luke called me to the telephone; and when he wouldn't tell me who it was, I walked away. I figured that Carlos would eventually give up; but three weeks later, I received a letter from him, and my curiosity got the better of me. He begged me to contact him and repeated over and over that he missed me, even suggesting that I return to Santarem to be with him. I must have read that letter three or four times before slowly tearing it into shreds and breaking down sobbing. I knew I still loved him, but I had my baby to think about.

By Christmas, I had gained twenty pounds and felt fat and unattractive even though everyone else said I looked marvellous. Marcy had been a real trooper and taken on a lot more chores, and Luke had done everything in his power to make things easier for me. On several weekends, Dad had shown up to do some of the heavy work, and Mum sometimes came with him to help out too. We decided to make the holiday really special that year and invited Jenny and Bridget and their parents for Christmas dinner. I had never met Mr. and Mrs. Kerrigan before and found them to be a charming couple who owned a small book shop in Oxford. I had always loved to read, so I was looking forward to seeing them and hoped to get an invitation to visit the shop and browse through the shelves of classics that Jenny had told me about. Mum had prepared dinner, with my help, and we sat down to the traditional turkey feast with all the trimmings and a wonderful assortment of desserts, including a brandy pudding, pumpkin pie and mince tarts. Everyone appeared to enjoy the day; but after all of the Kerrigans left, I noticed that Sammy had been very quiet and had ignored any of the turkey scraps we had put down for him. I was worried. "Do you think he's sick, Dad?" I asked.

Dad stooped down and stroked Sammy's head. "You've got to remember, Ariel, he's fifteen now, so he's pretty old. I don't expect him to be with us much longer."

"Don't say that, Dad," I said, kneeling down and cradling Sammy in my arms.

I had got used to not having Sammy around all the time, but I still got great joy out of seeing him when Mum and Dad came to visit, and I couldn't bear the idea of not seeing him ever again. When my parents left the next day, I settled Sammy in the backseat of the car, covered him with a blanket and watched with tears in my eyes as they drove away. Two days later, Sammy was gone. He died peacefully in his sleep, and I was grateful he hadn't suffered. Up until the last few days, he had been the wonderful dog we had always known, playful, loyal and affectionate. Luke did his best to comfort me as I grieved, but I know he was grieving too.

During the week after Christmas, I received two more letters from Carlos; but this time, I didn't read them. I just threw them onto the fire in the lounge and watched them burn. Luke shook his head when he saw me, but he knew from the look on my face that I had made my decision. I couldn't deal with Carlos anymore; now I had to think about my baby.

Early on, I hadn't wanted to know the sex of the little person growing inside me; but as my due date loomed closer, I became anxious to know if I was having a girl. I had always secretly hoped for a girl and was surprised to learn that it was not to be. For a brief moment, I was disappointed, but Mum was so excited that I eventually got caught up in her enthusiasm. Soon we were shopping together for everything blue. We decided to wait to decorate what would become the nursery because as soon as the baby was old enough, Luke would be moving out of his room and moving into Nana's old room at the back of the house. This way, the baby would be close to me upstairs. Mum and I spent what seemed like hours discussing names. She wanted me to continue with the tradition of naming the baby after a character from one of Shakespeare's plays, and I finally gave in after getting Dad and Luke's approval. I was going to name my son Marcus after Marcus Anthony in the play *Anthony and Cleopatra.*

Chapter Sixty-One

Marcus was born at just after midnight on Valentine's Day, which was ironic because later, according to Marcy, a huge bouquet of red roses arrived at the inn from Carlos, but it had nothing to do with the birth of our son. I was three days past my due date when I started to experience a severe backache, and Luke decided to ask Mum and Dad to come and stay with us, as he was sure I was going into labour at any moment. By the time they arrived just a few hours later in the middle of the afternoon, I was getting my first contractions. They only lasted about ten seconds and were fifteen minutes apart, and Mum said there was no reason to panic. Two hours later, I was having stronger contractions every ten minutes, and I started to get anxious, so Mum rang Dr. Rourke. He told us not to rush but suggested we start making our way to the hospital, as there was a lot of snow on the ground, and it could take some time to get there. All four of us piled into the car, and Luke held my hand, telling me just to squeeze real hard when I felt any pain. I was so happy he was with me because he had been helping me practice my breathing exercises for months, and I had no reservations about him being in the delivery room. Years earlier, when Luke and I were born, it still wasn't very common for fathers or other male members of the family to be present at the time of a birth, but times had changed. Nevertheless, Dad still couldn't be persuaded to be there, so he had to sit it out patiently in the waiting room.

I didn't have an easy labour, but there were no complications, and every bit of pain and discomfort I endured was forgotten when I saw Marcus for the first time. He was a big baby, weighing nine pounds six ounces, and had black hair and dark skin just like his father. I thought he was the most beautiful baby I'd ever seen, and Mum was smitten from the first moment. As for Luke, well, he just wanted to hold him and kept muttering, "I'm your uncle Luke."

They kept me in the hospital the next day because I was bleeding quite heavily; but as soon as it was under control, Dr. Rourke discharged me, and I headed home with my son in my arms, grateful in the knowledge that my family was with me. I honestly don't know how I would have coped without them. When I had trouble breastfeeding, Mum would get up in the night and prepare a bottle so that I could sleep; and when Marcus got cranky and wouldn't stop crying, Luke would sing lullabies to him. Dad kept commenting on what a great father Luke would make, and I prayed that it wouldn't trigger Luke's memory of the baby he had lost. I never really understood how deeply Luke had been affected by what Pandora had done; but seeing him with Marcus, it was obvious that he had a paternal instinct that I had no idea existed.

Mum and Dad stayed for three weeks. I think Mum would have liked to have stayed longer, but Dad wanted to get back to his workshop and finish a dining table set he had been making for a neighbour. At first, I was sorry to see them go; but after a day or two, I began to enjoy being left to figure out my role as a new mother and Marcus was already beginning to sleep right through the night. Two or three days a week, Jenny would come over and help Luke; but being off season, there were only four guests at the inn, so there was little to do. When she wasn't helping out, she would fuss over Marcus; and then one night, she confessed that she was longing to have a child of her own. I knew she had been training to be a paramedic, so I took the opportunity to question her about her future. "What about your career? Doesn't a paramedic have to be on call all the time? I would think it would be difficult to look after a child with a job like that."

Jenny lowered her eyes. "I'd give up any thought of a career if I had a baby," she said.

I reached over and grasped her hand. "Look at me, Jenny. Are you in love with my brother?"

She looked up and nodded. "Yes. I know we're both really young, but he's the finest person I've ever met, and I'd like to spend the rest of my life with him."

"Does he know how you feel?"

"I told him I was in love with him, and he said he loved me too, but he hasn't made any commitment."

"I think he needs a little more time. He's been through a lot this last year, and lately he's been so busy with the inn I don't think he's had much time to think about anything else. I do know one thing, Jenny, he thinks the world of you, and just between the two of us, I'd be happy to have you as my sister-in-law."

"Really, Ariel, you mean that?"

I nodded. "Yes, of course, I mean it. You've been such a help around here, and I love the way you are with Marcus. Just hang in there and everything will work out just the way you want it to."

A few months later, at the end of June, on a perfect day when there wasn't a cloud in the sky, I was relaxing in the garden, with Marcus sound asleep in his pram, when Luke showed up and sat down beside me. "Beautiful day, sis," he remarked.

"Mmm . . . it is. I was just sitting here looking at the flowers—they're so pretty."

There was silence for a moment, and then Luke said, "I need to ask you something."

I turned to look at him. "What is it?"

"How do you really feel about Jenny?"

I smiled. "I think she's a lovely person, and I enjoy her company tremendously. Why?"

Luke leaned forward and looked down at the grass. "Because I'm thinking of asking her to marry me."

I put my hand on his shoulder and made him turn towards me. "I think that's wonderful. I couldn't be happier. When are you planning to propose?"

"As soon as I buy a ring. Will you help me pick one out, sis?"

The very next afternoon, leaving Marcy in charge for a couple of hours, Luke and I drove into Oxford with Marcus and stopped in at Beaverbrooks', the jewellers that Mum had recommended. It didn't take long to pick out the perfect ring for Jenny. It was a dainty cluster of small diamonds set in white gold. "Now when are you going to give it to her?" I asked as we drove home.

Chapter Sixty-Two

Once Luke had proposed and Jenny had eagerly accepted, Luke didn't want to wait to get married. The wedding took place in September at Marston United Church in Oxford, with a reception in the Red Room of the Old Bank Hotel. Jenny looked like a dream in a strapless form-fitting silk dress, with flowers in her hair. She had asked me to be a bridesmaid along with her closest friend, Amy, and Bridget was the maid of honour. We all wore dusty rose, ankle-length dresses, and the colour was flattering to each one of us despite the fact that I was so dark, Bridget so fair and Amy a strawberry blonde.

Mr. Kerrington looked proud as he walked Jenny down the aisle, and I could see tears in Luke's eyes as he stood watching and waiting at the altar. I had been worried because he was no longer in touch with Jimmy and all of his other friends had moved away, so I had no idea what he would do about a best man. Luke wasn't concerned; and without hesitation, he announced that the best man, as far as he was concerned, was Dad. And so on that very special day, our father stood alongside Luke at the altar.

There were about forty guests, most of whom were invited by the Kerringtons. On our side, the only people there were a few good neighbours who we'd known for many years; but nevertheless, it was a wonderful evening with delicious food, good music and a lot of dancing. Bridget had invited Parker, someone she'd met just three weeks earlier, and Amy was with her childhood sweetheart, who she'd been engaged to for over a year. I felt a little left out, and I was missing Marcus. I had been reluctant to leave him behind with Marcy, but Mum assured me that she was quite capable of looking after a baby and urged me to relax and enjoy myself.

Immediately after the reception, Luke and Jenny left for their honeymoon in the Canary Islands, and Mum and Dad returned to the inn with me. I was so grateful that they had offered to stay until Luke and Jenny got back; and after a day or two, it seemed just like old times. In midweek, I got another letter from Carlos; and this time, I didn't tear it up or attempt to burn it. I think I was feeling a little lonely and just wanted some reassurance that he was still thinking about me. The letter had taken a while to reach me and was written just before he left on his second journey to Mount Aconcagua. I had forgotten that he had planned to go mountain climbing again and inwardly prayed that he hadn't come to any harm. He told me about a visit he had made to his sister in Australia. He had spent almost a month there but couldn't wait to get back to Santarem. He had also seen Ann and Miguel on a few occasions, and I couldn't help laughing when I read that Bandit had become the proud father of three endearing puppies after a rendezvous with the neighbour's poodle, Coco. The more I read, the more I realised how much I missed him, and I began to regret the way I had cut him out of my life. He insisted that he still loved me and begged me to get in touch with him, and I wanted to so badly, but how could I when I'd never even told him he had a son?

Seeing Luke and Jenny so loving and sweet to each other after they came back from their honeymoon made me feel even more remorseful, and I felt lonelier than ever. They seemed to sense that I was feeling rather low and encouraged me to help them with their ideas for expanding the services at the inn. Jenny was certain that she could provide an evening meal for our guests and suggested that we get a liquor license to maximise the profits. They seemed so enthusiastic, and I was happy to go along with their plans; so the very next day, Luke applied for an alcohol and entertainment license. By Christmas of that year, we were serving a hearty supper to our guests and managing the inn more efficiently than ever. I had to credit Jenny for the smooth transition. She was not only well organised but also practical, creative and very much attuned to the needs of our guests. It wasn't common practice in England to provide cream instead of milk with coffee; but when she discovered that's what Americans expected, she always made sure we had cream on hand to accommodate anyone who preferred it. It was all of the simple little things she did that endeared me to her and the way she doted on Luke, made me appreciate her even more.

Marcus was too young to understand all of the celebrations during the Christmas holidays; but at almost ten months, he was sitting up, crawling and babbling incoherently all the time. He was showered with toys from his doting grandparents as well as Luke, Jenny and Bridget, but he preferred the boxes they came in, like most children his age. The day after Christmas, late in the afternoon, I was watching him and thinking how much he looked like Carlos when Luke announced that there was a special delivery for me and handed me a FedEx package. He grinned as I looked at the label and saw that it was from Brazil; but when I frowned back at him, he backed out of the room and left me to open the package in private.

Inside the dark blue velvet box was the most exquisite diamond pendant in the shape of a heart that I had ever seen, and I was sure it had cost a fortune. Along with the pendant was a small card that simply said, "I am giving you my heart, my little *ganza*, with all my love, Carlos." I took the pendant out of the box and held it in my hand. As I stared at it, I couldn't help wondering why Carlos had sent me such a beautiful and obviously expensive gift this Christmas when the year before, I had only received two letters, which I hadn't even read. Was he missing me as much as I was missing him? Had time and distance made our feelings for each other even stronger? I couldn't stop thinking about him; and a short time later,

Luke came back to find me in tears. He rushed over and sat down beside me. "What's wrong, sis?" he asked, looking really concerned. I passed him the pendant and the note and heard him take in a breath. "Wow, that's some necklace," he said, and then he read the note and reached for my hand. "You have to ring him, sis. It doesn't take a rocket scientist to see that you still love him, and he doesn't look like he's going to give up."

I turned to him, with tears streaming down my face. "But what about Marcus? If I tell Carlos about Marcus now, he may feel trapped or he may never forgive me for not telling him before."

"There's another option. He might be ecstatic to hear that he has a son."

I shook my head. "No, I can't take that chance. There's no way we can be together anyway. He won't want to live here, and I can't move to Brazil."

"Why can't you move to Brazil?"

I looked at Luke in disbelief. "Do you really think I could leave Mum and Dad and you and go thousands of miles away?"

"If you love someone enough, you'd do anything to be with them, wouldn't you?"

I shook my head again. "I don't want to talk about this anymore."

Luke got up and put his hand on my shoulder. "Okay, sis, but I'm here to listen anytime you change your mind."

Marcus turned one year old on the following Valentine's Day, and he was beginning to stand, creep up the stairs, wave bye-bye and finally understood the word no. I loved him so much, but I felt like my life was slipping away, and I was beginning to suffer mild periods of depression. I was pretty adept at hiding my mood swings from Mum and Dad when they came to visit, but Luke and Jenny weren't fooled. Bridget had just broken up with her latest boyfriend, and so Jenny encouraged me to get-together with her sister and spend a night out in Oxford. When Bridget invited me to go to the Bridge Club on the weekend, I did my best to get out of it. I just wanted to stay home and wallow in my misery, especially as I hadn't heard from Carlos since Christmas and was disappointed not to get roses again on Valentine's Day. Bridget wasn't taking no for an answer and informed me that she would come and pick me up at eight o'clock on Saturday and to make sure I put my dancing shoes on. The last thing in the world I wanted to do was dance; but the very next day, Jenny was in my room, scouring through my closet, looking for something sexy for me to wear. She finally gave up and raced off to her own room, insisting that she knew exactly what she was looking for. I was surprised when she came back with a pair of black capri pants and a sleeveless white top, which was cut really low in the back. "I can't wear that," I protested. "It won't fit me, and who wears pants to go dancing?"

Jenny sighed, "Oh, Ariel, you've lost a lot of weight, and I know it will fit. Just try it on. As for not wearing pants, you really are out of touch."

I stripped off my jeans and tee; and after slipping into the outfit, I had to admit it looked really good on me. "See, I told you so," Jenny said, grinning. "Now if you wear your black sandals and these, you'll look fabulous."

I glanced at the silver drop earrings she was holding. "Mmm, those are really lovely," I remarked.

"Luke gave them to me, but he won't mind me lending them to you. You know he's really concerned about you, Ariel."

I nodded. "I know but tell him not to worry. I'll be okay, I promise."

Chapter Sixty-Three

I had never been to the Bridge before; in fact, other than the time I was seeing Zach, I had led a very sheltered life. Even in Brazil, Carlos and I spent most evenings at home or at Ann's and only occasionally went out to eat. I was never really comfortable in a partylike atmosphere; and as we drew up outside the club, I got really anxious. "You hop out and get in the queue," Bridget said, "and I'll park around the corner."

As I stepped onto the pavement, I felt really self-conscious; and when one of the young men near the front door of the club let out a wolf whistle, I felt the blood rushing to my head, and I knew my face had turned scarlet. After that, with head down, I raced to the end of the queue and tried to make myself as inconspicuous as possible. Just a few minutes later, I saw Bridget strolling towards me and obviously getting a kick out of the attention she was getting. It wasn't surprising because considering she was a little overweight, she looked amazing in a white mini dress, cropped black jacket and four-inch heels. "Aren't you a bit chilly?" I asked, looking down at her bare legs, as she stood beside me.

"Never let them see you sweat, and never let them see you shiver," she replied.

I laughed. "Did you just make that up?"

She just grinned back at me and then turned to bat her eyelashes at the man behind us, who looked like a younger version of Nicholas Cage. When we eventually got inside the club, I was overwhelmed by the flashing lights, the music and the crowd. The Bridge was the most popular club in Oxford; and even though it had two floors to accommodate a lot of people, it was always packed. Somehow, after what seemed like forever, Bridget managed to get us two glasses of wine, and we made our way to the edge of the dance floor, where people jostled for space. I was already wishing I was back at home when Bridget handed me her glass and said, "Hold this and don't go anywhere. I'll be back." Then I saw her being dragged off onto the dance floor by a short, dark-skinned man, and she vanished into the crowd. I stood there like a ninny waiting for the music to stop and for Bridget to come back, but she never did. In the meantime, I was hit on by several men; and at first I politely declined their request for a dance, but as my anxiety grew, I found myself snapping at anyone who so much as spoke to me. Eventually, I just gave up and worked my way back to the coat check, where I retrieved my jacket, and then walked out onto Bridge Street. Dad always said I was prepared for anything, and I had to admit that my habit of never leaving home without money in my purse proved to be a blessing that night. There were a number of taxis waiting at the curb; and a moment later, I was on my way home.

Luke was in the reception area when he heard the taxi pull into the driveway. He was curious to see who it was, as he knew the guests were all in their rooms, and his mouth dropped open when he saw it was me. "Sis, what on earth happened?" he asked as he met me at the front door.

"Bridget dumped me for some guy," I snapped back.

"Come on," he said, putting his arm around me, "let's go in the kitchen. I'll make you a cup of tea, and you can tell me all about it."

I spent the next few minutes telling Luke and Jenny all about my miserable time at the club; and when I finished, I burst into tears. Jenny was doing her best to console me when we heard the phone ringing, and Luke went to answer it. It was Bridget, wondering if I had shown up at home; but when she said she wanted to speak to me, Luke told her I'd already gone up to bed. I felt as though I never wanted to speak to her again. Later, as I held Marcus in my arms, I felt more depressed than ever.

By the end of April, when the world around me was starting to turn green again and everyone else was looking forward to summer, Luke insisted that I get some professional help. I had lost interest in food and had lost even more weight, and I could no longer hide my condition from Mum and Dad, so I had made excuses not to see them for almost three weeks. Luke made an appointment for me with Dr. Rourke, hoping that he could recommend someone who would be able to help me, but I never kept the appointment. It was after that, for the first time, that I can remember Luke got really cross with me, and that made me even more depressed. I think he was at his wits end, and that's when he decided there was only one way to get his sister back.

Chapter Sixty-Four

At the beginning of June, when everyone was enjoying the bank holiday, my whole life changed. It was the perfect day with a clear blue sky, above-average temperature and no humidity. That morning, Jenny had persuaded me to sit outside in the garden with Marcus and get some sun, and she had tried to tempt me with her freshly baked banana nut muffins, but I just didn't feel like eating. I looked at Marcus, who was sitting on a blanket with his favourite teddy bear, and thought how attached he had become to it. He was a good child, only on rare occasions subject to a temper tantrum if he was frustrated, like when he was learning how to use a spoon, and he was adventurous, wanting to climb up onto anything he could reach. He was handsome too and looking more like his father every day.

At noon, after Marcus fell asleep, I put down the book I had been trying to read and closed my eyes. I so desperately wanted to escape for a while; but after a few moments, I heard Luke's voice. "Sis, are you awake?"

At first, I decided not to react. I just wanted to be left alone; but when he put his hand on my shoulder and asked again, "Sis, please wake up, there's someone here to see you." I slowly opened my eyes. It took me a few seconds to focus; and when I looked up, Luke was leaning over me.

"What is it?" I whispered.

"There's someone here to see you," he repeated and then took a few steps backwards.

I turned in my chair and gasped as my hands flew to my mouth. It was Carlos. I tried to get up, but I felt faint, and Luke rushed over to help me. "Sis, are you okay?"

I nodded and slowly got to my feet and then turned to look at Carlos, who was standing motionless, staring at me. "What are you doing here?" I whispered.

He took a tentative step forward. "I couldn't stay away any longer," he answered.

Luke took my hand. "I asked him to come, sis," he said.

I looked at him in disbelief. "Why, what right did you have to do that?"

Carlos took another step forward. "Don't blame Luke, Ariel. He' s been very concerned about you. He thought he was doing the right thing."

"What, by bringing you here?" I cried, suddenly feeling trapped in a situation I never thought I would have to face.

Luke released my hand. "I'll leave you two to talk," he said.

I scowled at him as he walked away and then looked back at Carlos. "What do you want from me?"

He slowly shook his head. "I love you, and I think you love me. We can work things out, Ariel, but we need to talk."

Suddenly, I heard a whimper behind me and realised that Marcus was beginning to wake up. I glanced at Carlos and saw that he was looking past me at Marcus lying on the blanket. "Why didn't you tell me?" he asked.

"For the very reason that you're here now," I snapped. "Luke told you about the baby, and you felt obligated to come."

"I came because I love you even though you've always pushed me away. When Luke told me you were sick, I had already decided to come here, but when he told me I had a son, I got on the next plane."

"So now what?" I said angrily. "Are we going to play happy families?"

Carlos crossed the space between us and wrapped his arms around me. "Please, my little ganza, don't do this."

My knees started to give way, and I felt all the anger drain out of me and began to sob while Carlos continued to hold me and tried to console me. When I finally stopped crying, he looked into my eyes and said, "May I see my son now?"

I slipped out from his embrace and picked Marcus up. He had just opened his eyes; and when he looked up at Carlos, he looked a little fearful. "It's all right," I whispered to him, "there's no need to be afraid."

Carlos held out both arms. "May I hold him?"

I didn't answer. I just passed Marcus to his father; and when I saw their faces just inches apart, I was struck at how much they resembled each other. "He looks exactly like you," I remarked.

Carlos looked down at his son. "I don't know anything about him," he said. "How old is he? What's his name?"

"He's sixteen months old now, and his name is Marcus."

Carlos smiled. "Another Shakespeare character, I gather?"

I smiled back. "Yes, it was Mum's idea. She wanted to carry on the tradition."

"He's a fine-looking boy, and I'd like to be a father to him if you will let me."

"And how do you propose to do that?"

Carlos gently placed Marcus back on the blanket then took my hand and led me back to the bench at the other end of the garden. "Come and sit down," he said.

I had the feeling that I was about to learn something about Carlos that I wasn't aware of before, and I was filled with trepidation. Once we were seated, he continued to hold my hand and paused for a moment before speaking. "I haven't been entirely honest with you, Ariel," he said.

My heart seemed to leap into my throat. "What is it, are you married? Do you have a family somewhere back in Brazil?"

When he reacted by throwing back his head and laughing, I didn't know what to think. "No, of course not," he said. "It's nothing like that. I told you I had never been married, and I had no desire to be a father, but when I heard about Marcus all that changed."

"What are you trying to tell me? Please don't keep me in suspense."

"Living in Santarem was just a temporary stop on my journey and fishing was just a hobby. It was something to do in between climbing mountains or travelling the world. As you already know, I'm independently wealthy, and with the money from my parent's estate, I made a killing on the stock market and bought quite a bit of real estate in São Paulo. Over the years, I've become a very rich man, and now I want to share my good fortune with you and my son. I'd like us to live in São Paulo, and I kept my parent's villa in São Sebastião, so now we can spend time there too. I didn't tell you all this before because in the past, I've been involved with people who, I discovered, were more interested in my money than in me. It didn't seem to matter to you that I didn't have a real job and lived such a simple life, but before I could tell you the truth about myself, you were gone."

I squeezed his hand and leaned my head on his shoulder. "I fell in love with the wonderful man that you are, Carlos, and whether you had money or not wouldn't have made any difference."

"Does that mean you'll come back to Brazil with me?"

I sat up straight and sighed, "I don't know. What will you do in São Paulo? How can I be sure that you won't get restless and just take off?"

"I already had plans to go back to São Paulo before I got the call from Luke. I told you about my friend, Ben. Well, we've been thinking about starting up an agency specialising in mountain climbing. Tourists come from all over the world to climb the Andes, and they're willing to pay top dollar."

"Wouldn't that mean you'd be gone all the time? Because if it does, Marcus and I might as well be on our own."

"No, it doesn't mean that. I might go on one or two short trips a year just to keep my hand in but no more. I want to spend my time with you, and I want to watch our son grow up."

I sat thinking for what seemed like minutes while Carlos remained silent, and then I shook my head. "How am I ever going to leave Luke and my parents? São Paulo is so far away."

"You can visit them whenever you want to, and they can visit you. It's only a twelve-hour flight, and they can come every year if they like, all expenses paid."

I turned and faced him. "I do love you. In fact, I never stopped loving you, but this is such a big step."

He took my face in his hands and then kissed me gently on the lips, and I felt my heart start to race. I pulled away for just a moment, and then I kissed him back with a passion that had been pent up inside of me for such a long time. When it was over, I whispered, "Please stay with me tonight."

Chapter Sixty-Five

When I crept downstairs early the next morning, I felt a little uncomfortable. Luke and Jenny had already gone to bed when Carlos and I finally came back into the inn from the garden, but I was sure they were aware that he had spent the night in my bed. I could smell the wonderful aroma of fresh coffee as I approached the kitchen and wasn't surprised to see Jenny already preparing breakfast for our guests. She turned around from where she was standing at the counter when she heard me and smiled. "Good morning, Ariel," she said cheerfully.

I decided to take the bull by the horns. "I hope we didn't disturb you last night, Jenny."

"Not at all," she answered. "Is Carlos still sleeping?"

"Yes, but I expect he'll get woken up soon by Marcus."

We continued to chat as though it was the most natural thing in the world for me to have slept with Carlos, and I began to relax; and when Luke joined us, he seemed just as nonchalant about the situation. We were all on our second cup of coffee when I realised that it was past the time that Marcus usually woke up, so I excused myself and ran up the stairs to check on him. When I opened the door to his room and saw that he wasn't in his crib, I felt my heart skip a beat and was about to cry out when I heard a noise. It was Carlos, holding

Marcus in his arms. "Oh, thank heavens," I gasped, "I thought someone had stolen him."

Marcus reached out for me. "Mama," he murmured.

It was the first time he had called me "Mama," and I couldn't wait to tell Luke and Jenny.

After I had fed Marcus and put him in his playpen, Jenny dished up a huge English breakfast and insisted on piling my plate with eggs, sausages, bacon, grilled tomatoes and toast. "We need to fatten you up," she remarked.

I noticed that Luke was very quiet; and then suddenly, he glanced over at Carlos and then at me and said, "So have you talked about your plans for the future?"

I hesitated but I had already made up my mind. "Do you remember telling me, Luke, that I should be willing to do anything to be with the man I loved?"

Luke nodded. "Yes, sis, I remember it very well. I gather this means you're going back to Brazil?"

I reached over and took Carlos's hand. "Yes, we are going to be a family."

After that, both Luke and Jenny had dozens of questions, and then Luke suggested that I should ring Mum and Dad and invite them for a visit so that I could tell them my news face-to-face. The very idea of having to tell my parents that I was moving thousands of miles away was daunting, but there was no way of avoiding it. Two days later, Mum and Dad arrived for a three-day visit. They needed very little persuasion, as they hadn't been back for a few weeks and were anxious to see all of us. I didn't tell them they would be meeting Carlos for the first time and hoped it wouldn't be too much of a shock. Luke and I met them at the front door and walked with them to the reception area, where it was relatively cool, considering that the temperature outside was higher than normal. "Where's Marcus?" Mum asked.

"Oh, he's out in the garden with Jenny," I replied, taking her overnight bag and placing it at the bottom of the stairs.

"Isn't it a little too hot out there?" Dad said.

"It's fine, Dad," Luke answered. "They've only been out there a few minutes. I moved all the chairs into the shade, under that big oak tree. You go on out and say hello, and I'll bring out the lemonade. I'm sure you're both thirsty after the drive here."

Luke left us to go to the kitchen, and we started to walk towards the back door; but before we got there, I reached out and grasped Mum's arm. "Before you go out there, I have something to tell you."

Mum looked alarmed and glanced at Dad. "What is it, sweet girl?" he asked. "You look so thin. Are you ill?"

"No, Dad, I'm fine. I was a little depressed and haven't been eating much, but I'm getting better now."

Mum took my hand. "Then it has to be Marcus. Something's wrong, isn't it?"

I shook my head. "No, nothing like that. I should have warned you when I rang you, but Carlos is here. He's in the garden with Jenny and Marcus."

Mum dropped my hand, and I heard Dad take in a breath. "What is he doing here?" he asked abruptly.

"Luke rang him and asked him to come."

"Why, would he do such a thing? I thought you didn't want anything more to do with him."

"Please, Dad, don't be cross," I begged. "I was so depressed, and when Luke realised I was regretting my decision to cut Carlos out of my life, he took matters into his own hands. Ever since I left Brazil, Carlos has attempted to contact me. It was pretty obvious that he still cared deeply for me, but I just couldn't see any future for us."

"Did he know about Marcus before he arrived here?"

"Yes, Luke told him, and even though he never wanted to be a father, all that has changed now. He loves that little boy, and he wants to take responsibility for him."

Dad started to walk back towards the front door. "Where are you going, Dad?" I called out.

He stopped and turned towards me, and I could see a look of anguish on his face. "I don't think I can deal with this," he said. "You're going to tell me you're going back to Brazil with him, aren't you?"

Mum gasped, "Is that true, Ariel?"

I patted her arm and walked over to Dad, who was standing motionless in the hallway. I took both of his hands in mine. "Please, Dad, come back. You have to understand—I love him, and we're going to be a family. Yes, I'm going back to Brazil, but I'll be less than a day away. You have to listen to our plans, Dad. I'm begging you, don't leave. Come into the garden and meet Carlos. I know the two of you will get along if you just give him a chance."

Mum came towards us and reached out to my dad. "Come along, Casey. Let's at least hear what plans Carlos has for Ariel and Marcus. If this is what she really wants, then we mustn't try to stand in her way."

I was really nervous as we walked out of the back door, but that all changed, and I felt a sense of pride because the moment he saw my parents, Carlos jumped up from his chair and came forward with his hand extended towards my father. "Good morning, Mr. Regan," he said. "I am pleased to meet you." Dad shook his hand rather reluctantly and mumbled something, and then Carlos turned to Mum and gave a nod of his head. "Mrs. Regan, this is a pleasure. I have been looking forward to this moment."

I watched as Mum looked up at Carlos, and then she smiled rather coyly and said, "How lovely to finally meet you. We've heard so much about you."

I glanced over at Jenny and rolled my eyes. "She thinks he's hot," I mouthed.

Jenny, who was holding Marcus, buried her face in his hair to keep from laughing out loud. At that moment, Luke came out with a tray full of glasses and a pitcher of lemonade. "Why don't we all sit down," he suggested as he put the tray on the table.

Marcus was almost asleep, so Jenny laid him down on a blanket; and as we began to gather around the table, Carlos pulled out a chair for Mum, and I saw the slight blush as she sat down. I think Dad might have noticed too because he had an annoyed look on his face; and once we were settled, he didn't waste any time in speaking his mind. "So, young man, I understand you are intending to take my daughter and grandson back to Brazil. I'll be quite honest with you, I'm not happy about this situation."

"Dad, please," I whispered, grasping his arm.

Carlos intervened. "It's perfectly all right, Ariel, your father has a right to know what is going on." He turned to Dad. "Mr. Regan, I know this must have been quite a shock for you, and quite frankly, it's been a shock for me too. I didn't expect to fall in love with your daughter, and when she left Brazil, I tried to forget her, but it was impossible. Then when she wouldn't respond to my messages, I considered coming here, but I had no idea how she would react. When Luke rang me and told me that she regretted cutting me out of her life and that I had a son, I was on the next flight out of Santarem." Dad started to speak, but Carlos raised one hand. "Please allow me to finish, sir. I never imagined being a father, but now that I am, I promise you I'm going to do everything I can to take care of Marcus. You may be concerned about how I will be able to provide for my family, but I promise you, you may set your mind at rest. I have been very fortunate and have considerable wealth, and we have already discussed living in São Paulo so that Marcus will be able to get a good education and Ariel can take advantage of all that the city has to offer."

"And have you discussed marriage too?" Dad asked abruptly.

Carlos looked over at me and then back at my father. "I have to be honest with you, sir," he replied, "we have not yet talked about that, but I am hoping Ariel will agree to become my wife and allow Marcus to take my name."

Dad nodded very slowly. "I see. Well, you appear to have my daughter's best interest at heart, but you must understand how concerned her mother and I are about her being so far away."

I decided it was time I intervened. "It might seem like a long way, Dad, but it's only twelve hours from Heathrow, and Carlos and I want you to visit as often as you want to, and you can stay for as long as you like."

"It sounds like you're planning to leave really soon," Mum said.

I glanced at Carlos, not knowing how to answer. "Actually, Mrs. Regan, we haven't set a date, but I was going to suggest that I return to São Paulo first and have everything ready for Ariel and Marcus."

I felt a sinking in my chest. "We never agreed to that. Why can't we all go together?"

Luke chimed in, "I think Carlos is right, sis. It makes a lot of sense. You would have to stay in a hotel or somewhere like that until you find a house, and it could take some time."

Mum reached over and took my hand. "It's a very sensible idea, Ariel, and I'm sure it won't take Carlos too long to find a suitable home for the three of you."

I sighed, "Well, I suppose you're right, but I don't have to like it."

Mum turned back to Carlos. "So when are you planning on leaving?"

"I was thinking in a week or two so that I can spend some time with Ariel and get to know my son a little better."

Mum looked at me and smiled. "Why don't you let your father and me take Marcus for the next week, and then you and Carlos could go off somewhere by yourselves?"

"Oh, Mum, that would be fabulous, but where would we go?"

"How about the Lake District? It's beautiful this time of the year," Luke suggested.

Chapter Sixty-Six

The time that Carlos and I spent in the Lake District was magical. We stayed at the Ravensworth in Windermere, a wonderful hotel with rooms decorated in the Victorian style but with all the modern conveniences. The weather was glorious, with only one brief shower that soaked us to the skin and had us running for cover. We spent our days, hiking, biking, canoeing, kayaking and my favourite activity, bird watching. There were so many species of birds I had never seen before, such as eagles, falcons and owls.

One day, Carlos went mountain climbing with Jesse, an Australian we met one morning while having breakfast in the hotel dining room. They both found it a little amusing when they discovered that Scafell Pike, the highest mountain in England, was only 3,200 feet, especially as they had both climbed mountains in excess of 20,000 feet. When they returned about six hours later, they claimed it was a walk rather than a climb, although they had to admit that the boulder fields were a bit of a challenge.

Dad had let us use his car rather than take Luke's more unreliable vehicle, so we were able to see a lot of the country, eat in some of the quaintest restaurants and sample the local food like Cumbrian lamb and line-caught codling. By the time we got back to the hotel each night, we were exhausted but not too tired to spend hours making love and talking about the future.

On our way back to Abingdon, I was anxious to tell Mum and Dad all about our holiday. In the days prior to leaving the inn, Carlos had managed to bring about a profound change in Dad's attitude, and now one would think they had actually formed a real friendship. One thing they had in common was fishing; and one day, they spent the whole day together at the edge of the Thames, trolling for chub and bream. They didn't catch anything; but by the time they got home, one would think they had known each other forever. Meanwhile, Mum was totally smitten with Carlos, and Jenny and I found it all very amusing. Even Luke commented on how she seemed to light up when he was around. Then there was Marcy, who still came in to help three days a week. Any fantasies she had about Luke were now transferred to Carlos; and whenever she ran into him, she would blush and lower her eyes. She had no idea that within a week, he would be gone.

The scene at Heathrow, on the day that Carlos left to go back to Brazil, was heartwrenching. Mum and Dad had returned home the day before, and we decided to leave Marcus with Jenny. He was asleep when Carlos kissed him on the cheek and whispered, "Menino adeus doce." A short time later, Luke drove us to the airport. After arriving in the departure lounge, Luke shook hands with Carlos and then made himself scarce. That was typical of my brother; he always seemed to know the right thing to say or do. We had almost an hour to wait, but the time seemed to fly by; and half of the time, I was crying while Carlos tried to assure me that he would send for me as soon as he found a suitable house and had bought enough furniture so that we could be comfortable. I wanted to believe that we would soon be together again, but a small part of my mind kept telling me that he might be leaving for good; and when I saw the plane take off down the runway, I broke down completely.

Thankfully, Luke was there to try and console me and listen to my doubts and fears all the way back to Abingdon. He didn't say too much until we were about a mile from the inn, and then he pulled over to the side of the road and took my hand. "Sis, I know this man. I've watched him with you and Marcus, and believe me, he loves you both, and he's not going to abandon you now. Think about what happened when I rang him and told him how unhappy you were and that he had a son. Did he run in the other direction? No, he got on the first flight and came straight here. I believe that he's an honourable person and a man of his word and he wants you to be a family. I've had conversations with him when you weren't around, and he confided in me, sis. Up until now, his life has been an adventure, but he always felt there was something missing. None of the women he met measured up until you, and he's not going to let you go. I guarantee that within a month, I'll be driving you back to Heathrow, and then I'll be the one that's doing all the crying."

I squeezed his hand and put my head on his shoulder. "How did you get to be so wise? I'm the big sister, and you're supposed to lean on me, not the other way round."

Luke laughed and released my hand and then started to creep back onto the highway. "You seem to forget that you flew all the way to Brazil to find me and bring me home. I would say that you fulfilled your big-sister role."

Less than two days later, Carlos rang me from the Gran Estanplaza Hotel in São Paulo, and all my fears went away. He had already contacted a real-estate agent and was going to be looking at several houses before the weekend. He would be moving out of the hotel the next day to stay with Ben and begin working on the details for the agency business. Now all I had to do was wait for my passport to be returned, with Marcus's name added, and then get all the shots necessary to ward off any diseases like typhoid, yellow fever or hepatitis A. I hadn't been vaccinated at all the last time I travelled to Brazil, but I had no time to think about it then. Now I had Marcus to consider.

I decided to go and visit Mum and Dad for a few days just for a change of scenery; and although Luke offered to drive me, I took the bus to High Wycombe, and Marcus slept most of the way. It was so relaxing being with my parents; and during the day, when Dad was working on his furniture, Mum and I would sit in the garden and watch Marcus or we would go into town for lunch or to shop. It was a bittersweet time for all of us because in a very short time, I would be thousands of miles away.

I had only been back at the inn for a day when I got the telephone call from Carlos that I had been waiting for. He had found the perfect house in the south zone of the city, in an area called Morumbi. It sounded enormous with four bedrooms and five bathrooms, a pool, a balcony-type terrace and three garages. When I asked him how much it was, he wouldn't tell me, but it was obviously in an exclusive area of São Paulo and was close to a number of good schools. The house had been on the market for a month, and the owner was anxious to close the deal, as he was moving to Rio de Janeiro, so Carlos would have the keys within a week and was ready to shop for furniture. He assured me he would only buy what was necessary, meaning a king-size bed for the two of us, a single bed for Marcus, a kitchen table and chairs and a few pots and pans. All the rest would be up to me. By the time I got off the phone, I was so excited. I knew exactly the kind of furniture I wanted to buy, and Carlos had assured me that money was no object. I had to keep pinching myself to make sure I wasn't dreaming; and then every so often, a small dark cloud would enter my mind. I was about to leave the people I had loved all my life—Mum, Dad and Luke.

At the end of August, I was back at the airport with Marcus; and this time, the whole family came to see me off, including Jenny. Dad was the most stoic and kept asking me if I was sure I had everything I needed—tickets, passports and so on—while Mum took Marcus for a walk around the departure lounge to keep him occupied. I think she was really trying to keep busy herself and putting off the inevitable. Soon she would have to say good-bye, and I wasn't sure how she would manage to hold it all together. Meanwhile, Luke and Jenny did their best to keep my spirits up, telling me jokes and teasing me about my new haircut, which they claimed made me look like a Vidal Sassoon model.

Walking towards the gateway with Marcus, I tried not to turn around and look back at my family, but I couldn't help it. Dad had to pull Mum away from me after she refused to let me go, and she was still sobbing now as I grew further away. Meanwhile, Dad was blowing kisses, and Luke and Jenny were waving like crazy people, and I thought my heart would break, but I kept walking forward until they were out of sight. I had to leave the past behind for now and think about my future with Carlos and our son.

Chapter Sixty-Seven

I loved the house that Carlos had chosen for us; and over the next few weeks, I furnished it in all the colours of nature I loved—brown, umber, terracotta and forest green. The role of wife and mother began to fill my whole life, and I even learned to cook after some rather disastrous attempts. Right after I arrived in São Paulo, I met Carlos's partner in their new enterprise. Ben was a little younger than Carlos, short in stature and slim, with coal black hair and rather piercing brown eyes. I liked him immediately; and when he introduced me to his fiancée, Felicia, I knew I had found a friend.

Felicia was well educated and spoke perfect English, so I didn't have to struggle with speaking Portuguese when I was with her. She was a legal assistant for one of the well-known lawyers in the city; and despite the fact that she worked long hours, she went out of her way to help me find a sitter for Marcus. She interviewed at least ten people, and we finally settled on Sophia, a middle-aged woman with three children of her own. Having Sophia available, I was able to take advantage of what the city had to offer. At least once a week, Carlos and I would go to dinner with Ben and Felicia; and while the men talked business, Felicia would fill me in on all the best places to shop and all the tourist spots I must be sure to visit.

Every week, I rang Mum and Dad, or Luke, to be sure that everyone was all right. The first few times, either Mum or I always ended up crying; but as time went on, it got easier. I think they had finally accepted that my life was now in Brazil and that I was happy. I still missed them all terribly, especially Luke, and I made a promise that I would come back for a visit the following summer.

Carlos kept his word; and in the year since we settled in São Paulo, he only went on one climbing expedition even though the business seemed to be thriving. Most of the time, he was involved in marketing, finance and recruiting new guides to cope with the increasing number of interested tourists, while Ben dealt with supplies and led three expeditions on Mount Aconcagua. They made a good team, and Ben had no issue with Carlos taking time out to spend with his family. In October, we went to the villa in San Sabastião, and Marcus was in his element, making sand castles and wading in the ocean.

Then at Christmas, because Carlos knew that it would be the most difficult time for me to be away from my family, he hired a private jet, and we flew to Santarem to stay with Ann and Miguel. Seeing them again brought back so many memories, and we spent hours reminiscing and catching up on all that had happened since I left. I hadn't realised Luke had kept in touch with them and was surprised to learn they knew all about Jenny and Marcus. It made me feel terribly guilty about cutting off all contact with them, especially after all they had done for me and Luke, but they just shrugged off my apologies. Ann was enchanted with Marcus, and he was over the moon when he met Bandit and a new member of the household, one of Bandit's offspring appropriately named, Mutt. After seeing him together with the dogs, I knew we had to get a pet for ourselves, and Carlos wholeheartedly agreed.

We spent Christmas Day with Ann and Miguel; and the next day, we went to Carlos's old place and listed it with an agent. Afterwards, he signed over the papers for his boat to Miguel and handed him the keys. Miguel was stunned and protested over and over, but Carlos was insistent. He wanted to repay Ann and Miguel for their kindness and explained that we probably wouldn't be returning to Santarem for some time, so there was no point in holding onto any property.

After we got back home, Marcus kept asking for a dog of his own, so we finally went to the animal shelter and picked out a fox terrier named Riley. He was the perfect pet for our family, and he had the same temperament as our beloved Sammy, whom I still thought about so often. I don't think I could have been any happier, except that I missed my family back in England; and then on Valentine's Day, Carlos asked me to marry him and presented me with a ring, which looked so expensive that I was almost afraid to wear it. Two weeks later, in a civil ceremony, with Ben and Felicia as witnesses, I became Mrs. Escada; and later that month, Marcus was officially declared an Escada too. When I rang Mum and Dad to tell them my news, they were thrilled; and when I told them we would be coming back in July to be formally married at Marston United Church, where Luke and Jenny were married, they were over the moon and couldn't wait to see us.

With Luke's help, most of the arrangements were made; and in mid-July, we arrived back in Abingdon, with only two days to complete preparations for the wedding. Mum and Dad were arriving later that afternoon, and although I was dying to see them, I wanted to spend a little time alone with Luke and Jenny. Felicia had helped me pick out my wedding dress, and I couldn't wait to show it to Jenny; but first, I had some news to share. We were sitting at the kitchen table while Marcus was having his afternoon nap when I looked at Carlos, and he nodded. "I have something to tell you," I said.

I noticed Jenny glance at Luke and grin. "You're pregnant," she announced.

I made a face. "How did you guess?" I asked.

"Well, let's put it this way. You've put on a little weight, but you still look fabulous."

"Darn," I said, "I wanted to surprise you."

"Never mind that," Luke said, getting up and coming around the table to hug me and then shaking Carlos's hand.

Jenny jumped up to give me a hug. "How many weeks are you?"

"Fourteen, and we already know it's a girl."

Carlos cut in. "Yes, and believe it or not, we already have a name picked out, and your Mum is going to love it."

"Oh oh," Luke remarked, "not another Shakespeare character?"

"Good guess," Carlos responded. "What do you think of Portia?"

Jenny clapped her hands. "I love it," she said. "Now I wish I could come up with a name for our baby."

Luke grinned as he watched my mouth drop open. "What? Are you telling me you're pregnant too?"

"Yes," Luke replied, putting his arm around Jenny.

"I'm only twelve weeks, and we don't know whether it's a boy or a girl yet."

Carlos and I both got up, and we were all having a group hug when it was interrupted by the sound of a car pulling into the driveway. "That must be Mum and Dad," Luke said. "Let's not tell them about the pregnancies until after the wedding. Otherwise, Mum will be a basket case."

The night before the wedding, Luke found me alone with Marcus. I was lying beside him as he was drifting off to sleep. "Can I talk to you for a minute?" Luke asked.

"Of course," I answered, slipping off the bed. "Why don't we go to my room? Carlos is downstairs with Dad, talking fishing again."

Luke followed me down the hallway, and when we got to my room, I thought he looked rather serious. "Is something the matter?" I asked.

He shook his head and replied, "Not really, but I thought I should tell you what's happened."

I felt a sense of alarm. "Has something happened between you and Jenny? Is the baby all right?"

He took my hand. "No, everything's perfect, and that's why what I have to tell you isn't really important anymore. You see, sis, when Jenny told me she was pregnant, it all came back to me. I remembered what happened with Pandora and the whole abortion thing."

I gasped, "Oh no, I'm so sorry, Luke. I was hoping you'd never have to go through all that pain again."

"It's okay, sis," he said, squeezing my hand. "It doesn't matter anymore. Pandora was just an infatuation, and I feel sad that she aborted our child, but it's all in the past. I love Jenny, and I know I'm going to love our baby."

I nodded. "What else do you remember?"

"Not too much, except for working on the *Artemis* and arriving in Santarem. After that, it's all a blank. I don't want you to tell Mum and Dad or Jenny any of this. It will just be a secret between the two of us."

I gave him a hug. "I promise, no one will know—not even Carlos."

"You're the best, sis," he said, hugging me back.

The church was decked out with yellow flowers, and Jenny looked amazing in a pale lilac dress, which suited her fair complexion. She had agreed to stand up for me, and as she preceded me down the aisle with Mum and Dad on either side of me, I felt like a princess. The wedding went off without a hitch, and afterwards, we went back to the inn for the reception. All of the guests staying at the inn had been invited, together with several neighbours, and I was thrilled when Bridget showed up despite the fact that we had hardly spoken since she abandoned me that night at the Bridge. It was almost midnight when everyone went home or retired to their rooms, and only my family was left to reminisce about the day. "This has been so wonderful," Mum said. "Let's have some more champagne."

"I don't think that's a good idea, Mum," I said.

Mum looked a little annoyed. "Are you implying I've already had too much to drink?"

"No, Mum," I said, grinning. "It's just that Jenny and I aren't allowed to drink right now."

Mum frowned. "And why is that?" she asked.

Luke decided to put her out of her misery. "I think Ariel is trying to tell you something, Mum."

Mum looked at Dad and saw that he was smiling; then she turned back to look at me and Jenny. Suddenly, it was as though a lightbulb turned on above her head, and she gasped and placed her hand on her chest. "Are you telling me—"

Jenny and I cut her off and in unison announced, " both preggers, Mum."

"Oh my god," she said and broke down in tears.

This wasn't the reaction we expected, and I rushed and put my arm around her. "Why are you crying? This is news."

She looked at me with tears and mascara running her face. "This has been the second best day in my whole she said.

"Really, not the best day, Mum?" I asked.

"Almost, but not quite," she answered, looking up at "The best day ever was the day you brought Lucius home